Daughter Of The Sea

DAUGHTER OF THE SEA

Sarah Woodhouse

GUILD PUBLISHING
LONDON

This edition published 1987 by
Book Club Associates
by arrangement with Century Hutchinson Ltd

Typeset by Rowland Phototypesetting Ltd
Bury St Edmunds, Suffolk
Printed and bound in Great Britain by
St Edmundsbury Press Ltd, Bury St Edmunds, Suffolk

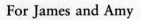

For James and Amy

1

The day was very hot. By narrowing her eyes Théo could make sea and sand blur into one fierce haze of light.

'You're squinting,' said Louise promptly, 'you'll get wrinkles.'

'You must allow me one wrinkle at twenty-eight.'

The shrieks of the children were borne to them on the barely perceptible breeze. Clarice, the nurse, had allowed them a game of cricket, a panting, wild, slippery sort of game. Her French lace and starched pantaloons were often on show.

'I want something to *do*,' said Théo – through clenched teeth.

'*Allez, allez*,' cried Clarice at some breathy pause in the proceedings as one of the boys pursued the ball to the water's edge. Yes, thought Théo, *allons* by all means, but where and with what purpose? She leaned back against her rock and closed her eyes tight against sun, sand, sea, Pierre in mock attack on the whooping Clarice, the charming eighteen-month-old Lou in her captivating white bonnet. Where? Where? God help me, she thought, I'm twenty-eight, no sense of direction, no kind of vocation. She felt she ought to have one, she felt it very strongly. She was acutely conscious of life's absurd brevity and its inherent uncertainties; it should not be wasted in speculation.

'My dear, you should marry Monsieur Varges. He's a perfectly sound proposition. It would get you away from Mama and allow you – well, allow you to be your own woman.'

'Varges' woman, you mean. And he's only interested in me

because he's under Mama's spell and she is forcing him in my direction.'

Louise turned her head so that her straw sun hat did not obscure her view of her youngest sister and looked for a long time at Théo's sharply-defined and decidedly unwrinkled features. 'Mama feels . . .'

'Oh, Mama considers it a slight to have a daughter still unmarried at my age, especially since she has lied about her own ever since Papa died and wishes . . .'

'Théo! It isn't true! Oh, I know she entertains a great deal now, and flirts a little with Mr Semple and Monsieur Varges, but I'm sure she considers La Croix your home for as long as you wish to stay. Why, what would we do without you? And where could you go? She only wants you to be happy. She's told me so herself.'

Théo's eyelids flickered but did not open. She sensed the faint false note that meant Louise lied. Mama did not consider her youngest daughter's unhappiness for the simple reason that she did not grasp the first essential of anything which might contribute to it. Her own world, the narrow social world of Jersey's most distinguished families, was all she knew or cared about, and a restless spirit who wished solely to escape it was not only exasperating but more than a little frightening. How much more satisfactory to have Théo married off quietly to some worthy gentleman who might prevent her creating scandal and confusion. Caroline de Faurel had never imagined, as she had once surveyed her three disciplined, becomingly dressed young daughters, that the smallest and apparently most insignificant one would cause her so much trouble. She had been acutely aware that her husband had hoped for a son – the old family business had passed father to son for generations – and her final child had been named Théophile for that very boy she would probably never bear. In some way this made the child particular from the start, and then so had her closeness to her father, and so had the four-year gap between her and Louise, a gap occasioned by the miscarriage of two other babies. This mere four years meant that during the three or so years Caroline was exerting herself to bring into society and marry off her two eldest daughters, the youngest was to some extent neglected by her; but Théo was not too young to take note of what was happening, of Caroline's methods, stratagems, machinations and ingenuity, of her sisters' feelings and ultimate achievements.

Théo had always watched a great deal and said little, a supposedly virtuous accomplishment Caroline found irritating at first and infuriating ever after.

'It's time to go,' said Louise, stirring. She tipped back her parasol and looked along the bay. There was a gull searching the waterline, descending now and then to pick over the empty mussel shells. Far away she could make out Clarice, Pierre and Bon hanging on her arms, paddling with little screams of pretend horror. Well, it was June. Perhaps the water was still very cold. But the girl was always noisy, always vigorous and unexpected and noisy.

'She adores the children,' remarked Théo, following her gaze, 'and they think the world of her.'

'So do I, so do I. It's simply that . . .'

'She exaggerates, tends to the hysterical, and laughs far too loudly. She's unquestionably just right for them.'

The two sisters laughed and stood up, brushing out their skirts. It would have been difficult for a stranger to tell they were sisters: Louise, like Marguerite, being tall and fair, a softer version of Caroline, while Théo was slight and mouse brown. Encumbered alike, though, by the *de rigueur* beachwear of 1853, including three petticoats each under their silk dresses and great quantities of lace, tucks, pleats, ribbons and cording, not to speak of the whalebone stays, they looked rather hot. Louise sighed and walked to scoop up the flushed toddler, calling to Clarice.

They walked back in a straggling line, Théo first with eight-year-old Pierre's hand tucked in hers and their heads coming together frequently over the secret contents of his pockets. Then came Louise with Lou, six-year-old Bon with the parasols, and Clarice with everything else. They meandered across the wide expanse of St Brelade's Bay until they reached the place where Luc waited with the carriage.

'I don't understand why you must have something to do,' Louise began again as they came slowly down the hill to St Aubin, 'as if you were idle – you, with the whole house to run. Why, Mama and I do nothing, nothing. And you have Mrs

Roach and the fishermen's children, and those awful Bible classes, and Madame Pol and her everlasting embroidery for the poor or whatever . . . Théo, you never have a spare minute.'

'They're just . . . occupations to pass the time until . . .'

'Until what? Until you marry. Dear love, Papa may have considered you as a partner in the business but the business is gone. Gone.'

'There must be something else.'

Pierre, sitting solemn and curious on the opposite seat, suddenly brightened. He beamed up at his favourite aunt. She had taught him to sail after all – though most secretly, so secretly she had been driven to brazen deceptions, to the very pit of guilty contrivance.

'Would you like to run away to sea?' he asked.

'Pierre,' murmured Louise warningly.

But: 'Only in my own ship,' said Théo mildly, 'and with a purpose.'

'Always a purpose,' cried Louise, gazing from beneath the sunshades at the long sweep of this, their most familiar bay, the sands of which she had known since she had tottered at her own nurse's side from the shelter of the big granite house just a little way from the waterfront. 'Why must you always be looking for a purpose?'

Théo too was staring seaward, but perhaps now as they turned the last corner only to avoid looking at La Croix, its terrace clothed in wistaria, the upstairs windows open, their blinds drawn against the sun. That she should so dread entering such a beloved place showed what they had come to, she and Caroline, in their uneasy and complicated relationship.

'I suppose,' she said as they climbed down in the narrow street, 'we shall be told off for taking the carriage again.'

'Well, we know the carriage is kept for show not for any practical use,' said Louise brusquely.

They entered by the garden door, and it might be expedient, they told Clarice, to avoid carrying the shells and embalmed shrimps and the still-living mussels into the house in case they should come to the attention of Madame de Faurel.

'Of course, Mama uses the carriage to go to St Helier,' Louise continued, untying the bows of her hat and breathing as deeply as she could in view of her tight lacing.

4

'But so infrequently the whole town pauses to point her out –
ah, there is the beautiful widow from St Aubin, look at her
clothes, did you hear about her dinner parties . . . Dear Louise,
Mama is very well aware of the advantages of exclusivity.'

Except that all Jersey knew how much less exclusive Caroline had become since her husband's death, and to what great
trouble she had been to marry off her youngest daughter. But
was not little Théo made of the sterner stuff of her island
ancestors, quite as stubborn as her renowned Grand-père
Bonespoir de Faurel? It remained to be seen, though, if she
turned out to be as resourceful.

'But of course it was too hot to take the children on the
beach,' Caroline declared, leaning back on the chaise and
looking at her daughters with a critical eye, 'and Luc was to
have fetched the new chairs from the harbour this morning.
It is too inconsiderate. I would have expected you to have
more sense.'

'Yes, Mama.' Louise sat down with a rustle of her new
cherry-red tarlatan, the first colour she had worn since she
came out of mourning for her husband, dead two years now.
It was a colour that might have suited Clarice, with her black
hair and cheerful disposition. Caroline, who had counselled
grey, or brown, or lilac, found it as stimulating as a slap on
the face. Instinct whispered that Théo had had a hand in it,
Théo who was apt, at unexpected intervals, to splinter the
conventions of her upbringing.

'I have rung twice already for luncheon,' Caroline complained now. 'And Théo, what is all this about Adele?'

'Adele? Adele is going to marry her fisherman, Mama, so I
have asked Goosie to find a replacement.'

'Goosie! You asked the cook! But . . .'

'Goosie is just the person to find a new maid. It was she
who found us Adele all those years ago, remember?'

Caroline did not remember, she had never concerned herself
with domestic arrangements. It had long been the custom that
Théo was allowed a completely free hand in the running of
the house, and as she ran it very well and had done so these
nine years, it would not do to fall out over the kitchen maid's
passion for a Breton crabber. To be sure Caroline would

5

have liked to criticize Théo's housekeeping, Théo's general demeanour, Théo's approach, but she hesitated to step, as she now thought of it, into a viper's nest. Experience had taught her the futility of quarrelling with Théo, who succumbed, if at all, with such ill grace and in such a manner there was never an ounce of sweetness in the victory. She could not be sure any more if Théo might not stand up to her, might not fling up her head and challenge her. It had happened more often lately. Caroline had found she did not like it, could not cope with it. How insufferably stubborn she could be, she thought now, looking at Théo's curious, intense face, those strange green eyes. Marguerite had been accident prone as a child, Louise fractious and demanding, but this – this changeling – had never been any trouble until she grew up.

'Are you cool enough, Mama?' Louise bent over her. 'Shall I fetch more lemonade?'

'Yes, another glass would be nice. But ring for Marie, don't fetch it yourself.'

Théo moved from the window where she had been standing looking steadfastly at the tiny line of blue sea she could make out all down the edge of the blind, and she reached the door before Louise could rise.

'Never mind. I'll go down to see why the meal is late and I'll bring up more lemonade when I come back.'

For a moment she glanced at Caroline on her couch, the upturned, disdainful face. She perceived it to be disdainful, she sometimes felt it had always been so when looking in her own direction, but anyone else might have seen nothing but blank incomprehension. It was a lovely face, each prominence and hollow a delight, and the blue eyes were only a little less beautiful than they had been when Philip de Faurel had brought her to the island as a bride of seventeen. She was fifty-one but she never reminded herself of the fact, and only she and her maid Laurente knew how she kept her fine hair that particular shade of blonde. Louise would be like her one day, but without the firm set of the lips, the remoteness, the deep, deep sense of what was due to her wealth and position.

Poor Louise, thought Théo, closing the door behind her, she fares little better than I do, except that she doesn't mind being at Mama's beck and call all day, doesn't mind the fancy needle-

6

work and the gossip over the morning calls. It's terrible but I can see it happening, she'll grow old here in Mama's shadow, caged up like a poor bird . . . It's a waste, a waste . . .

Down the wide cool hall, across the black and white tiles, into the kitchens. Yes, there was dear old Goosie bent over the hot stove, the colour of bricks and with perspiration trickling into her collar, and there was Adele, hovering anxiously, wisps of hair all over her hot forehead.

The soup was misbehaving, Goosie informed Théo with customary bluntness. It was Madame's favourite. She needed five minutes.

'It's quite all right,' said Théo, 'but you know Mama's feelings about punctuality.'

'Hah!' was Goosie's comment, she who had lived and worked in this house forty years and therefore could remember distant days before a certain English bride had imparted her views on timekeeping to the domestic staff.

Théo put the lemonade on a tray and began to ascend slowly to her mother's drawing room. How remarkably reluctant she felt, as if every instinct for self-preservation screamed out that she should not enter. She stopped in the hall by the french window that gave on to the terrace under the wistaria and she looked longingly at the blue sea, the boats, the glimpse of sand, that was all she could see between the garden wall and the steep roofs of the houses one step further down the hill towards the quay.

Mama had never liked the position of the house. It was too near the water, the boat-menders and builders, the fishermen, for the residence of an ancient and honourable Jersey family. True, it was a large house, and it stood in large and gently sloping gardens sheltered from the west and north. But it was right in the town, could not in any way said to be aloof. It rubbed shoulders with its neighbours, and its very front door – noble and capacious front door that it was – opened into the steep street that led directly to the waterfront. Her husband had adored it, indeed had been born in it as had his father and grandfather, but Caroline pressed him to find something grander, something a little inland and perhaps nearer St Helier. He refused, as indignantly as such a gentle man could, and even insisted, equally gently, that his children be born there too. They would hear her screams on the quay, Caroline had protested the night she gave birth to Marguerite, and what would the honour of the Faurels be worth then? They would hear her screaming like a common fishing woman.

It did not occur to her that the screams of a great lady and those of a fisherwoman might not be told apart, and that the hubbub on the quay was generally such that no one would take more than a passing notice of either. She thought only of her own dignity, of the position she felt she must live up to, and so she kept the one in the teeth of great adversity – she bore none of her babies well – and lived up to the other with undeniable courage, while her endearing husband went down to the quay to buy half the town beer and wine to celebrate his daughter's birth, and was clapped on the back, wrung by the hand and kissed by every sort of man: attorney, sawyer, rope-maker, priest.

Théo knew none of this, gazing from the window, though her eyes noted every familiar landmark her father had passed by that long-ago riotous night. But she had watched and suffered Caroline's easily bruised dignity many times since she herself had been toasted in sound old Burgundy on that selfsame quay. She could not remember a time when she had not been told to mind this or that because Mama would not like it, or to be quiet because Mama was resting, or to be on her best behaviour because Mama had visitors. The house was oppressive for one always had to take account of Mama. It was bearable when she was a child because she was allowed great freedom and was seldom indoors, but later, growing up, she had come to fret at being confined, always aware of her mother in the next room or upstairs in the cream and white bedroom where her father, she somehow sensed, had long been unwelcome. She was a sturdy, wholesome child, learned to sail with Goosie's grandson, a fisher boy, climbed rocks, ran barefoot, offered nothing at the shrine of dignity. Had she known Caroline would have been horrified, hysterical, but Caroline found her youngest daughter unprepossessing, unexplainable, was slightly unwell for some years after her birth and took to her couch, creating a sort of court at La Croix to which all the island society came to pay her homage. She did not inquire if Théo was playing virtuously

8

with her dolls upstairs or was picnicking in the garden, so no one told her Théo was afloat on the bay, learning to wrestle a lugsail in a tricky wind.

There was the clatter of feet on the polished floors: the boys had escaped the nursery. Poor little Lou had been left behind, she had no guile as yet, perhaps never would have. The wail of a distraught Clarice two storeys above pierced the very fabric of the house.

'Oh, Aunt Théo' – a hushed exclamation accompanied by a conspiratorial grin. Théo opened the french window just enough for them to slide through, returning to the drawing room with a gleam in her eyes that Caroline, noticing it at once, took as a personal affront.'

'Well? And have you spoken to Goosie?'

'She's making your favourite soup, Mama. I said we would forgive her five minutes.'

'But the meal is half an hour late already. And Mrs Stoner is visiting this afternoon.'

Caroline leaned back and she and Théo exchanged fleeting and acrimonious looks. What a disaster this child of hers had turned out, Caroline was thinking, so quiet and insignificant, so strange and unpredictable. She might have been forty, a determined old maid, she showed such lack of spirit, of . . . of personality. That she herself might be responsible for any diminution of Théo's spirit did not occur to her. It would certainly never have crossed her mind that the defiant spark that lately had caused such bitter argument, such recriminations, such outrageous conduct, was the last of Théo's stifled passions and undirected longings and confused ambition.

For her part Théo saw an elegant woman on an elegant day bed whose sole purpose had sometimes seemed to be to thwart whatever vague plans she had had for her life. Caroline had always been at her best on that couch, she thought, pretending to be an invalid. It had given her an excuse never to stir from the house. Everyone had been forced to visit her, and this drawing room with its Chinese rugs, the Aubusson carpet, the pictures and porcelain from the family home in Hampshire, had become the meeting place for all the wealthy and fashionable families on the island. Even Grand'mère Honorine de Faurel had come here, invariably accompanied by one of her parrots, though she called Caroline's behaviour nonsense and faradiddle.

The three girls had been put on exhibition in this room, seated in the background among the *objets d'art*. They were not expected to take part in the conversation, so were provided with suitable flimsy sewing, the general impression being one of industrious beauty. Caroline had languished exquisitely, had accepted the compliments on her daughters with the same graciousness she accepted those on her wit or her complexion.

Marguerite, Louise and Théo, denied the carriage – only Caroline should be seen in the carriage – walked everywhere. 'You will develop healthy lungs and strong hearts,' said Caroline, who cared for neither, keeping to her beautiful room where the green blinds were always drawn against the weather. They were not expected, however, to acquire well-muscled legs and brown skin. Marguerite and Louise resorted to large hats, parasols and cucumber cream in quantity, but Théo had shunned all these and grown tanned and freckled. Often she went with her father to the company office in St Helier, ambling along the sweep of the bay, drawing rein to talk to fishermen and boatmen he knew. Those days were treasured memories now, those last sweet days before Philip had drowned on one of his regular visits to Bordeaux, and Caroline had let up the green blinds a little and risen from her couch more frequently until she was the undisputed queen of Jersey society.

Perhaps after all, Théo thought, she had been as good as the son her father had never had. Although he and his brother John George had inherited the wine shipping company of Faurel Mannelier from old Bonespoir, John George had died young and only one year after his father, leaving his only son Alexandre in his place. Philip had nothing in common with this obdurately grave, cautious boy. He did his best, but they were destined to gaze at each other with bleak incomprehension across a great divide. So it was as well perhaps that Philip had his other love, medicine, to sustain him. No one was too humble to receive his attention, but he also had distinguished patients, so that in society he occupied a strange middle ground, the kind of middle ground his family had occupied for anything up to a thousand years, men of wealth but not fashion, professional, often professional adventurers: lawyers, doctors, wine shippers, smugglers, privateers. And Théo became his nurse, his clerk, impressed his patients, impressed Vautier, the manager at Faurel Mannelier, seemed capable of anything. She had shared Philip's love of ships, his interest in and incomplete understanding of the new power of steam. One day, he had said, Faurel Mannelier would pay for a frivolous, an indescribably beautiful steam yacht and they would call her the *Théophile*. They had laughed over this, father and daughter, their amusement sobered by deep hope, excitement, determination. Each saw a real *Théophile* tied up beside the quay. But there had never been any yacht, for Philip had drowned and cousin Alexandre had no interest in steam – nor in anything his mild convivial Uncle Philip had sketched on some of the office paper in a fit of eccentricity.

Thus had ended Théo's liberal and mostly happy childhood and the pressure was on to find her a suitable station in life. She was twenty, a rather boyish, gauche child with impeccable intentions, rather more intelligence than she was credited with, and no particular style. Anything that smacked of passion or ardent individuality had been battened down long ago behind the rigid control of her corsets; passion and individualism were not the required attributes of a young lady from a good family. There was still the occasional stormy eruption but on the whole Théo's nature was of the fiercely loving kind, like Philip's. She was desperately eager to please, hated to disappoint those who cared for her, and this included even Caroline, whose affection for this difficult daughter was usually impossible to discern. So the storms passed, control was regained, life went on. Théo was put up for auction – or so it felt – and there were no bidders.

In a restricted society where nearly all the eligible young men had been her companions since childhood she was doomed. She was not pretty and it is the pretty women who find husbands quickest, as Caroline knew; to be attentive and inquisitive and too short was no use at all. She had a rather elfin face, with a long nose, and odd flyaway eyebrows. What was a mother to do? She did everything required of her, as might be expected in a woman of acumen and foresight, but apparently it was not enough. Théo was dutiful but dull, danced but did not sparkle, charmed but did not captivate. She said she wanted to help with the wine business, a proposition Caroline vetoed with a fainting fit. She had never enjoyed the connection with 'trade', had longed and longed to be rid of it ever since coming to the island, and Alexandre, who was terrified of her, never troubled her about the company, even though most of her income depended on it.

The time came when every eligible bachelor had been accounted for and Théo was introduced to those not so eligible but labelled charitably in Caroline's private thoughts as 'passable'. All these Théo treated circumspectly, correct in every detail of dress and behaviour; she could not be faulted in anything except lack of vitality. Her father, had he been alive, might have accused her of hiding her light very firmly under the bushel, but then she had always hated social gatherings and he was no longer there to lend his sympathetic support.

Then Monsieur André Givard from Bordeaux, visiting Alexandre on business, took on the amusement of this staid and retiring young woman while Caroline was laid low with a fever and an unexplained rash. He was thirty-five, married, was as charmingly French as possible, and was kind. It was his kindness that touched Théo to begin with, his small attentions, the consideration that was so new to her. At a dinner given by Alexandre he had kissed her cheeks as they had walked in the garden and then, as she remained pliant in his arms, her soft innocent mouth. He had smelled of the cigar he had come out to smoke and he had roused feelings she had not known she possessed, she who had never received any open affection since her father died. She did not know if it was love – she vaguely and naively supposed it must be – but her longing terrified her. It was perhaps mostly a longing to be held and comforted in the old way, but André Givard was not, after all, her father, nor had she ever been kissed by a man before. Her one other meeting with him, in St Helier and quite accidental, and which resulted in her lunching alone with him at the best hotel in the town, was known to Caroline before they had finished the strawberries, and brought recrimination, hysteria, copious weeping, and a dictate that Théo would never, never, never meet any man – who could call him a *gentleman*? – alone again.

Théo grieved but the grief was short-lived. She was not schooled in deception and had been raised in a strict morality: the man was married after all. She was kept busy at La Croix anyway, Marguerite coming home from Guernsey very ill after her first miscarriage and Caroline determined there would be no time for mischief. In six months she had grown up enough to feel ashamed of the incident, conscious of her complete innocence and a little angry Givard had taken advantage of it, but most of all she felt sorry that her unsatisfied craving for ordinary affection had led her into Givard's arms. On the other hand he had opened a door to a world she had not known, had forced her to be more cautious in her dealings with men, and had caused her to take a new and dispassionate look at her position at La Croix with Caroline. If only her father had been alive, to whom she could have confided her constant desire to do something, anything, save stultify her energy and intelligence with the exchange of gossip and the choosing of new dresses. Sometimes, walking along the hard sands of the bay, she felt very close to him, and asked him what she should do, where she could go if she left La Croix – oh, it would break her heart to leave the island – and what purpose God had allotted her. There were no answers, of course. And the fishermen only saw a small wiry figure passing on doggedly for the town, her face troubled, her eyes unseeing, and would nod and shrug and call some witticism – out of her hearing – about Madame at La Croix and the merry life she led now the good doctor had gone, God bless him. But was this one not a throwback, the spit of the old Faurels, hardy and true?

The spit of the Faurels smiled kindly at their greetings but was not comforted.

The responsibilities of motherhood outweighed its compensations, said Caroline, who had just come from a frustrating half hour with a mutinous Théo. But no task was too difficult to accomplish with good sense, determination, and the grace of God. She was certain of this, having been educated at one time by nuns: nuns took a sanguine view of worldly problems for they knew what it was to wrestle with the eternal.

'I've decided what to do with her,' she said to Louise that evening, 'I shall write to Millie and arrange it.'

'Millie Boswell?'

'Millie Boswell. She's quite as eccentric as ever, I know, but she has money, position, and a very wide circle of acquaintances. If she can't find Théo a decent husband before a year is out no one can. And in any case it will do us all good if Théo goes away for a while. My nerves have been ruined these last six months.'

'You shouldn't have pushed Monsieur Varges so much, Mama. You know Théo doesn't want to marry, and a middle-aged man with such dreadful whiskers and a stoop . . .'

'You make him sound grotesque; he is nothing of the kind. He is perfectly amiable and well-bred, entirely suitable in every way. Of course she must marry. Of course she must.'

'But what are we to do without her? She runs the house just as we like it, she adores the children, she keeps the servants in order, and she has all her committees and charities and poor old fishermen . . . Dr Frere will break his heart if she leaves. Why not forget about marriage and let her do what she wants?'

'But surely you see? The house, the charities — they aren't what she wants. She wishes to do something more, Heaven knows what. She can't be content with orphans and old fishermen. She'll start some scandal, interfere at the highest level somewhere, bring the name of Faurel into disrepute. I know she will. No, there's only one thing to be done, she must be married and settled and beyond reproach.'

'I fear she will never be that.'

'Of course she will. It needs planning, that's all. I shall write to Millie and see if she can't go to London for a year. It would do her so much good. The house in Russell Square, entertainment, interesting new faces — you never know, there might be the very man, the very man we've been searching for so long.'

'I think,' said Louise slowly, 'that you and Théo are alike in one thing after all. Neither of you knows when to surrender gracefully.'

Caroline gave a snort of disgust.

'I can scarcely credit sometimes she is a daughter of mine,' she declared. 'We must see what Millie can do.'

*   *   *

The boys were in the rock pools. '*Attention!*' Clarice flew by, shrieking about shoes, wet stockings, Pierre eating shrimps.

'Just because he caught one once and ate it alive,' remarked Louise.

'I will not go,' announced Théo in her flattest tones from beneath her parasol. A wisp of bleaching hair blowing in the sea breeze was all that was visible. Louise hardened her heart.

'Think of it as a holiday. It's only for a short time after all. And Mama will simply grow more cantankerous if you refuse. In any case, Millie Boswell is an extraordinary creature, certainly worth a visit. I've read some of her letters. I find it so strange she and Mama have remained in touch all these years though they've only met once since they were at school together – and Millie was only at the school six months. She was an only child, no mother, and her father a Hussar; she went on campaign with him, inherited a vast fortune when he was killed at Waterloo. Théo, are you listening? Théo?'

It was exile, thought Théo, squinting through the July haze to the blue, blue sea. She was being exiled for no fault of her own. Was it a crime to wish to remain single?

'Perhaps,' Louise continued, hoping to strike a happy note, 'you'll discover something to do in London.'

'While being paraded for the benefit of all those suitable elderly gentlemen, I suppose.'

'Goodness! Why should they be elderly?'

'Miss Boswell must be so by now. She was a girl at Waterloo. That was almost forty years ago.'

'But why suppose she knows only elderly men?' And then, losing patience and suddenly distressed for Théo's sake: 'Oh, for Heaven's sake marry an old man. He might die of a stroke on the honeymoon and you can be a happy widow, like Mama.'

Such bitterness was unusual coming from placid Louise. Théo reached out her free hand, Louise took it. They stood in silence looking at the sea. There were ships, brightly painted crab boats close in along the shore. It was a long time since Théo had been in a small boat, a long time since she had revelled in the freedom of those stolen hours under sail. Barefoot, her hair loose ... Those days were long gone. She wondered if she would ever sail again, unfettered, unrestricted, laughing at the bubbling water. Assuredly she never would as the wife of a suitable elderly gentleman. She wondered a little at Millie Boswell's alacrity in taking her on. Had not Mama described in the minutest detail the horrors of her youngest daughter?

It was a good thing her corset and her tight bodice and all her overstarched underwear was holding her up. She felt like sinking down beside the rocks and weeping. But she would not weep. She would not give Mama the satisfaction of knowing how deeply she was wounded. She would . . . She would go to London and behave with impeccable propriety and in a year return, unmarried and unrepentant.

Louise started forward with a cry of anxiety and annoyance as Bon slipped knee deep into a pool, flailing about and shrieking with laughter. Théo was left alone under the parasol, twirling it in her thin brown fingers, looking across the lovely stretch of sand. Something Grand'mère de Faurel had said years before came back into her mind, something about hard knocks: 'Hard knocks are nothing. You can't expect to get through life without them. It's the day you stop being interested you'll know things are really bad, the day the sun in your eyes and the wind on your cheek don't make you glad to be alive . . .'

Grand'mère de Faurel with her neat little figure, her inventive bonnets, all those garrulous parrots. She had been eager and interested to the last day of her life.

Louise was waving. They had found a sheltered spot and were preparing to spread Bon's pantaloons to dry while he capered about in his underwear. Théo started after them, holding up her full grey skirt.

'Come on,' Louise was crying, shading her eyes and longing for the parasol. Théo was being so slow.

Théo was stepping deliberately from one wrinkle of sand to the next. I will sail again, she thought, and I will come back. Gulls swooped and turned above her and she waved the parasol at them, smiling now, her face lit by secret resolution. And I will not marry.

There seemed enough in these three promises to keep her busy for a year in England at any rate.

2

Weymouth in the rain looked dull and dispirited but some of this could be attributed, no doubt, to Théo's mood. She had been seasick on the packet, an unbecoming process, and homesick too, a physical pain equal to any she had known. No wonder she arrived with a grave, grey face and a compressed mouth. She was dressed very finely – never let it be said Caroline did not provide the best for her offspring – but the hues were sober and her bonnet was approaching starkness. Her hair was confined severely in a net and not one tendril escaped. There was nothing to soften her haggard expression as she stepped ashore except the raindrops on her cheeks.

For a moment Millie, poised for an embrace, thought she was crying.

'My dear, my dear. Was the crossing so terrible? What weather! And the brute old tub five hours overdue.'

Théo saw a bright-eyed, desiccated little woman with a hook nose sheltering inside a flamboyant green bonnet and under an equally dramatic green umbrella held over her by a stooping, shuffling figure in a shako and a cloak that swept the ground.

'I am so pleased to meet you,' she said in her soft, exact voice with stunning politeness. Millie Boswell looked suitably stunned, took a step forwards, hesitated, frowned, and then bore away, obviously coming to some decision.

'You're not like poor Caroline in the least,' was the statement blown back to Théo, and was there the smallest trace of relief in the voice? 'My dear girl, you look knocked up.

Come. The carriage is a step along this way. Jack, Jack, the carriage! We shall all be soaked.'

The carriage was expensive and discreet. In its sumptuous interior Théo examined her hostess properly and her hostess gave her back her stare with a wry smile. She was fifty something, Millie Boswell, and looked as if she had been fifty something all her life. Long ago she had cultivated a fierce glare, a sort of predatory blaze, that had struck dumb the great and influential, the sycophants, and the merely silly, at twenty yards. She had an indomitable air, well spiced with pride, and her voice was clipped and well-bred and penetrating; she did not care what she said, she had been brought up in a more scandalous age. It was difficult to imagine she had ever been young though, had ever danced all night with the officers of her father's regiment, had ever whispered in corners, kissed in passages, grown passionate for ice creams. But the lines about her piercing black eyes were laughter lines, for she had always laughed a great deal, had Millie, and often at herself.

'I've engaged a room for the night here in Weymouth,' she said, as they started forward with a jerk and she thumped her umbrella handle on the roof to show her annoyance. 'I thought you'd be so tired after such a stormy crossing. Then tomorrow we travel to Oxford. Oxford has the misfortune to harbour several relatives of mine, strange dour academics every one, and I pay them an annual visit in September every year. I find it quite tiresome. They are never in the least glad to see me. But I've somehow got into the habit and Oxford is my home town, you know; it makes me feel young again.'

It occurred to Théo that like Grand'mère de Faurel, that other notable eccentric, Millie Boswell had never stopped feeling young. She smiled across the carriage, her first genuinely warm smile, and Millie, comforted at last, pushed up the brim of her bonnet with the umbrella handle and grinned.

'We'll stay in Oxford a week, then I must return to London. Caroline was quite explicit as to what I was to do with you, you know. She has even written me several letters with numbered paragraphs, setting out exactly what you're to spend on clothes and what sort of clothes and how often I am to allow you to ride in the park or dance with the same gentleman at balls. Balls! My dear, I detest balls!'

'So do I. Don't attend for my sake.'

'Oh, I have been sent your views on balls, on dress, on dinner parties and on gentlemen in the minutest detail. No, don't blush, girl. If I can't read between the lines of Caroline's letters after forty years I deserve to be hung. You refuse to be put into the mould, that's all, or should I say refuse to turn out of it in the proper shape? She is bewildered and a little frightened, and consequently takes your insistence on being an old maid as a personal affront. Anyway, we must go to some dinners and dances, dear girl, just so that I can write and say I've done my duty by an old friend. And between the dances we must find something more interesting to pass the time.'

Théo smiled widely. Millie nodded in approval. The carriage lurched on its superior springs as they drew up violently in the yard of a well-known, exceedingly fashionable inn.

'Dear me,' cried Millie, sticking her head out in the rain, 'I shall have to find another coachman if Hardy insists on throwing us all about like this. Hardy! Hardy, are you drunk?'

Hardy was six foot four, remarkably stout, and was camouflaged by a great deal of whisker. He was sober, he asserted, how dare she cast aspersions? His watery blue eyes twinkled at her with undisguised affection. He was sober as an archdeacon, was she going to pick an argument?

'How I manage to acquire such cantankerous servants I never know,' said Millie, and she looked with exaggerated ferocity at the shuffling little man with the umbrella who was following them inside with his peculiar gait. 'Do you, Jack? Do you? No doubt you'd say I deserved you all. Hah!'

There was a very large bedroom, a bathroom, a small sitting room. Millie told the startled maids to turn up the mattress and she prodded among the covers with the tip of the umbrella. It all seemed satisfactory. The call went down for the boxes, all the boxes, and sharp about it.

There seemed to be innumerable hat boxes and one that contained a small white terrier with a patch over one eye.

'This is Nelson,' said Millie. 'He really belongs to Joss.

Jack! Jack! Tea, man, see if you can make them fetch us some tea.'

'Who is Joss?'

But Millie was dragging back the curtains to come at a better view of the dirty window panes and did not hear. In another moment she had briskly rearranged two small tables, a chair, and a painted screen, and had returned to the window to fling it up, exclaiming as she did so: 'I would rather have the rain in and some decent fresh air. The most extravagant prices and the place smells as if they'd stabled camels in every room . . . Where is Polly?'

Polly was her maid, a plump, motherly, simple girl.

'I believe she's gone down for hot water.' Théo sat in one of the chairs Millie seemed disposed to leave alone and Nelson climbed in her lap. She loosened her bonnet and took it off, feeling tired, so tired, and if she closed her eyes she could see Louise on the quay with the children clutching her skirts and waving . . .

'I'm afraid you are overwhelmed.' Millie discarded hat, pelisse and umbrella here there and anywhere. 'We are a strange crew, I admit it. Polly was in an orphanage all her life but she isn't quite right in the head so couldn't get a place when she grew up; how could anyone turn an innocent like that on to the streets? And Jack, Waterloo Jackson was my father's servant. I seem to have inherited him.'

The door burst open. 'Tea,' announced Waterloo Jackson in person, 'such as it is. There ain't no discriminatin' guests at this 'ere establishment, I told them, if this is what you calls tea. But there you are. And there wasn't no cream.'

He set the tray in front of Théo. 'Looks poisonous,' he said, 'I shouldn't partake too free meself.'

Théo grinned. 'It can't be worse than the jet-black brew they gave us on the packet.'

'Hah, sailors!' Jack snorted, 'sailors never could make a christian cup of tea.'

'I'm afraid,' said Millie as the door closed behind him, 'he has the soldier's contempt for anyone afloat. It's a great pity. He even treats my godson to pithy comments on naval etiquette and naval deficiencies. Still, Joss takes it in good part, the dear boy.'

'Your godson is in the navy?'

'My dear, he is an Inspector of Machinery Afloat. I confess I too was taken aback when the title was first sprung on me. It means he is a chief engineer in one of Her Majesty's steamships. You'll like him. He has an extraordinary history. He is exactly the sort of person Caroline would bar from the house.'

'But a commissioned officer?'

'Commissioned? Oh, certainly. Those absurd old men at the Admiralty were forced to it in forty-eight, though their hearts bled, no doubt. Engineers, dear Théo, are exceedingly highly paid but despised beyond measure – which just suits Joss, he has a contumelious nature. But to compound his unsuitability as an acquaintance, he is illegitimate. He doesn't care to exercise his manners much and he's far too outspoken to be safely left alone in a drawing room with anyone of a delicate disposition. Oh, you'll like him, you will indeed.'

'But how did he come to be your godson?'

'He was born in my house. His mother was the daughter of one of my oldest friends. Being thought likely to die he was christened at once and I was his godmother. One day when we're all less tired I'll tell you his story. He might tell you himself, he is not ashamed of it, but his head is full of engines, engines . . . and he isn't a man to put himself out . . . Now, drink some tea and tell me about Louise and Marguerite, and Caroline, Caroline the toast of St Aubin. Yes, do tell me. How I would love to see her again.'

'I think you would find her remarkably unchanged.'

Millie put her small feet up on a footstool and drank deeply of the obnoxious tea. 'Alas, I fear I would indeed. It is a grim thought, is it not, that however we struggle for perfection we can never alter our essentials?'

'Dear Joss,' Millie wrote,

she is the dearest girl and fit for anyone's wife, too fit for most, too honest and sensitive. How she must have come to grief with Caroline! She is rather wary with us as yet, alert and standing off wondering whether we are going to be friendly or not. She is rather sober, dresses in dull colours – beautifully cut clothes and the best material, but dull, oh so dull; I wonder if she ever wore white and roses in her life. Clothes seem to mean little to her, except they are neat and clean and presentable, but mud-brown and stone-grey! All these years when I thought of her at all I thought of blue, bright changing blue like the sea, like her quick moods.

Her hair is brown, nothing to commend there, and she has a longish straight nose – for looking down at the lesser families, *ma fille*, as her Grand'mère de Faurel apparently said – and her eyes are green, quite certainly green. It is a curious face, everything sharply defined so that it draws the eye and yet nothing satisfying or attractive. She is very sure of herself though reserved, not in the least witty. She does Caroline credit at the same time as showing up Caroline's omissions: all the poor girl's gifts have been left undeveloped. She is musical but plays badly – no time for lessons, she has the house to run – sings but could do better, ditto, draws well but but but ... On the other hand she can talk knowledgeably about sailing, fishing, wine, cider making and iron bridges, topics that must be unusual in Caroline's stifling drawing room. All her energy and fervour have been damped down or held in check all her life – or at least since she grew to womanhood. Do you know what Caroline wrote: She has no figure, no conversation and no desire to attract men. The first two are lies, the third certainly true but then she has been frightened half to death by a succession of elderly suitors and has never been given the chance to fall in love. What can anyone expect?

What indeed? Joss Westover on his steamship smiled and smiled and reflected briefly on Théo de Faurel's chances with an unorthodox chaperon like Millie. He hoped some good would come of it. He wrote back saying as much to his irrepressible godmother who was, it appeared, about to fire a broadside into Caroline's careful plans. But he was only faintly intrigued. By the time he got home on leave the girl would be engaged or safely returned to her island. What had Théo de Faurel to do with him? In the close, dark, intimate world of his ship, confined with his beloved engines, juggling the demands of a skilled and dirty job with the elusive niceties of the wardroom, a social chaos, Millie and Théo seemed understandably remote.

*   *   *

The carriage pulled up with its customary lurch in the narrow confines of Holywell. Here, in a toppling medieval house, Millie always took lodgings for her annual week in Oxford. The house belonged to . . . But here her explanation to Théo was drowned in the din of the raging carriage horses, who had taken an intense dislike to a vegetable barrow and a bob-tailed sheepdog. Théo caught the words 'college' and 'uncle' and 'dotty old fool, foot in the grave' before she found herself swept in through a dangerously low doorway and propelled up some suicidally steep stairs.

The house was tiny, poky, low-ceilinged. There was a smell of soot and very old, probably unsound wood. And then they emerged into a charming, lop-sided little sitting room, all chintz and fruitwood and ticking clocks.

'Shocking,' said Millie, looking out to see her horses careering like circus animals, 'shocking. I shall have to find a proper coachman,' and she flung wide the tiny casement and poked out her head, shrieking down instructions with piercing and disdainful clarity.

After this she slammed the window shut and turned round to see Jack heaving a trunk up the winding stairs, the mute, anxious figure of poor Polly close behind him. The room had been furnished for some other lady, Théo thought, not Millie. Her little green figure gleamed and shifted among the pale pinks and blues like some exotic jungle bird in a canary cage.

'I wish it would stop raining,' said Théo an hour later, watching the wet spattering on the panes, 'then I might walk up the High Street.'

'You mustn't be depressed by the weather. Don't let a spot of rain put you off. Why, in Sicily . . .'

'Yes?'

'Ah, Sicily. No, I forget. Perhaps it was Spain. We had such floods.'

'You've travelled a great deal.'

'Turkey, Egypt, Jamaica . . . Jack and Polly and I have voyaged and ox-carted and camelled and muled over what seemed like half the world, and never a decent map or anyone who knew the way. It was all very frivolous and pointless, no doubt, though there were times when . . . well, when the spirit was lifted.'

Théo was feeding small pieces of biscuit to Nelson. 'And this is the first time I have been away from Jersey in my life.'

Millie leant forward to lob a slipper down the open well of the staircase; Waterloo Jackson stuck up his head.

'Tea, I think. Some of the best, Jack. And tell Polly to run out for the cream.' She sat up with a satisfied air, beaming round at Théo. 'Your saying that, about it being the first time you have ever been away from home . . . It reminds me of the time I came down here to fetch Joss. It was the first time he had been away from the farm on Otmoor for longer than half a day. Did I tell you he is an Oxfordshire boy? We went to St Giles' fair, he was so keen to go. He was only fourteen, quite incorrigible. We had to pay to see a mermaid and a tent full of snakes and a fire-eater. And before I could turn round the wretched boy had discovered a steam organ and had got into its entrails. You never could keep him out of engines.'

The mermaid had been only a small disappointment: they could both be merry about it afterwards. Joss had acquired some horrible sticky sweets and they had sucked them in companionable disgust through several more phenomena: the snakes, the fire-eater, the baby with two heads. Millie's bonnet had become a little tipsy, her thin face a little flushed, and the fire in her eyes had been replaced by resigned humour. Then the afternoon had been given over entirely to oil and smuts. What had she let herself in for? What had she, Millie Boswell, to do with a fourteen-year-old boy and pistons, pumps and regulators?

Théo gave Nelson another biscuit. 'Tell me about Joss,' she said, and she watched Millie's face change subtly, grow girlish and delighted.

'Ah, Joss, Joss and his engines.'

She had been bequeathed Joss in 1837, his mother dead, his foster parents anxious to put him to work — but what work and where? Was he not in reality a Westover of Martagon House?

It was in the library at Martagon Millie first made his acquaintance, the lofty, splendid library, alien territory for both of them. She had been oddly afraid the moment her hand had hesitated over the ornate brass knob on the heavy door. What would she find within? Well, whatever, by a stroke of fate – and Miss Amelia Boswell knew all about fate's whimsical strokes – it would be her very own responsibility.

So that was how they had first met, Millie poised like a strange little green fairy – how she loved green – with both hands clasped round her umbrella, and Joss at bay by the fireplace, his head up and his chin forward, his eyes defiant in his square, ordinary boy's face.

'So you are Joss,' Millie had said, advancing. 'It's nearly fourteen years since I saw you last.'

'I don't see . . .' he had begun.

'No, I'm sure you don't. It was your mother's last wish I should take care of you. I'd be failing in my duty if I didn't take you on. Anyway, Mrs Gurden says it is time you were put to some proper work.'

She had had nothing to do with children, she was thinking, and this one was already more than half a man. She thought it very vexing of Rose to make her responsible for him, a boy brought up behind the plough. But there it was. Who else might do it? She had always managed the little money put in trust, paying the Gurdens, sending extra for clothes, schooling, books. But what *was* an old spinster to do with a farm boy?

How like Rose he was and how, in the manner of children, completely unlike. Perhaps his father had contributed the long upper lip, the large hands, the promise of size and strength. And that humorous, pugnacious look was not at all Rose, though the blue eyes were hers and the dark straight hair.

His accent was Oxfordshire, she could see the dimpled river and the ox-eye daisies in drifts as he spoke. He knew next to nothing about himself, thought his father was a tinker; she had to disabuse him of *that* idea. She had tossed away umbrella and bonnet with total disregard for where they fell and had bent to wield the poker.

'What a shameful little fire, a couple of twigs and damp too; and in this musty cavern. Have you ever felt such a chill? I never did like this house,' and she had glanced around, all the humour and curiosity and good nature in her face put out, extinguished by the old memories. 'Your mother was brought to account in this very room. I was here. I shall never forget it. Old Mr Westover, your grandfather, stood there behind that desk and howled at her for an ungrateful and unnatural child for a full thirty minutes; and she defied him, chin up and eyes blazing. She said your father was going to marry her as soon as ever he returned from the West Indies where his regiment had been sent – he was a private in the artillery, dear boy, not a tinker – and that she loved him, she would not give him up. Only of course he never did come home, being dead of a fever long before you were born. What a to-do! I took Rose to Russell Square when her time came and that was how I first met you, stood by while that daft old curate named you Henry – after your father – and Jocelyn – after old man Westover, little he did to deserve it. And then you were taken away by the Gurdens, good kind people every one.'

It seemed so long ago, Millie thought, blowing ash off her fingers and watching the sulky logs splutter, all the scandal and rows, the tears, the ridiculous, prolonged, unnecessary agony, the hasty and somehow shameful christening, and Henry Jocelyn borne away by dear ruddy Mrs Gurden in a country cart with no springs. And Rose had not wept, had not asked to see the baby at all, even to kiss him goodbye, and afterwards, when a very large settlement had induced Frensham to overlook her unspeakable past, she had apparently become a quiet, dutiful wife. But there had been no more children, a fact Millie found significant by instinct rather than reasoning. Now all the Westovers were dead and Martagon, damp and unlovable pile, had been inherited by very distant cousins, a widower with a severe and impressive spinster sister, the Barnards, and an only daughter, a pretty little thing still in the nursery.

It was Joss who was heir to Martagon, she had thought suddenly, looking at him, Joss who spoke with the cheerful rounded vowels of the deep country, who had been used to tramp the open spaces of wild Otmoor and swim naked in the river, chewing watercress while netting the sticklebacks; Joss who had swung a sickle at haymaking and knew a good cow when he saw one. Rose's son; what in the world was she to make of Rose's son?

'She never came to visit me,' was all he said of his mother. 'Her husband would not allow it.' A pause, words of comfort eluding her. 'Of course he would not. But if I believed in broken hearts I would say hers broke the day she gave you away and it never mended, but broken hearts are most likely tomfoolery, dear boy, most likely.'

Miss Barnard, who had thought it inappropriate, a perfect disgrace, to bring the boy to Martagon, had found him and the odd little Miss Boswell almost too much to bear. Here was this eccentric enthroned before the fire, practically alight and with smuts on her chin – and worth all those thousands a year, who would have thought it? – and the boy, great country lout, lounging back in the chair opposite, arms akimbo. They had quite stared her down, black eyes and blue turned on her together, and she had had a deep sense of intruding on some warm, affectionate intimacy . . .

'Ah, Miss Barnard,' Millie had said, 'come to offer us tea.'

Théo could picture it all. She could picture the long gloomy library at Martagon, so different from her father's airy, untidy study at La Croix, and she could picture Millie toasting her neat little boots and giving back Miss Barnard stare for stare. She could picture Joss, tall for his age, straight dark hair, *that nose* as Millie described it, perched on the edge of a little pink and gold chair intended more for show than honest service. And the curricle? She found it harder to imagine the curricle, a racy vehicle in no way suited to a middle-aged lady, in which Millie had driven herself to Martagon to meet her godson and in which she was to drive him away. How they had charged the gates, drawn by the pair of peppery greys with foaming lips, and how they had sent the gravel spraying and had fled out on to the high road. An ill-assorted couple, a dispassionate observer might have said, and brought together by a misguided, wilful girl who had disgraced an old and honourable family with the son of a Cornish farmer. But the ill-assorted couple had been in high spirits all the way to Oxford, and their immoderate laughter had only encouraged the maddened horses.

And then the question of what to do with Joss; Théo could appreciate Millie's predicament. Joss himself had apparently had no doubts, and had regarded his being ousted from the farm into the hands of this capable and benevolent godmother the opportunity to achieve his dearest ambition. Steam engines were his whole life.

Millie might have bought him a commission in the army, but what influence she had left was with the cavalry and Joss was no great figure on a horse. He could not be moved from his engines, either, and engines were not yet to be found in the army. So what else was there? The navy? She had a hazy notion there were such things as steam tugs in the navy. Did she want to see Joss in a tug? She recoiled from the thought, more for Rose's sake perhaps than from her own prejudices, but made inquiries none the less. All she knew was that there was a most important book called *Bunnythorn's Arithmetic* and that the life of a boy at sea was unmitigated hell. She found out that steam was anathema even though the First Sea Lord, Sir James Graham, was prepared to encourage it, for the navy was more full of diehards than the army, the custom of the service was sacrosanct. Engineers were non-commissioned officers, treated as if they had some deadly infectious disease and generally sunk out of sight in a dark, cramped world of their own on the lower deck. They were tolerated because they were needed, though Nelson's ghost might wring his hands over the great sails smutted by filthy Newcastle coal.

Joss, wiser than his years, pointed out that in a new branch of the service he might rise faster to the top of the tree. The man who controlled the engine controlled the ship, he said, with a wry, somewhat elderly smile of anticipation. And what other way up was there, even supposing Millie could purchase him a place? Ancient half-pay lieutenants were common; the running down of the navy that had fought Napoleon had left some curious and awkward legacies, not least some thousands of officers who would never go to sea again. The Admiralty's reluctance to retire any – even nonagenarian – officers of flag rank created a dangerous blockage, a heart-breaking hold-up in promotion for the able men lower down the ladder. Engineering at least held out hope of advancement, of promotion on merit even. But a warrant officer, a lowly scrub of a warrant officer, a man to whom a proud captain might never speak such was the general prejudice – was that at all suitable for the last of the Westovers?

Joss was stubborn; in the end he turned out to be more stubborn than Millie, which was something of a phenomenon along the lines of the mermaid and the two-headed baby. He held out for the navy and for steam until she buckled, trotting off reluctantly to see a very lordly person at the Admiralty whom she hoped to stun with a wickedly expensive new bonnet and her sharp, intelligent black eyes.

The lordly person was shifty and apologetic. It was true to say that he was stunned. He hoped he might get rid of this forceful little woman by being suitably compliant; she did not look the sort to be pacified by elusiveness. Yes, he said, he could find young Mr Westover a berth as an Engineer Boy; it would be a four-year training period after which he might qualify to become a Third-Class Engineer Officer. Wages? Fourteen and sixpence a month. Soon, of course, very soon, he assured her, engineer officers would be commissioned, the day could not be put off much longer, the opposition of every captain afloat notwithstanding.

'Dear Bos,' said Joss, who had meanwhile been learning to un-round his vowels a little and to eat asparagus, 'I knew you could do it. A ship! A ship with an engine!'

'I believe it has sails. I was not paying proper attention but I feel sure I was told it has sails as well as paddles.'

'It doesn't matter,' with the hauteur of fourteen, 'there's an engine. And one day . . . Have you heard of screw-propellers?'

'No, thank God.'

'You will,' Joss said, deep abiding enthusiasm glowing in his face, 'you will.'

And to be sure Millie had heard enough about screw-propellers and valves and horsepower over the next ten years while Joss had blazed up the path of his chosen profession. In forty-eight the despised Engineer Officers had been commissioned at last, for steam had proved irresistible – as irresistible as Joss himself, said Millie.

'He isn't a man to be turned from his purpose,' she ended, gazing sagely at Théo de Faurel over the teacups in that little room in Holywell. 'I'm sometimes a little afraid of him.'

'Yet you said he had no ambition.'

'Nor has he, in the ordinary way; he is not set upon wealth and power. And he never cared much for anyone else's good opinion, his achievements are for his own satisfaction. Still, when he sets his heart on anything he will not be shaken off, can be unpardonably tenacious, savage, irrational . . . It is a side of him you might never guess was there, hard, selfish; thank God we see it so seldom. I always think . . . I think it is something to do with Rose, with his life with the Gurdens, what he was, what he might have been; but I am no philosopher, my dear.'

And Théo heard Bonespoir de Faurel's voice, huge and hearty, booming down the years: 'I'm no judge, *chérie*, but I would guess the man was miserable, was suffering . . .' He spoke of her father, of course. She had not understood at the time but later, striving herself to cope with Caroline, she had begun to, little by little.

'Théo, Théo, you are very tired,' sighed Millie, leaning to pat her knee. 'We'll dine early tonight, and tomorrow I'll show you Oxford.'

Nelson jumped on to her lap and she rubbed his perky little triangular ears. 'He's Joss's dog, found in a railway carriage. I have a monkey in London, also Joss's, and half a stuffed elk. Were the elk alive, and Miss Cole's pickled reptiles . . . well, we could set ourselves up as rival to the Zoological Gardens.'

'I haven't heard you speak of Miss Cole.'

'Ah, Miss Cole inhabits my top floor. She is the sister of a man who once wanted to marry me – dead now, poor fool – and ran away with a wild genius of a boy who left her destitute. She has lived with me for twenty years. Lizards are her joy. If some idle, wealthy gentleman were to get up an expedition to some remote and fearful place swarming with the things she would go at once, lame leg, squint, and all. She would drive him witless with her erudition and her obnoxious glass jars full of specimens, and she would create an absolute scandal among the inflexible men of science by knocking all their dearly held theories over the head one after the other. She is perfectly harmless. Had that scoundrelly actor married her when he should she would have turned out the sweetest wife and mother, no doubt; but he did not, and so she puts all her energy into the lizards.'

It was time to light the lamps. Jack appeared, carrying a

30

taper. Théo stood up to draw the curtains at the tiny low windows.

'Get away then,' said Jack to Nelson, who had slipped off Millie's lap to worry his bootlaces, 'get away, you horrible hound. You wait till Mr Joss comes 'ome, he'll very likely teach you some manners.'

'Is Joss coming home soon?' Théo asked Millie when he had gone, and they were restored to quiet, Jack's faltering rendering of 'Lilibulero' dying away down the stairs.

'Well, we haven't seen him in nearly two years. It's quite time. I had hoped to persuade him back for my ball in November.'

'I thought you detested balls?'

'I do, I do. But this is by way of being my annual party. My mother always gave one for my father's birthday at the end of November, always, no matter where we were, no matter the difficulties, the shortages, the extreme measures that had to be taken. We have celebrated in a row of tents in mud six inches deep and thought nothing of it. I suppose I was sentimental enough to want to keep up the tradition. I'm afraid I don't have a gift for entertaining, and throw everybody together pell-mell, high, low, old, young, Tory, Whig . . . If they cannot be reconciled by dancing and champagne they have only themselves to blame.'

Théo laughed. She supposed the extraordinary Miss Cole would also dance and grow merry on champagne.

'She does her best,' remarked Millie darkly.

'And what am I to do? Has Mama left copious instructions?'

'Oh, I know exactly what to do with you. I will give you to Joss.'

She implied nothing, meant only that they should be friends. It was not that the eventual coming together of her two 'children' as she called them had not crossed her mind, perhaps at the moment she first saw Théo on the ship, small and resolute, clutching simultaneously at skirts and bonnet in the wet, gusting wind. Why not? They were both decent, good-hearted people, healthy, unexceptional. But Millie considered, amongst other things, that their ages were too close. In her opinion Joss needed someone much younger, someone less independent who would give him the unqualified adoration he had never known – make up in some undefined way for his mother's desertion. He saw it as desertion still, she knew, and not all the Gurdens' genial affection had lessened the bitterness of it. A constant loving wife might do wonders, she naively supposed – she would readily have acknowledged the naivety of all her impractical hopes – to lighten that dark side to his temperament. And Théo de Faurel was not at all the sort of woman to do it.

'Tomorrow,' she said now, watching Théo turning up the lamps, seeing that inquisitive, chiselled face thrown into relief, 'we ought to visit Martagon. I generally call. I am wicked enough to enjoy Miss Barnard struggling to be affable in the teeth of her inclinations, especially when I give her news of Joss. She thinks him a scandal. The shame of having once entertained him under her roof – *his* roof, Heaven knows! – will never leave her. Yes, yes, tomorrow we must go to Martagon.'

3

Théo's first impression of Martagon was of a grand old stone house at the end of an elm avenue, rather oppressively surrounded by ornamental box and clipped yew. Sir Francis Westover had paid for it to be built the year Charles II had returned from exile, to celebrate the repossession of his estates, to impress his neighbours, and because he was passionately in love with Architecture. Martagon was an extravagant piece of self-indulgence.

Self-indulgence was not in general a failure of the Westovers, at least, not in the accepted sense; they were tenacious in their ambitions to a fault though, which might come to the same thing. Money ran out before the house was finished and Sir Francis married, with indecorous haste, a young heiress with whom he was totally unhappy simply, it was said, to ensure the walls were plastered and the doors put on. A hundred years later his great-grandson died childless and the house passed to other Westovers, hardier stock, all of them professional soldiers or seamen. And what had dedicated army officers and naval captains to do with a large country estate, a dozen tenanted farms, two thousand sheep? Everything and nothing perhaps: they continued in their professions while wives and bailiffs coped with the tenants and the sheep. But though none of them would have built Martagon still it was theirs, and they cherished it and struggled feebly to improve it and mortgaged themselves to death for it with that old Westover determination Sir Francis would have understood.

Then there were no more wars and no more chances of

prizes, a new world of railways and furious manufacture and ruthless enterprise outside the gates. And as if to seal their fate Jocelyn Westover had no son and his only daughter, having disgraced herself with a common soldier, took Martagon to her surly husband Frensham and so to the Barnards.

The Westovers were done, Millie said crisply as her glossy carriage careered beneath the elms, when Jocelyn refused to allow Rose's marriage to Tregarron and would not have his baby in the house. He came to regret it, she was sure he came to regret it: he had left Joss a brief impersonal letter and a gold watch.

'Even at the last he was too proud to do more' – Millie, as a preliminary, was taking a very firm hold on Nelson's collar – 'but I suppose, bearing in mind he had ruined Rose's life and his own for the sake of pride, a gold watch and a letter were enormous concessions.' She looked out, Nelson in a stranglehold. 'The Barnards have money, have put some of the land in better heart, though I fancy they have a blackguard bailiff, nothing looks quite as prosperous as it should. But the house . . . It's less like a home than it ever was. And I've not been warm inside it one minute since Rose died.'

She was to be disappointed again. In spite of the clear yellow autumn sunshine outside, in spite of a respectable sort of fire, Martagon felt cold and damp. Its furnishings were expensive but unsuitable, its panelling hidden by huge pictures, drapes with tassels, carved screens. Miss Barnard, a tall thin lady in charcoal grey, welcomed her visitors with chilling politeness, staring in horror at the saucy Nelson under Millie's arm. She made an effort to be pleasant to Théo, who had novelty value as well as impeccable references, but it was quite clear Millie was anathema, that one of the peacocks straying into the drawing room could not have agitated her more than the sight of that bright, exotic little woman picking her way towards the best armchair.

Then young Miss Barnard came in, just returned from an invigorating ride through the park – did Miss Faurel ride, was it not exciting to ride in a strong wind? – and the atmosphere brightened. Miss Sophie Barnard was an accomplished horsewoman, her aunt informed Millie and Théo with satisfaction. Sophie, who had changed hurriedly and looked charmingly windswept, gave them a sweetly proud smile. She was twenty, considerably taller than Théo, dark and striking; in ten years she would be a very handsome woman. It became clear she was pursued by a score of anxious gentlemen, too anxious perhaps: one or two had been pressing, had been troublesome. Mr Barnard, who had no desire to see the darling of his life married too soon, recommended a year in London, a complete break, new faces, new interests, a broadening of horizons. They were to leave, Sophie told Théo, in two weeks. She did not seem to care much for the troublesome suitors, evidently none of them had touched her heart.

'Then you must have an invitation to my ball,' said Millie, feeding macaroons to the irrepressible Nelson. 'Of course you must come.'

Miss Barnard was torn between gratification and apprehension. She was aware Millie's ball was a well-known social event and equally aware its doors might be open to all manner of undesirables: Joss Westover, for instance.

'I suppose your godson will be at sea,' she said hopefully.

'I don't think so.' Millie relinquished a last macaroon and pushed Nelson away with the toe of her shiny little boot. 'I have altered the date this year so that he might come. He's being promoted to a larger ship and has some leave.'

'A larger ship,' echoed Miss Barnard faintly. 'How he does get on.' The vision of a face, broad positive nose, strong eyebrows, rose in her mind. She would not acknowledge him a gentleman but she could not fail to be impressed.

The macaroons and tea coming to a natural end they made a tour of the house for Théo's benefit, a tour which ended in the Long Gallery where generations of Westovers gazed from the walls. The Gallery was shut up, Miss Barnard explained, sniffing at the damp, it was too cold, too draughty, too inconvenient. The portraits had been left – who cared for them?

'It's a disgrace,' Sophie said as they retraced their steps to the drawing room, 'that Miss Boswell's godson should call himself Westover. I do believe his father was called Tregarron, was the son of a smallholder.'

'What else could he call himself but Westover?' demanded Théo, brushing dust off her wide skirts. 'And his grandfather left him . . .' How very little had been left him . . . 'Left something in his will.'

'But I thought he'd refused to even see him for years and years, that he never spoke of him? How fortunate Mr Westover' – a subtle emphasis – 'seems to be in the matter of wills. Miss Boswell's will make him a rich man.'

What were they talking about, Millie wondered, watching them sit side by side on one of the hard sofas. Théo's sweetly polite expression had gone to pieces and she was grave, furiously, burningly grave as if she had just been offered a mortal insult. Sophie bloomed beside her, unaware.

'I find Miss Faurel delightful,' remarked Miss Barnard in Millie's ear, 'but . . . unusual.'

Teased and plucked and rearranged a score of times by Caroline, all to no great effect, how could she fail to be otherwise? Knowing she was not pretty her self-confidence was of an inquisitive, aggressive variety, though it was not so much what she said as what she looked with her strange eyes that made onlookers uneasy.

Millie sighed, and exchanged further banalities with Miss Barnard: London in the summer, the variable efficiency of the railways, the merits of red flannel. Out of the corner of her eye she saw dark brown and pale brown head meet over a magazine, a fashion magazine presumably, Sophie's morning reading. Théo's heart was not in it, her downbent eyes were fiery. For a moment Millie felt the cold shadow of Caroline's misgivings.

She was promising material, Théo de Faurel, promising in every way except that she was twenty-eight. She had an unblemished lineage, dressed as befitted a woman with French connections, was bilingual, graceful, and could dance. Besides, her fortune was large enough to make any man think twice before rejecting her. But twenty-eight? She was no naive child to be wooed by compliments and flowers, though Heaven knows, Millie thought, she had received few enough of either. She had attended Caroline's whims for years, had run La Croix unaided, had nursed Marguerite through two miscarriages and a terrible childbirth. This naturally gave her an outlook on life somewhat unusual in a girl about to enjoy her first London ball.

36

'How bored you must have been,' Millie said to her as they drove away from Martagon in a series of short bursts, Hardy standing on the box like a circus performer, 'I'm sorry. Perhaps you should have stayed in Oxford.'

'I wouldn't have missed it for anything. It's a beautiful house.'

'Well, it beggared the Westovers, and I'll be rash enough to wager you a hundred guineas it will beggar the Barnards too.'

'A hundred guineas is a great deal of money.'

'And I don't make wagers lightly. So! But what did you think of Miss Sophie?'

'I thought she was charming.'

'Oh, indeed she is' – wicked look from under the bright, feathered bonnet – 'and how the Barnards ache to rush her away from temptation down here and give her new interests in London. I fancy they'll find she makes a dozen more conquests, all equally unsuitable, and becomes twice as wilful because of them.'

They took the wrong road and went some miles out of their way, put back on it by a small boy in a dress, muddy to the knees, who informed them Oxford was that way – a wide sweep of his thin arm to the right. Millie gave him sixpence, an extravagance that made his eyes pop out, and Hardy sprang the long-suffering horses into a canter with a great jolt that threw Millie off the seat.

'I can't stand it,' she cried, rescued by Théo, 'I can't stand it! I must advertise for a coachman. Hardy must hoe the garden or carry the coal.'

Théo laughed, a deeply amused laugh that startled Millie into poking back her bonnet for a better look.

'I do declare you look quite radiant when you laugh,' she said, 'almost like . . . Like Marguerite. And how is Marguerite? Is she happy?'

'She has her little boy Robert,' replied Théo carefully.

Marguerite's marriage to one of Guernsey's leading citizens, arranged with infinite care by Caroline, had never been a success. She had been very ill after losing her first two babies and Théo, who had brought her home to La Croix to recover, had found out how very unhappy she was and with no possibility of escape – unless circumstance should make her a widow. But it was gentle, pretty Louise, so very much in love with her dear Edmund, who had been the victim of circumstance.

'How you feel for them all,' cried Millie, peering into Théo's face. 'You are the strangest mixture of passion and cool good manners I have ever met. Lord help anyone who has offended you if one day the passion gets the better of the manners, eh? Now what?'

For they were at the foot of Shotover Hill and Hardy had pulled up. The bays were sweating and distressed, all nerves and anticipation; Millie said she feared for her old bones and got out to walk. She and Théo struggled up beside the coach, clutching their skirts and shouting disjointed conversation. At the top they paused to take in the view along with a great deal of blowy air and Millie said: 'How I remember . . . I grew up here, ran quite wild till I was ten or so and then was snatched away to follow the army. The smell of the grass brings it all back.'

It was inconceivable the grass on Shotover should smell any more richly than grass elsewhere, but Théo was not one to deride that sudden strong pull towards the lost, kindly places of childhood: she only had to close her eyes to feel the soft air of Le P'tit Clos des Pommes, to be overpowered by the smell of apples at the cider-making . . . She gazed about her at the wide view, the trees, the pale fat moving shapes of distant sheep, and a great wave of the homesickness she thought she had conquered rushed over her.

'I often wonder,' Millie was saying as she climbed back in the carriage, 'what Martagon means to Joss.'

No doubt his attitude was ambivalent, Théo thought, as was her own to her loved La Croix.

'Well, at least it will never beggar *him*,' she said.

They were on their way again, and in a sort of stampede, several shaggy donkeys and a tinker's pony accompanying them in a furious gallop. For one horrific moment a pig in the ditch caused the horses to shy violently, shooting Hardy in the air, but he was naturally agile and had had a great deal of practice at staying aboard in a crisis. They righted themselves, even Millie, who was on the floor murmuring 'Jehu, Jehu,' in a mournful undertone.

'Hardy must go!' she cried as they reached Holywell at last, 'Jack must drive us to London or we'll all be killed!' and then, hustling Théo towards the door, 'My dear girl, do put that dog down. He has four perfectly sound legs and is no more tired than I am.'

'But he is full of macaroons,' said Théo.

The clash between upbringing and inclination was all too evident. 'An attentive husband and a baby will cure her restlessness,' Caroline had written, with the optimism of someone who has temporarily relinquished responsibility. Millie disagreed, and wondered if a trip to France, Italy, Egypt, might not be the answer. She had thought her travelling days were done but for Théo she would attempt anything.

She was still pondering Egypt – Egypt was so very far from Jersey – when she and Théo arrived in Russell Square. The house was large, the front door might be expected to open on opulence within. Instead there were bare boards, a few, very few, pieces of exquisite furniture, and an air of imminent departure as if the absence of furnishings were due to their just this minute having been loaded into the removal van . . . Théo found herself allotted a grand bedroom in which stood a splendid eighteenth-century bed hung with damask, a Louis XIV chest of drawers with a jug and basin on top, a candlestick, and a chamber pot.

'I do hope you like it,' Millie said, casting about anxiously, 'I believe I can smell mice. Do you hear that crashing? That's poor dear Di coming downstairs.'

Poor dear Di, otherwise the Miss Cole of the bottled lizards, appeared on the threshold and stared in. Her gaze was pene-trating and disconcerting, partly because of the squint, or perhaps because her height and extreme thinness and large, jutting nose combined to produce an impression of maniacal alertness and eccentricity.

'How nice to meet you,' were her words to Théo, crossing the room with long jerking steps and stooping to peck her cheeks. 'Millie has written so much about you.'

She smelled of lavender water and when she smiled her strange beaked face glowed with deep and innocent kindness.

And then there was Polly with the hat boxes, overjoyed at being home; and there was Nelson, running in pursuit of some small brown frantic animal that shot up the curtain with an angry chattering; and there was Jack, in a clean coat and a turban, coming to ask if they wanted tea.

'I never imagined it would be like this,' said Théo faintly, sitting down on the bed. Caroline had obviously not imagined it either, or she would never have suggested a visit. Théo clutched the elderly cream damask hangings and laughed.

'Oh, how I would like to see the lizards,' she said.

She saw the lizards, and Miss Cole's fine, detailed anatomical sketches, her library of reference books, her letters from great naturalists, explorers and men of science; and she also saw the half an elk which had been banished to the butler's pantry, and the stuffed parrot which sat on its perch in the huge bare drawing room, and she saw Millie's oddly voluptuous bedroom which, though it boasted no more furniture than any of the others, still managed to convey the idea of an eastern harem, with its vivid silks and peacock cushions and the Turkey rugs on every wall.

Two days passed, three. Friends and acquaintances called. Millie entertained all her visitors with madeira and anchovy toasts, a habit which added a certain flavour to morning calls. The drawing room might hold at any one time several eminent scientific gentlemen conversing with poor dear Di, an equally eminent surgeon, a struggling young doctor, Lady Elmhurst and her three pretty daughters, one or two Hussars, a Lancer perhaps, and a banker. The monkey was generally in evidence, and Nelson who was, as Millie said with a sigh, the very devil for anchovy toast. So apparently were Lord Palmerston, some ardent freethinkers, some disciples of Robert Owen, and some learned members of the Zoological Society. Millie's assertion that she threw everybody together pell-mell had certainly been the truth.

'You mustn't expect a dull moment in this house,' Miss Cole told Théo over the ritual of afternoon tea one dull November day, 'the door is always open to whoever cares to come.'

'So long as they do not begin any childish disputes,' said Millie, tinkering with the obdurate old samovar she insisted on using. 'Théo dear, do come and turn this. It leaks, the old knave that it is. No, no, the tap! Ah, that's better.'

Théo sat down again, smoothing her blue wool dress. The monkey reached for bread and butter with long, acquisitive fingers. He felt the cold terribly but distrusted the fire, sitting on a chair back with his spoils.

'Will everyone come to the ball next week?' Théo asked, dismembering a muffin for him.

'Almost everyone. Miss Barnard is bringing Sophie, did I tell you? She will be occupied keeping the poor girl from importunate Hussars. If you give that monkey any more he will be sick.' And then, above the hissing of the samovar: 'We must harry the dressmakers, I suppose.'

The morning found her fingering Théo's best aquamarine silk and acknowledging she had seldom seen anything so fine.

'Caroline always had impeccable taste,' was the remark.

'She wasn't happy with the colour,' said Théo, who was being laced into her corsets by Polly, 'that was my choice.' And here a pink, perspiring look of defiance.

Millie looked round. 'You look thinner than ever. Aren't you well? Aren't you eating? Are you still homesick?'

Why, she was thinking, the girl was slight and fragile, with a narrow waist and round young breasts. Corsets! Who would want to constrict such a pliant, perfect figure? How different from her own girlhood, those flimsy high-waisted dresses that flaunted the flesh and left nothing to the imagination, nothing. The General had breathed his delight into her ear often and often on the dance floor. Her face lit up with the memory, the memory of his arm squeezing the life out of her plump little person, his watery eye glazed over.

'Is something amusing?' demanded Théo.

'My dear old General, bless him. He would have found you a most unsatisfactory armful.'

'I believe you were very fond of him.'

'Perhaps I was, in spite of the glass eye. He was certainly fond of me. He was a good man, a simple old rascal. But there, he's dead and gone, oh years, years.'

Polly was hooking up Théo's dress. The face half hidden by drifting hair showed two spots of colour high on the cheekbones, looked exasperated, rebellious. Millie was

41

conscious that however brilliant and stimulating the company in Russell Square, Mlle de Faurel would rather be elsewhere, would like to go home – though on her own terms, not Caroline's.

Even Millie, who missed very little, could not know how acute her longing had become. She missed the beaches, the tarry quays, the harbours and houses and little hills; she missed Louise more than she had imagined possible, Louise whose tastes were so very different from her own; she missed La Croix with its secure granite walls keeping out the Atlantic blast; most of all she missed the children with their open, unqualified love: Lou's fat arms round her neck, Bon's shy, eager curiosity, Pierre's confidential and adoring smile. She wrote to them every week but it was not the same. She was afraid they would forget her, that they would not know her when she saw them again.

London was exciting, she could sharpen her mind in Millie's drawing room, but her heart was elsewhere. Often it was outside among the sick and poor. She had never seen so many human beings in such squalor. Why was nothing done, she asked Millie? Where were the philanthropists, the benevolent moralists?

'Men of words and not of deeds,' snapped Millie, who perceived the kindling of that crusading spirit Caroline deplored, 'but there is some progress. Shaftesbury is a great soul. Lunatics, Ragged schools . . . Yes, there are steps being taken.'

Théo's indignation was not assuaged. While the reformers took their cautious steps, men and women died for want of common necessities. She burned with revolutionary fervour, all the more fierce because she felt so helpless.

Heavens, thought Millie, and rushed her away to the dressmakers. It was only a momentary diversion, Théo was not interested in clothes, but anything would do, anything. After all, Caroline had made a generous allowance, why shouldn't Théo be encouraged to be frivolous for once? Jade and turquoise, subtle, shifting shades, spilled across their hands: the colours of Théo's eyes, Théo's loves – the sea and sky.

'Yes,' said Millie, 'those are just right.'

Caroline would have chosen mauve or sage green, as if by

restricting colour she could restrict Théo herself. Millie and Théo looked at each other, knowing it, and smiled.

'I am determined you will look the part at my ball,' Millie remarked as they climbed back in the carriage.

'And what part am I to play at your ball?'

But Millie shook her head. She was not yet entirely sure herself. Indeed, she was finding it increasingly difficult to imagine what role Théo de Faurel was going to play in life, but it had occurred to her once or twice that in spite of appearances to the contrary, and all Caroline's unremitting efforts, it might not be an obscure one.

'And will Joss be there?' asked Théo, knowing there was still some doubt, that his ship had been in Malta for repairs.

'Joss? Joss will be there, dear girl, if I have to petition the Admiralty to get him back in time.'

4

He was a big man, dark-haired, with a square intelligent face. He stood in the doorway rubbing his cleanshaven jaw with his large hand, quite unconcerned, quite innocent of the fact he was something of a spectacle. He appeared to be lost in thought, his eyes sweeping dancers and onlookers almost without seeing them.

Where was she, he wondered, and then, remembering how long it was since he had last seen her, he decided he must have missed her, mistaking her face, and began a leisurely survey of the room all over again. It was hot, too hot, and he could feel the unwelcome tightness of his collar. There were plenty of bare white shoulders, flicking fans, bold glances which he met with studied blankness, drawing down his agile dark brows. But Millie . . . Where was Millie?

'Joss! Joss! Dear boy, you look . . .' and she was hanging on his arm. He looked sullen, politely savage, but she only caught a glimpse before she was enveloped in his embrace.

'You haven't changed a bit,' he said, holding her away for inspection as if she had been a doll, 'and in green too. Dear Bos, I don't believe I've ever seen you in anything but green.'

She had reasserted herself, had hold of his cuff, was steering him round the dancers. 'I had to have the parrot stuffed,' she told him, 'he shrieked in the night.'

He heard her indistinctly, which was just as well; the parrot had cost him a great deal of money and the whole of his unreliable temper for a week. But: she never changed, he was thinking, was as jaunty and vital as ever. What streams of letters she had written him down the years, just as jaunty and vital and impulsive as herself, letters that had caught him up in remote corners of the world, arriving in soaked packets and scarcely legible, letters that contained in one breathless page politics, philosophy, misquoted Latin tags, and six sovereign remedies for staying healthy in the tropics. 'The food is like boiled dishcloths,' he had written back once in the early days, cramped below decks in the reeking hole given over to the engineering boys, and back had come the prompt reply: 'Nothing worthwhile is ever easy.' She would have lived off boiled dishcloths for a decade to achieve her aim. 'Do your best,' she had told him, 'make yourself indispensable without being obsequious.' He had done so; he had succeeded. He had grown accustomed to the life, still at times so brutal, and to the sea, which he did not care for much, and because he had a genius for the mechanical he prospered. He had long ago set his heart on rapid promotion and the determination of the Westovers was legendary; his promotion was spectacular.

Millie tugged at his sleeve. She was bobbing up and down and trying to see someone. 'Now where is she?'

'Bos, you know I hate dancing.'

'I know, of course I know. But women, surely you don't hate women?' Her bright little eyes shot a speculative glance at him. He looked stubborn and affronted. Just what had he been up to in Malta?

'Well?'

'Well, I want you to be especially kind to Théo.'

A moment later a small figure in palest aquamarine turned round with a start and Joss found a pair of subtle green eyes on him. 'How do you do,' she said with remarkable formality.

'I'll leave Théo in your care,' said Millie optimistically, acknowledging someone's frantic wave with a distracted one of her own.

Joss, encumbered, prepared to make the best of it. He roused his good manners and asked Théo to dance. To his surprise and relief she refused, said she would prefer a glass of wine, and took his arm. Her voice had the trace of an accent, he noticed. She was slight and graceful, and yes, she did have a distinguished, patrician nose and bony, passionate face – but it was a damped-down passion, she did not sparkle.

They squeezed through the crush. Then they were face to

face with a tall severe woman in grey and a dark, merry, laughing girl in pink.

'Oh, Miss Barnard!' exclaimed Théo with gentle surprise. 'Miss Boswell was so glad you could come. May I introduce Mr Westover? Have you already met?'

They had met, though only once in the long years since Millie had whisked him away from Martagon in her curricle. Joss bowed slightly, so slightly and with such a look of animosity he might as well have slapped the woman's face. Sophie, however, stepped forward boldly and held out her hand. She seemed to have left her prejudices at Martagon, or perhaps the champagne and a desire to shock her aunt had got the better of them. She smiled at Joss and asked some pretty questions about his journey home, and how large his new ship must be, and how long he would be staying.

Miss Barnard wore a look of perfect anguish.

'Did you see that old biddy's face?' Joss demanded as he and Théo passed on to the other side of the room, 'she thinks I'm unspeakable.'

'Well, what you thought of her was written quite clearly on your own face,' as she received her glass of wine at last.

'You realize that enchanting young woman will inherit my house?'

She had never considered he might view Martagon as his own property. She had not received the impression he was vindictive or grasping or uncommonly sentimental. When she had thought about him at all it had been as just Joss, not as a Westover or a Tregarron, but Millie's beloved Joss of the mermaid and the two-headed baby and *Bunnythorn's Arithmetic*.

'I don't expect you to understand,' he was saying, taking a large mouthful of wine and looking round darkly, 'I scarcely understand myself. But I resent it, that girl having Martagon.'

It was absurd, of course, for he had never seen her before. Perhaps what he really resented was the immediate, entirely instinctive pleasure he had taken in her lovely eyes and smooth bare shoulders.

'I didn't know you were interested in the house.'

'I'm not,' and he shrugged and finished his wine. 'It's a great sprawl of a place. I can't say I even like the look of it.'

But Théo knew he lied; the certainty of the lie made her

46

lost for words. Joss did not notice her sudden silence, he was busy looking about, but then, as if he had just remembered she was there: 'Tell me about Jersey.'

She told him a little with polite obedience, something of La Croix and the steep old town of St Aubin, about her sisters and their childhood under a succession of strict governesses, French and English. She did not think she had given a true picture of the island, of the pebbly inlet where she had beached her secret boat, of the cliffs, the little orchards, the ships. But after a while she grew conscious of Joss's intense blue gaze, of his undivided attention, of an odd intimacy that had sprung up, of a sort she had never known before, that was to do with his knowing what she meant and imagining as she spoke the very gulls shrieking and squabbling over the garden at La Croix.

'And what do you propose to do with yourself during your year in England?' he asked at last.

'Millie is going to take me to her refuge for foundlings.'

'You will catch the smallpox.'

'I hope not. Don't you think I could be useful?'

She looked up at him with a passionate appeal, as if he might find her some fulfilling occupation, as if he, from his much greater height, could perceive the way she was to go.

'Well,' he said slowly, 'the foundlings are all right, poor mites, but I thought . . . I thought Bos had to get you married.'

Théo blushed. She felt herself blush deeper and deeper. When she looked up he was reaching for another glass of wine and scanning the room again, too absorbed to notice her embarrassment. In fact he was following the triumphant progress of Miss Sophie Barnard, who was trailing at least six young cubs with undisputed breeding and no prospects, two clergymen, and a cavalry officer. She had obviously slipped her leash. But then a little figure in green bobbed up and dispersed the philandering young gentlemen right and left, detaching the cavalry officer and leading him towards the buffet.

'Théo, Joss, this is Captain Alex Trent. Captain Trent, Miss Théo de Faurel and Mr Joss Westover,' and Millie's eyes twinkled at them. Joss sensed a mood of playful machination. Was she matchmaking? The man looked as if he might be everything Caroline had ever hoped for: fair, good-looking, a man of means and family. Joss, who was none of these, took him in at one glance, inclined his head with complete and boorish lack of interest, and remained mute.

'Miss Boswell tells me you're an islander like myself,' Trent said to Théo, and with a broad, affectionate smile as if there could not possibly be any doubt to which island he referred, 'I have a house at Rozel.'

Rozel: sun on green water and the gulls above the rocks. Théo smiled, said how glad she was to meet him, why had they never met on Jersey? She had never seen him before, this elegant, immaculate young man with the marvellous whiskers, the sculptured moustache. How had Caroline missed him?

Joss was craning to see someone.

'Miss Barnard,' said Théo, following his looks of profound interest, 'how pretty she is.'

'Yes,' said Joss, 'excuse me.'

'What a very dull fellow,' said Alex Trent, watching him for a moment. 'Surely he's not the engineering prodigy, Miss Boswell's godson?'

Since Théo received this rather seriously, her eyes stormy, he took refuge in talking about Jersey. He was not island *born*, he said, he was the son of a Kentish gentleman and had lived all his life in England until he was fourteen. On his father's death his mother had moved to the house in Rozel with a companion, a Madame Legrange. He knew of La Croix of course, it had been pointed out to him, and everyone spoke well of the Faurels, but his mother had been an invalid and generally unwell, she had no social life, depended on Dr Frere. Within two years of the move to Jersey she had died, Madame Legrange had returned to her own family, and Alex, complying with her last wishes, had found himself an ensign in a cavalry regiment. During the last few years he had visited Rozel infrequently, he preferred to live in London, but he had indelibly happy memories: of the house, the harbour, the island.

Indeed, his tenuous connection with the island, with darling old Dr Frere, caused Théo to view him with a deeper interest. Here was someone who knew all those landmarks that were so unutterably important to her, who had walked the same roads and looked at the same pattern of little fields. Joss might accompany her there in spirit but Alex Trent was the next thing to a Jerseyman. The deep festering sense of being rejected, of being cast out of La Croix because she had not measured up, was eased by talking to him; the kinder, older memories surfaced and made her happy. When Joss returned – he had been told by Millie he must dance with *someone* – he found them laughing over some shared recollection.

'Would you care to dance?' he demanded, handing her wine glass to the startled Alex who took it meekly, 'I'm sure Captain Trent won't mind looking after your drink.'

Théo found herself borne along, Joss's hand under her elbow and Joss's large person clearing the way. He did not like dancing, said his expression, but he would indulge in it for the sake of good manners – for Millie's sake.

On the dance floor, Théo found, he had developed the art of improvisation to an unlikely pitch, and as his great height and reach allowed him to swing most ladies off their feet he scarcely bothered what his partner was doing.

She said: 'I see you're a desperate man for going your own way.'

'I'm sorry. Have I trodden on you?'

'Good Heavens no! My feet hardly touch the ground. But tell me, has no one ever taught you the steps?'

They turned a corner abruptly, so abruptly her beautiful skirt flew out in a shimmer of silk. He was grinning.

'No, well . . . Shall we call it quits? We've been round twice. Surely to goodness that's enough to satisfy Bos?'

'So you only asked me out of a sense of duty?'

'You seemed the obvious choice. Did you want to talk to that affected young fool all night?'

'Yes, if he talks about Jersey. You've no idea how homesick I am. He even knows all about my grandfather Bonespoir.'

Bonespoir had been a giant with red whiskers, who habitually went to sea with two monkeys and a mastiff. He had brought back to Honorine a whole aviary of parrots, which she hated, and which had become famous. Now, of course, they were part of the legend. He had been the youngest of the family but had inherited equally with his elder brother Henri, who promptly denied him any share in the business. Bon was not suitable, he said, he drank too much, he chased women, he risked the ships by sailing them too hard. There had been terrible rows, audible to the greater part of St Helier. Then Bon had stolen one of the ships — all the men loved him, would sail with him anywhere — and sailed away, no one knew where. He had come back ten years later like the poor boy in the fairy tales, remarkably respectable, remarkably rich. Cocoa, rum, slaves, he had carried them all. He returned with six ships and a fortune, bought Henri out of the family house in St Aubin and married the daughter of a Guernsey seigneur. His ships took the trade from the company, for he deliberately set up a rival wine shipper's, naming it Faurel Mannelier after himself and Honorine. He was implacable in his revenge.

How the young Théo had loved him, climbing on his knee for stories of pirates, slavers, dark deeds in the tropics. How his flamboyant style had appealed to her in contrast with Caroline's genteel resetraint. She adored her father, that relationship was secure, a rock of known dimensions; but with Old Bon she could reach out to new experiences, be unashamedly, unreservedly exactly what she liked. Discipline he understood, ships at sea were unsafe without it, but decorum was an unknown quantity. He had had a small farmhouse in the north of the island where Théo had spent some of her happiest hours, sitting with him under the vines at Le P'tit Clos des Pommes, listening to his great carrying voice.

'So that was Bonespoir,' said Joss, and then: 'Let's dance. They'll be playing the last soon.'

'I believe I'm engaged to a Mr Sandwich,' said Théo, not consulting her card but staring with a wrinkled brow at a small weasel-faced man pushing towards them.

'I thought you might like to be deprived of the pleasure?' and Joss seized her arm, backed her away to the dance floor.

They progressed eccentrically, Théo a little dizzy. She caught a stray glimpse of Sophie dancing with one of Millie's young Hussars and looking . . . what? Wistful, furious, disappointed? Perhaps all of those or none of them. But she was looking at Joss with feeling, there was no doubt of that.

'Poor Mr Sandwich,' said Théo as they galloped on.

'He is probably a perfect gentleman, he will think it was he who made the mistake. Or if not, Millie will comfort him. That wasn't your dress tearing, that odd sound?'

'I rather think it was the skirt of the lady in blue. Maybe we should slow down.'

'I don't see why. I'm enjoying myself. I never enjoyed dancing before.'

Nor had she, not with quite such wild delight. She could feel the perspiration starting on her forehead and between her bare shoulder blades; her necklace, the aquamarine necklace her father had given her, was stuck to her skin.

'I'm not sure, strictly speaking, it could be called dancing,' she said, her head thrown back.

Alex said as much too, claiming her for the last. Joss relinquished her with a wry smile and went to raid the debris of the buffet, noticing Millie consoling Mr Sandwich over the incomprehensible mix-up and laughing rather harshly and unsympathetically.

Millie was tired; the evening had been a success but it had drained her. She might have just come from a mule ride up a Turkish mountain. Théo found her saying goodbyes, encouraging the stragglers, interrupting even Alex's protracted, starry-eyed leavetaking.

'To bed,' she cried, when they had all, by some means or other, been ejected, 'leave everything till the morning.' She plucked the green feathers from her hair, shooing the two young maids and Hardy away from the chaos and unlovely ruin of the feast, shutting the ballroom doors with finality.

Jack appeared. 'Mr Joss is in the library a-partakin' of the leftovers.'

He was. He had carried a plate there and a last glass of champagne. His coat was thrown over a chair and his shoes were kicked in the hearth. Opposite, propped upright but fast asleep, sat Miss Cole, snoring gently.

'You look debauched,' said Millie, who never minced words.

'I mean to have her,' he replied inconsequentially, 'I mean to marry young Sophie.'

'You're drunk. Why would you want Sophie Barnard? For Martagon?'

'Damn Martagon.'

'For the money then.'

'There may not be that much money. There may be several

mortgages and a great many debts.' He looked up, placidly chewing.

'That place,' cried Millie. 'Why must you always become irrational where Martagon is concerned?' He had looked like this once before, she was thinking, when she had opened another library door and found him standing there, wary and defiant and ready to bite. She bit her lip. It came to her that this was not, after all, a fit of momentary madness. He had thought about the possibilities long ago, and often through the years, and now Sophie Barnard had shown him the means to achieve . . . whatever it was he longed to achieve. Not Martagon? Not the money? A posthumous revenge on the Westovers?

'Revenge is a sour pudding,' she told him, 'as you will find out.'

She had gone, the door had closed. Nelson, sensing a change of atmosphere, slid from his hiding place beneath Miss Cole's chair and begged shamelessly for the remains on Joss's plate. Joss stood up and stretched. 'I didn't mean to upset her,' he said.

Théo's head was aching from the wine. It was morning now, outside the grey cold dawn was breaking. Her own voice sounded dull and slow.

'Do you really want Sophie Barnard?'

'She's very pretty.' It was all he was going to say. He took up his jacket and swung it over his shoulder. And then: 'Dear Théo, which of us would have his motives examined too closely?'

'Then it isn't Sophie?' And when he did not reply: 'They would never agree to it, never. You would have to elope.'

He laughed, put an arm round her shoulders and bent to drop a kiss on the parting in her smooth hair. Then he went to the door and opened it, waiting for her to pass through.

'We must send Polly down to wrap up old Di,' he said with an affectionate glance at the queer old lady in the chair. 'If I were you, Théo de Faurel, I would forget Sophie Barnard and worry about what you're going to do when Captain Trent comes calling, kissing your hand and begging you to marry him.'

5

Captain Trent knew nothing of elliptical approaches, of the many virtues of subtlety: he wooed with a maddening, even perverse punctuality and to a strict pattern. He always brought flowers, he was always available to ride during the afternoon, and he called promptly at two every day whatever the weather.

'He means to have you,' said Millie, half amused, half uneasy, 'I swear he means to have you.' She had a moderate opinion of his intelligence, his prospects, and even his motives, but she gave him credit for such single-minded pursuit. She also had an odd ambivalence of feeling towards Théo herself, Théo whom she longed to see happy and prosperous. She did not feel Théo's happiness and prosperity depended on a young captain of the Lancers, however charming; material comfort she might have, certainly, but what about spiritual comfort? She could not see it as a marriage of true minds, and that was what Théo needed, a proper mate, a man to whom she was totally committed, or else she would be away after satisfaction and fulfilment God knows where . . .

Théo meanwhile was trying not to look on Alex as a fortune hunter, trying not to turn his constancy and generosity into blatant self-interest. He was younger than she was and though he expected to inherit a decent amount of money one day he was not rich, not nearly rich. Caroline had had a nose for shabby young men seeking to improve their position in life and she had taught Théo how to recognize the signs; this meant that Théo, who was aware of falling short of womanly perfection, distrusted every man's motives, however innocent.

She refused to ride with him: she was an indifferent horsewoman, nervous and inept; she danced with him only when it was unavoidable; she was out when he called as often as she could be; but in the end, the very end, she must acknowledge his peculiar persistence and decide what to do about it.

'You'll only fuel the fire if you refuse to meet him at all,' said Joss one morning two weeks after the ball, tackling with his usual gusto the large breakfast his enormous frame seemed to require. He had real reason to feel this was an inescapable truth: he was twice as eager to see Sophie Barnard having twice been refused admittance to her house on the flimsiest excuses. He had even written a disgracefully – or so he felt – obsequious letter to Miss Barnard asking if he might call before he joined his ship and had received a frosty reply to the effect that of course he was welcome, but they were distressingly busy, a return to Martagon planned for the very near future. It was a rebuff, as plain a rebuff as could be, and couched in terms intended, rather optimistically, not to offend Millie.

'I like him,' said Théo, pushing her plate and looking sorrowfully into her cup of tea, 'but I don't want to encourage him. I don't . . .'

'Strikes me women can never make a decision. Tell him to go away or let him see you now and then. Don't keep him dangling about hoping . . . If he's any kind of man at all he'll get irritated and cause trouble.' Joss crunched bacon heartily, occasionally poking a piece under the table for that opportunist Nelson. 'I can't abide these part-time soldiers,' he said at last, 'on half pay, joining in for the parades and the applause, letting better men fight the battles and get the real glory. And what happens to those better men? I've seen them time and again, left out in some hot, disease-ridden hole, badly paid, badly provisioned, badly led in all probability, and then expected to perform miracles. How they do I don't understand, but they do, and the rich spoiled children back home march up and down once or twice in their fancy uniforms and get all the credit.'

There was a silence. Théo, strongly inclined to his view, nevertheless felt an irrational urge to defend Alex, who was the most amiable of men; to question his courage touched on the courage of all Jerseymen. She thought of him as a Jerseyman. She was about to jump in with some reasonable explanation for Alex being always on half pay – was it not almost obligatory for the sons of good families? Whoever expected them to share those hot, disease-ridden holes with ordinary soldiers? – when Joss said: 'Where's his regiment now?'

'They were in India. I'm not sure if they're home.' She watched him raid the sideboard and come back with the last of everything.

'There. You see.'

'No, I don't see. Alex couldn't go to India. He was advised against it by the doctors.'

'Doctors no doubt make a great deal of money advising young idlers not to risk their health in dangerous climates. As soon as there's any real fighting to be done there's a rush to get a featherbed barracks post or go on half pay.'

The door opened. 'Arguing again?' asked Millie.

'Joss was telling me why he disapproves of Captain Trent.'

'Heavens, you should take no notice. Joss disapproves of nearly everyone, his standards are so exacting. Has Di not come down? My dear, is there any hot tea or should I ring for some more?'

There was hot tea, muffins, marmalade, peach conserve and even a last, overlooked boiled egg. Millie eyed the range of empty dishes on the sideboard with resignation. She turned to Joss, who had just finished reading something that he tucked, deliberately and with a thoughtful expression, under his plate.

'Is that your recall?' she asked.

He leant back and undid his waistcoat. 'The end of next week.'

'Then we must try to make the rest of your stay as exciting as possible.'

'Not more parties, Bos. I can't abide them. I thought I might go down to Portsmouth by way of Oxford, see the Gurdens.'

'Of course. I expected it. Are we invited too?'

Joss stretched, began to refasten his waistcoat buttons slowly, and gave her a lopsided smile. 'Now would I leave without you, Bos dear? And I need you, after all, to conjure me an invitation to Martagon.'

55

Millie looked at him sadly. 'Are you sure . . .' she began, but then applied herself to her toast, after another moment declaring airily: 'I shall absolutely refuse to call on Uncle Joseph again. He has no idea of a good sherry.'

There was a familiar knock, not at all discreet. Jack, who fulfilled his role of butler with idiosyncratic aplomb, stuck in his head. 'Captain Trent is in the 'all and begs pardon but can he have the honour of a quiet word with Miss Théo?'

'Good Heavens!' exclaimed Millie on a mouthful of toast.

'It's far too early to call demanding private interviews,' said Joss. 'Surely you aren't going down?' as Théo rose.

'Dear Joss, Théo is quite old enough to conduct her own life without help from us or from ridiculous social convention. If he wishes to see her and she wishes to allow it we have no right to interfere.'

Théo smiled. It was a shadow of her usual smile but it was a smile bordering on the defiant, and she walked resolutely to the door.

'Perhaps you should have a chaperon,' said Joss, standing up.

'Do sit down,' said Millie, 'Théo's quite capable of talking to a man alone without losing her reason or her virtue. Sit down. You still have a whole toastrack of toast to clear up.'

Joss sat, leaning back with his hands clasped across his stomach. 'Be careful,' he said, 'you ought to have serious reservations about a man whose health is in doubt.'

Théo refused to give him the satisfaction of shattering her dignity; she would *not* laugh. Something told her too that he was quite serious, that beneath his affable exterior was an altogether harder Joss Westover who felt nothing but contempt for half-pay soldiers.

'What is wrong with his health?' Millie was demanding, as Théo stepped out and Miss Cole, in her usual morning disarray, stepped in. 'He looks perfectly well to me.'

'You'd better come quick,' said Waterloo Jackson, capering down the stairs ahead of Théo, 'Nelson has him cornered in the parlour and is worriting his trouser legs.'

They need not have hurried. Alex had given Nelson a

shrewd whack with a candlestick seized off the mantel and the dog was now crouched on the hearthrug, growling. Théo called him, scolded him, and ejected him in an instant, shutting the door firmly and turning to see Alex replacing his weapon next to the silhouette of Millie's grandmother.

'She looks as if she were pretty,' he said, embarrassed to be caught at such a disadvantage and trying for a neutral subject. 'As much as you can see, anyway.'

'According to Millie she crossed China on a donkey. It may be apocryphal, of course. But it seems to run in the family, a sort of eccentric wanderlust.'

Alex, whose regard for Millie was not very high, apparently decided it might be better to plunge in at once without waiting to dip his toes. 'Forgive me for calling so early, but I am rejoining the regiment; there isn't any time . . . I have to leave tonight. I wondered . . . I tried to consult Miss Boswell about this a few days ago but she refused to discuss it, said she wasn't your guardian, that I ought to write to your mother . . . Will you marry me?'

She had her back against the door, leaned a little for support. She had avoided marriage so long, with a mixture of total innocence and desperate cunning, that a direct proposal, made across ten feet of room and with no one else present, caught her unawares and left her breathless. All she could think of was that Millie had known about this for several days and had said nothing, had not seen fit to warn her or, just now, given her any hint of it at all. But then Millie would have said she ought to have seen it coming for herself, that to avoid looking at the truth was a form of cowardice Millie especially despised, and that at least she had had the grace to let Théo manage it all on her own, something Caroline would never have done.

'I am . . . honoured,' she began, hearing Joss laughing loudly in her ear as she spoke.

'Honoured! Honoured be damned!' cried Alex with an impatience she had never seen before, crossing the rug and taking her hands, turning them palm up and kissing them. For a moment she stood absolutely still, looking down on his fair head, the stiff, ornate collar of his uniform coat, the gold lace, the hilt of the sword.

'I adore you,' he said, 'surely you can see that?'

No, she had not seen it; no doubt she should have. She felt naive and gauche suddenly, an insensitive, unwordly child. But then Caroline had not encouraged any gentlemen, however eligible, to kiss her daughters' palms and declare themselves so shamelessly.

'I don't know what to say,' Théo whispered, at bay.

'Say you care for me. Say you feel something.'

She felt exasperation, and inexplicable fright. She tried to withdraw her hands but he had been prepared for that and would not let her. He gazed with an earnestness it was not easy to dismiss lightly. She cast about for some sensible words, a kindly phrase of absolute rejection. Nothing. Her eyes beseeched him to let her go. He did not.

'If your answer is no, tell me I may ask again. Tell me that much at least.'

'Of course the answer is no' – a grasp on her courage at last – 'We've known each other a few weeks, that's all.' It was a thin excuse, would not have been entertained by Caroline, who passed or rejected marriage candidates within an hour of first acquaintance.

'But let me see you again.'

'I think it might be better if you didn't call. You'll be in barracks. You'll be . . . busy. It will be easy to forget all this as . . . nonsense.'

He let go of her hands abruptly only to take her shoulders and stoop to kiss her cheek, her forehead, her mouth. It was remarkably improper. Even Millie might have hit him over the head with a poker for it, an alarming punishment she had once meted out to a Turkish bandit who had tried much the same thing.

Théo had not been kissed since André Givard had taken her in his arms on the terrace all those years ago, and he too had tasted of cigars. The longing to be held and comforted, the overwhelming need for reassuring physical contact, and the excitement of novelty, caught her unawares again. Alex's kisses were pleasant, restrained enough not to frighten her; it was an exhibition of chaste adoration rather than frantic passion. When he let her go she stepped back, only a little short of breath, and said: 'Perhaps you should go,' with an *hauteur* her mother could not have bettered.

'We could live at Rozel,' he said unexpectedly as if he had not heard her, 'I would give up the army.'

'You must never give up anything on my account. In any case, you've only just rejoined the regiment.'

'But I don't care for it much. I could leave any time without regrets. It's only that there might be some excitement . . . The Turks, you know, the Russians.'

'And you'd exchange the regiment for a life of idleness and boredom at Rozel?'

'Long ago I did once wish to train as a doctor, but my mother was set on the cavalry. Ask Dr Frere. He and I have spoken about it often. He was always hopeful, said it didn't matter if I started late, that dedication and determination would see me through. Would you object to being married to a doctor?'

She was the daughter of one, how could she object? The mention of Dr Frere brought all the homesickness back. How often she had smiled at his wrinkled, cadaverous face framed in its wild white hair: her father's friend and colleague, her own mentor as she coped with the destitute fisherwomen, the orphans, the iron-willed benevolence of her charity committees. All her loves stirred and beckoned suddenly: the sea, the cliffs and rocks, the granite stronghold of La Croix. What she would not give to be rid of corsets and morning calls and importunate young men with moustaches and be quite alone in a small boat, pulling round to Petit Port in the sun and wind the way she had used to during those stolen hours of freedom.

She shook her head, not to Alex's question, but to the memories. She must not be sentimental about this, her life was in the balance. How could she begin to care for this man? True, she felt some vague affection, but that was because he was a likeable man and was linked, however remotely, with all she deeply loved. He was very young, an undeveloped twenty-four. It ought to mean nothing, he was far more experienced, she supposed, in so many ways, but twenty-four . . . If she had expected a proposal at all it would have been one from a middle-aged widower, a man who wanted a mother for his children, a sound, competent woman to keep his house in order. But this . . .

Théo found she was dazzled by the brass buttons, by the gold lace. Her thoughts wandered, became confused, and her voice, when she managed to speak, was not her own.

'You mustn't expect me to change my mind.'

'Oh, but I do. Théo – I may call you Théo? – I'll ask you again. I'll write. You would be so right for Rozel.'

Had he known it he touched her on the only spot she was vulnerable, for there were moments when she felt she could sell her very soul to see the island again. Had he known it? He knew she had twelve thousand pounds of her own and judged by her manner she had been kept as close as a nun. Could such a woman resist the spirited assault of a handsome young Lancer?

'I will ask you again,' he repeated, and thought the high colour in her face was guilty pleasure.

After he had gone out she stood for a moment, listening to the front door closing and Nelson's distant, frustrated yapping.

Then: 'Dash it,' said a voice, 'I don't want to go to the opera. I shall have to dress up, choke myself with a starched collar, and be polite to that hideous Lady Fox. You can manage without me. Better still, take Di along. She'd love to talk reptiles to Mr Barker.'

'Joss. Joss!' Millie was pattering down the stairs after him. 'Oh, what a disgrace you are! You refuse all the invitations. It's so ill-mannered, so . . . perverse. And it's Lady Ford, not Lady Fox.'

'I'm sure I don't care if it's Lady Foley. D'you remember old Lady Foley? She used to go visiting with her curl papers in. Now there was a woman who knew what to do with etiquette.' He had reached the foot of the stairs. 'Hello, Théo. Did you accept him?'

'I think you could have warned me.'

'You didn't accept then.'

'Of course not.'

'Of course not. Think how inconvenient if every time you wanted to travel abroad he pleaded ill health and a delicate liver.'

'Oh Joss,' said Millie, reaching up for his arm, 'don't tease the poor girl so. Joss . . . come back . . . You *will* go to the opera Joss . . . What *is* that dreadful barking?'

'That's Nelson,' remarked Joss over his shoulder, putting on his hat, 'he doesn't like soldiers either.'

The house in Russell Square had made her welcome; for all its peculiarities Théo thought of it as home. Yet still more than anything she wanted to return to the island, wanted to sit in a small room of her own overlooking St Aubin's fort, wanted to have time to herself safe from Caroline's interference, to have time . . . Time to help the children grow up, to explore all the rock pools, to teach Bon to sail, time to persuade Dr Frere she could make him an admirable assistant, time to read, time to paint.

'What are you smiling at?' Joss asked her one morning as they sat over a disgracefully late breakfast.

'Oh, at a mental picture I had of myself in a few years' time, a rather starched, proper spinster, my glasses on my nose, helping old Dr Frere wind bandages. I expect that's all he would ever allow me to do if I were to ask him.'

'Dr Frere? But I believe there are schools for nurses. I don't know about this country but abroad . . . My last captain had a sister who ran away to go to one.'

'How spirited of her. I'm a terrible coward. I could never run away. My conscience would stop me. I feel . . . Sometimes I feel so responsible for other people's peace of mind: Mama, Louise, even my cantankerous committee ladies. I suppose you couldn't understand that. You don't care about conscience, you can do as you please.'

Joss grinned. 'What do you think?'

Nelson emerged from under the sideboard. Théo reached down to catch his collar and lift him on to her lap.

'Now *that* toadie would never criticize you,' Joss told her. 'You could run away with a Russian count and dress in wolf skins and he would still die for you.' He was tucking his post under an accommodating plate and as he fingered the pages his look became deep, introvert, considering.

'Bad news?' asked Théo gently from the far side of the coffee jug.

'There's going to be war with Russia. The signs have been

61

there a long time but now there's more and more talk . . . This is from Lieutenant Devlin, he was with me in my first ship. We're much of an age but he, poor fellow, can't get any promotion at all, no influence, no money . . . I outrank him by far, of course. It's a sour thing between friends. I'd move heaven and earth to get him a ship of his own, but there are no ships, at least no ships for the able and deserving. Well, Devlin says it's war for certain.'

'But it's Turkey who is at war with Russia.'

'For the time being.'

Théo poured her coffee thoughtfully. She had not considered that England might seek to keep the tottering Turkish Empire on its feet for the sake of denying Russia the Mediterranean. Her grasp of world affairs was not very firm, her views on the stratagems of ambitious politics rather naive, and she found she did not really care who held power in Constantinople; she had dimly supposed only the people who lived there were likely to have strong opinions.

'They won't send the cavalry to Russia, will they?' she asked abruptly as her thoughts ran on.

Joss frowned. 'You wouldn't care a toss for him if he weren't masquerading as a Jerseyman and always reminding you of home.'

'He's perfectly good-natured and inoffensive.'

'My God! Are those the qualities you appreciate in a man? You would sell yourself for thirty years of inoffensive good nature! And I thought you meant to reject him completely. I thought you were a woman of sense!'

Théo moved the coffee pot the better to return his furious stare. 'I'm sorry you don't like Captain Trent. I never said I wanted to marry him – I have refused him once if you recall – but he's always amiable and always good company . . .'

'Meaning I am not. Nor is any man unless he's playing a part or was born a saint. But it seems to me you think a great deal more of him than you pretend: I only mention Russia and you imagine him dead on some battlefield. Yes you did. I saw it in your face. Well, I tell you this, my girl, I'm far more likely to die in a war against Russia than your darling Captain Trent. They've a fine fleet and a strong base at Sebastopol . . . And we haven't seen proper action for years and are commanded by old fools still fighting Trafalgar and the Nile.'

Théo pushed back her soft obedient hair. Her coffee was cooling, her breakfast was uneaten. From the angry flush that had coloured her face when Joss had challenged her about Alex, she had been reduced to a tired pallor, every feature twice as sharp as usual.

'Captain Trent really wants to be a doctor,' she said after a long time and in the expressionless voice of someone tentatively holding out an olive branch. Joss, however, was not a man who easily concealed his contempt.

'Doctor! So he has two baits to his hook! Jersey and medicine. There's more to that young cub than meets the eye. He knows how to make an effective breach in your defences, doesn't he? And what does he say about your ambitions? About your wanting to be a nurse?'

'Nothing. I don't want to be a nurse . . . I don't know what I want. I would love . . . I always hoped I could run Faurel Mannelier.'

Joss hooted with laughter and his heavy face brightened. His eyes narrowed to a gleam, a blue gleam of humour, horror, admiration.

'Follow in the footsteps of your disreputable red-bearded grandfather Bonespoir, you mean.'

'And why not?' She was fiercer than he had ever seen her in an instant, her eyes open very wide and glowing with a strange light. 'My grandmother Honorine ran the entire business quite competently while he was away at sea, and he was away two years together sometimes. He left it all to her.'

'Your grandmother of the parrots,' mused Joss, remembering.

'Oh,' said Théo, wholly serious, 'I believe I would manage better without the parrots.'

6

Dr Crale had treated Millie in her girlhood when he himself, as he constantly remarked, had been not much more than a child. Those had been heady days when he had served as the assistant of a renowned physician whose patients had included all the important Oxford men, the more expensive undergraduates, the infamous, socially brilliant women. He was nearly seventy now, a short, quick, wiry little man, of a height and vivacity to match Millie herself. He dressed out of fashion — *she* said deliberately — and often, to her consternation, in breeches and boots like a country practitioner. He rode about on a shaggy white pony, a tinker's pony, a ragman's pony, an ambling, placid beast fit for a child, an idiot, to bestride. Dr Crale, however, rode by guess and by God, and there were often some miles separating him and his kindly steed. Millie, who came on her mother's side from a whole family of brilliant riders, who had ridden to hounds with the verve and determination not usually associated with elderly ladies, who had mounted camels with equanimity and had won many a difference of opinion with opinionated mules, Millie hid her eyes when she saw him approaching on any kind of quadruped and had been known to refuse to see him.

He had retired from practice now and lived off the fortune he had made out of bored ladies, for whom he had made up many harmless pills, beautifully coloured and shaped, nothing less than works of art. Millie called him mercenary to his face, and took delight in reminding him of more stirring days before he had become fashionable and cunning, or cunning and fashionable, there was some dispute as to which had come first.

He had come to the conclusion at Millie's ball that Mademoiselle de Faurel was something special in the way of elegant and wealthy young women. She understood his medical vocabulary for one thing, and did not object to his cigars. He did not approve of her interest in nursing, it seemed more than was appropriate, and he held that ladies should nurse only their own children and immediate families; but he approved of common sense, a modicum of intelligence, a steady nerve. And if Théo in aquamarine silk and adorable décolletage had charmed him, Théo in quiet grey, and with ringlets, smote him to the heart.

Théo was aware of his qualified admiration, much, she supposed, like that of Dr Frere who indulged her for her father's sake and that of enduring friendship. The devil of rebellion leaped up and singed her heart. But she received Dr Crale in Millie's place that morning before they left for Oxford with grace and aplomb, explaining that Millie was out after some sort of new, very new, almost secret, probably unobtainable, telescope. Miss Cole had insisted she must have one.

'I have attended saner women in lunatic asylums,' said Dr Crale morosely, following to the library where Théo had been writing, 'I hope I haven't disturbed you, Mamselle, I do hope I haven't disturbed you. I never stand on ceremony with Miss Boswell, we are too old for it, know each other too well.'

Théo shut up her long letter to Louise, cleared away pen and ink, and rang for Jack. It was in the nature of the Russell Square house that Jack did not answer, but that Joss put his head round and asked what she wanted, only coming in for a perfunctory handshake when he realized Dr Crale was present and going out at once without anything more than 'Good morning'.

'There is a bone under my chair,' said Dr Crale, reaching down as the door closed on Joss's broad, indifferent back. He forbore to say it was, in fact, half a carcase.

'Millie leaves the doors open, Nelson takes his bones wherever he likes,' Théo said, taking one look and thinking it would be prudent to ignore it, 'then she wonders why there are chicken wings under the sofa.'

'I am sure you find her very eccentric.'

'I find her quite delightful,' said Théo with feeling.

'I'm glad you think so, glad indeed. She is my oldest friend. But I wouldn't blame you if you found her overpowering. She has overpowered greater characters than you or I, Mamselle, oh dear yes. She has brought sultans to their knees, I believe.'

Joss re-entered. A thunderous look made Théo and her guest stare at him nervously.

'I am not to join the ship until Monday now,' he announced, setting down the coffee tray he carried, 'and Di has returned without Bos, apparently lost her in the Observatory or some orangery, I can't make out which. And they didn't find the telescope and she came home in a cab without any money, I had to pay the driver before I could extract her, he was quite rightly indignant. I'm not sure she should be allowed out alone.'

'I believe Dr Crale would agree with you.'

'I'm not saying she's not clever,' Crale said, taking his coffee, 'but it is often the way with genius, one part of the brain develops at the expense of others. She would be incapable of looking after herself and yet her work on reptiles is so highly regarded she is consulted by Sir Richard Owen, entertains practically every member of the Zoological Society in that stinking attic of hers. God save us from intelligent women.'

Dr Crale sank deeper into his deep chair, watching the rain fly up against the windows and hearing its hiss in the chimney. It was a miserable day, a cold and miserable day. He had determined to get himself invited to luncheon if it could be done, he would so dearly love to sit next to this charming girl who spoke with such a pleasant inflexion, whose keen and strangely-coloured eyes were so easily kindled.

He was destined, however, for Miss Cole, who wished to consult him on some personal medical matter, and who drew him away and upstairs to her stinking attic. Joss laughed shamelessly at his evident distress and drank up the coffee, remarking between mouthfuls of small biscuits: 'He is frightened to death of Di, that's the truth of it. He doesn't understand a word she says, she talks to him as if he too has a great scientific brain, which he has not. Here, would you like the last one? Lord, you've no idea how I long to be back on a ship.'

'But what about the wooing of Miss Barnard?'

'Oh, that's no great matter.'

Théo cocked an eyebrow at him, saw grinning self-confidence, a blaze of roguish enthusiasm. Was he so certain of success?

'You told me I wouldn't care a toss about Alex Trent if he weren't a Jerseyman; it seems to me you might ask yourself why you care so much about Martagon. I can't see why you need to be so touchy about the place.'

Joss leaned back, crossed his legs, and then reached along the sofa to pick up her hand, turning it over much as Alex had done. Instead of kissing it – what an impossible idea, she thought, Joss being Joss – he traced the lines upon her palm with the long forefinger of his other hand, and smiled.

'Have you ever had your fortune told? I believe my Cornish grandmother had the second sight.' And then, quite seriously: 'Bastards are always touchy, didn't you know that?'

Jack and Polly were sent on ahead to Oxford to prepare the lodgings owing to the landlady's disinclination – as Millie put it – to air the beds or beat out the fleas. The carriage containing the two ladies followed a day later, scampering along in the usual harum-scarum manner, Hardy in his element on a fast road crammed with other traffic, singeing the wheels of goods waggons, gigs, all the more sober travelling chariots and a nobleman's brougham. Joss, prudently, had gone by rail.

'He won't arrive before us, oh dear no,' Millie told Théo as they cracked along at their foolhardy pace, 'not if he gets his nose inside an engine shed. D'you know, I've been plagued more by Joss's steam engines than by Di's lizards.'

She was right, Joss was not to be found in Oxford, Oxford in the rain, the streets streaming, the trees tormented. Polly was in tears because she could not get the fire to draw, the draught being all contrary, and Jack was in a dour mood because the weather had gone to his bones. There was nothing to be done with either of them in this mood, said Millie, closing the door on them and tackling the fire herself; the weather had got to Jack's bones once in Turkey and she had been carried off by bandits right under his nose, spending two very uncomfortable days in a cave, sleeping on goatskins and eating strong cheese.

'We all have our bad days,' she ended cheerfully, 'I expect it's all this talk of war, it's brought back the memories, stirred his blood. It's a cruel thing to have one's blood stirred at his age. Go and shout for muffins, dear girl, we'll have a feast.'

Polly brought the muffins and a note from Miss Barnard inviting them to supper at Martagon.

'It doesn't mention Joss anywhere,' said Théo, as they sat toasting side by side.

'No. Well . . . I wouldn't expect it to. We'll take him anyway.'

'You don't think . . .'

'Sophie? The Barnards will do everything to stop it. I must rely on them to repulse him, I can't. They won't countenance their pretty heiress marrying an illegitimate naval officer with barely a hundred pounds a year over and above his pay. Oh, nothing will come of it, nothing. Joss will come to his senses, of course he will; there is something about Martagon that makes him unreasonable, but he can't be unreasonable for ever, he is not that kind of man.'

Nelson was pushing between them for crumbs, knowing he only had to wag his stumpy tail to be indulged. Théo looked down, smiling.

'You don't sound very sure,' she said to Millie.

It was debatable whether the Joss Westover who travelled the road to Otmoor in the winter of 1853 was substantially changed from the Joss Westover of sixteen years earlier who had charged along it in Millie's daring curricle, holding on for his life. Then he had been dressed in clothes that were rather too big for him, hand-me-downs of Pa Gurden's, and Millie had wondered if he really had such very large feet or if his boots too were someone else's. Now, setting the lean grey horse into a canter on a level stretch, he sat in the gig with his face abnormally sullen, as morose, as cast down, as if he were on his way to a funeral. Théo kept silent, staring at the road ahead. She had innocently expected he would be pleased to visit his foster home, indeed the only home he had known until the age of fourteen; after all, surely this was why he had come to Oxford?

He still has large hands and feet, Millie might have told

her, but it is the dark side of his nature that causes the most concern.

They turned down a narrow lane, even narrower than the last, and the horse slowed of his own accord, staggering a little in the deep-gouged ruts of the farm waggons. There was a house ahead, low and simple, nothing much more than a stone cottage with a range of buildings attached, a tiny yard full of boisterous bullocks. Joss pulled up; there was something almost savage in the way he pulled up. He handed Théo the reins.

'Hold him a moment, will you. They may not be at home. There's no point in your muddying your dress for nothing.'

He jumped down, picked his way to the gate and hallooed over it, a nautical bellow that sent the bullocks slamming against the far wall and a plump, short woman running out in consternation.

If Théo had expected a grand scene of reunion, Joss not having been back to the farm for nearly ten years, she was disappointed. It was clear that, for the briefest moment, his foster mother did not recognize him. When she did she was in two minds about him: he was not an easy man to embrace, six-foot-something in his large boots and not offering himself up for kisses. She took one of his hands and smiled and smiled, quite incoherent but careful, mindful of their respective positions . . . Had she forgotten, Théo wondered, how she used to box his ears? Could she not find any trace of the child she had raised in the gentleman who stood before her?

But perhaps it was Théo who caused her the most anxiety. The parlour was not swept and there was no tea in the house until Will came back from Oxford. She threw open the back door, reddening, and ushered them into a fragrant, smoky interior. There were pies and pastry on the table, the oven was stoked and smoking, and three or four nephews and nieces were ranged on a settle licking jam off a spoon.

'Oh,' cried Théo, 'we've interrupted your baking.'

'My dear, think nothing of it.'

But it was evident they felt they must think something of her, Théo de Faurel, and not only for her own sake but because they wondered at her relationship with Joss. She explained she was, in a sense, only another of Millie's god-

69

children, but that did nothing to clarify the situation; god-children were not, as far as Mrs Gurden knew, written down in the table of consanguinity as forbidden to marry. Thus they all beamed on her, plied her with hot tartlets and strawberry wine and scones, believing that shortly she might become Mrs Westover and, though it would remain unspoken for ever, a daughter of the house.

Mrs Gurden, who had known him intimately from two days old, got over her awe of the mature Joss in half an hour and sent him out into the fields to find his brothers Tom and Harry, who were mending the gaps and looking to the ditches. Old Pa Gurden was dead, but then Joss knew that and if it was any kind of grief to him kept silent on the matter. He did not even care to change his boots for some more manful ones belonging to the absent William, he simply ducked out through the low doorway and vanished without a word.

Her three sons ran the farm, explained Mrs Gurden, count-ing over her pies, though two were married now and had families of their own. Last year they had managed to buy in twenty acres of marshy level beyond the woods and Tom's dearest wish was to see it sweet grazing for the sheep; and Harry and his wife did not always agree, she was a Witney girl and had worked in a mill, found Otmoor strange and remote, its people contentious and intolerant; and Will was a wild boy, the youngest, her darling, and wanted to enlist in the infantry. All this Théo absorbed while sitting on the settle with one of the children on her knee while the pastry steamed in and out of the oven and the wine went to her head. There was a quality of solidity, of timelessness about this place, the sort she had met with in the old farmhouses on her island where she had visited with her father, the sort she had known at Le P'tit Clos des Pommes with her grandparents; the welcome was assured, unvarying and unqualified.

It must be strawberry wine, Théo thought, but she felt drowsy and warm. The smell of new bread, and pies, and the burning fruitwood logs in the hearth brought back the memories of La Croix in the days before she had been required to play the lady, of Goosie standing over the pots and the kittens tumbling by the open door. She felt that if she sat on the settle long enough she would regain her confidence, would

70

find that Théo of the lugger, the contented, self-reliant, barefoot Théo who might have grown into such a different person; she felt that in a while she might be able to face Caroline without recoiling, might be able to declare her intentions of becoming a trained nurse, or a great traveller, or even ... God willing, even a doctor. If she married Alex he might help her to become one.

Joss, coming in at that moment on a draught of bullock-scented air, his breath curling frostily, saw her wide-eyed, startled look as if something had just been made abundantly clear to her – but what it was he could not guess. She seemed to have made herself completely at home, a facility, he had noticed, that she shared with Millie, who never let a sense of her position get her down.

'We must go going soon,' he said.

'But you've only been here an hour,' was the instant response from the hearth, and Mrs Gurden's stricken face peered from the steam and smoke. 'Stay to eat. You must stay and eat.'

It was the custom of the country; it would be bad manners to refuse, an insult to the house. And then again Joss, whose appetite was rarely assuaged, could not resist the promise of beef and dumplings, apple pie, the best ale brought out in his honour. His resolve to be away before the familiar sights and sounds of this place made inroads on his emotions melted at the mention of the dumplings and the ale. In any case, he had the oddest suspicion Théo was a little drunk – Théo, who had been brought up on the greatest wines of France! – for she moved with a deliberate care and spoke very slowly and clearly, that French intonation a little more pronounced, her hands a little more graceful; she would be the better for a good meal inside her.

The good meal was a boisterous and prolonged affair, young Will arriving late, the ale jug replenished over and over, the talk all of scour and drainage and the price of fat beef. It was assumed Théo understood all, would join in, had a valuable opinion. She was the very person, Tom declared, to tell them about Jersey cattle. She could milk a cow, she said, beyond that she was ignorant. There was a moment's complete silence, while they all looked at her, as if suddenly remembering what she was and how she came to be there, and that it was incredible she could know how to milk a cow, it was not the usual occupation of fine ladies. Then Mrs Gurden, as red as her fire, made some remark about Will's visit to town and the oddity of his purchases from the drapers and the grocers, and the awkward minute was over and forgotten. But Théo finished her meal slowly, not speaking again. She had been excluded, was no longer one of them. They were independent, respectable small farmers but she was gentry, the representative of inherited wealth and frivolous idleness. No matter her father had been a doctor, that the Faurels had been in the wine business for centuries, and in privateering and smuggling and shipbuilding; no, no matter. Théo was a lady, and all that implied cut her off from them as surely as if she had been sitting behind glass. The irony of it did not escape her, the sour irony, for had not Caroline been trying to sever connections with Alexandre and the business for years in order to appear exactly what, it seemed, her daughter Théo had become?

The food, the ale, fortified both Théo and Joss for the farewells. He shook hands heartily with his brothers and embraced Mrs Gurden with circumspection, for fear of being seen to kiss her too fondly perhaps. He gave each of the awed children a shilling, an untold fortune, and accepted a large piece of cold pork pie in a cloth. And Théo? Théo was nodded to by all the men, who looked at her uneasily, and was aware of Mrs Gurden's floury cheek against hers and her bonnet being rescued from the smallest nephew and Joss holding the door for her and the cold bright winter daylight suddenly hurting her eyes . . .

'They're good people,' was Joss's only comment as they tackled the ruts again and climbed away from the level, but he did not look back to see if they were clustered at the gate. It was Théo who looked, and saw Will and Mrs Gurden arm in arm at the side of the lane; it was Théo who waved, though she was a lady and should not have stooped to it.

Two miles from the city the horse cast a shoe. Joss, as morose now as when he had travelled in the opposite direction that morning, said nothing but inquired the whereabouts of a smithy. They walked there in the frosty dusk, and had to wait while a great sway-backed cart mare was shod amid cursings and shoutings and a great scrambling this way and that. Some wouldn't stand, not for nothing, the smith informed them, grinning over his fire, once they'd been ill treated in their young days. He offered Théo a seat — a broken-down country chair off which he swept the dust and horseshoe nails — and put Joss to ply the bellows, talking all the time. The grey horse proved more tractable than the other and dozed over his shoulder as he worked.

How Caroline would have stared, Théo thought, to see her daughter seated in a forge with her skirts brushing the earth floor and her nose assaulted by the reek of singed hoof; and in the company of an unpredictable fellow who had already dirtied his good coat in a farmyard and was now smearing it liberally with ashes and rust. How far he was from La Croix after all.

The short, blue, biting dusk of winter deepened into night. The smith advised looking to the lamps. Théo edged her chair nearer the leaping fire and the horse snorted and threw up his head at the shadows. When the time came to leave she felt an enormous reluctance to step out into the cold and dark, and only Joss calling, and the feeble flickering of the gig lights, the smith offering his arm to help her up, drew her away from the warmth.

'Millie will think we're overturned,' she said, pulling the rug over her knees.

'I doubt it. She'll think we stayed on at the farm.'

They overtook a waggon, a farm cart with no lights. They heard the distant rattle of a train, and the hoot of a hunting owl, and there at last through the mist a glow, shifting and fading, a few lighted windows, that was Oxford.

The horse stumbled. Joss put out an arm to save Théo falling, and she looked up to thank him, saying something ordinary and not totally coherent about the bad roads and the strawberry wine . . . And on impulse he bent to kiss the pale blur of her face and missed her cheek and came upon her mouth, a warm, surprised, amenable mouth.

He let her go abruptly. He did not know what had prompted him to it, except that he had felt a brief, burning gratitude for her unspoken support through the day, for the way she

73

had greeted his family, for the way she had sat, smiling and patient, in the debris of the forge ... He had the feeling tonight, as always, that nine-tenths of Théo de Faurel were being kept hidden, that her occasional moods, her tussles with authority, those hungry looks, were simply the preliminaries of a volcano.

'You mustn't mind it,' he said, 'sailors always take liberties. The mist's getting thicker. Is that the toll ahead?'

'It's quite all right,' replied Théo weakly, 'I assumed you were practising for tomorrow.'

'What's tomorrow?'

'Dinner at Martagon and your conquest of Sophie Barnard.'

'Good Lord,' cried Joss, slowing as the toll gate loomed ahead, 'I'd quite forgotten.'

7

Théo closed her bedroom door with extreme thankfulness and lit another candle from the one she carried. It gave sufficient light, she found, to see all she wanted of her own face, a face that seemed to her immeasurably different since Joss had kissed it. She took off her dress and wrestled with her stays, and then, momentarily defeated, sat by the small mirror to let down her hair.

He had meant nothing by it, that was certain. He had kissed her for much the same reason Givard had done so all those years ago, simply because she had been there and had looked up, so to speak, at the wrong moment. There had been nothing contrived about it, nothing preconceived. If the motion of the gig had altered it might, after all, have turned out a chaste kiss on her forehead and nothing else. Joss had brushed it away lightly, had let her go as if she had burnt his arm, presumably through a sense of shame, and had hardly spoken to her since. He had delivered her to Millie and gone out again immediately to return the gig to its stables.

It had been a difficult evening though for all kinds of reasons.

Firstly Polly had been in tears because Nelson had escaped and had not returned. Millie had been driven to fortify her with cherry brandy while Jack went out to cry about the streets. The inevitable outcome was Jack returning at nine o'clock blind drunk and no Joss to help him up the stairs.

'I've never been lucky with my servants,' was Millie's only comment as she and Théo left him sleeping noisily in the entrance passage, wrapped against the cold in a blanket, their only effective assistance. Nelson came home by himself five minutes later, his muzzle cut about and his eyes full of devilment.

'Where's Joss, I wonder?' Millie retired to the fire with the bottle of cherry brandy. 'He's in a dark mood tonight. The farm, no doubt.'

'But he chose to go there.'

'Of course. He loves them dearly. Deep inside he still thinks of it as home. But they did take him in for money, after all. It demolishes his self-esteem, his sense of belonging. The fact that Lizzie Gurden would take in any motherless child for nothing means very little to a man who feels he was sold in the market by his own family. Oh yes, yes, he loves them dearly. But their love for him . . . He can't accept it for what it is. He can't forget the sum they were paid – a substantial sum, remember – to bring him up.'

Théo tended Nelson's bleeding nose and did not look up. 'And will he come home as drunk as Jack?'

'I hope not. I've never seen him the worse for drink. What he gets up to in foreign ports I couldn't say, sailors being sailors, but I've never known him lose himself in a pint pot or a wine bottle, not my Joss.'

But the night drew on and he did not return. Millie, who knew about such things, wondered if, sailors being sailors, he had found some measure of required oblivion in the arms of a street girl. Théo, who also knew about such things because the great Dr Faurel had treated such girls for nothing – unknown to his wife – thought about it too. She was astounded to find that she wished with her whole being to be that girl, to enjoy whatever it was that was enjoyed, or endured, at such a time. It was a deeper and more furious longing than any she had ever known, quite different from the desire for safety and affection she had felt in the arms of Givard and Alex Trent. It was a shameless longing in a young woman brought up in ignorance of such things, for whom the mysteries of the marriage bed might well remain mysteries for ever. Caroline would have been scandalized.

She did not care what Caroline thought. Had Caroline herself never burned like this for anyone, not even the dear

76

doctor in those early honeymoon days? Had none of those clever flirtations come to this?

Millie saw that she had grown pale and strained, that she seemed to be making rather much of Nelson's wounds, and she sighed. Such a grave, introspective look – what had Joss said on the drive from Otmoor to bring the girl so low? She suspected Joss for certain, he was inclined to be insensitive or outspoken, or to the pretence of them; he would not notice if he hurt Théo's feelings.

And Théo's feelings had been disregarded far too long, thought Millie; a man might trample on them at his peril.

Breakfast brought burnt toast and Millie in conservative purple, a bad sign. Joss had risen early, she informed Théo – had he even gone to bed? – had devoured the better part of their provisions for three days, and had gone out to rouse Hardy with the carriage. He had been his usual pleasant self, dutifully polite, astonishingly hungry. He gave no sign that he had been keeping any company other than his own, that he had been drinking heavily, or that he had been up to any mischief whatsoever.

He had not intended mischief, had only hoped to walk Théo de Faurel out of his system. For a long time he had wandered about the narrow dark streets he knew so well, and then, because he was tired of walking but did not want to return to Holywell, he had made his way across Magdalen bridge to the Plain and sat down by the toll gate. An old woman smoking a pipe had joined him, and a man with a squeeze-box and a monkey. The mist had been thick about the river and the low meadows and hour after hour the bells had sounded out muffled and distanced. Joss, anonymous in his dark cloak, had broadened his speech and slipped back in time to a familiar country; it was a more successful return than his foray on to Otmoor, and he found himself relaxed and laughing for the first time since leaving London. Then it had been morning, the mist whitening across the road, his limbs stiff and cold, and the man with the monkey, seeing what he was, touched his cap to him and called him sir.

Well, he had rid himself of any lingering desire for little Miss Théo, God bless her green eyes. Yesterday had been a fleeting aberration, the result of being strung up about the visit to the farm, his confused feelings of belonging and yet not belonging. Certainly Théo had made it easier for him to pass the time there, and pass it pleasantly. Had that impulsive kiss been simple gratitude after all? Had the subsequent urgent longing been for Sophie Barnard, whose dark hair and untouched perfection lived in his memory? Perhaps. She was a damn fine girl, Sophie, would make an excellent wife – she had been reared from the cradle to make some happy man an excellent wife – and he wanted her, for herself, for her money, and for Martagon, an irresistible combination. But he wondered, striding back to the little house in Holywell, what this contained, unfathomable girl from Jersey was really like and whether she would eventually marry that good-looking young fool of a Lancer and learn from him the delights or otherwise of physical love, and all the other sorts of love, and compromise, and patience that might be said to make up marriage.

At Holywell Théo was still in bed, but Millie was up and looking militant, chasing Polly for the teapot and the marmalade. Nelson hurled himself across the floor barking and Joss swung him up and tucked him under one arm.

'Well,' said Millie, 'you both look remarkably smug. I shan't ask you what *you* have been at; *he* has been at the bacon.' And she passed on, her little chin in the air and her eyes blazing.

Joss stuck his head round the dining-room door. 'I hope he left some.'

'Some what?'

'Bacon.'

'I have often observed' – this as she re-set the table Polly had laboured over half an hour – 'that by and large men are quite intolerable until they have eaten.'

'That's what you get,' said Millie, 'for causing a crisis.' She was referring to Miss Barnard's baldly unenthusiastic welcome, a face in which a thousand emotions were at war.

'I don't see what is wrong with Joss. He doesn't stand on his head to recite or lap his soup, does he?'

'No, no, I don't say he can be faulted – apart from his

insatiable appetite. No, I've known him grace several dining tables quite prettily. Her objection is moral, poor woman. That is not to say it might not be overcome was he a captain in the Guards and his fallen mother a member of some remote northern family. The trouble is she hasn't the least notion what an Engineering Officer is, doesn't even grasp his rank properly, and then he is, most decidedly, a true Westover: the very spit of him used to hang over the sideboard until it was banished upstairs. She will be entertaining him, you might say, at his own table, dining him off his own plate.'

Théo, who was struggling with the mass of her hair, laughed at this, though she was aware of a certain sympathy for Miss Barnard. Who would care for Joss, seething with injured pride, brooding at her dinner table? It was not as if he were a self-effacing, inoffensive sort of man, a man who would refuse to rise to the occasion.

Polly came in, disapproved of Théo's efforts, and proceeded to arrange a complicated knot from which the hair fell in loose curls. She had been overawed by the house, by the servants, by the unremitting chill; the whole of the house in Holywell could have fitted in the entrance hall.

'We look very fine,' eventually remarked Millie, who was dressed to shock in the brightest emerald, gazing at Théo's palest blue in admiration. 'How that style suits you. You have such nice shoulders. You know, I do hope there is going to be a decent fire, I'm always so cold in this house.'

There was a fire but it could best have been described as unpretentious. Millie nearly set herself alight in an attempt to feel its benefit. But the party was large and Martagon, being remote, was lit by candles. Soon, very soon, the heat began to tell; ladies took out their fans and moved away to the cooler corners. Miss Barnard was growing heated for different reasons, reasons to do with Joss Westover, his inescapable size and unsuitability. She had invited all the local gentry she considered of sufficient standing and wealth to enhance the dinner table, but that had been before she had realized Millie was to bring Joss. Now she had the horrible experience of seeing one couple cut him dead and in the same instant old Sandiway come up to wring his hand, chattering on about old Jocelyn, dearest Rose, something to do with rare days, great deal of sport, terrible thing to happen, and lost a leg at Salamanca. On the other side of the room two more regretted guests were holding court, a brilliant Oxford professor and his eldest daughter. The professor, though he had been perfectly correctly attired when Miss Barnard had made his acquaintance, now stood unconcerned in canary yellow breeches like a footman and grey stockings with outdated buckled shoes. His daughter was very pretty and very well aware of it, without the least particle of modesty, and had had every man's eye on her since she stepped through the door.

But the dinner was destined to be a success, even if the hostess was brought to close her eyes at frequent intervals. She had placed her brother, a puritanical, judicious man, as far from Millie and Joss as was possible, and had placed little Miss Faurel between the professor and Colonel Paget. There was nothing more she could do. She could have to rely on the wine and food to work the miracle: she was deeply conscious of the need for divine intervention.

Théo felt for her. She had a ready sympathy even for those she disliked, a virtue or a failing – who is to say? – that often left her vulnerable: Caroline had worked on her sense of duty, her natural desire to please, for fifteen years with great success. Tonight it had struck her forcibly that in twenty years she too might be another Miss Barnard, making the most unconscionable fuss about the trivia of life because they were all she had for consolation. The mirrors on the wall showed her she had some way to go, however, to achieve Miss Barnard's state: the dress left her shoulders bare and her ringlets were uncurling sweetly on her neck. The Colonel, who had already mellowed with the good wine, found her endearing.

Meanwhile the professor's daughter was concentrating only on Joss, at whom she directed the sort of glances guaranteed to strike dead most men of her acquaintance. Joss continued to eat unperturbed, and to address commonplace remarks to Mr Sandiway. If he minded being dined off his own plate he gave no sign of it, and if it had not been for his uncanny resemblance to the portraits in the Long Gallery and the vibrations of moral outrage issuing from the Chisholms at the other end of the table, he might have made the perfect guest.

Millie said: 'Poor Sophie! She's always been the centre of

attention, and now she's met her first real siren and is at a complete loss. How that girl flirts with Joss!' She and Théo were making their way to the drawing room, leaving the men an uneasy party taking refuge in port and thick smoke.

'Joss seems not to have noticed,' remarked Théo.

'He has. To be sure he has. But it suits him to give no sign of it. He is after Sophie.'

He gave no obvious sign of that either, except that during the inevitable piano entertainment he never took his eyes from her face. She played very prettily, perhaps with more enthusiasm than ear but very prettily. Miss Barnard looked gratified. Afterwards Théo was prevailed on to take her place.

Théo played much better than Sophie but she did not smile over her shoulder so perhaps it went unnoticed. The song she sang was in French, was charmingly melodious, and was obviously about love.

'It wasn't about love at all,' Théo protested to Joss, 'it was about seagulls.'

'How dull,' and he prepared to look amiable for the last fifteen minutes while coffee was brought round. 'Was there a moral?'

'I don't think so. Would you have preferred one? It was simply about seagulls.'

'Hmm,' said Joss, gazing steadfastly at Sophie across the room. She looked up and met his eyes and blushed crimson.

'Silly little moth,' was Millie's verdict as they waited to say their farewells.

'She has never met anyone like him,' said Théo, who knew the irresistible pull of novelty.

'Of course not. And look how that silly woman practically elbows between them, determined they should be parted. It will have the opposite effect for sure. Her Sophie will be in his arms the first time he asks her.'

'But,' asked Théo, as they approached Miss Barnard with smiles of polite gratitude for their stimulating evening, 'does he really want her?'

'Heaven knows. But Martagon brings out the worst in him, I told you, and sometimes I fear the worst might be very bad indeed.'

Miss Barnard's thin cold hand, cloaks, gloves, outdoor

shoes, Hardy wrenching open the carriage door. Behind them there was a flutter of silk on the steps that might have been Sophie.

'Hi my, what an evening!' said Millie.

They went to Portsmouth and were allowed to set reverent feet on board the new ship, although they were not allowed below to a view of Joss's vast, complex charge deep in its bowels. They were entertained to sherry by the captain and did their best to charm him for Joss's sake, pretending a most disgracefully contrived ignorance of the sea and ships.

At last it was time to go. Millie forbore to kiss Joss goodbye, even in the privacy of the deserted wardroom, aware he was of the nature and stature to be embarrassed. Théo thought she could not bear to touch him in case her feelings showed but when he took her hand in his and shook it once, twice, hard and affectionate, she was aware only of her bones being crushed and the momentary fierce pain.

'If you marry that bow-legged Lancer don't expect me to come to the wedding,' he said.

'His expressions are never very delicate,' said Millie as they blew on the cold rampaging wind towards the grey shore, clutching their fur collars tight under their ears. 'He means nothing by it. He would be the first to congratulate you and send you the most impractical wedding present you could think of.'

'Yes,' said Théo.

8

Syntax meant nothing to young Bonespoir. It was true he had been introduced to punctuation but he had not pursued the acquaintance. His letters were legible only to a fond and loving eye, and Théo's was passionately fond and devotedly loving.

'It has bin cold and Goos hins wud not lay,' was the gist, 'Granmama was cross and I dur Pierre to et a worm and he did and had som trikle and was sik . . .' The wandering and disjointed words, the shaky kisses added by baby Lou – aided by Clarice – Louise's calm and chatty pages, and a papery pressed moth included by Pierre, reduced Théo to tears for the first time since the summer. She went to her room and shut herself in, lying down on the bed and pressing her cold hands to her hot cheeks, trying not to see the familiar waterfront, the masts and spars, the old women helping to mend the nets, and at La Croix Goosie's hens, which so often ended in the pot at the least sign of intransigence, going off lay at the first real squall of winter to ruffle their feathers.

It was Di who noticed the evidence of this excess of nostalgia and who spent the afternoon showing her interesting things through a microscope in order to take her mind off it. She kept up a surprising flow of information, illustrating every point with evidence from her comprehensive library, groping about the floor for those authorities who had escaped the bookshelves. Théo began to feel dizzy. She was rescued by Nelson, who scratched at the door with maddening persist-ence, his nose on fire with the reek of bottled lizards, his internal clock telling him it was time for muffins.

'You would make me such an excellent secretary,' said Di with feeling, as they descended to the tea table a few minutes later, 'and I did so hope this proposed expedition to Africa ... But there, Millie won't put up the money, says I will be eaten by crocodiles. What an absurdity! Crocodiles! Can you imagine anything wanting to eat a leathery old thing like me? She tries to find excuses ... She has no feeling for what it means to broaden our knowledge, to discover new species. All that gadding about abroad and what for? Nothing. Just because she couldn't think of anything else to do.'

It was not said unkindly, she had no idea it might be seen as unkindness. She loved Millie deeply, an unspoken, unqualified love that had grown up over the years as they had passed their dissimilar lives in this large, eccentric house: she would no more have been unkind to Millie than fail to draw breath. But she could be selfish, irritating, perverse and ungrateful like everybody else, though seldom for long, and she had no capacity for being devious, disputatious, or sour.

'You're too old for it,' Millie asserted over the muffins, no unkindness intended on her part either, 'you're too old for scampering about in jungles, and as far as I can see the "gentleman" who suggested it is a man of questionable virtue and misplaced optimism. He admires your mind – and wishes to use it, his own being defective.'

Millie's sitting room, her own private sitting room, was heavy with the smell of damp coal and toasting muffins. It was a small room tucked away at the back of the house which she had crammed with mementoes of her travels and furnished with the bizarre opulence of her bedroom. The stuffed parrot, which had moved in for the winter from the vast drawing room down the passage, went well with the colour scheme. The monkey lived there all the time, could not be persuaded from its warm, stuffy atmosphere, and he sat on Millie's lap now, half asleep. All over the tables, obnoxious eastern tables with sharp corners and perplexing carving, lay books and magazines and pieces of newspapers, and at Millie's feet more newspapers, some marked with black ink in great, furious strokes.

'I can't imagine what they're about, scrapping round the Mediterranean like schoolboys round a bag of sweets. No one can say a good word for Napoleon and yet we must have him as an ally, kiss his hand, bury all differences, and fight a Christian country for the sake of a rotten, corrupt, confused Muslim state that dislikes us as heartily as we dislike it,' Millie said, gazing down at her handiwork.

'But if Russia were to take Constantinople . . .' began Miss Cole.

'My dear Di, there's no point in arguing about it. I don't give a toss for the rights and wrongs at heart, only the senseless waste to come. The Russian navy will have to be destroyed, Joss says, and all those old fools at the Admiralty are still fighting Trafalgar . . . I wouldn't be surprised if half of them didn't think France is still the enemy.'

'And what does your Palmerston say?' demanded Di, peering round her remarkable nose.

Théo did not hear what Palmerston said, she had drifted away on the last few waves of her homesickness and was standing in the entrance hall at La Croix. There in her lap were her small hands with their blunt, cared-for nails; ringless hands. She had defeated Caroline after all over the question of marriage. She *would not* marry. She would not suffer exile from Jersey for ever. She would return and become . . . What would she become? Would Dr Frere tolerate her even winding bandages?

There would be war with Russia. Everybody wanted it except perhaps the Russians. One country could not impose its will on the rest of the world, must not be allowed to contemplate it even. And Russia! Why, Russia was a country of savages who must be taught their place.

She had received a letter from Alex, unexceptional and circumspect, the sort of letter a girl's mother might read and find perfectly correct. He did not waste time in charming asides for which Théo was grateful, though perhaps it was only because he had no time to waste. His time was not his own. Everybody in the country, it seemed, had the right to it except himself. The days were endless drill, the getting oneself dressed up for it or down for it, or brushed and polished for dinner with the Colonel or a review or a trot through all the neighbouring towns as a prelude to the recruiting drive that was sure to come. Alex, who described all this in Théo's letter, had all a young boy's enthusiasm for the panoply of war and none of an adult's apprehension of its horrors. Red coats but not red blood, thought Théo, and then smiled wryly, remembering the Lancers were got up in blue and grey.

'Are you all right? Théo? Théo!' Millie had tipped the poor monkey off her lap and was leaning forward.

'All right?' A blank, confused look.

'My dear, you were miles and miles away.'

Théo smiled, a strange fey smile, and folded her ringless hands together. She said: 'I want to go home to Jersey.'

Millie chewed her lip. Behind her the samovar burbled gently and steam rose from unexpected places.

'It's almost Christmas,' she said.

'Why not come and spend Christmas at La Croix?'

'The sea,' cried Di, flapping the monkey away from the remains of the seed cake, 'think of the sea at this time of year. The crossing would be terrible.'

'And there I was,' murmured Millie, 'thinking about a trip to Egypt. Or Italy. You would so like Italy.'

Théo rose, a small blue figure in a jungle of red and green. The monkey plucked at her hem, and she put down a finger, lifted him, tucked him into the crook of her elbow. She said: 'I want to go home, Millie.'

It was not that she was not grateful, that she did not enjoy life in Russell Square, that Millie and Di with their oblique views of life were not the perfect antidote to Caroline with her rigid perceptions. But Russell Square was no more for her than was marriage to Monsieur Varges, and now that Joss had gone . . . And she so missed the children.

She felt strong enough to face Caroline's disapproval, strong enough to face anything, provided she was on home ground; strong enough to ignore what she felt for Joss Westover: once at La Croix it would be a laughable memory.

'Oh well,' said Millie, 'life is nothing much if you don't put it to the hazard now and then. A sea trip in December is just the thing, a good strong wind and all those fearful rocks around Jersey . . .'

Théo was smiling, smiling, with relief, with sheer exultant joy. She would not be caged and restrained at La Croix, and would take rooms somewhere, or a cottage, would badger Dr

Frere until he relented, swallowed his prejudices whole, would storm her genteel committee ladies into more practical charity, would see about that home for the sailors' women and children her father had dreamed of so many years ago ... She was a Faurel, if she did not care for the poor and the damned of the island, who would? She had position and wealth and a starving intellect. Who would dare turn her aside?

The vision of Théo de Faurel the pragmatic philanthropist blinded her with its brilliance: in forty years all St Helier might turn out with songs and flowers to thank her. It was like a great fire leaping up from the little spark she had kept alive so long and with such painful difficulty; she could not see the absurdities, the inescapable absurdities of such a Théo. And for a while, because this deep a joy, this furious, implacable resolution was new to her, she could not see that the only certain end of such a Théo was not songs and flowers but a sad heap of ashes.

And: what will Caroline say? Millie was thinking.

After three hours at sea in a more than contrary wind priorities shift: Théo was used to the sea, to big ships and small, had taken the wheel of a little St Malo schooner when she was ten years old, had listened to her father's patient instructions, had watched his satisfied smile; but endless rain and a near-gale, the pitching and tossing and heaving to and backing off and coming round again, made her feel ill, ill . . . She did not care for philanthropy, she did not care for the sick and the poor and the outcast; she was aware only of the physical wreck that was herself, her shivering clammy flesh, her throbbing head, her aching bones. Freedom from the tyranny of her duty to the family meant nothing now, freedom was a concept of that mind which had ceased to function; she wanted nothing now but to survive.

On the afternoon of the third day they sighted one of the islands, and the rain eased a litle and drove away north-eastward. Théo felt drained and half dead, only her tight bodice, her high collar, her puritanical bonnet holding her together. She clung to the rigging where it met the side, while the wind tried to tear her away and out to sea and the spray flew up and stung her cheeks. Air at last, lungfuls of raging air, and the islands on the horizon; what could life offer sweeter than this? She grinned, turning her face away from the flying spume as the sodden canvas went up and the packet struggled valiantly back on course.

The captain crossed over to pay his respects. He was aware she was a Faurel, a lady of consequence; he had once skippered a brig for her grandfather. Those were the days, he said, though she had been a crabby, slow little thing, slab-sided, unlucky. Old Bon had sold her in Marseilles, done a deal over a Spanish xebec that had taken his fancy and they'd run along the coast to Genoa . . . sardines and red wine, plenty of wine . . . those had been the days. Mademoiselle de Faurel smiled a small, enigmatic smile and said nothing. He enthused a while longer about the xebec, condemned Genoa roundly: filthy, funny little alleys, quarrelsome natives, knives at the least provocation; then, just as it seemed he might lead himself by natural degrees to an indiscretion or two, he pulled himself up with a gruff: 'Going home, eh?'

'Yes.'

She looked as well as any woman could under the circumstances, he thought, her hair plastered to her forehead, her cloak soaked, her face thin and wet. She looked like a Faurel, small and light-coloured mostly, every one of them, except that great red devil Bonespoir, rot him. Yes, small and fair, nothing much to look at but tough, clever, argumentative and resilient. He doffed his hat with exaggerated respect.

Millie, who a short time ago had apparently been dead, refused to rise until they tied up in St Helier. She then put on her bonnet and her cloak and her boots, all she had taken off, and ordered tea while they waited for the carriage from La Croix, which could not be seen along the quay, they were assured, and no wonder, the packet two days late. The tea revived Millie absolutely, and in five minutes she looked as she always looked, like a small ferocious hawk. There was no answer to seasickness, she informed Théo, except perfect immobility and dry biscuits.

The carriage arrived, Louise inside restraining a crowing baby Lou who had been allowed to accompany her. She did not stop to look at Théo but enveloped her in a hug that knocked her bonnet askew and brought bright pink to her hollow cheeks.

'How we have missed you! You have no idea!'

She cast a glance of awe at Millie, but Millie dispelled her doubts by climbing into the carriage and taking baby Lou on her lap, producing a string of beads from her purse to put round her fat little neck.

'Mama is a little . . . indisposed,' said Louise as they made their way slowly through the harbour traffic to the road. 'She has been to three parties this week. For my sake,' in a lower voice. 'She thinks I should marry again.'

A look passed between the sisters. Millie, talking dolls to Lou, affected not to notice.

'Does she want you out of La Croix then?'

'Oh hush, Théo . . . No. At least . . . No. Don't talk about it now. I should never have mentioned anything about it.'

'You can say anything in front of Millie.'

'But it's impolite, discussing personal matters when Miss Boswell's only been on the island five minutes. It's such wretched weather too, we'd given you up. Mama said you would never attempt it.' And hoped you would not, she might have added, hoped you would remain in London, would behave.

By now they had reached St Aubin, the little harbour, the steep streets, and La Croix. Luc handed them out, smiling, and flung open the door for them, and there was Goosie in the hall, playing truant from the kitchen, wiping her hands on her vast apron and crying out a welcome in the familiar patois, and behind her the new maid shy and curious. Millie shook out her skirts and looked about with interest. Louise went upstairs to tell Caroline they had arrived.

As if it were not self-evident, thought Théo, the row they were all making. Even the dogs, shut up in the back regions, were joining in now. She took Millie up the curving, shallow stairs. She thought: if I had been a natural daughter I would have run up here the moment I stepped through the door; and perhaps Mama would have come to the hall and held out her arms . . . But that's not Mama's way, she's never done it, and won't start now even for a dutiful daughter who means the world to her. She thought: do any of her daughters mean

89

the world to her? Marguerite is dutiful and loving but I couldn't say if Mama cares for her ... How odd. I never thought much about it before, I took it for granted Mama loved us, only that she didn't like me, that I was a disappointment ... They were at the top of the stairs. Théo was not aware of it but she straightened her already straight back and lifted her head a fraction. Only children ran into their mothers' arms, she thought, only little children like Baby Lou. Women of twenty-nine who were not particularly liked had to be content with a token kiss on the cheek.

The cheek Caroline offered to be kissed was cool and dry and smelled of good perfume. It was a familiar fragrance and it sent Théo's stomach and mind into instantaneous revolt. A thousand memories crowded back and knocked her good intentions sideways, her resolutions, her ambitions, her new, blazing hopes. She retreated a step or two and answered Caroline's questions about the journey mechanically, politely, feeling her courage already on the ebb.

'My darling Théo, how elegant you look,' said Caroline, which was true: much thinner, and something had happened to her face which perhaps could be put down to the dreadful crossing, but elegant, yes, and with her wild hair in a heavy chignòn, quite tamed.

'You're not ill?' asked Millie, coming forward to plant a kiss on Caroline's forehead, a gesture Caroline was not expecting and had no time to avoid. 'You always were one for lying about pretending to be delicate.'

A reproachful look from the couch. 'I see you haven't changed at all. I have had a migraine, have not been able to lift my head for nearly two days. Amelia, have you a whole bird of paradise on that hat or only half of one?'

'I don't like unobtrusive hats,' said Millie, poking at the blinds until she came at a view of the gardens. 'Anyway, it helps one to get along if people can see one coming. Tall women can have no idea of the vexations of being short.'

Louise took Théo to her old room. 'The boys are out with Leonie,' she said, 'I thought it was for the best. Mama has been so irritable this last week since she received your letter saying you were coming home. We argued a little about it. She was going to forbid you to come. She would have done too had it not been for Millie – I do believe she couldn't think up an excuse to put off Miss Boswell. Now I've met her I can see why.'

'And why has she suddenly decided you must remarry? And who is the gentleman she has chosen?'

'A man called Foster. He is a banker. Nothing will come of it.'

Théo loosened her hair from its chignon and brushed it out. Louise came to take the brush from her hand, looking over Théo's head at their reflections in the mirror for a moment.

'You look so young with your hair like that, so different. I wouldn't mind being married again, not now, but I don't want Mama's choice. Can you understand?'

'I know all about Mama's choices, remember? What about Monsieur Varges? Have you met anyone?'

'No, but then I hardly go out now. It's only in the last month Mama has suddenly accepted every invitation and we've scarcely been out of our best dinner dresses for two days together. We have even called on Alexandre and Leonie – though only because they had some Italian count staying, I think – something we hadn't done in years since Mama took to turning up her nose at the business.'

'You know, you should have gone to London, not me. You would have enjoyed it.'

'And left you here managing the house and looking after the children, I suppose. And minding Mama.'

'I'm used to managing Mama.'

'But you can't quite do it. Oh, you do it better than I do but she still . . . She still wins. The only consolation is that she finds you just as difficult.'

They smiled at each other in the glass. Louise pulled the soft fair hair back from Théo's face and began to brush.

'Tell me about London. And the packet. Was it terrible? Luc said you'd be drowned. According to him the seas of the world are choked with drowned Faurels.'

It was not the same Théo, Louise was thinking, who sat smoothing the blue cashmere of her skirt while the mass of her hair was folded back into its chignon and pinned. She could not understand exactly what was different, but something was; and then she saw the swift laughter in the change-able, mysterious eyes and she remembered all the old restlessness, the barely contained energy, the unsatisfied craving to do something. If Théo stayed at La Croix sooner or later there would be a battle with Caroline, an all-out, tumultuous, brutish sort of battle.

'I can't run the house as well as you,' said Louise, 'I didn't even try. I whispered to Goosie that everything must go on as before, as if you were here, and it has; well, more or less. Mama thinks less, she's always complaining. Things are too hot or too cold or lamps haven't been lighted or food isn't fresh. You know. And every week she "speaks" to Clarice because of her singing, or being familiar with guests, or showing her underwear on the beach – and Clarice becomes twice as French as usual, feigns hysterics, swears she will pack her bags within the hour and will catch the next ship to Malo. It's remarkable. She should be on the stage. But the result is Mama has to back down and Clarice goes on singing twice as loudly. Oh, you've been sadly missed, I assure you.'

And so she had. On the landing she met Clarice herself, and poor flustered Leonie, Alexandre's wife, and the two boys in full voice and so happy to see her . . . All her dignity flew out of the window and she found herself kneeling with their treasures in her lap: shells and bits of bottle and corks from the warehouse, and a pair of sailor's earrings.

'Do mind your Aunt Théo's dress,' cried Leonie, trying to rescue her and taken aback by the thin, vivid, laughing face she could not remember. Something had happened to the girl in England. Was it love? Caroline had said there was a cavalry officer in the case.

'It's quite all right,' said this stranger. 'Oh Leonie, you look so pretty.'

It was true. She was expecting her second child and pregnancy became her. She smiled happily, glad of a completely spontaneous compliment. She had never been quite sure of Théo, finding her elusive and moody, a dispiriting mixture of the self-assured and the totally vulnerable; she had also had reported to her the scandalous affair with Givard – unkindly reported, for it was an affair never forgiven her husband's family by the redoubtable Caroline. But this new positive Théo, quick to jump up and press a truly affectionate kiss on her cheek, this was a Théo she could appreciate.

So lunch was a happy meal, helped by Millie's conscious and unconscious drollery. What a relief, she exclaimed, not to have to eat dry biscuit ever again! The rain had blown away and it was a fresh, cloudy afternoon, the creeper tapping at the panes. Théo stared out at the grey framed in the bare, blighted stalks, and ached to be away, to be able to forget the inevitable interview to come, the inevitable reproach, the inevitable guilt. It was Caroline herself, however, who chose to postpone the moment, for after the meal she closeted herself with Millie in an attempt perhaps to regain whatever intimacy they had once shared. Throughout the last three hours she had looked long and anxiously at her youngest daughter, suspecting a new poise and therefore a new challenge in Théo's smiling face. She did not know if she was up to the challenge, she felt tired suddenly, honestly tired of all the years of battle and resistance, of attack and repulse. If the girl promised to settle down at La Croix, to give up these crazy ideas of throwing herself hand and heart into the front line of some charitable organization – prisons had once been mentioned, Heaven forbid! – then Caroline was prepared to cease to push for marriage. Perhaps with Louise married again Théo could be persuaded it was her duty.

She thought she might ask Millie's advice, but she found Millie unnerving, and put aside the hope of a serious discussion for another day. Millie apparently only wished to indulge in some honest-to-goodness nostalgia, recalling names, and recounting tales from their brief, shared schooldays. Caroline, for once, lost her grasp of the conversation entirely. She had the feeling Millie was steeped in trickery, that every word was false, but she knew she could never get the better of Amelia Boswell, never, never. She lay down again on her couch and allowed herself to remember those good, good old days, the days before she had had any daughters to cause her such heartache.

Théo was in St Helier with Pierre. Louise had connived their escape, had made a sly suggestion they should return Leonie

93

to her own house in the smart part of the town and stop on the way back to buy some badly-needed lace.

'You have enough lace in your workbox for half a dozen petticoats for Lou,' said Théo, kissing her goodbye.

'But this is very special and has been on order three months. In any case,' in an undertone, 'it will give you an excuse not to hurry back.'

At the charming house in St Mary's Road Théo was begged to stay for tea, a sherry, a glass of wine. She took a glass of wine, had even offered her cheeks to Alexandre to kiss, something she had never done before, such ordinary intimacy having been discouraged by Caroline. Alexandre had never thought much of Théo, since his innocent introduction of her to Givard had never been forgiven him; he had suspected she was too clever for her own good, that her moodiness was caused by her thinking herself superior to other women in some way, he had deplored the way her father had encouraged her to take an interest in the business, on that alone he was in wholehearted agreement with Caroline. But now . . . She was so slight, so poised, so . . . electric. Her very smile was daunting in its sincerity. She reminded him suddenly and forcefully of their grandmother Honorine.

'You must visit us more often,' he said when she left, and meant it.

Théo asked; 'What would you like to do now?'

Pierre gave a wide, gappy grin and said: 'Look at the ships,' which was all his delight apart from Lepidoptera and going barefoot.

They drove down to the harbour and left Luc to take the carriage home, saying they would walk back along the bay. Then they wandered hand in hand to the waterfront where the wind still whipped the water and the gulls rose and fell, lamenting and complaining. There were a great many small craft packed in the shelter of the quay, French fishing boats blown in on the storm, Portuguese with painted eyes, and a lovely little three-master off course for the West Indies. Pierre wanted to see them all, was passed from hand to hand across the decks while Théo looked on torn by horror and bubbling amusement at his audacity. Louise would have died to see him shaking hands solemnly with old Breton skippers and the

Norwegian mate of the fruit schooner. Sometimes his glossy dark head in its round blue cap would be lost from view below, to emerge in a moment, while the words '*Ma tante, voilà!*' would drift across the water, and half a dozen pairs of curious eyes would scrutinize Théo from the top of her bonnet to the soles of her smart little boots.

If I had been a boy, Théo thought, I could have walked on board any of those ships, could have worked a passage to . . . where? Anywhere. What would it matter? If she had been a boy she could have followed in the footsteps of old Bonespoir and no one would have considered it more than mildly scandalous especially if she arrived home richer than she had set out. But as a woman? What could she do that would not close some doors to her for ever, would not lose her her reputation, would not make her as unspeakable as the whore of Babylon? The very poor could escape, she supposed, and the very rich, and even the very eccentric, like Millie or Miss Cole. Millie had been born in a baggage cart in the middle of the Indian monsoon and had had, by any standard, an unconventional upbringing. What hope was there for a girl brought up on the best principles and groomed to be the perfect wife and mother?

'You look sad,' remarked Pierre, straddling a bollard and trying to whistle.

'Oh, I'm not sad. I was thinking about . . . about your great-grandmother.' Another age, said Théo's inner voice tartly, Grand'mère Honorine was the daughter of another age, less formal and smug than this, less concerned with the minutiae of class and occupation and respectability; an age of revolution and of war.

'Look, another packet,' cried Pierre, tugging her arm. 'It's got a jury mast. It must have been in your storm. Was it so bad? Luc said you might be drowned. He made Goosie cry.'

They contemplated the packet, squeezing into the crowded harbour. The few passengers – were they only the passengers capable of standing on their feet? – stood about on deck, morose and silent, like dead men who wonder if they have reached paradise. A trim, soldierly figure caught Théo's eye.

'Aunt Théo, Aunt Théo! What's the matter? Oh, look! Look! There's a Faurel dray and Monsieur Vautier. Aunt Théo?'

She turned to look down at him, and then glanced up as quickly to see Alex Trent vanish below decks.

Then: 'Mademoiselle Théophile, how we have missed you,' said a voice, and Vautier was in front of her, Vautier the misogynist whose admiration for her was genuine and, now she was forbidden the waterfront, undisguised. 'Come, come. We shall have a glass of wine in the office. Step along. Your Pierre knows the way, he comes with Luc sometimes on his way home from his aunt Leonie's . . . He likes to look at the ledgers, to look at the old plans of the ships. He can tell you every ship we have ever owned. Not a Faurel in name but a Faurel for all that, eh?'

9

It was the sort of day Caroline did not venture to leave the
house: a great blustering adventurous wind was howling
down the steep narrow streets about La Croix and the sea
was loud and furious. She did not mind her daughters going
out though, in spite of yards of petticoat and even pantaloons
being on display as they battled staunchly with their skirts.
She did not mind Millie accompanying them, she was even a
little thankful, for Millie was too robust, too keen in every
way, not least keen-sighted, and she had spent an uneasy
night wondering if those snapping black eyes had penetrated
to her very soul and seen all the shameful desires and ardent
selfishness there.

The carriage was not called for. It had been out now two
days in succession and Caroline's edict kept it in the coach
house even when Louise had the temerity to ask for it on
Millie's account: they wanted to show her St Brelade and
L'Etacque. Caroline would not hear of it and acquired the
symptoms of another migraine the moment she judged, with
growing horror, that Louise, amiable, placid Louise, might
be about to protest. How much better when Louise was
married again, away from Théo's influence, thought Caroline,
stung by the belated realization that rebellion might have a
momentum of its own, that her whole household might be
set on fire for independence and free thought.

So it was that the three ladies, armed with umbrellas – it
was far too windy to put them up – and gabardines and their
stoutest boots, set off on foot for St Brelade, as if, indeed, to
throw down the gauntlet to the grand lady of La Croix, who

drew her blinds and tried unsuccessfully to languish upon her couch, tormented by indignation and anxiety. Had she looked out of the window instead she might have had the gratification of seeing Louise and Théo catch Millie deftly as she was nearly blown into the ocean by a freak blast, and the further joy of knowing that wherever the intrepid adventuresses reached in the next two hours, it was unlikely to be St Brelade unless they were transported there by the wind itself. It was all they could do to keep upright.

But Louise and Théo had faced worse before, back in the days when they had ruined their complexions in the pursuit of just such vicarious freedom; and Millie Boswell had been undaunted by marauding tribes and sandstorms in North Africa, was she to be put off by a good honest blow from the Atlantic? They held on to each other, occasionally shouting snatches of conversation above the noise of the wind, occasionally helping each other up, occasionally laughing. By the time they had walked a mile they were exhausted and descending into a debilitating mood of humorous despair. In another moment they would have to admit defeat, turn round, and be blown back to La Croix. At the top of the hill they paused to catch their breaths, and looked back.

A carriage was ascending in their wake, the horses thrown into their collars, ears flat, eyes distraught behind their winkers. One of the carriage occupants had elected to get out and walk for their sakes but the other, an elderly little man, hung out of the window.

'*Les belles de la Croix!*' exclaimed this wizened person as the carriage drew level, 'Madame Fontaine, Mademoiselle de Faurel! What a pleasure! What a pleasure indeed!'

'Dr Frere,' said Louise, holding out a hand with difficulty, the other raised to her bonnet as the wind got under its brim, 'I didn't recognize you in such a grand carriage!'

He looked sheepish, and waved to the young man who had toiled up behind, a young man enveloped in a huge greatcoat and with his hat rammed down hard over his ears.

'I have been driven to hire it for the sake of young Trent, who made some shameful remarks about my old two-wheeler. He is staying with me. His house at Rozel has been shut up six months and he has come back unexpectedly, the place is too cold and damp to live in. Captain Alex Trent, Madame Louise Fontaine. And Mademoiselle de Faurel. But I believe you have met.'

Alex was cheerful and polite, avoided Théo's eye, and greeted Millie effusively. When he doffed his hat and smiled his ingenuous smile he looked handsome enough to make Louise give him an unmatronly and speculative look, the look perhaps of a still-young woman who has long been deprived of any interesting male company. She raised one fair eyebrow at Théo and the corner of her mouth lifted.

The wind rioted about them, it was no time for idling. They agreed to meet again. Louise, enjoying herself, asked Dr Frere and Alex to La Croix for a 'quiet' evening, though what might be involved Théo could only guess. Then the carriage toiled on up the hill while the ladies contemplated the long toil down again.

'So that is your cavalry officer,' said Louise, slipping her arm through her sister's, 'I liked him. What on earth made you refuse him? I can't see anything to object about. And Mama said he had good connections and owns La Prairie at Rozel.'

Théo wore her mutinous withdrawn look, and made no reply for a long time. Then, as the restless water of the bay came into sight again and Louise, missing her step, leaned heavily on her arm, she murmured: 'Mama would say I refused him because I am a fool.'

'My love, we all want to see you happy.'

'You may never live to see that,' said Théo lightly. 'I believe I was born contrary. Or so' – and here a strained, tilted smile – 'Mama tells me.'

The 'quiet' evening was a success, though less quiet than Louise had intended. Caroline took things into her own hands. In two days an intimate dinner had grown out of all proportion to include six more couples besides Dr Frere and Alex, a box of presents, parlour games, and Christmas puddings. When the old shutters were closed and the heavy curtains banished the last draught of furious sea air, when the lamps and candles were lit, when the huge fire in the ancient stone fireplace in the dining room was stoked until the flames leapt up the chimney, when Luc entered with a tray of punch, then the whole proceeding was invested with the warm, kindly, old-fashioned hospitality of the house, in which generations of Faurels had done their festive entertaining. Caroline certainly knew how to make an occasion, thought Millie, who had had misgivings.

Dinner was a loud, friendly meal, the conversation ebullient rather than intellectual, and afterwards Théo reluctantly sang her song about seagulls, every word of which brought back memories of Joss Westover. Alex paid her attention, but not too much, for which she was grateful, seeing that Caroline had passed him fit to husband a Faurel within the first ten minutes and was busy devising the means of bringing them together.

'I never thought he had it in him to chase you here,' Millie said to Théo behind her fan. 'Perhaps he's short of money after all.'

'What a cynical remark! You made it deliberately just to tease me, didn't you? Apparently he's been allowed a few days' leave to settle things at Rozel – in case his regiment is sent abroad.'

'Couldn't he have written to Dr Frere?'

'He might be away years. He might be . . . killed.'

'All the more reason to put it in writing. How absurd! Are you going to reproduce all his excuses verbatim? I may be getting old but I'm not a fool yet, I hope. He came here to ask you to marry him. Will you refuse him again? Your mother is his champion already.'

'I don't want to marry anyone.'

'My dear, your attitude will be as incomprehensible to Caroline as bootlaces to the monkey.'

And so it was, though she expressed her opinions of it to Millie and not to Théo, not feeling up to the verbal parry and thrust that might ensue and the wild, unpredictable moodiness that surely would.

'Nothing has changed, has it?' she demanded, after she had shut her door on the last guest and retired with Millie to her drawing room. 'Nothing. A completely personable young man pays her attention and she brushes him off without a thought. Well, she's not getting any younger. In a year or so she will be glad of any man, any man at all.'

Millie pursed her lips and said nothing. After a while, for distraction's sake, she tried: 'There is going to be a war, you know.'

'War? I can't think what the fuss is about. What difference will a war with Russia make here in the islands?'

This was Caroline's only response to the deepening crisis in Europe. If she thought seriously about it at all it was to feel irritation at the idea of the French as allies; she did not like the French, though she spoke their language beautifully and entertained what remained of their aristocracy at her dinner table. She could admire them as enemies but found it difficult to imagine her countrymen calling them friend on the battlefield; it struck her as unnatural.

Millie looked at the matter from a different angle: Joss's angle. She, who could face anything, began to think it must be old age that was making her so anxious over the threat of war; after all, she believed in risk, had had no qualms throughout Joss's long service career. And if he were killed she would not be alone, there would be thousands of mothers and wives mourning their own men; it was a grief she had always been prepared for, or so she had thought. It was old age making her faint-hearted, she confided to Théo, whom she called to add a postscript to her latest letter to Joss; it was the thought of a lonely decline without Joss to warm the cockles of her heart.

Théo, whose heart was warmed at the very thought of him, found nothing to say. She picked up the pen and laid it down several times before piously hoping, in a rather cramped hand, that the conflict could be averted. Joss, vivid and egocentric Joss in the hot bowels of his great ship, was more real to her than anyone she touched or spoke to every day, except perhaps Millie. She sent her affection, which was natural and proper, seeing that Millie herself thought of them as almost brother and sister – what Caroline might have thought was another matter – and then signed her name with a flourish that was the expression of the hardy spirit which lurked some-where still in the closely kept inner self of Mademoiselle de Faurel.

And then there was Alex.

'Will he make a good doctor, do you think?' she asked Dr Frere when he called the next morning. 'He spoke to me about it again last night.'

'A doctor? Young Trent? Whatever gave you that idea?'

'But he's so keen to take up medicine. He wants to leave the regiment. I thought you knew all about it?'

'Hmm,' and he took off his glasses and polished them carefully. 'Is that what he told you? Yes, yes, perhaps he did mention going into medicine, but a long time ago, a long time. He seems more taken up with spitting Russians on his lance now, don't you think? How irrational men become in an instant when war is projected.'

A part-time soldier, said Joss's voice in Théo's ear, what could you expect? How genuine was his desire to be a doctor? She would have been exceptionally naive not to suspect a ham-fisted machination, to further his cause, to impress her. But he did not strike her as a man who practised deception as a matter of course, who ought to be distrusted. After all, his current enthusiasm for fighting Russians was equally suspect. How real was that enthusiasm, or was he simply a young man bored by pleasure and pursued by unpaid debts or predatory women? It occurred to her she did not understand him in the least although he seemed good-natured, affable, quite ordinary.

He was to prove unexpectedly tenacious. He called one morning and kissed Caroline's beautiful hands and invited them all to Rozel on Christmas Eve.

'I don't want to go,' said Théo to Millie, with all the stubborn fury of a small child.

'If I were you I would go with a good grace and confound them all by being sweetly amenable. After all, he can't bite, and Caroline can't force you to do anything against your will: you're of age and have your own income. My love, all the cards are in your hand.'

Théo took a deep breath. The window panes rattled and she looked up. It was going to be a stormy Christmas in more ways than one, she thought.

'I was never very clever at cards,' she said quietly.

*   *   *

It was a huge old house standing in a tangle of gardens facing the sea. The romantically inclined would have said an air of the Sleeping Beauty's castle lay over everything. Nine-tenths of the place was still under dust sheets and what remained had been polished and prettied and furiously heated in their honour. Millie blew the dust off a window sill and peered out.

'Fine views,' she said.

'It could be so lovely.' Louise was poking in forgotten cupboards. 'Can't he get a decent woman to housekeep while he's away?'

Below the murmur of voices told them Alex and Caroline and Dr Frere were admiring the drawing room. Théo sighed and looked down at the agitated grey water beyond the green sweep of the hill.

'It would be a waste of money. And now with this trouble in the east . . .' Her voice trailed away. Oh, how she longed to be out there, the spray in her face and a whole ocean to conquer, her beautiful underwear, her expensive merino dress, her charming little hat all left behind on the beach.

The rooms smelled musty and were cold. It was a beautiful house going to ruin. All that was practical and constructive in her nature ached to set it to rights, but La Prairie would remain neglected until Alex had a wife. She shivered. They all thought it would be so suitable – *so* suitable – all except Millie who kept her own counsel, who expressed no opinion.

'I'm going to look at the garden,' she said suddenly, and gathered up her skirts and ran down.

Alex found her a little later crammed into the shelter of an old mulberry tree, looking out to sea. He was glowing with Caroline's encouragement, and with his own new, deep excitement. He was excited by the thought of war, of glorious action, a mad dream of patriotic purpose and acclaim.

'Are you sure you aren't cold?' he asked. Théo was part of his excitement, he had never come across such a heady mixture of innocence and independence – and all allied to twelve thousand pounds and an impeccable pedigree. Charged with this strange elation, this glorious sense of anticipation, this longing for action – military action, military honours – he was determined to have her, had come here expressly to win her.

'Théo . . .'

'I've been here before.' She was looking back at the house. 'My father called here. One of the two servants had the measles.' It had been years and years ago, perhaps about the time its present owner was taking his first steps in his Kent nursery.

Measles? He was momentarily at a loss. What an extraordinary creature she was. She had turned back to her silent contemplation of the restless water; she might have been completely indifferent to good-looking young cavalry officers: he only had to appear in uniform and he made instant conquests. Well . . . Caroline had warned him Théo was strikingly modest, deeply shy of men – and what girl would not be wary who had so often been pursued by fortune hunters? When he put a hand on her arm she blushed and pressed back against the tree, a perfectly understandable reaction. She was overwhelmed, of course.

'Say you'll marry me and we'll tell them now – they will be so pleased. And we can make this Christmas unforgettable. Say it, Théo. Say you'll marry me.'

She turned then, gazing at the house, and in the doorway Caroline, exquisitely dressed as always, pulling on her gloves and glancing to see how well Alex might be doing. She will never let me set up my own house, thought Théo, not without the most bitter, bitter fight, and then she will make me an outcast, will tell all Jersey I'm an ungrateful, unnatural, uncharitable child. She will make my life misery, she'll drive me from the island. How unbearable, how absurd . . .

All this in a second, her face whitening. Dr Frere had emerged now, his straggling locks blown anyhow, and had offered Caroline his arm. What had Louise said last summer? A married woman had such great freedom, an unmarried daughter none. So was this the price she had to pay to escape Caroline?

'You haven't answered yet,' said Alex, conscious of the figures approaching over the grass.

'No,' and Théo looked with a bright fierce longing at the leaden sea as if her dearest wish was to run straight into it. 'No, I haven't.'

She felt nothing for him: Père Guillaume would say it was

a sin to think of marrying, caring nothing, nothing at all. She knew he was staring at her, trying to gauge her mood.

'Théo!'

She swung about then so that he instinctively stepped back to be out of the way of her skirt, and she ducked out under the branches with decision and walked quickly to meet her mother and the doctor.

'Have you . . .' began Caroline.

'I'm going to find Louise, Mama.'

She was almost at the house when Pierre ran out with the news that they had found some bats, dozens of bats, a whole attic of bats. Théo put an arm about his thin shoulders, laughing, but it was queer laughter, she could not seem to get her breath. It was the tearing wind, she would be all right indoors. She would certainly not look back. No doubt Caroline was already preparing a devastating rebuke. No, she would go in, would find Millie and Louise. Pierre grinned up at her, still explaining the discovery of the bats. When had she last felt such enthusiasm for anything, Théo wondered, except running away with Joss Westover who would never ask her?

'Your mother appears to be consoling Captain Trent,' said Millie, who had cobwebs in her hair after the bat hunt, 'I wonder why?'

Caroline was disinclined for battle: she saw they were beyond it. And Millie had shown her true colours at last, had been very forthright in telling her to let Théo manage things alone. She could only hope then that Alex's continuing optimism was well founded — and had nothing to do with her own description to him of Théo's character, so largely falsified.

So it was that Théo woke on Christmas morning to find an extravagant silk wrap, obviously expensive, laid out on the end of the bed with a note from her mother pinned to its folds, and no hint of rebuke or recrimination. She sat for a moment folding the paper over and over, listening to the sound of bells and muffled shrieks from the nursery accompanied by Clarice's uninhabited foghorn voice. A married woman, she was thinking, almost entirely free to do as she pleased . . .

Now she came to face it in this steely frame of mind — this post-Joss frame of mind — it seemed after all the only sensible solution. As a married woman she would be able to form her own circle, to meet whom she liked, to go where she liked. If Alex left the regiment and studied medicine what help and encouragement she might give him. He was amiable, she had never seen him other than amiable, and if he swaggered a little and exaggerated a great deal and was easily flattered he was no different from the majority of idle young men of his age and class. He had charm and good looks; none of her other suitors had possessed either.

'I believe,' said Millie, who came in while she was dressing and recognized the signs of warring emotions, 'that you were born out of your time and place. You're a salamander, you thrive in the destroying elements – only there are none in our sane, idle, comfortable lives. We talk and talk but we do nothing, go nowhere, adventure no further than the back doorstep. You would make a Joan of Arc, but can you see Joan of Arc in Miss Barnard's drawing room talking Socialism or fringes or flannel chemises? The ordinary world is so dull for anyone made for greater things.'

Théo laughed.

'If I married Alex would you ever speak to me again?'

'Why should I be so unreasonable?'

'Because I think you are against it.'

'Well, I'm no judge of these things, I never married. I only care that you make up your mind yourself. That's why I've never tried to discuss it with you, why I cautioned Caroline to leave you alone.'

'So it's your doing, this truce. How do you manage it?'

'I scare her to death, I really don't know why,' and then, after a long contemplative pause: 'Let's look on the bright side: perhaps marriage will be the very challenge you've been looking for all along.'

Théo pulled a brush through her hair, once, twice, three times. Through the soft mass of it falling across her cheek and forehead as she tipped her head, her eyes were emerald green, bright and fixed as if she looked into the future.

'The destroying elements,' she said.

The day passed, bright, clear and windy. They went to church in the customary procession, Caroline and Millie with Louise,

106

Théo with Alexandre and Leonie and lovely Marguerite who had come for just two days. Behind were the children, all the children, and the servants. And the whole of St Aubin was out, calling greetings up and down the streets and along the quay.

In the afternoon Théo and Millie set out in the carriage for St Helier, bearing presents and comforts and baskets of edibles for the orphans, those abandoned children of sailors' whores, and for the destitute wives and a few ancient fishermen. Somehow Théo's heart was not in it, though it was Christmas, though her committee ladies were touchingly glad to see her again. She was wearing a dark blue velvet cape, braided and tasselled, and a blue-checked dress and a dark fur hat. She wished she had worn something older and plainer, something more suitable. But perhaps it was only the meeting with Marguerite, her first in eighteen months, that had brought on this awkward irritable mood; the sight of Marguerite had reminded her – had warned her again – how destructive the elements of a bad marriage could be.

Dr Frere was there, dispensing brandy and bonhomie, making the old women cackle and the young ones blush. He kissed Théo affectionately, wished her the joy of the season, and toasted the memory of *le vieux* Bonespoire, God rest his soul. And then there was Alex, standing a little to one side, unable to understand half of what was being said and ill at ease in a room full of what he could only suppose were women of the town. Théo was shaking hands with them, allowing her fur hat to be admired, speaking at length in that infernal bastard French. He called it as much to her face when she cared to stop and take notice of him at last, and she seemed affronted, gave him a lecture on its origins, its purity . . . He felt exasperated, helpless.

When they left Millie expressed a desire to walk back to St Aubin across the sands, she had put on her thickest cloak on purpose. Dr Frere agreed walking encouraged the circulation of the blood, cleared the lungs . . . He looked doubtful though. He said it was a long time since he had walked the whole sweep of the bay.

The carriage was sent home. Alex, who had been invited to Christmas dinner at La Croix, offered his arm to Théo, who refused it, folding her hands implacably inside her velvet muff. The wind ruffled the fine fur above her forehead and colour was stung into her cheeks. She walked beside him but apart, a good yard apart, and she walked with her face turned towards the sea where it broke roaring on the distant grey sand.

'It looks like rain,' was Alex's unpromising beginning.

'It's turning colder,' said Théo, gazing inland suddenly at the ominous overcast sky.

They pressed on, passing slipways, moored ships heeling over, some old men playing cards; and St Aubin looked as far away as it had done twenty minutes before.

'Théo,' and he stopped and turned to face her, catching her arm, 'Théo, marry me.'

She swayed a little in the wind, and above the deep blue of her cape her face was very pale except for the spots of colour under the cheekbones.

'Yes,' she said.

He began to smile, a grin of delighted achievement. She was just the wife he needed: well-bred, accomplished, and with money of her own. And she attracted him, not as some other women had done perhaps but in a subtle way: she had a strange elfin innocence at times that touched him to the heart.

'I don't love you,' she was saying, 'it would be unjust not to tell you so.'

How formal, the tone so clear and precise. What an adorable, inexplicable child she could be! He stepped forward and swept her up bodily, and because her hands were still locked together in her muff she could not resist him. He kissed both her cold cheeks, French fashion, as he had seen everyone kiss her this afternoon, and she closed her eyes, the brown lashes hiding everything.

'You'll come to love me,' he said, 'and we'll be disgracefully happy at La Prairie.'

She did not smile though he had expected her to, and on her face was that burning desire for God knew what, intense, electric, infuriating.

'I want to come with you if the regiment's sent overseas,' she said.

'Come with me?' It seemed an odd thing to discuss on a blowy Christmas day, their feet sinking in the sand, the rain threatening.

'You won't leave me behind,' and then: 'You promise me?'

Of course he promised. Miss Boswell was hurrying back towards them, and Dr Frere was standing flapping his arms to keep warm, and all the clouds were massing over the huddled roofs of St Aubin.

'Are you all right?' asked Millie.

'It's the happiest day of my life,' said Alex.

Théo said nothing.

'The wedding is in two days and where is she?' complained Caroline, looking out of the window as if by staring hard she might pierce the very fabric of the island to come at a glimpse of her daughter. 'Where is she?'

Millie remained silent. She did not know, but if she had known she would never have told Caroline. She scuffed her little feet on the Aubusson carpet.

'Why aren't you pleased now you've achieved your heart's desire?' she asked, and the sour amusement in her voice made Caroline turn slowly round and come to sit down, as if only by doing so might she keep her dignity.

'Of course I'm pleased, but is Théo? If she is she gives no sign of it. You would think it was to be a funeral not a wedding.'

Oh Théo, thought Millie, why weren't you born hard and uncaring? Why weren't you born with the spirit of crazy old Bonespoir? But you're too sentimental, you love this house and the island, love all the Faurels too much . . . Look what you're doing just to gain your independence from Caroline, *and* stay on Jersey, *and* not fail in your 'duty' as a daughter. How foolish! For years you're put upon and under-appreciated and restrained and devalued and yet still you strive unconsciously to do what Caroline wants. Why? Do you hope that one day, after all, she might love you?

'You look tired,' remarked Caroline's beautiful voice, 'you really should take more care. Women of our age must pamper ourselves. Fancy walking across the bay last week! Still, he proposed again and she accepted him. At last! At last a suitable, decent marriage – though what a rush having to arrange it all within a fortnight. Do you really think his regiment will go overseas?'

Millie made no reply. She was thinking of her own drawing room and the stuffed parrot, Jack tinkering with the samovar, dear old Di thundering down the stairs. After a moment, seeing her rapt face, Caroline continued.

'I wish I knew where she was. I shan't be happy till I see the ring on her finger. There's no telling with Théo, she's always been so unpredictable.'

'I would have said she was generally quiet and dutiful.'

'Generally perhaps. You would not believe some of the battles we have fought. She refused to give up her charity work – those dreadful women! Those stinking old men! And she's said some things in the past that struck me to the heart.'

'I see,' said Millie, reflecting on the nature of human hearts and coming to some grievous conclusions.

'Oh no, you don't see. Once she accused me of selling Marguerite – her very phrase: selling Marguerite. She said I was responsible for all the unhappiness and grief, that Marguerite had never wanted Julien . . . It was all too absurd! But I shall never forget it. Imagine it, dear Millie, if you please. Théo said she would never forgive me for what I had done to Marguerite and that I would never do the same to her. Oh it was all over a man called Varges, a perfectly harmless creature who was really very fond of her . . . Millie, are you awake?'

'No,' said Millie.

Théo was along the beach, her hair blown from its chignon, her skirts dampened round their copious hems, her feet soaked. She was elated, furious, frightened, and in an agony of guilt. To the sea and the sky and the secret places of her childhood she was always truthful, and the truth was that she did not think she could ever come to love Alex as she should, and that it seemed now a fearful thing to have on her conscience. The sea raged beyond the rocks and something in her raged and howled for fulfilment and Alex . . . Alex was not the person to satisfy that inexplicable craving.

She scooped up her skirts and began to climb. The wind at the top took her breath away and tore down the last of her hair, so that she had to put up both hands to push it away and stood, buffeted and pierced with cold, watching the tide come in and in. In the summer it would come in with a hushing, soothing noise, creeping up the pebbly inlet to where the whelk shells and mussel shells had been plundered by the gulls. The water would be warm and foaming only at the very edge. There, high up out of its reach under the overhang of rock, Théo had hidden the old sailing boat.

It was not there now. Goosie's grandson had sailed it round to St Aubin the year Philip had been drowned, and it might be seen yet, painted a different colour, bobbing among the others. But Théo stood on her rock staring at where it had lain, and at another Théo, thin and brown and with her hair in a pigtail, who sat on the shingle leaning against its planks lobbing stones at a crab shell.

Late that night she wrote to Joss — Caroline would have been horrified — to say how sorry she was he could not come to the wedding, that it had been arranged in haste because Alex had to return to his regiment, that she hoped Joss did not still think of him as 'bow-legged Lancer'. She wrote and wrote, trite, stilted phrases for the most part, telling him about Christmas, about the island, about the ships in St Helier. The candle flame flared and died in the draughts, and the scratching of her pen seemed loud in the sleeping house . . .

'We leave for England the day after the wedding. The regiment is waiting for orders. I am not sure how I will make out as a cavalry wife . . .' She laid down the pen, walked to the window and back. Once she glanced at the bed, the bed she had slept in most of her life. She was a little afraid of sharing that other bed, as yet unseen, at Rozel with Alex. Instinct told her that all her doubts, like the proverbial pigeons, might come to roost in that bed.

'Wish me well,' she finished, and signed herself Théo, nothing more; then she altered the line suddenly to: 'I hope you wish me well.'

She hoped he did. She knew it was a strong possibility he might not. As she wrote his name 'Henry Westover' she thought she could see his cynical smile in the shadows by the wardrobe.

10

It was a shocking day. Even Caroline, whose sense of occasion was seldom shaken by vicissitudes, shuddered at the sheeting rain, the leaden sky. She was not the sort of woman to count them an omen but she grieved for her new and indescribably charming bonnet, her fur-edged cloak, the noble sweep of her train. Millie, whose cases had not included wedding finery, was at her fiercest in strident emerald like a predatory insect. She felt ill and old. She was afraid Théo had escaped from one cage to another that might prove, in the long run, more closely barred and infinitely more closely guarded.

And Théo? Théo was almost beautiful, for after all it was her wedding day, but it was a hollow, haunted beauty. She seemed to have lost all her colour, and the pale grey silk was ethereal and unflattering, the grey velvet cape edged with pink ribbons and pink silk roses darkened by rain before she got inside the church porch. Alex looked dashing – had he packed his uniform for just this purpose? – and youthful and touchingly proud. Only once or twice as they made their vows did he look down at Théo and wonder what she was, what spirit moved her. He was aware of deep, infinitely deep ignorance on this point, in spite of all Caroline had told him.

The rain, do what it might outside, could not dim the candles in the old, old church, could not drown the rousing singing of those stout friends and relations, invited or chance-come, who had gathered to see Théophile Marie Ursule de Faurel walk away as Mrs Trent.

Théo was aware Alex had moved, that there was a ring on

her finger, that Père Guillaume had just said something in his most portentous tones. What had he said? That she and Alex were man and wife? It was a charade, she did not love him; it was a sin, a mockery of the sacrament . . . What were they saying now? Her face lifted. She saw the benign wrinkled face of the old priest, and then . . .

And then Alex kissed her.

The wedding breakfast was sedate. Only close friends and relations had been invited. Even so it had a sense of style. No one but Caroline could have organized everything to the last detail within a fortnight and made such a success; she was regal with satisfaction.

The children were eating too much and getting out of hand; Clarice was strident with defeat. Bon contrived to sit with Théo, squeezing between her and Alex on the window seat where they had retired for a moment of peace. He put his small hand in hers.

'I don't want you to go away.'

'It won't be for long. Then I shall come back and live at Rozel.'

'It's all cobwebs.'

'It's going to be repainted and furnished and made all bright and sunny. I shall keep a boat in the harbour. I'll teach you to sail the way I taught Pierre.'

She realized suddenly that they were speaking French, that Alex was frowning. Did he imagine it was a deliberate slight? Théo smiled reassuringly but he still frowned.

'Go and find your mama,' he told Bon.

'He's really still a baby,' said Théo, watching Clarice catch him as he tried to hide behind Dr Frere.

'What were you talking about?'

'I'm sorry. I thought you'd understand.'

'Not when you gabble that peculiar patois. I didn't catch a word.'

'I was telling him I'd teach him to sail when I came back to Rozel.'

Alex drew back, horrified. 'Not now you're my wife you won't. You'll drown yourself – and the child too.'

'But . . .' But he had stood up, for Caroline was coming

towards them with outstretched hands, her eyes becomingly moist.

He was solicitous. Was she cold? Was she tired? But he was young and too eager to gratify frustrated desire. She was not entirely sure what he would do, Caroline had not ventured an explanation, but he did it with the assurance of a man who has learnt all he thinks he should know with one or two accomplished women and who has all the selfishness of youth and masculine pride. He did not consider any bruises he might have given her other than fleshy ones, did not consider he had failed her in any way.

He did not say he loved her, he did not say anything. He went to sleep immediately with his head in the crook of his arm.

She watched him sleeping in the last gutterings of the candle he had left burning on the bedside table. She thought she ought to feel tenderness, perhaps the same sort of tenderness she felt when Bon and Pierre flung their brown young bodies at her feet in the sand and she saw their slender bones almost piercing the skin. Surely she ought to feel something? She was determined not to fail him. It was the least she could do.

She shifted gently away from him and leaned to blow out the candle. She felt very old suddenly. She felt she was an old woman looking back on her life and finding she had not achieved anything, not even the simple happiness of being loved by and loving a good man. And as for the duties of married people – as Caroline had put it – they were not so much frightful as ridiculous. Was this what she had imagined Joss doing that night she had ached for his touch?

The rain was hurled against the panes and the noise of the sea grew louder suddenly, the tide on the turn. Théo lay awake staring into the darkness, feeling the draughts, listening to the thunder of the water on the rocks. It came to her that she had not kept two of the promises made last summer: she had married, and although she had come back, she was leaving again and who knew for how long. There remained only the sailing.

'I shall keep a boat in the harbour,' she had said to Bon.

She would perhaps, for all Alex had forbidden it, but she

knew with certainty that was as irrational as it was powerful, that it would not be this harbour and that it would not be Alex or Bon or Pierre that sailed it with her.

11

'Dear Joss,' wrote Millie, dashing into her letter without stopping to think of its composition,

You should have seen the dear girl on the deck of the packet, looking quite white and done up, extraordinarily reserved. She submitted to Caroline's blandishments with good grace, of course, but had to make a great effort to save herself when little Bon nearly strangled her saying goodbye and cried all down her front and into her collar. Alex was his usual charming self, smiling and unaffected. He does not seem very possessive or loving but I suppose it is only to be expected. I'm afraid he will come to regret his choice, he is young and impetuous, and I am sure she is not at all what he imagines. She has brought him a great deal of wealth and excellent connections, but money runs out and pedigrees cannot be slapped on like poultices when two people are intent on injuring each other. She has promised to write to me regularly and I know she will, but will she write the truth?

I keep abreast of the times with a strange collection of newspapers, some very outspoken on the subject of this war with Russia; some are from England and some from France and make an interesting comparison. I don't understand the hysteria that has broken out at home, the bellicose inhabitants of my graceless nation huzzaing at the street corners while the recruiting sergeants go by. How despicable they are, those poor deluded fools. How merrily they encourage others to spill their blood in a dubious cause. I am holding my breath in anticipation of calamity, how large a calamity remains to be seen.

Before he left Alex said that if he is ordered to the east Théo will naturally go with him. This must be her doing. I have the impression – very foolish old woman's impression founded upon no facts whatever — that he would prefer her to return to Rozel if he has to embark. But there, I expect all the other officers' wives are intent on turning the whole thing into a grand *fête de champêtre*, and will reside in splendour at Constantinople a long way from any fighting. Poor children. Neither Alex nor Théo have the least idea what battle is like, but I fancy she will face the realities better than he. You see from this I have a sad opinion of his character, think him amiable, lazy and a coward, but then he is so young — though he does not think so — and has been fondly mothered and allowed to idle about in bad company on the excuse of tender health. I hope for the best, but how far short of the ideal the best might be I daren't contemplate.

Your own last letter was indescribably slip-shod, told me nothing, hinted darkly at unsatisfactory shore leaves and between-deck squabbles. Are you pursuing a failing love affair or have you an inadequate captain? I have been puzzled to make it out. You are lucky to be able to go your own sweet way, you rascal, without being pulled up short by a sense of duty — I do not impugn your sense of honour — and an over-sensitive conscience. Can you even conceive what drove Théo to use marriage as an escape route? Caroline wept on my shoulder this afternoon, quite human after all apparently, saying that if there was a war Théo would be killed, and Alex would be maimed or disfigured. Perhaps there is real affection in her after all. But I suspect, because I am a wicked old woman too cynical for her own good, that she had only just realized how completely Théo *has* escaped her and was weeping for pure chagrin.

I have received a note — no more than a note, three scant lines and a scanter PS — from Miss Barnard, shivering at Martagon. They have been pursuing the usual dreary round of country society, it seems, but the weather has been bad and they're often confined for days together. Sophie is courted by half Oxfordshire but her heart isn't anywhere but on the *Satyr* with you. I never doubted you would make an impression but what an impression! How I hate self-assured men who have good cause for their self-assurance! You are a scoundrel and you know it. You care for her no more than my stubborn little Théo cares for that harmless handsome Lancer. Surely the world is a sad enough place without deliberately adding to its miseries? Do you really think you would find any kind of happiness with a girl brought up to be so much a lady, who thinks of nothing but society and going about in it and what she might wear in it and how she might entertain and be entertained in it? You would be better off to propose to dear old Di and her lizards.

Still, I will write and tell them how you fare, for that is what Sophie thinks about. As for you, I will pray for you in this dark business of Tzars and Pashas, that you come safe home again, as whole as might be expected. And if by the remotest chance – I do believe most faithfully in chance, you see – you meet Théo, give her my love.

'Remarkable,' said Dr Frere, when Millie pressed him to post this plump packet for her the following day, 'how such a small thing can travel across hundreds of miles and come at last to the right hands.'

'Yes, remarkable,' replied Millie, shooting up her umbrella and giving him her most sardonic smile, 'especially in this case, for I have no idea where the ship might be. Let us hope the Admiralty has.'

Millie's departure from Jersey at the end of January was accomplished to the languid fluttering of Caroline's handkerchief out of the carriage window, and Louise's tears which fell thick and fast, soaking three flimsy bits of cotton and lace and outwearing even Millie's famous stoicism. It was flattering to be regretted, she felt, but her collar was quite sodden.

In England at the same time Théo was dressing for a regimental entertainment, a dinner with Alex's fellow officers and dancing afterwards. It might be the last such gathering before they were ordered overseas and Alex had asked her to wear the rose silk with the deep flounces and the low tight bodice with its myriads of little roses and pearls. It had been Caroline's choice for her trousseau, horrifyingly expensive. Along with a pearl necklace and some tiny diamond earrings it had formed Caroline's wedding present. It was exquisite, but it was not Théo, the pink was too positive and made her look pale and sharp. It did show off her slender shoulders though, those faintly freckled shoulders with the small horseshoe-shaped scar where she had once cut herself falling out of the lugger.

She wore the dress obediently, conscious of Alex's desire to show her off, to prove he had not married her for money alone, something she now guessed had been whispered around before they had arrived back from Jersey. She did not care for dances, or even for dinners, but her behaviour would be irreproachable, he would never have cause to complain. Alex would never know how this forced frivolity, coupled with an excess of ardent patriotism, offended her, try as she would to associate herself with this military world. It had occurred to her more than once, watching him in the company of his fellow officers, that he did not dislike the army as much as he had made out, that the sense of belonging, of comradeship, of group purpose, was important to him. Théo found all the men immature, indescribably insensitive, unbearably jingoistic, and their exaggerated slang, their ridiculous affectations had once or twice made her long for permanent escape.

She gave no sign of it. She was even a mild success, gaining a reputation for sympathetic attention rather than wit; but sympathetic attention given by a charming lady in the latest French fashion and with the trace of an irresistible French accent could not fail to go down well. Alex said she was splendid, he had never doubted they would all love her, and because she did not want to be made unhappy but wanted dearly to make something of this marriage, she did not stop to wonder if he lied.

Tonight, at Major McCready's dinner, she would do her best as she had done her best these last few weeks, to appear the ideal young officer's wife.

'You must save a dance for your poor husband,' said Alex when they were ready to leave.

'I expect I shall have several to spare.'

'You underrate your popularity.'

She did. Of course she did. She had not been used to being the centre of attention, and although they would all soon find another new and younger wife to lionize, just for the moment she was queen. She would have shrunk from it as she had when Caroline had pushed her forward in the past, but it pleased Alex, it pleased him immensely; she would do anything to please Alex.

She danced as long as dances were played, her feet quite sore. Alex did not even manage one with her, though he made no serious effort to claim her, preferring to watch from the table where he sat with his closest friends. She was conscious she was in demand both as a novelty and for her own sake:

they really were very nice shoulders. There was also sometimes a startling air of innocence about her, the kind which appeals to certain men who regard it a challenge to their experience. Several gentlemen with hot, stupefied eyes squeezed her waist too tightly in the crush of the small dance floor and looked meaningfully, hoping for a response. It reminded Théo of Millie and her General. She was also reminded of dancing with Joss, Joss who had whirled her so cavalierly about the ballroom at Russell Square, steering his erratic course while talking oscillating engines and cogged pinions. She would have exchanged any of her partners at Major McCready's for the welcome, impersonal strength of Joss's arm, his loud laugh, his voice with its occasional warm curl of Oxfordshire adding point to some remark. She thought of him with a deep affection – she had tried to put out of her mind that mysterious physical longing – and she smiled to consider how refreshingly pragmatic and irreverent his views would be in this roomful of consequential cavalry officers.

She retired with Lieutenant Monkton, hardly more than a downy boy, to consume the largest ice of her career. She glanced about: no Alex in sight. She had no chaperon, no overseer, no one to restrain her; she could do anything. But what was there for her to do? Simply be elegant and polite and try to spare young Monkton's blushes, he blushed so very easily.

Grand'mère Honorine, she remembered, biting into angelica, spooning up cherries, Grand'mère Honorine had gone to balls alone and had not been above some merry flirtations, had been considered scandalous, had been imputed lovers of every sort and station, and had been universally adored. Once she had lost all the parrots, had called out the Centeniers, and had had the whole island parrot-catching for a week. Country people had brought the captured birds in cages and wicker baskets, the Centeniers had brought them in police wagons, and Honorine had entertained them all willy-nilly to strong cider and plum cake.

'Why are you laughing?' demanded Lieutenant Monkton, who thought she looked quite another person when she laughed.

'Oh, just a memory. I do beg your pardon.'

He thought she was very fine, and even in that dress, that gorgeous, fairy-tale dress, much more approachable than most of the other wives. He pressed her to another ice cream and she declined, smiling, asking him if he would find Alex for her, it was so very late.

It was late, but few had made any move to leave. Were they all thinking this was the last time they could enjoy such frivolous gaiety, that next time they might be in the midst of war? And then Mrs McCready, a plump, squat, unlovely woman with a coarse, red-veined face and the same unbreakable fibre as Millie, came over to remonstrate – why was she all alone?

'Heaven knows when we embark,' she said. 'Rumours fly like little birds, all different, darting in and out again. But what a way for the poor horses to go – you would think they might spare a steamer. Why, a steamer could reach Constantinople in a week and the dear things spared all that suffering.'

'They do not have enough steamers,' said Théo dryly, 'for all the deserving cases.'

'It might be as well, I suppose. I had relatives upon the *Amazon* you know, the ship that caught fire and sank with such loss. If it weren't for the horses I would trust myself to sail every time.'

Teddy Monkton reappeared, without Alex. He had a hang-dog, apologetic air.

'Captain Trent is engaged at cards,' he said, very low, very strained. 'He has arranged for you to be taken home by the Allisons.'

Théo inclined her head. Reassured he stumbled on: 'I am . . . He has asked me to bring you to them.'

'My dear Edward,' cried Mrs McCready, 'I will take Mrs Trent myself. Mary Allison is my particular friend.'

Teddy Monkton looked furiously disappointed and blushed deeply. He had felt there was great charm in being entrusted Mrs Trent's comfort. He had thought Alex too casual about her by half, would never have stayed at cards if he had had a bride of one month as sweet and pleasant as this woman who stood before him in her rose and pearls. As if she understood his vexation and appreciated it, she held out her hand, looking up into his boyish grey eyes fringed by their heavy lashes.

'You've been very kind,' she said. 'Good night. I hope we meet again soon.'

He was scarlet. He barely touched her hand in case he held it too long and he stood aside to let her pass with a jerk. He watched her bustled away by Mrs McCready as he had often seen stately little craft bustled from the river by pilot cutters.

He hoped she was coming out east. He had the deepest, vaguest, most irrational sense of premonition.

He did not want to go.

'We embark on Thursday,' Alex said, flinging himself down on the sofa in their shabby sitting room. 'Four days. Dear Théo Trent, four short days.'

There was a withdrawn look about her these days, he thought, as if she did not fully attend what he said. He had done his best to make her happy, certainly these last five weeks had blessed them with a merry social life, but she did not like his friends — she did not say so but he was quite sure of it — and of the wives only Mrs McCready, that rather vulgar woman, Beth Fullerton and Mary Allison called to pass the time of day with her. He found her increasingly restless, uncomplaining and yet remote, troubled. He had wondered once or twice if she was expecting a child, they had ragged him about it in the mess, but she had said nothing and then denied it, and almost vehemently, when he had tentatively asked. That practical streak in her, which had made her the excellent housekeeper at La Croix and her father's trusted assistant the year before he died, Alex found less admirable now. She was inclined to overstep those invisible but universally acknowledged boundaries of propriety. She had been downstairs to help another tenant in childbirth, an act of common kindness deplorable in a lady of her standing; how he wished there had been time to find better lodgings for the last weeks left them in England.

Now she took the definite date of their embarkation calmly, she had long ago applied to accompany him and she would have at least Mrs McCready for company on the passage. All she asked was time to go and visit Millie, currently terrorizing Holywell again as she had felt 'cooped up' in London, or so she said, after the blustery tranquillity of Jersey. Alex, glad to see Théo active and positive, encouraged her to go, provided she did not miss the transport.

'How could you think I would let you go without me?'

'You sometimes keep time according to your own clocks, dear Théo. If you are one minute late we might have sailed and you will have to stay behind.'

'I should pay a bold fisherman to bring me out to you. You'll not crack along with fifty horses on board, all confined and hobbled and whinnying with fright.'

He laughed. Sometimes he adored her, and that irritating practical side of her was an asset after all; at any rate now, when it was not in conflict with his ideas on what was socially permissible.

'Have a nice time with Miss Boswell,' he said, cupping her face, 'give her my best wishes.'

She nodded, withdrew before he could kiss her. It struck him that she often withdrew, not only physically but with her whole being, retreating to some remote place he could not reach her. Once or twice he had thought she had done so during his lovemaking, which had offended him, but perhaps it was to be expected from a well-brought-up virgin of twenty-nine. He was sure he gave her some pleasure, and suspected it was as much as she would ever feel.

How grave she looked now, and still with that untouched, innocent air as if she had never yet lived nor felt deeply. Yet how popular she was, they thought him a lucky beggar to have her at all, some of them. He would hate her to miss the ship, he knew she was a good sailor and he hoped to show her off on board. He had made an excellent choice, he thought, she was good, generous, quite charming in her own way, and she had breeding and a fortune and unshakable good manners.

The excellent choice smiled. 'I'll go by train,' she said, 'I'll leave tomorrow morning.'

She arrived in Oxford somewhat smutty. She had made the mistake of opening a window shortly before they had passed under a bridge and clouds of vile smoke had enveloped her. Millie met her, umbrella aloft against the first cold drizzle of the day. She had walked, but had asked Jack to bring the carriage in her wake in case of baggage.

'My dear, you look . . . extraordinary.'

'It's soot.'

'But so thin. And my dear Théo, you have rings under your eyes.'

'We've been to so many parties and dinners. I haven't had an early night for weeks.'

Jack came alongside. He might have been driving a steam omnibus, his rigidity and look of terror was absolute. Hardy had a cold, was indescribably weak in the head and arms, so the horses, the fiery, unpredictable, overfed horses were Jack's for the day.

'Hardy prostrate and Jack in a foul mood,' declared Millie, 'I suppose we may as well get in. Oh, and Polly lovelorn for a most unsuitable Lothario of a groom at the George. I'm plagued by them all, sighing and sniffing all over the place. Only Nelson is in his normal spirits.'

Nelson poked his face from under her many petticoats and hung out his tongue.

It was like coming home to Théo, coming to the narrow old house with its sloping casements and crazy staircase, its faded chintz and threadbare rugs and bowls of greenery. Polly, a little pink about the eyes, helped her change her dress, and even looking into the old mirror and contemplating a night in the high lumpy bed was comforting. Nelson lay on the coverlet, head on paws, wagging his stumpy tail. It was as if she had never been away.

'Sophie Barnard has written to me,' said Millie at dinner, 'and wickedly enclosed a note for Joss. It's quite improper. She only hopes he is well, of course, and in good spirits, all perfectly innocent. I shall send it, it will make him smile, no doubt.'

'They keep her too closely guarded,' said Théo, who knew all about such things.

'Well, let's hope she falls violently in love with some suitable Lord this that or the other before Joss lands in England again.'

A little later: 'You look so tired,' Millie was moved to say, reflecting that parties and dinners and late nights would not have half the effect on a young woman who was truly happy, however much she disliked them. 'It isn't a child, is it?'

Théo smiled and shook her head.

'Good,' said Millie, 'a baby's the last thing you want on a sea voyage and in a strange heathen place with no proper friends to help you. But I suppose it will come. Plenty of women have had their babies in the shelter of gun carriages.'

'I believe that officers' wives, such as are going, will be accommodated in handsome apartments a very long way from any gun carriages.'

Millie shot her a look, hooking Nelson from under her chair with her toe, and lifting him on to her lap. 'That's what they tell you, of course. But it is most amazing how wars never progress by the book, how certainties are reduced to rubble in five minutes by those very guns that are supposed to be so far away.'

For a moment she and Théo looked at each other by the light of the candles. Millie stroked Nelson's ears.

'They are commanded by old men,' declared Théo, and passionately: 'It's not their age that is objectionable but their lack of experience. They squabble for the honour of leading this or that when they have never led anything more exacting than a cotillion in their lives. All the good knowledgeable men who have been in India are disregarded, looked down on. Everything is show – who has the best horses, the prettiest jackets, the . . . oh, I don't know. It's all so false and foolish. Some of them know it is, a few, the real soldiers, and worry about it, but the others go on in their exaggerated pride and silly patriotism and drown out their objections. They think . . . They think the Russians will turn and run when they come in sight.' And she thought of Teddy Monkton, scarcely more than a boy, telling her that he wished they were not going, that he was sure the infantry would accomplish whatever had to be accomplished with ease, and blushing because he would never have confided in anyone else and dreaded being thought a coward.

'Then we must pray,' said Millie, 'that the ordinary soldier, who has endured hell these thousand years, will make up in courage for the shortcomings of his leaders. Now, have a last glass of madeira and tell me about Alex.'

Théo closed her eyes. The candlelight gilded her soft,

straying hair. 'He's like a boy,' she said softly, 'like a boy waiting for Christmas morning. I wish . . . I wish we could see the future. I want to know how all this ridiculous piece of theatre will end, what will come after the cheering and the church bells and the bellicose speeches.'

'Why not go back to Rozel?' The question was fired from the half-dark beyond the candle flames.

'That isn't what I want. I'm not afraid to go east, only afraid for Alex, he has such dreams of glory, such . . . expectations.'

Millie considered. 'Do you feel you belong to Rozel?'

'Belong? I was brought up on the island, how could I not belong?'

'Oh, to the island, yes. To St Aubin, La Croix, even to Faurel Mannelier. But to La Prairie at Rozel?'

'I don't understand you.'

'You understand me perfectly. Your intellect has never been wanting. You married Alex to escape Caroline and to own the house at Rozel. But is it what you really want? Is that house where you really belong?'

Théo was silent so long Millie thought she did not intend to answer. But then she looked up, her eyes tawny in the light, unreadable, her mouth pulled up gently by a wry, sweet smile.

'I don't know where I belong,' she said.

Miss Sophie Barnard belonged at Martagon, in a purple dress with a blue polka and with her hair *à la Turque*. Miss Barnard, raising her glass, said that Théo looked charming, marriage suited her, and did not mean a word of it.

They would not take off their bonnets, they had not meant to stop, only to pay their respects, declared Millie, thrusting Nelson from the remains of some small cakes with the handle of her umbrella. Miss Barnard looked but said nothing with a noble self-restraint, but it was all lost on Millie who had found herself in possession of a collar but no dog, Nelson having slipped away to some further mischief behind the curtains. He came out some moments later with something feathery sticking from the side of his jaw and Théo, seeing her chance of escape, ejected him into the gardens and let herself out with him.

It was a cold gusty day and she had to hold down her skirt.

There was no one about. Nelson walked beside her, giving the false impression of an obedient and amenable little dog. They paced on together, skirting the lawns and striking down some gloomy yew walks to a sort of Chinese pagoda. It was a very small dilapidated pagoda, the haunt of spiders, beetles and dead leaves, but there was a seat, and a fine view of Martagon across the level sweeps of grass. Théo sat, Nelson beside her, and contemplated the tall windows of the Long Gallery behind which hung all those martial Westovers and their important wives.

Nelson crept nearer and put two paws and a nose in her lap. She fondled his ears absently, thinking of Alex. She did not miss him, and oh the relief of sleeping alone last night, and of being far from all those pompous young men with their moustaches and their boasting, their childish, irritating gossip. She could not bear the thought of several weeks cooped up in a ship with them.

'I will take you to Russia,' Alex had said that first morning when she had woken at Rozel, 'I'll take you to the east, to Turkey, to India . . .'

He was a dreamer, impractical; if any of these things were to be accomplished it would be she who led, he who followed. Not that she knew any more whether she wanted them accomplished. She felt adrift with no stars visible, and no land and no friendly light.

But she had made a sort of bargain and she would stick to it, that was one certainty. She would be a dutiful wife to Alex. Her loyalties might be subtle and divided, her heart uncommitted for the rest of her life, but to the world, to Alex, she must be seen to be dutiful: it was the price of her freedom from Caroline.

But it was a sobering thought. She sat ramrod straight and squeezed of breath by the wind and her corsets together, and her face was serious and a little puzzled, like a lost child, as she picked her way delicately through the maze of contradictory hopes and resolutions. After a long time she stood up and tried breathing normally again, calling Nelson and setting off for the house with a drunken step, buffeted and choked by the freezing wind. She must hustle Millie from her pleasantries or she would miss the train, the tide, the waiting ship.

Sophie wept and kissed her on parting, no longer the proud young lady of Martagon, while her aunt whispered in the background that the poor sweet girl was delicate, so delicate, this cold weather quite threw her down.

'Hmm,' said Millie.

But Sophie was clinging to Théo's arm, her dark head bent, her back to the elderly ladies. 'If you should meet Mr Westover,' she said in Théo's ear, 'tell him I think of him. Oh, Mrs Trent, how lucky you are to be going!'

12

If Théo's life had been a little less dull in the past, and if the choices it had so far presented had been more obvious ones, she might, standing by her baggage on a deserted quay, have been better able to come to a firm decision. It is practice makes perfect as Millie, who could be *so* irritating, would surely have said. But Millie was not there, she was snug in Holywell with a spirited little fire and Polly to bring her the newspapers and the writing things for the all-important letters to Joss. Théo was alone. She was alone and she had never been in such a predicament. All her rigorous training as housekeeper and tender sister and dutiful child had not prepared her for such a wretched, sinking, desperate state. She had missed the ship, and all for the sake of two hours which she had lost because of a broken coupling and the propensity of the cabby's horse to fall on his knees every twenty yards. She, who had been schooled in punctuality, one of the first lessons for a lady, now found herself facing the disintegration of her whole life because of two hours wasted and the prompt sailing of an elderly ship.

So how to get to Constantinople, her money scanty and her virtue in the balance?

The first thing perhaps was to apply to travel with one of the other cavalry divisions still waiting passage; after all, she had an official pass, it was not as if she was trying, like some poor women, to sneak on board disguised. A whole day in Portsmouth, knocking up officials, taught her that while in some instances official passes were everything, in others they might be nothing at all. The difficulty was that space was at a premium, and also that she knew no other officers' wives except the ones in her own regiment; there were no friends to call on, no influence to be exerted. She might as well have been a soldier's woman disappointed in the lottery and howling with grief and rage, and there were plenty of those. So then what? She was advised to go home, it would be by far the best thing, the rigours of the east were well known and not to be undertaken lightly; she was advised to travel out by steamer, a great number of the ladies who had chosen not to accompany their husbands in person were set upon following in this manner.

The idea of the steamer appealed, though it meant extra expense and she had no companion, no servant – she had been going to share Mrs McCready's Peggy. Well, it could not be helped.

The inn she stayed in that first night was gloomy and cold and too near the harbour for respectability. In the morning she walked to the water's edge and watched the comings and goings of the little craft between the troopships. There were two troopships. An old man on a bollard, spitting accurately at an inoffensive seagull, told her they would sail that afternoon, he didn't know what regiments, pack of red-faced fools the lot of them, marching about to their confounded tunes and drums, all their women caterwauling. Most of them were packed aboard already, and good luck to them, there was a nice swell and the *George Fraser* was scarcely watertight, a converted Indiaman, saw service back in the nineties, laid down before jolly old Clive ha, ha: just look at her roll!

Théo looked, and because she knew about ships, she shuddered. Beside her a little sniffing dab of a girl in grey looked with equal interest but more innocence: 'It looks low in the water.'

'Low? Bless you, she's overloaded, that's why she looks low,' from the bollard. 'Wouldn't surprise me if she capsized.'

The girl stood biting her handkerchief, distraught. Théo put herself between them.

'My husband has already sailed,' the girl said, hoping this might seem a neutral sort of remark.

'Oh, has he?' a wet look, another sniff.

'My Tom's on the *George Fraser* and I should be with him,

I drew a place in the lottery. He's a corporal. But they embarked early, I was saying goodbye to my family — they're Portsmouth people, you see — and someone came running up the street to say the men were going on the ship and why was I not there?'

Théo sympathized. How could she do anything else, since her own experience had been so similar? By the time Mary Anne Brewster had reached the quay the *George Fraser* had been towed out into the river and now wallowed there inaccessibly waiting for her pilot.

'Can we get a boat?' Théo demanded. 'Will they row us out there?'

''Spose so.'

'She looks all in,' said the waterman, regarding Mary Anne suspiciously. 'How come she ain't on board? They won't let you up, you know, they'll think you're ladies of easy virtue.' He might have put it more strongly but the young woman holding tight to the arm of the other, though she was dressed in quiet, sober colours and wore no ornament except her wide gold wedding ring, had the air of a person to whom the word whore might not be mentioned. Well, if she got aboard that rascally old ship it would be a word she came up against for certain. He spat. What did he care? So long as she paid him to row them over.

'D'you think they won't let us on?' whispered Mary Anne as they bobbed forward on the choppy water and the gulls complained on all sides.

'They'll let you on,' said Théo with conviction, more conviction than she felt. Bureaucracy could be cruelly inconsistent.

There was the miserable, shaming business of hailing the ship, the inevitable rope ladder, and a crowded deck of staring men. But Mrs Brewster's right to be there was confirmed in a second, her husband's sergeant being crammed up against the after hatch and vouching for her loudly, and somehow in the confusion — the pilot coming up the ladder after them in a tearing hurry and a bucolic temper like an outraged ox, why no one knew — Théo was hustled below with scarcely a passing glance at her dress, her condition, her expensive little carpet bag which was all she had brought. It was a known fact the officers of many ships turned a blind eye to 'extra' ladies, for what was six wives to every hundred infantrymen, the official figure?

There was a noisome dark in which the lamp dimmed ominously. She had not been prepared for the smells, the noise, the overcrowding. She was not pampered or spoiled or even ignorant but nothing in her life had prepared her for this. She hesitated, her comforting arm about Mary Anne's thin shoulders, and then a voice shouted out, and someone pushed in front of them, and a boy – hardly more than a boy – said: 'My love, I thought I'd lost you,' in the accent of the Sussex downs.

Théo was explained – though not as an officer's wife, for even Mary Anne did not know that – and made welcome. She was accorded a piece of deck and an all-round scrutiny that showed how little they thought of other regiment's wives taking up space when their own loved ones had had to be left behind.

Half an hour later they had weighed anchor for the east.

On the third day it occurred to Théo how scandalized Caroline would be to know a daughter of the Faurels was in such a place as this. It was not as if her virtue was in danger: a code of morality as rigid (ostensibly rigid) as Caroline's own might be found in the stinking half-dark of the gundeck. She was treated with rough kindness and left to herself, insofar as anyone could be said, among so many hundred, to be by herself. But virtue for Caroline had other dimensions, and she would have declared in horror and hysteria that on the *George Fraser* was neither decency, sensibility, nor God. There were certainly whores – though they were expected to do the washing like the other women – and there was bad language and filth and an inconceivable smell; throughout the bad weather they were, to all intents and purposes, battened down where they could cause no trouble.

Théo, who had been brought up to be polite in unpromising situations, simply endured. She salvaged what dignity she could from the situation because that was all she could do to keep herself from tears. She had often cried years ago out of self-pity and frustration when Caroline had driven her too hard, and it was something she had tried to grow out of, tried to avoid. It would be absurd to give in to this unseemly desire to howl just because she was not being treated as a lady. She was, after all, treated as a superior being, someone having assumed she must be a sergeant's wife and according her the natural privileges. Mary Anne was unfailingly attentive, conscious she would not be on board but for Théo. Truly, she had no cause to complain.

She had none, nevertheless she was troubled. She was troubled by the difficulty of finding Alex once they reached Gallipoli – she was certain the Lancers had gone to Constantinople – and she was troubled by lice, a new experience, and by the inescapable lack of privacy. But she endured. La Croix had been built out of the Jersey granite and perhaps the Faurels, too, owed something to that uncompromising rock.

The gales of the Bay gave way to hot weather in the Mediterranean. Théo, whose spirits had reached a low ebb, wondered if perhaps she should have acquainted the captain with her situation as soon as they had been safely at sea and insisted on being treated as the wife of an officer. It would have been ungentlemanly of him to tip her back into the misery of the gundeck and he could hardly have tossed her over the side. But in the early hours, when the lice and the heat and the indescribable noise of the ship brought her to this reflection, she would dismiss it by thinking of Mary Anne, who seemed to have come to depend on her, clinging to her first through the bouts of sickness that left her white and helpless and now the prostrating heat that cooked them in their airless hole.

At the moment when they felt they could not survive another day of it, the washerwomen came down to tell them Malta was in sight.

They were short of water and had painfully dry throats else they might have cheered.

Malta was hot, full of English, French, Swiss, Italians and staff officers who viewed Théo's determination to be reunited with Captain Trent as just a trifle irritating. The Lancers were at Scutari – or they had been and they had left, or they were to be, it was unclear. Thirty thousand men, all these blasted horses, the forage, the equipment, the ammunition . . . and one small importunate young woman asking for Captain bloody Trent of the 17th Lancers.

Théo knew no one, so got nowhere. Kind offers to 'see what could be done' came to nothing in the welter of paperwork and the effort to see the expeditionary force was sent with the least delay wherever it might be going – which place was as yet uncertain. It had been most irregular to travel out on a transport along with the wrong regiment and as a common army wife – and she lost caste, poor Théo, through admitting it. She received no congratulations for perseverance, nor did anybody see anything romantic in the gesture; a lady would not have done it, therefore she was no lady.

Malta, besides frustration in abundance, provided the wherewithal for a decent wash and a change of clothes; Théo burnt those she had worn for the long weeks on the *George Fraser*. She took a cheap lodging in a house run by a drummer's wife, a large, rascally, opportunist of a woman who had quarrelled with her husband on board ship and now saw no reason to leave what little business she had made for herself on the island. She regarded Théo with suspicion, for no woman of any station would choose such a mean lodging; she imagined Théo had married beneath her – perhaps not married at all? – and had been deserted, was following her feckless lover because she had nowhere else to go.

Théo, who thought she had done well to survive the *George Fraser*, to manage without a maid for the first time in her life, to rent a room and feed herself and all for very little money – her money was running very low – ignored Mrs Batty's unsubtle probing and pursued her cause. It was a hopeless pursuit, she was blocked at every turn, and she grew more and more weary and anxious and helpless as the days passed. She wrote letter after letter to Alex and sent them off in good faith, but she received no replies and concluded they could not have reached him. She also wrote to Millie, in the false tones of an amused adventuress, joking about the primitive conditions and the apparent inability of the staff to discover Alex's whereabouts. She was rather proud of the absence of complaint or self-pity in this letter; she was feeling depressed and had no one to confide in and it was all too tempting to write the truth to Millie. She did not, she fudged and lied and was wholly optimistic. And after the thing was signed and sealed and sent on its way she sat down on her narrow, iron-hard bed at Mrs Batty's and cried her eyes out.

'You shouldn't take on so,' said that corpulent lady, coming in without knocking. 'Have a sip of this, bring the roses back.'

It was gin.

'Is he worth it? No, all right. You still want to find 'im. My dear, my dear, Poll Batty knows what it is to have a sore heart. A baby is it? No? Well, that's a blessing. Here, have another mouthful. You don't need to come over all shy with me. Far better to tell me the 'ole story. I could help p'raps.'

'There's nothing to tell. My husband is Captain Trent of the Lancers and I wish to be with him.'

'Well, why can't their lordships help? They can't have lorst the Lancers.'

'I think they could help if they tried. They don't want to try. It's an underhand way of discouraging me from joining the regiment. They keep telling me how much better off I would be in an hotel in Constantinople, or even here. And I can't get round them . . . I don't have a title, or friends in the right places, and I don't have . . . I don't have the *nerve*.'

'True. I said to myself when you arrived: that one isn't made of what she needs to be made of, turned loose in a foreign seaport with only a weddin' ring to protect her. But sometimes it don't take nerve so much as cunning, a little bit of careful thinkin' and proper-laid plans. My dear, my dear, you can count on old Poll. I'll see what I can do.'

'But what can you do?'

'You'd be surprised. I've knocked round the military all my life, and besides, I've opened gin shops and eating houses in foreigner parts than these. I know certain people who will always help others less fortunate – for a price, you understand, for a price.'

'Yes, of course,' said Théo wearily.

The *George Fraser* had gone, there was a self-important little paddle-steamer in her place, one of the seamen tossing a bin of rubbish into the calm blue water. Théo, who could feel the beads of sweat on her brow, down her straight spine, stood and watched. Then a young French lieutenant came up and asked if he might walk with her, at which she blushed crimson and said she thought not, perhaps he had mistaken her for someone else, all in the perfect, upper-class French of Caroline's dinner table. He blushed himself, and retreated, but he looked back several times, his eyes accusing: if she looked like a whore could she blame him for the mistake?

She was thoroughly demoralized but was beyond weeping about it. She returned to her lodging and discovered Mrs Batty screeching choice military obscenities at the score of starving cats who haunted the back entrances.

'Well, well, I never saw you,' she said, leaning on the door jamb to catch her breath. 'You walk like a nun, dearie. Those cats'll be the death of me, they get me that worked up. Oh, I've done a little askin' about on your behalf – they say the Lancers are at Varna, God knows where that is for no one I've spoke to does.'

'Have they been there long?'

'Just landed by all accounts.'

'And how can I get a passage there? I'll never be allowed on another transport.'

Mrs Batty cackled wildly. 'How you got on the poor old *George* is a mystery to me. P'raps you've got nerve enough when it comes to the point. If you have . . .' a sly look, a dramatically wicked smile for effect: 'If you have, dearie, I might be able to find you a passage.'

Théo felt it would be undignified to ask how and when and how much with that sort of eagerness she knew Mrs Batty might expect, and if her daily brush with dilatory bureaucracy had taught her anything it was how to wait. She said: 'I'll see what I can do on my own account first. But what I really came to ask you . . .' and she smiled her sweetest smile, 'do you know where I could buy some more clothes?'

She could have bought them in the shops. Mrs Batty grasped her predicament at once.

'Cheap, you mean? Somethin' suitable to the climate, eh? Well, I know someone as deals in second-hand stuff, pretty good, and all for a small sum.'

Which resulted in Théo visiting a sort of clothes shop in a back street, a narrow dirty disagreeable shop overflowing with garments, men's and women's, and none of them washed or pressed or even hung up to catch the eye. The old lady who ran the place let her poke and pry across the boxes and the makeshift counters without comment, expecting to have to haggle the price almost to the death: one could never tell with Impoverished Gentility. In fact Théo was undemanding, stating the most she would pay and asking with amazing politeness if that was all right, if perhaps the habit shirt should not be left behind. The shirt was thrown in, along with the cotton skirt and the brown jean dress with the torn cuff that had belonged to poor little Miss Tindall, now dead. Théo did not wait to learn how she had died, there were deaths enough in this heat and general overcrowding. She allowed her purchases to be wrapped – folded and tied with string – and then fled back to Mrs Batty's.

'What about that passage?' asked Mrs Batty as soon as she stepped through the sagging door, blinded by the dark after the brilliant sunlight, 'I need to know, see.'

'It depends. It depends how much it costs.'

'Haven't you 'ad any money from home? I don't understand it, you writin' letters morning noon and night and no replies, not one. You'd think they were glad to see the back of you. Are you sure you didn't run away from home? Families can be funny. I know. I ran away from mine and they'd never let me acrorst the step again, not even when I come back destitute and two babies to feed. Cruel some people are if you touch 'em in their pride. Well, as to what it'll cost to get you to Varna, you'll have to sort it out yourself. I know someone who'd take you there, that's all.'

So Théo went into the tiny paved courtyard that was common to all the neighbouring houses and proceeded to wash her new purchases in a stone trough, determined, at the least, not to wear other people's fleas, and Mrs Batty sat beside her on the edge of the trough, talking. She would be sorry to lose Théo as a lodger, if only all lodgers were so quiet, so well-behaved, such prompt payers. In all her life she had never had such a good lodger.

What had happened to the babies, Théo asked, and to Mr Batty?

'Oh, they wasted away, poor mites. There's slums in parts of old England, dearie, as you've never set eyes on where babies die just like that, you'd think the very air was poisoned.

S'pose it is. There never was a Mr Batty, but I weren't goin'
to call myself Miss now, was I, not at my age and tryin' to
run a decent house. No, never was any Mr Batty.'

'But . . . but the drummer?'

'Well, we was married but he had a wife livin' so it ain't
legal. And I'm well rid of him, dearie, he was a terrible
complainer and mean as you like, not capable of anything
but banging that terrible old drum.'

Théo watched her hands turning wrinkled in the cold water.
A strand of hair fell over her forehead and she blew it away.
It was cool in the courtyard compared with out in the street
but the heat was still intense. She straightened a moment,
rubbing her back.

'I'm sorry about the babies.'

'Well, to tell the truth I wasn't at the time, though I am
now if you know what I mean. I had no means to feed them,
did I? If I worked on the streets the pimps took all the money.
They're better off dead, dearie, better off.'

Théo bent over her washing again. Is that how she would
feel, she wondered, if she bore Alex's child in a place like this,
far worse than this, unable to find him, unable to join him?

The dress, the skirt, the shirt, pummelled with savagery,
were hung in the sun to dry. Théo wiped her hands and pinned
back her hair.

'Now what about Varna?' demanded Mrs Batty, bringing
her fresh lemon juice and a jug of the dubious local water
where she sat on the edge of the trough. 'Are you going? Or
do I tell the captain you aint interested now?'

Théo mixed her curious lemonade and sipped it, staring up
at the pattern of the roofs against the intensely blue sky.

'How much?' she asked.

'I told you, you'd have to bargain between you. I'm findin'
you the means, that's all.'

'But what about your cut?'

It was an astute question, apparently out of character. Mrs
Batty had grown used to her lodger being unfailingly meek
and rather cast down, obviously struggling with life on her
own. She raised her faint eyebrows and stared.

'Well, you're shrewder than I give you credit for. But what's
a few shillings between friends? Look, I've known the captain

since I was runnin' a beer shop in Gibraltar, and he's done favours for me in the past, turning out the roughs, makin' sure the cash was paid down proper. He wasn't often in port but he always looked me up. How you doin' Poll, he says, how's life in Trade? Never too high and mighty, though in them days he had three ships, had his own line you might say. Then his partner went sick and after a year or so died, poor man, and the ships had to be sold. But he got himself another, carried cargoes here there and wherever till he had the means to buy a snug schooner of his own again. A hard man to put under, my Mr Griffith.'

'And he's going to Varna?'

'Well, he's goin' in that direction he says. But if you was to have second thoughts he could drop you off at Constantinople, you'd find friends there, like as not.'

Théo sighed and continued to sip her lemonade, which had a curious taste and might have an even more curious effect. The brown dress hung limply, a nondescript, possibly home-made dress that even the youngest, newest maid at La Croix would consider beneath her. But it was clean and modest and had only cost a shilling, all tremendous considerations.

'Where do I find this Captain Griffith?'

'Well, as to that, I believe he'll find you, dearie. If he likes the look of you he'll take you along, and if he don't, well, five hundred pounds won't bring him to a bargain. He once told me,' and here she shifted slightly, an implication that her words were intimate, considered, philosophical, 'he told me he'd seen enough of the world to judge a rascal at first acquaintance, but he owned it his privilege to choose what racals he'd do business with. He said,' and a little croak of her peculiar laughter issued from her vast bosom, 'that in thirty years at sea he'd never met a truly honest man, that he wasn't surprised what's 'is name couldn't find a decent soul in Sodom, 'cos there never was any and wouldn't be now if he come back to try again.'

'It's a point of view,' said Théo.

If there are any true pointers to a man's character in his possessions then the *Aphrodite* suggested other things about Captain Griffith than his cynical view of humanity. She was a Baltimore schooner, flush-decked, fast, and immaculately kept. No warship could boast a cleaner deck, nor rigging, sails, paintwork in better order. The figurehead, voluptuous even by the standard of the time, gazed across the crowded harbour with understandable satisfaction, for already someone had fondly tended to her yellow hair and carmine pout, badly flaked by rough weather in the Bay, and had put the finishing touches to her remarkable breasts and the cream waves out of which they rose.

Théo, in her brown dress, its cuff mended and her only good collar setting it off as best it could, had just come from another shattering interview with officialdom, in which the landing of the Lancers at Varna was admitted but her requests to be allowed to join them turned aside with all the old arguments. If she wanted to find her husband she must pay her own passage to do so, they could not help her. In a bitter mood, part humorous resignation and part flaming indignation, she had begun to make her way back to the lodging by way of the waterfront: to look at ships had always been her pleasure. She saw the *Aphrodite* at once: in an imperfect world such perfection rates second glances.

That someone on the *Aphrodite* saw her, and pursued her with a telescope, she had no idea. She was being careful not to linger long enough to be mistaken for a prostitute, though she looked far too respectable in the brown dress and a charming wide-awake hat to be in much danger this morning. In any case, a great many people along the waterfront, seeing her so often, treated her with the friendly respect of old acquaintances, even the French officers, who knew the meaning of the word gallant. Her progress was punctuated by civil greetings, bows, inquiries after her health. She smiled at these, was every inch a lady, and even had to refuse three offers to carry her purchases: two very small parcels. It was her air of gracious vulnerability that appealed, of courteous shyness. She was an oddity, respectable and yet alone, which no respectable woman would be by choice. So the French and Italians and Maltese smiled and paid their respects and watched her go by with affection.

The gentleman with the spyglass on the *Aphrodite*, however, watched her go by with an altogether different interest, and astutely noted the sadly crushed shabbiness of the wide-awake hat — which had survived the ordeal in the *George Fraser* — and the lowly origins of the brown dress. He also took in that mixture of boldness and hesitancy, of self-possession and indecisiveness that was Théo Trent, the expressive face with its eager, hungry, fearful look.

That evening the gentleman himself was admitted to Mrs Batty's lodging, was hugged, petted, made much of, and sat down with a bottle of wine — very good French wine, he had brought it himself. In five minutes Théo had been summoned, thank God she had not already gone to bed, she kept strictly virginal hours, said Poll Batty lovingly, oh the sweet girl she was, like a kitten turned out in a thunderstorm. Captain Griffith, aware his hostess's colourful smile was the result of gin and the expectation of a few shillings down, reserved his judgement until Théo herself stepped into the room, closing the door behind her and leaning back on it, apparently not breathing. He had never seen anyone struck so rigid with fright — he supposed it must be fright — in his life before.

He had seen too much in his life, however, to be ill at ease in the presence of a retiring dab of a woman, though she were Queen Victoria herself reduced to penury. He put down his glass slowly and looked her over close to for the first time, not really liking what he saw, she had no physical appeal whatsoever; she might as well be in some safe drawing room persecuting a piano or sewing a firescreen or whatever else well-reared young women did with such dedication, instead of being adrift in the lower ranks of Maltese society, lodging with an ex-harlot and beer-shop keeper, wearing the dress of a servant. There was no spirit in the lift of her head, and now he saw her without the hat, her hair was perfectly ordinary, fairish brown, swept back in a simple knot. She moved well; when she finally left the door she walked with a grace and deportment that suggested hours of practice with a book and a poker. She was an uncomfortable combination, he decided, of the innocent and the accomplished.

'Théo, dearie, this is Captain Griffith. He don't mind takin' you to Varna.'

Théo sat down. It put her at a disadvantage, she thought, she felt humbled on the scruffy little chair the other side of the table; but then she was at a disadvantage already, what did it matter? Mrs Batty had on her best, she saw, a glossy black bombazine rescued from or maybe wrested from some widow or other, kept carefully mothballed for moments of celebration and favoured guests. So what was so favourable about this particular guest? He was not strikingly tall, had a rounded, undefined face with wide-apart blue eyes, a good mouth; an amiable face in repose. When he spoke it was with the trace of a once-strong Welsh accent, lost after years at sea. His voice had an edge to it, a bite. His voice was not amiable in the least.

'I can take you to Constantinople,' he said, 'or Scutari. I'm not chartered for Varna. But I know where you might get a ship.'

'Mrs Batty was sure you were bound for Varna itself.'

'Dear old Poll has no more idea of where Varna is than she has of where Moscow is, or Paris for that matter.' A deep, smiling look passed between him and the fat woman at his side. 'You can have a passage to Constantinople. Take it or leave it.'

'How much?'

He put his head on one side. In the shadowy little room his eyes seemed to be the only colour and Théo felt they missed nothing, they could see through to her soul.

'Five pounds.'

She wanted to say how ridiculously cheap; she did not know if it was or not but she could afford it, she could afford it and still eat. She sat trying to look unmoved while relief flooded her through and through and she began to tremble with it, relief and gratitude.

'I told you if he liked the look of you he'd take you, didn't I, dearie?' asked Mrs Batty, rising to find two more glasses on a draught of camphor and Russia leather – used to keep the moths at bay from the black bombazine.

'I'm so glad,' said Théo, feeling stupid, slow-witted, slightly faint, 'I thought . . . I thought I might have to stay in Malta for ever.'

'What about your fine friends at home? Why can't they help you?'

She turned to look at him, unable to think of anything to

say. What use was it to say her letters had not been answered? After all, there was no reason for such a long silence, there were mail packets in the harbour, post brought regularly to every respectable breakfast table on the island. She shook her head.

'I don't think my letters have been delivered.'

'If you've written any, you mean. Oh, there's no need to play the innocent wronged woman with me, I've seen your like before, running away from a decent home for the sake of some red coat and an hour of guilty kisses. Mrs Trent indeed. The ring looks loose to my cynical old eye, Mrs Trent.'

Théo twisted it. She seemed to have lost whatever spirit she had once possessed, whatever she had salvaged from Caroline's long suppression. She could not reply to him as once she might have replied to Joss, in those strange happy days in Russell Square revelling in her first glimpse of freedom, of self-determination. She felt cowed, defeated.

'I'm thinner than I was,' she said quietly.

'It was that bleedin' transport,' asserted Mrs Batty, appropriating some of the wine and handing a glass to Théo with a fond look, 'not fit for dogs. I've been in some stews, I can tell you, but none to beat a transport in bad weather. How can you expect a girl to look her best after six weeks of hell battened down in the hold?'

The wine was good, a generous, full-bodied Burgundy. Théo closed her eyes and was back at Le P'tit Clos des Pommes, seeing the sunlight strike into the full glasses at Bonespoir's table, the squawk of the parrots all around. When she opened them she became aware of Mrs Batty and the captain deep in conversation about his charter, luxuries for the Europeans in Constantinople by the sound of it, tea, coffee, Fortnum's marmalade. He had crates of delicacies in *Affie*'s hold, a nice clean cargo that was no bother and paid exceptionally well. Half Europe, it seemed, wanted to sit in a grandstand and view the stage of war while eating potted beef sandwiches, not to speak of the officers and staff officers who assumed they would have plenty of time to do justice to this fine old wine. Not like some cargoes he had carried: coal, rice, pig iron, hay. He had known some nasty moments, the rice damp, the iron shifting in high seas, the hay on fire. They said a man shipwrecked three times could not drown. He had been wrecked four and knew how easily it might be done.

'You haven't spoken any ships of Faurel Mannelier these last few weeks, have you?' asked Théo in a low, determined voice, the wine warm inside her.

'Faurel? Only the *Honorine* out of Bordeaux. And what's your connection with her, Mrs Trent?'

She found she could not tell him. It was probable he would not believe her anyway, but to sit here in her sad dress in this dirty little room and confess she was a daughter of that ancient and respected house . . . No. She could not do it. She objected to those blue, searching, dismissive eyes, to his veiled insolence, his unnecessary, unkind remarks about her wedding ring. She was silent but her eyes met his, defiant for the first time.

'None that would interest you,' she said.

She thought his expression changed slightly, but so slightly she could not be sure. He seemed to take stock of her again, but gave no indication he liked her better now than he had twenty minutes ago. He drank off his wine and stood up.

'I sail in the morning,' he said. 'Don't be later than six. She's the schooner with the fanciful figurehead you showed such interest in this morning.'

'The *Aphrodite*.'

He was standing now, reaching for his hat. For the first time Théo noticed he was dressed with sober respectability, the only jarring note a lack of any stock or neckerchief. He pulled his blue hat down over his short greying hair.

'Known fondly as *Affie*,' he said. 'Even a goddess can't stand on her dignity for ever.'

13

The *Aphrodite* left Malta that morning in the second week of June with all her huge sails set to catch the light airs and Théo standing rather self-consciously on the pristine deck waving goodbye to Poll Batty who had commandeered a bumboat. It was thanks to Poll, who was in fact letting her go with misgivings – would the girl assert herself, stand up to old Griff as she ought? – that she had, besides her carpet bag, another crammed with a choice selection of garments from the second-hand clothes shop. She felt she must wave until Poll was out of sight, if only from gratitude. Across a hundred yards of vivid blue sea – two hundred, three – she could not see Poll's obvious anxiety or her fat cheeks mottled by half real and half pretended grief. She leaned on the rail and watched Malta slip astern with that old lifting of her heart: she was at sea.

She had been at her happiest on ships, from her borrowed lugger to the St Malo schooner and the stately old *Honorine* who had only last week put out from Bordeaux on her homeward passage to St Helier; how many times had she sat in the saloon of the *Honorine* while her father and Vautier and the ruddy Captain Brissac talked vintages, tariffs, insurance? Once, she remembered, there might have been a ship called the *Théophile* . . .

'You're spoiling the look of my deck,' said a voice. 'If you go below they might serve you some breakfast.'

She looked up, shading her eyes. He was two yards away, in an open-necked shirt again and the blue hat.

'Are you saying I can't walk on deck at all?'

'That would be unnecessarily cruel, don't you think? But you must think of the men's morale, the effect of a good pair of legs and some French lace. They may have sated themselves in the dens of Malta but a day of this kind weather, a day of complete abstinence, and they'll be revived. Believe me, Mrs Trent, their appetites are prodigious. Not to speak of the fact I had to resort to the crimps for three or four scoundrels to make up my complement, some of my boys getting into the clutches of the unscrupulous and going adrift. So altogether . . . It would be better if you were not seen much and not heard at all.'

She was a furious red, a furious, furious red. The helmsman had overheard and was grinning; there were one or two curious, amused faces aloft as well.

'I don't think you need be afraid I'll cause any trouble in your ship, Captain.'

'I'm not, else I wouldn't have offered you the passage. But a warning or two doesn't come amiss; simple-minded innocents can be just as much bother as pretty flirts, I've found.'

She was stung, and stung again, but she could not blush deeper, it was not humanly possible. So she put up her head and faced him squarely, a great storm of resentment throwing down her caution and all her good resolutions, and bringing her, as it had done so often with Caroline, to the edge of the battlefield.

'You make it sound as if your ship is often crammed with women, Captain. I'm surprised you find the time to carry proper cargo.'

He laughed, turning his back. 'Women are bad luck, didn't you know, like priests; it doesn't do to challenge a sailor's superstitions.'

'Then why take me on board?'

'Because I took pity on you for Poll's sake, she was worrying about you like a mother. I wouldn't waste pity on you for your own. Any woman who wanders about like a lost lamb in search of a reluctant red coat deserves all she gets.'

'I see,' and she started down the deck after him, incensed, aflame, scarified, 'and what do you think I will get, Captain? Typhoid? Cholera?'

146

He swung about, laughing.

'Raped, robbed and deceived more like. But all the same, your deserts, dear young lady, your just deserts.'

She could say nothing to that, but plunged below, refused the breakfast she was offered, shut herself in the cabin he had assigned her, sat down on the locker and clenched her small fists.

It was too much. On top of losing Alex, of the *George Fraser*, of Malta, she had to find herself in the hands of a man without an iota of respect for anyone, anyone. She might as well have been abducted by pirates. But after a while the fact that she had left some respect for herself, and that, whatever her fears, she was determined to join Alex at Varna, made her get up and repair her hot, ravaged face, and emerge to see if there was any lunch, just to show him she was not entirely defeated.

It was, after all, better than pirates. The *Affie* swept along in a generous south-westerly, the limpid blue eyes of her figurehead gazing towards the Aegean, and the cook was a Frenchman, and there was another bottle of excellent wine, and the water was the best she had tasted since leaving Oxford. Captain Griffith did not join her, for which her gratitude knew no bounds, and his steward was ham-fisted but utterly respectful, an endearing man.

In the afternoon she was allowed on deck but no one spoke to her and she presumed she was not allowed to speak to anyone herself, so she stood with the wind on her cheek and wished she had the wheel of this fine ship between her own strong, eager hands, and that all her grace and speed and liveliness was at her command. Slowly the clouds lifted, the clouds of doubt and guilt and bitter introspection, the disappointment at receiving no replies to her letters, the shame of being reduced to bartering for other women's cast-offs, the deep suspicion she was not up to fending for herself, that all she was good for after all was to be Caroline's housekeeper and perennial disappointment. It was impossible to be standing here with one hand on the rail and the other shading her eyes from the setting sun, watching the wake curl and broaden, and not be happy; it was impossible to smell the clean smell of warm open sea and watch the helmsman shift his feet and ease the spokes gently, gently, without remembering all the glad memories from her childhood. She pulled off her hat so that she could feel the wind on her forehead, and closed her eyes. I shall keep a boat in the harbour . . . I shall keep a boat in the harbour . . .

Captain Griffith did not join her for dinner that evening, nor did he the next, but the next, when they were hardly eight hours sailing from the Dardanelles. He entered the tiny saloon just as she sat down.

'I hear you speak perfect French, *comme une duchesse*. That explains why you splutter your words when you're angry; not at all English. But I can't believe you're a runaway member of the French aristocracy, so what are you? Poll, bless her heart, who hasn't had much experience of ladies, thought you might be a governess; she has this idea that governesses are always badly trated. She thinks you must have been badly treated, you see, to leave a comfortable place for a no-good soldier. She doesn't have any time for passion or undying love, old Poll, and she thinks you're a sensible woman at heart and wouldn't give up everything for them unless there was a baby in the case – which there isn't, she assures me – or you believed life out here must be better than life back there.'

Théo stared at her plate and could think of nothing to say. The French cook Albert came in with duck, what looked like pigeons in wine sauce, and something else which he said, only a little apologetically, was as tough as a gull. His little eyes glinted at Théo, he wished her *bon appetit*, he closed the door.

There was a strange intimacy about this meal, she thought, something to do not with the proximity of the man but the quality of the food. She was used to the best but even so . . . It was very good. The 'gull' was not tough at all. It all reminded her of that ill-starred lunch she had shared with Givard. A feeling of guilt and sudden nameless panic shook her. She glanced up and saw the captain demolishing the duck with brutal concentration.

But: 'Well?' he asked fifteen minutes later, refilling her glass.

'Well what?'

'Well, who are you? And what sort of man is this Trent?'

It was the wine, no doubt, gone to her head. She said: 'This Trent is my husband. I had official blessing to travel with him to the east but I missed the ship.'

'Excellent, bravo. Fanny Kemble couldn't have spoken with more conviction. Why don't I believe you then?'

'You may believe what you like, all I've asked is a passage to Constantinople – my reasons for travelling there are entirely my own.'

'What a prickly child you can be. And have you ever wondered, prickly child, what might generally happen to unaccompanied young ladies who accept berths from passing sailors?'

She looked straight at him but he stared her down. His large eyes were shining with humour, such a bland face even middle age had not discovered the bones of it.

'Well, what a virtuous prickly child you are, to be sure,' he said softly, 'all blushes and confusion. How many times did your mother warn you to beware of strange men? You really aren't fit to be loose in this black old world, are you?'

Albert knocked and entered with ice cream. Théo would have liked to ask him how he did it, make strawberry ice cream fit for an emperor, for Louis Napoleon himself. She would have liked to beg him to stay, she did not want to be left alone with his master.

'I don't understand why you refuse to believe I'm Mrs Trent,' she said, still chastened, not looking at him for fear of blushing again like a silly girl, the young impetuous Théo whom she had hoped was gone for ever. 'Look . . . I have a picture of my husband in my baggage. Wait a moment.'

She was back in a rush of petticoats, thrusting the photograph at him. It had been taken in St Helier the day before the wedding at vast expense; Alex had been discomfited both by his collar and the impending ceremony.

'A Captain of Lancers indeed. What exquisite whiskers! A very handsome young fellow. I congratulate you.' He laid down the picture and reached out to seize Théo's hand, twisting the loose gold band. 'It doesn't fit very well though, does it?'

She freed herself, snatched up the photograph, went to sit down as far from him as possible. She was silent, and so was he. Of course the ring was too loose, it had always been on the large side and she had lost weight in Malta; it sometimes slid right down her finger. But she stubbornly refused to take it off. It was the symbol of the bargain she had made, the price of her escape; and it was a symbol of her status, her virtue: she was a wife, not a whore.

'Funny how women set so much store by a little gold band,' said Captain Griffith, holding up the wine bottle with a jerk of his eyebrows, and pouring himself the last glass when she shook her head. 'You really might as well put a ring through your nose, you're as much his property as a pig bought in the market. And all for what? Respectability.'

'I see you have no morals, Captain Griffith.'

'Morals, is it? Oh, I have morals, Mrs Trent, but I hope to God they aren't the general kind.'

'But what would you have women do? What is there for us if we remain single?'

'How should I know? Obviously not much or you wouldn't have hazarded your life with that young puppy with the moustaches. But perhaps if you all cared less for the unwritten rules . . .'

'Like Poll, you mean.'

'That was unkind, and I won't hear my friends insulted: she cared for you in her own way. What chance did she have to make anything of herself growing up by the river? By the time she was seventeen she had two babies, had been deserted, and her family wouldn't take her in. She got on with life though, she didn't whine. She wouldn't ask for your sympathy, Mrs Lancer Trent.'

Théo, more chastened than ever, looked out of the stern window and rested her cheek on her arm.

'I think I shall go to bed,' she said as retreat seemed the only possibility.

He opened the door for her. He was too close for comfort in that cramped space and he smelled of wine.

'What a proper little person you are, so starched and refined. If it's adventure you're after I should be careful, you might get more than you expected. And I should swallow your pride and put that ring in your pocket, dear Théo, in case one of those dastardly Turks steals it in the night.'

'I wish . . . I wish you would . . .'

'Be comforting? Be kind? It's not a comfortable kind place you're going to, and in any case I don't approve of virginal children trying their luck in the bazaars.'

'I thought you said we ought to care a little less for the rules of society? Isn't that what I'm doing?'

He grinned, and ran one square brown hand through his short hair. 'Oh, yes, that's what you're doing all right. But you're making such a mess of it.'

Albert brought her breakfast two mornings later with a tigerish look, with a smile that showed all his large white teeth. If she looked out, he said, she might see the golden domes of the city. The captain had left a message that she was welcome on deck. At her startled glance he shrugged; it would be a shame to miss one of the glorious sights of the world, said that shrug, for a small difference of opinion.

And it was an extraordinary sight, the great glittering city of Constantinople on its promontory, the harbour packed with ships, and the *Affie* gliding in on the merest breath of wind, the men waiting for the order to take in sail.

'There is Scutari,' said Griffith, pointing to the opposite shore, 'you might find you were misinformed and the Lancers are still there, though I doubt it, Poll's sources of information are usually reliable.'

She had no hat on, she would grow horribly freckled; she did not care. It was heaven to feel the breeze on her face and the sun on her head. And it must only be a matter of days before she found Alex. She was looking forward to it. She had not expected that. She had not even thought she was fond of him. But the feeling that she should be at his side, that she wanted to be, was strong, and a naive hope still flickered that she might learn to be fond of him, that in this coming fight they would be drawn closer together and afterwards, at Rozel, they might find some sort of happiness. Théo did not probe this puny hope too much in case it died; then she would have nothing.

In Constantinople however, she was destined to find she had not been forgotten by Millie at any rate, for if Millie's letters had not reached Malta, they had reached the Golden

Horn and even now were causing panic in some quarters, even now as Théo stepped into the boat that was to take her ashore.

How smug was *Aphrodite*, she thought, settling her skirts and staring up as they shot forward and under the bowsprit, and how that glorious bosom was making the natives blink, plying their way between the anchored craft with their baskets of fruit and fish and knick-knacks.

Captain Griffith, who had a cargo to discharge, nevertheless saw fit to escort her to the British Embassy, a pointless exercise since the ambassador had gone for a picnic and there was no one who could see her.

'I'm damned if I shall leave until I see Mrs Trent attended to,' declared the Welshman with all that stubborn rage Théo had come to know so well. 'If Stratford isn't here what about the secretary? What about Napier?'

Lord Napier was out.

To Théo's horror Griffith sat down on a beautifully gilded chair and stuck out his legs, folding his hands over his waistcoat and staring with animal ferocity at the gang of clerks who sought to turn him out.

'I shall sit here and wait,' he said, 'and I assure you, boys, there'll be trouble if you put a hand on me. Lord Napier knows me.'

They did not believe him. He was obviously a merchant captain and no gentleman and he was about to rock the dainty legs off an antique chair. But how could they argue with him? He did not look pugnacious but he had a fighter's build, and his was one of the hardest jobs, taught a man how to use his fists. They retreated, not so much deferential as wary.

Théo sat down.

'Well, and are you about to dissociate yourself, pretend we never met? Or are you depending on that poker face and your very, very good manners to carry you through? They would have had you out of doors by now if you'd come alone. They don't let suspicious ladies into this palace uninvited.'

'What about your cargo?'

'It can wait an hour,' and he pulled out his watch and shook it. 'If no one comes to deal with you by then I'll dance a hornpipe in Napier's office.'

'You wouldn't. They would throw you out for certain then.'

He tipped back the spindly chair, grinning. 'Oh, Théophile, Théophile, what a coward you are!' and then, considering her with that challenging stare: 'Only a little pink this time – you must be growing hardened. By the way, why in the name of Aphrodite did they call you Théophile?'

Griffith did not have to dance his hornpipe and Théo had some of her bruised dignity salved: Napier returned, wrung the captain's hand and announced he had had an urgent, peremptory communication from Miss Amelia Boswell, a lady he had once known well.

'You have friends in high places after all,' said Griffith as they returned to the stinking alleys of Constantinople, leaving the glorious palace far behind. 'This Miss Boswell seems to have felled half the civil service with a stroke of her pen. I think I should like her.'

'I believe you would.'

'What is she to you?'

'I suppose you could say a sort of godmother.'

'And who is this Howard whom she has deputed your guardian in the east?'

'I have no idea.'

There was nothing for it but to return on board the *Affie*, Griffith would not hear of her loose in the town and declared the harbour a more healthy place. It was on the *Affie* that Mr Howard found her, brought out at prodigious expense by a caique and puffing a little in the afternoon heat. He was shown into the saloon by Albert and he stood a moment, looking about anxiously, mopping his forehead.

'Mrs Trent, what a pleasure! You must have had a terrible time, terrible time. I have been charged to take care of you as if you were my . . . hmm, daughter, to draw on the bank, to fetch you whatever you need, to be at your . . . hmm, complete disposal.'

He was a strange little foursquare man like an amiable baboon, and he was dressed with scrupulous Western propriety even down to a rolled umbrella. There seemed too much whisker for the size of his face but it gave him an aggressive look – he could not have been a milder, more retiring man – which perhaps was all to the good in these damnable foreign parts as he called them. He had come out as an onlooker, a disinterested observer; the strategies of war fascinated him. He was something of a scholar, a potterer among books. He was, in fact, a friend of dear Miss Cole, whose fine analytical mind he so admired. Miss Cole had suspected him of being in Constantinople, he had outlined his plans to her some months ago, and so Miss Boswell had written to the ambassador and to Lord Napier – who had once, long ago, graced her dinner table.

'I am going on to Varna,' said Théo.

'I don't advise it, dear lady, I don't indeed. Why, a great many of the officers' wives are staying at the Hotel d'Angleterre at Therapia, so beautiful, cypresses, views of the bay. It would be so much more suitable than a cavalry camp. Your husband can't possibly be expecting you now.'

'But I want to go there.'

He sat down, still chasing the beads of perspiration with his blue handkerchief. He was a solitary and timid man, he did not think he could cope with belligerent young women.

Albert brought wine and water, and little almond biscuits that reminded Théo of Martagon and the macaroons. It was strange, she thought, how she did not feel homesick out here, so far from Jersey, from everyone she loved . . . Love . . . The thought of Joss burned through her. She had tried not to think of him for so long that she was somehow taken aback, caught her lip between her teeth, turned so that little Mr Howard might not see her face in case all those confused and guilty desires should be visible there like moral wrinkles.

'Well, I could escort you to Varna,' he was saying tentatively, a reluctant hero if ever there was one, and momentarily burying his face in the blue handkerchief as if he already regretted his chivalry.

'You?' said a voice. 'You take her to Varna? You've just paid double the usual price to come across a hundred yards of water. I wouldn't like to guess which of you is the more innocent, the lamb or the kitten.'

'I'll have you know, sir, I've spent a lifetime in Asia and Europe. I am no ignorant traveller, sir.'

Griffith grinned. 'The caique boy might have his own opinion.'

Howard opened his mouth and closed it again, looking flustered. Griffith, like the caique boy, was evidently a superior force; it was not poor Howard's nature to oppose them.

'I have been trying to persuade Mrs Trent to abandon all idea of this expedition to Varna,' he said in as conciliatory a tone as he could manage, 'I'm sure you agree with me how unsuitable an adventure it might be for a lady of good family and quite unsupported.'

'But it's adventure she wants, you know, and is quite determined to get it. You will stay for dinner? You'll eat as well here as anywhere on shore.'

Mr Howard, who was beginning to feel outmanoeuvred by Millie and this irrascible, quick-speaking sea captain together, not to speak of the plain, even dour young woman with the sea-green eyes, accepted the invitation with misgivings. How much better to drive the girl to the Hotel d'Angleterre, provide her with enough money to engage a maid and feed herself royally, and write hastily to Russell Square to say he had discharged his duty. He had a strong premonition – his was an anxious nature – that he was about to be entangled in some scheme he would not like, not like at all.

Two hours later, mellowed by Albert's exquisite offerings and another bottle of matchless Burgundy, he was as amiable as a tame bear cub, squinting above his whiskers at his charming host. There was no doubt Griffith could be exceedingly charming when he wanted. Théo said very little, could not really be considered an asset, and she was not very decorative in that shabby old dress, but even so . . . Howard began to think it would not be any great hardship after all to escort her to the Lancers' camp, that he might even contrive to cut a dashing figure, riding in with her at his side. It had not often been given to him to play the chivalrous knight.

'I suggest, you know,' began that clipped Welsh voice, so soothing and mellifluous now, 'that you charter the *Affie* to Varna which would cost you as little as you'd have to pay . . .'

'I was thinking of asking Mr Munro if I could not travel on his steam yacht . . .'

'Does Mr Munro have a French cook?'

Howard stared. 'Cook? Cook? I have no idea.'

'And will Mr Munro also accommodate a young woman with no baggage and no maid and very dubious references?'

Théo half rose but his look made her subside. And after all, with her current wardrobe and all, or most, of her finance depending on Howard, how much better it might be to remain on the *Affie*, where she could have absolute privacy, enviable meals, and only the discomfort of matching her opinions to those of Captain Griffith. If she stayed she would be in Varna within forty-eight hours, if she left to take her chance with Howard in Constantinople she might never clear the Bosphorous.

'Mrs Trent,' Howard was saying with some irritation, 'was a Faurel, sir, a Faurel of Jersey. I beg you reconsider that last remark of yours: you insult Mrs Trent deeply.'

'A Faurel? I didn't know. So that accounts for your interest in the old *Honorine*. For the accent too. How they'd stare if they could see you now.'

The *Affie* swung and groaned; there was a wind rising. She rode high without her cargo and her movements were lively. Mr Howard, who was devoted to the land, began to regret his second helping of ragout.

Albert came in to clear away, his white-aproned bulk filling the doorway.

'Another bottle, Albert,' said Griffith, pushing the empty one towards him, 'Mr Howard and I have business to talk over.' His eyes rested on Théo, who was fiddling with a napkin: 'I thought it was customary for the ladies to retire to the drawing room?'

'What drawing room?' demanded Howard, glancing about mystified. 'Do you mean to say you have such facilities on a merchant ship of this size? Well I never. It's a revelation to me, a revelation.'

Théo, flaming pink, rose unsteadily as the *Affie* rolled.

'I believe this is Captain Griffith's oblique way of asking me to leave you,' she said.

'But we shall join you in a trice, dear lady.' He did not grasp her meaning, was all innocent smiles. 'A drawing room on a little ship like this, fancy! I do hope there's a piano.'

Théo caught the Captain's glittering eye.

'I'm afraid I sold the piano in San Francisco,' he said.

156

'Oh well, perhaps in Varna . . . Who can say? Even on the march armies must be entertained.'

Théo reached the door, was outside, was leaning back on it with the laughter rising in waves, choking her, making her eyes water. And she just heard Griffith, muffled through the wood, remark genially: 'I rather think Mrs Trent was hoping for a bath in Varna.'

14

Baths might be had for free, or for a paltry sum, and failing baths there was always the kindly sea, but first it was necessary to make oneself known. Théo, approaching an officer of the 8th Hussars, found his attention difficult to get and more difficult to keep. As far as he was concerned she was a camp woman, a soldier's wife or his whore, it made little difference. He scowled, turned his horse and moved away.

'We must find Headquarters,' said Mr Howard, gazing about short-sightedly, hoping perhaps to see it in front of him. But Varna was all confusion, the little white town with its sandy bay a scene of administrative chaos, troops and ammunition still coming ashore, boxes, baggage, mules and men in turmoil on the quay.

Be decisive, Millie had always said, in a crisis do something, don't stand about. Théo made her way up the main street, pushing through the crowds, avoiding the filth. It had once been a pretty town, clean and peaceful.

'This will never do,' said Howard, thrown up against some baggage mules and struggling to keep his feet, 'it's too hot. My dear Mrs Trent, let us return at once to the landing place. There is bound to be an officer . . .'

But Théo had captured a boy, a boy in uniform, and only by the expedient of putting her hand on his arm and holding on, crying for news of the Lancers above the hubbub. He shied away but she did not let go, and she repeated her question. The regiment was at Devna, about nine miles away; she could walk, said the boy, or there were baggage carts going up all the time, she might get a lift on one of those, other women did.

Riding on a baggage cart, however, did not strike Mr Howard as dignified.

'We must find Headquarters,' he said again, swiping his umbrella at six small boys crowding in hopefully. 'You are exhausted. Captain Griffith would not approve of you wandering about in the streets.'

There was nothing for it but to turn back. Her bags were still on the *Aphrodite*, swinging gently at anchor between the warships and the transports in the bay. She was aware she did not look like an officer's wife, that her dress was creased and tired, that her face was probably ringed with dirt, that she was not wearing a hat – the wide-awake had blown off and drowned in the bay.

'Mrs Trent? Mrs Trent!' A voice called from behind and above. She looked back to see Teddy Monkton on a thin, rangy-looking little horse. 'Is it really Mrs Trent?'

He looked older, she thought, and depressed. She stared at him, trying to equate this dusty, frowning young man with the diffident boy who had carried her ices. She could find nothing to say. She was so relieved . . . At the same time she felt the first chill of irrational premonition.

'Do you know . . .' She could not smile and her voice sounded parched, 'do you know where my husband is?'

He dropped lightly to the ground, shielding her from more labouring mules, wringing Mr Howard's hand with a sort of cheerful gratitude as if he, and not Alex, was the happy bridegroom. He had a message to take to Headquarters, he said, but he would meet her on the quay in an hour, would find her some kind of transport, or failing that would offer her his Bulgarian pony. He said goodbye to her glowing with good intentions, but the frown never left his wide forehead. In truth he hardly recognized her, she looked gaunt, sun-tanned, unsmiling; and he was worried about her meeting with Alex, he had heard some harsh words from that quarter when they had sailed without her.

His misgivings and anxieties grew when he returned to the quay to find her standing by two small bags and attended by two strange characters who had obviously taken her welfare to heart. One was the vague, ineffectual little gentleman he had met before and the other was a taller, squarer individual with the face and general demeanour of a man accustomed to being obeyed.

'Mr Howard has rented lodgings in the town,' said Théo, 'the very last to be had, it seems.'

'I will be happy to call on you at the camp, will bring up any necessities,' said Howard, twirling his umbrella nervously.

'That would be very kind.'

The captain's face expressed his exact feelings on this civil exchange.

'I hope,' he said, 'life with the army is everything you imagined.'

Théo held out her hand. 'You mean you hope I will be thoroughly uncomfortable.'

He did not take her hand. He simply moved to help her mount the mule Teddy had purloined for her, an anguished, irritable mule who did not like the unaccustomed military saddle.

'I had no idea where to find a lady's saddle,' confessed Teddy with an apologetic sideways glance. 'I have seen Mrs Duberly upon one, of course, and another lady, but as to spare ones . . . I had a tussle to acquire the mule, I was nearly knocked down by a French private who thought it should be his.'

It was quite all right, said Théo, abandoning the hope of being able to ride astride with decorum and crooking her right leg round the pommel, a perilous position.

'For God's sake,' said Griffith, viewing her with derision, 'swallow that damn pride of yours and put your leg over. He only has to step sideways and you'll be off.'

She did as he said reluctantly; all her precious petticoats, the only fine things she had left, were now on show. She gathered her reins anxiously. She had never been much of a rider, even on the old pony with a decent saddle. She looked down suddenly into a blaze of laughter as Griffith let go of the stirrup and stepped back.

'It's the price of adventure,' he said.

At Devna they were circumspect; Teddy was conscious of the enormous indignities of entering the camp at the side of a strange young woman astride a mule. He was embarrassed enough to wish she looked a little more like Mrs Théophile Trent and that there was less lace exposed to the general view, though he would have died to defend her.

Alex, just that moment sitting down to his lunch, was taken by surprise.

It could not have been a worse, a more ill-starred meeting. Here he was, on the point of draining his second glass of the thin local wine, laughing at some joke of his fellow officers — they were six in a merry circle about the makeshift table — when Théo, dishevelled and dusty, in a mannish felt hat, was precipitated into his presence. He did not know what to say, what to do. There was a long, complicated silence, during which Teddy Monkton turned deeply crimson and someone cleared his throat awkwardly. And then Timms, a capable, hearty boy, greeted her with false effusion, offered her his chair, demanded to know how she had come there, what ship she had come out on, who had befriended her.

But: 'Théo' was all Alex said, in a low, shocked voice, and he made no move to touch her or greet her in any way, just 'Théo' and a look of pure astonishment.

She sat, she refused food but accepted a glass of wine. It was like sweet water. She nearly choked. She was conscious they were all trying not to watch her, all solicitous but alarmed.

'I thought you were in Russell Square,' was Alex's sole contribution; surprise was giving way to exasperation.

'Perhaps,' said Théo, rising, 'I could go somewhere to wash and do my hair.'

Alex shared his tent: their privacy was counted in minutes. He stood by the flap while she fumbled at the basin with the tepid water the orderly brought her, hearing the sounds of horses and carts and men outside without really hearing them at all. She washed carefully, her hands shaking, seeing there was so little time, that Alex was still shocked, that nothing was as she had supposed.

At last, making a brave attempt to put her hair in order, she turned to face him.

'You wish I had not come,' she said.

'We've had some cases of cholera,' he said by way of answer.

'The train . . .' she was conscious of gabbling but could not seem to help it. 'A coupling broke. Then chance put me on the *George Fraser*. I was weeks and weeks in Malta. I wrote to you.'

'How could it have been weeks and weeks? I never received any letters. I've been writing to Russell Square, I thought you might be there. I thought . . .' he was hunched, miserable, vehement: 'I thought you'd deserted me.'

'But you aren't pleased to see me.'

'It's not that. Of course it's not that. But you can't stay here. You must find a lodging in the town or go back to Constantinople. Mrs McCready will help.'

She stood quite still, her hands by her sides, her eyes on his face. If there was appeal in those eyes he could not see it. He rather resented her for having the courage to follow on alone where many a woman might have turned back for the comforts of Russell Square. If she had arrived in style, properly escorted, he would have been gratified, touched. But instead she had made him look a fool in front of his friends, so shabby and travel-stained, her hair on her neck.

'Aren't you at all glad to see me?' she asked.

His romantic fervour, his naive enthusiasm, had already been bruised. Lord Cardigan, complex and irascible man, did nothing but sit in the shade eating fruit and issuing orders: about whiskers, washerwomen, picketing the horses. Nothing seemed too trivial to escape his attention. It had worn them all down, had ceased to be amusing and become intolerable. This was the man, they remembered, who had once been removed from the lieutenant-colonelcy of the 15th Hussars, a blow from which no one but a man of extreme influence could recover; this was the man who had held fifty-four courts martial in his first six months as lieutenant-colonel of the 11th. It was not going to be the picnic Alex had cheerfully imagined; it was pipe-clay, drill, unbearable heat, lame horses and sick troopers. He had felt a fool when Théo had not turned up in Portsmouth, had had to endure the inevitable teasing of his friends, the chagrin, the mortification; he had felt more of a fool when she had entered just now, such a haggard, plain-looking, dingy figure she might have been one of those controversial washerwomen; he was not going to let her make a fool of him again.

'It's no place for a woman,' he said harshly, 'I wish to God I'd never encouraged you to come.'

'You didn't. You always had reservations. It was what *I* wanted.'

He was cocking his head to catch the approach of footsteps, one hand grasping the flap. Any senior officer finding them together would be justified in thinking Théo was a camp woman. Where was the elegant Théo de Faurel he had married?

'Alex?'

'You'll have to go back to England.'

'But I only arrived this morning.'

'Constantinople then. Scutari. Therapia. There's something about this place. It's not healthy. Théo, you must go home.'

She could not use coquetry, it was not in her nature, and in any case, though Caroline was a skilful practitioner she had discouraged it in all her daughters; she could not use rational argument, nothing, rational or irrational, would weigh against the fact that if she stayed she would put him at a social disadvantage. It seemed there was probably nothing she could say to move him, no compromise to be struck. But she would *not* be sent all the way home, she could not bear another sixty days at sea, every day reminding her of what she had endured on the journey out.

'There are other wives in Varna surely? Why shouldn't I stay? Are you so ashamed of me?'

'I don't want you in Varna, the place is more like a pigsty every day. It was a mistake to think you could ever be comfortable out here . . .'

'I didn't expect to be comfortable. I expected to be of some use.'

'Doing what? There's nothing you could possibly do in this place except die of heat or cold or some sort of fever. It won't do, Théo. I realized it when we arrived. I was sick with worry about you while I was on the ship, wishing you were with me, but once I got here I saw how absurd it was to expect you to put up with . . . all this.'

It was true Varna was deteriorating fast, that the lovely

town, the harbour, were sinking into chaos and squalor. She had seen that for herself. No, there was no rational argument, and yes, her presence in the camp embarrassed him. She turned away, tucking up a last stray wisp of hair.

'Perhaps I should call on Mrs McCready,' she said calmly.

He nodded briskly, still looking irritated. He made no move to kiss her. He stood aside politely and she stepped through the flap and out into the hot sun.

Mrs McCready threw wide her ample arms and became voluble which was guaranteed to embarrass Alex further. She shot several accusing stares at him meanwhile, aware of something lacking in his attitude – grace perhaps. He looked like a mutinous small child prised from the strawberry bed and told to wipe his fingers and say sorry. He looked handsome but sulky and temperamental, the nervous state of a man who has just taken delivery of a wife he does not want.

Mrs McCready inhabited the upper floor of a small house near the harbour, almost too near the harbour for comfort now it had begun to resemble some of the more stinking basins of the Thames. Meg McCready did not care though, she liked to be in the thick of things, would have felt painfully isolated in any of the prettier, more socially acceptable quarters. She had a cramped living room in which she entertained other wives with that studied formality she felt was their due, when all the time she would have been far happier sleeping on the ground in the major's tent at Devna, acting as confidante to the washerwomen, tending the small ills and the easily wounded pride of all the young subalterns and lieutenants. Her husband had risen from the ranks, helped by superhuman perseverance and the legacy of a mad uncle, but although he was beloved by his men, he was not beloved by Headquarters: he was socially inferior, so was his wife.

Alex fell back on Meg's good nature because he had nothing else to fall back on except his own resources, and he feared they might be inadequate both financially and emotionally. If Théo refused to go home he would have to find a respectable lodging – there was nothing left but hen huts and pigstys – or a room in an hotel. Meg McCready, though such as Lord Cardigan would never have spoken to her even though she was a major's wife, would accept Théo as she might have done her own daughter, would keep her safe, would force her to mix with the other wives, and would prevent her running up unfortunate bills. He hated to admit it – he rather despised Meg's unashamed homeliness, her brash gaiety – but it was the ideal solution.

As for Théo, she assented, more out of exhaustion and disappointment than anything, the heat had melted her resistance along with, or so it felt, the greater part of her flesh. She could see Alex was relieved, though she perceived from a distance now as if she had suddenly become a disinterested onlooker. She knew instinctively that he had been afraid she might become unreasonable, even belligerent, might weep or try to plead with him, when he had hustled her from the camp and brought her back here, and that because she had not and because Meg had welcomed her with all her usual warmth, he was unutterably relieved, ecstatically relieved. He kissed her hand on leaving, though it was still quite grubby, and said he would visit her as soon as his duties permitted.

'He isn't being very gallant, silly boy,' said Meg as his footsteps died away down the stairs.

'I think I gave him a shock.'

'But of course you did. He had given you up. I do believe he thought you had changed your mind, had abandoned him completely. He was in quite a state on the ship, and then some of the others ragged him a little which didn't help. And I must say, you are not the smart little Théo I remember. Was Malta as hot as this?'

Later, washed, unlaced, practically deloused, and heartened by her first food since disembarking from the *Affie*, Théo confessed the misery of her voyage on the *George Fraser*. Meg, who had been brought up in genteel army poverty – her father had been a sergeant in an infantry regiment – made no comment of the kind Théo might have expected from any of the other wives. She simply looked serious a moment and said: 'My dear, how ridiculous not to go to the captain or one of the officers. But then ... This Mary Anne, what happened to her?'

'I wish I knew.'

Théo twisted her hands together under the table. She

wanted to cry, to put her head down among the plates and howl. She could hear her own voice, a defiant, infuriated voice: And what do you think I will get, Captain? Typhoid? Cholera?

Raped, robbed and deceived more like . . .

'Théo, dear, are you all right? You look strange. You ought to lie down.'

'I have some letters to write.'

'I really think you would be better to lie down. Can't they wait until the morning.'

Half an hour later, throwing down her pen in weariness and exasperation, she conceded they could. Her head was heavy, her eyes sore, her hand – odd she had not noticed until now how sunburned her hands had become – was shaking. She stood up and walked to the window. Her room was a small dressing area that led off Meg's spartan bedroom. The absence of luxury, the absence of furniture, reminded Théo of Millie and Russell Square. And the memory of Millie made her smile. She looked up and out at the view for the first time, as if the world had only this moment become truly interesting, the world beyond herself and Alex, that was.

A great many masts, spars, tangles of rigging, funnels: there were ships of all kinds busying in and out of Varna, still bringing in troops, ammunition, forage. Amid them all must be a graceful little Baltimore schooner with a dashing rig and a gaudy, overblown figurehead. Théo looked and looked but could not see her.

'We're very short of candles,' said Meg, bringing her one before bedtime. 'There are so many things in short supply. Or else someone has purloined all the boxes and is waiting for the price to rise.'

Théo prepared for bed, but her head still ached and her hands still shook. In the end she threw all thought of laudable economy out of the window and kept the candle burning into the night. She could not sleep, she could not pray, she could not even think coherently, and she had not been as frightened as this ever, not even in the unsavoury recesses of the *George Fraser*, not even in Malta, accosted by those brash young officers.

And a candle was a comforting thing to watch in the hostile dark.

15

Joss had received four letters from Millie in the same post, a common enough occurrence once but one he found particularly trying this time. He read them out of sequence so that nothing made much sense and when he came to the one about Théo's wedding, he sat brooding over it with such grim concentration his subordinate, who had come to present him with a problem to do with temperature gauges, slunk away without daring to disturb him. And then, of course, there was Théo's own letter, if such a flimsy thing could properly be called a letter. He crumpled it up in a moment of savage temper and threw it away.

He regretted her precipitate marriage. He would allow himself no stronger word than that, though that could be menacing enough spoken through gritted teeth. He thought she had thrown herself away, that she had given in, admitted defeat, done her duty. Millie's description of Caroline's overwhelming relief at getting the girl off her hands, of achieving at long last a more than respectable result, sickened him. And had the foolish girl come to the war? Had she?

He looked out over the anchorage at Scutari, and thought of Constantinople which he had lately left. It was hot. He would not normally read his private mail on deck but there was an air of slack indecision over the ship and here was a quiet corner out of the way. He studied the golden-domed city that shimmered across such a narrow stretch of unruffled blue, a fairy-tale extravaganza, like everything out in the East, including the plans for the disposal of the British army, somehow unreal. He stared at it and stared at it and supposed he must send his congratulations, it would be boorish not to, and yet he so disliked having to write lies. He sighed. The sun was damned hot. He ran a finger round the tight, elaborate collar of his uniform and sighed again.

He did not care in the least if Mrs Théophile Trent – what a ridiculous name! – was entertaining the cavalry in Varna or wherever; she was a muddle-headed, opinionated, spinsterish little . . .

'Excuse me, sir,' and there was young Pemberton, showing his young white teeth in a placatory grin, and standing with his young gangling limbs all neatly aligned; he was terrified of Joss.

'Yes?'

'Mr Seymour wonders if you can spare him five minutes, sir. It's . . . it's to do with Mr Bennet.'

It was to do with a flogging matter. Nobody could remember when Mr Westover had last had a man up for flogging but this was a dim, criminal business that must end with the lash. That was navy discipline, that was the rule. And there were some rules even Mr Westover would have trouble bending to his satisfaction.

'Tell Mr Seymour I'll be along directly,' said Joss, shoving his letters into his pocket, 'and don't let me see you slouching round the deck with your hands in your pockets again.'

'No, sir. I . . . I didn't know you were there, sir.'

'Evidently. Well, if you're sent to look for me in future you can look a bit more businesslike about it, can't you?'

Pemberton scuttled away, looking as businesslike on his return journey to the waiting Seymour as a man who has to announce the enemy in sight. Behind him on the deck Joss paused to look out for a last time across the bay of Scutari, at the milling craft, the shore, the vast yellowish barracks, the hills. A pleasant enough place. No one knew what they were doing here, what they might be doing in a day, or a month, or a year; but a pleasant enough place. The thought of war seemed faintly absurd.

It was not quite the end of June. They had a few more weeks of complacency left them, of leisurely moments to admire the view.

And: Married! thought Joss, reaching the glorified cupboard

he called his cabin and adjusting his offending collar, well, he hoped she would be very, very happy.

And he tossed all Millie's letters in his sea chest and went out, his eyes kindling, to charge his usual bloody-minded way through naval etiquette and tilt with all the ferocity he could muster at the iron god of naval discipline.

It might be supposed that a man who had been married only weeks before being sent overseas on active service would find time to engage in some of the more obvious pursuits of conjugal life. It might be supposed he would not mind his wife carried to him in a carpet like Cleopatra or in the baggy trousers and tasselled cap of a Zouave. So Mrs McCready supposed anyway, having allowed Alex a few days to recover from the shock. She invented a score of improbable errands to take her out of the house the moment he knocked at the door, back in his old good spirits and glowing with anticipation. But Alex did not knock, simply sent down promissory notes, none of which, she began to suspect, he intended to honour. Days went by and Théo grew browner and thinner, but nothing in her face gave any hint of frustration or understandable disappointment or the bitterness of rejection; whether she felt any or all of these was a mystery. But Meg McCready, whose courage was of the dashing, unsophisticated kind, felt enough of all of them to send a private, stinging note up to Devna on the perilous subject of a husband's duty.

Alex, however, stayed away, and who were Théo and Meg to say his reasons were not legitimate? The cavalry was disordered by two madmen, Lucan and Cardigan, between whom rivalry might be said to have reached the bitter limit, and further disordered by the first of the cholera that was to take such a hold in the next few weeks. Théo buoyed up her sinking spirits with the knowledge that life was not all it could be at Devna, that after all Alex undoubtedly knew best. His infrequent messages, usually delivered – how did the boy contrive it? – by Teddy Monkton, spoke of stale eggs, no meat, dysentery. After the raising of the siege of Silistria by the Turks, the job for which the British army had come to Bulgaria, Lord Cardigan on one reckless reconnaissance had deprived the Light Brigade of nearly a hundred horses through heat, starvation and overwork. They would soon be reduced to foot soldiers, wrote Alex in an anxious scrawl, there would not be a horse left alive.

Mr Howard, the indefatigable TG – Travelling Gentleman, as they were known in this most curious war – brought her fragmented news that confirmed all this, for he had acquired a refractory mule and rode about between the camps. He wore a broad-brimmed straw hat and a scarf over his mouth to keep out the dust, and he used his rolled umbrella to belabour the mule. The mule, as ingenious and stubborn as any other, had been fortunately reduced by hard labour and starvation rations, which made him responsive to the umbrella if not the convulsive movements of Mr Howard's short, ineffective legs.

Had Théo been able to get hold of a side-saddle she might have borrowed the mule herself; Mr Howard was painfully willing to lend him and act as escort on foot. Lack of the saddle – and lack of courage, she wondered? – kept her on her own two legs and in Varna. She frequently called at the hospital, the most terrible place on earth, Meg called it, where the cholera cases died amid the lice and rats and there were no supplies and apparently no hope of supplies, though the paper requests flew to and fro with astonishing rapidity. The doctors and orderlies shooed her away. She would return to Meg in a wild, bitter mood, one Caroline would have recognized only too well, one that did not last – she did not know how to sulk, whatever Caroline might say about that – but while it was on her made her curious eyes as tawny as a cat's and brought that urgent, hungry look back to her bony face. She felt she was not wanted anywhere, by anyone, and that she had come to this place simply to waste away until she died or was put back on a ship bound for England.

She wrote to Millie:

We sit here and sit here. The army grows apathetic. Discipline is weakening. There are men drunk everywhere and the harbour now is a foul sink of corpses, not all of them animal, I think. Men are dying from cholera in scores, and from other things. The doctors at the hospital say the drinking compounds matters, hastens death, but of course they won't let me help. The soldiers' wives go in and out, wash the linen, are on good terms with the orderlies, but they won't let me pass the door for I am a 'lady' and if I die someone will be held responsible. None of them is prepared to be held responsible for anything, not even, I believe, the saving of their poor patients' lives. I suppose there must be good men, caring men, but they are hard to spot, or perhaps so much suffering has turned them all brutish. Perhaps they are so disgusted by their own helplessness they have taken refuge in a sort of studied callousness. At any rate, I am no use to them. I begin to feel a parasite, for food is very short; if all we extra mouths went home there would be more to go round, I suppose, but results do not always bear out the theories.

I have had one letter so far, a fat, fat letter from darling Louise, who is worrying about me enough for twenty and has apparently given Mama a dozen migraines in as many weeks. She has refused to marry Mama's choice of second husband and has actually taken over one of my charity committees because the other ladies begged her so prettily – well, they would, seeing none of them wished to make the effort to run things. She says she understands now why I found them so tiresome and always wished to cook the soup and distribute the blankets by hand in case it should not get done but only get talked about. She says she has no time for fashion magazines, nor needlework, and has engaged a governess for the children entirely on her own and without reference to Mama, who was furious. She sounds quite ridiculously happy when she is not wondering if I am dead and buried. The children have sent drawings, Bon's is of Grandmama having a headache, which is very wicked and irreverent but as Louise points out, so very like! As for any other letters, I do believe they have been dropped in the harbour along with most of the refuse of Varna. Ships come and go but never a word for me. Dear Mr Howard goes to see if anything has come every single day and returns very glum, he feels so for me. He has just lost his mule, baggage animals being in such short supply it was bound to be requisitioned sooner or later, the wonder is he has kept it so long. Meg and I, however, suspect the poor suffering creature ended on a staff officer's plate to be washed down with champagne. There is very little meat but a great deal of champagne if you know how to get it.

I have seen the *Satyr* on the horizon, at least so I was told. She has not yet had any orders to come to Varna, which is just as well. Joss is in a far better place than all these poor souls here, dying for the want of a few necessities. There is talk of splitting up the camps

owing to the cholera cases but nothing has been done yet. I have
seen Alex once and that at a distance. He was here to chase after
stores with six of the largest, fiercest men in his troop – stores are
a matter for hard bargaining apparently – but they all looked quite
absurdly smart, though rather dusty. It is not that they haven't lost
men, and horses too, but that Lord Cardigan keeps them on parade
all the time, polished and pipe-clayed. Teddy Monkton says they
are forever re-buffing their boots and re-buttoning their collars,
everything must be done as it would be done at home. It is a
contrast to some of the other regiments, whose officers sport
huge beards now, and turbans, and oddments of civilian clothes,
though it's strictly forbidden. They are all reduced to frustration
and apathy.

Apathy prevailed. This was the lull before the proverbial
storm, said Meg, who could read the signs. With the crisis in
Silistria over there was some debate as how best to deploy
the troops currently wasting away at Varna. More went to
waste while the debate continued. The Light Brigade moved
thirty miles away to Yeni-Bazaar hoping to escape the cholera,
but they took the cholera with them, and the only cheering
thought was of winter quarters in Adrianople. Rumours blew
about that an attempt was to be made to invade the Crimea,
but rumours had blown by before and been forgotten. The
disease in the infantry camps worsened, Varna smelled of
death.

But Théo endured, with that same stoicism she had dis-
played on the *George Fraser*, a stoicism she herself felt was
attributable to upbringing and not anything in her nature.
She received seven letters from Millie in one post, which must,
even Mr Howard felt, have taken great ingenuity on behalf
of the military postal authorities. They were full of Millie's
most strident encouragement, her plans for Mr Howard's
rescue – where *had* these dried-out pages been lying all these
long weeks? – and contingency plans for Joss to abandon his
post and lend her assistance in the best traditions of chivalry.
In extremis, wrote Millie, anything is permissible – well,
almost anything.

They were not quite *in extremis*, though on the tenth of
August some Greeks set fire to some houses and nearly reduced
them to that state. Théo had been at Headquarters poring

over a map that showed her Yeni-Bazaar and Isseyteppe, where the light cavalry and the horse artillery had gone; it might be as well to know where her husband actually was even if she never saw him again, something she had thought about more often recently, the communal graves overflowing and the hospital little more than a charnel house. She also hoped to investigate the part the cavalry was to play in this proposed invasion of the Crimea – the infantry were supposed to be embarking on the transports on the sixteenth. The map was forthcoming but no one would confirm the orders; the cavalry might be left at Isseyteppe until it died of old age along with disease for all anyone was prepared to tell her. Théo, infuriated by this pig-headed reticence – was it the first thing taught to aspiring staff officers? – went out to find fire raging in the town and a scene of confusion and destruction. And she found Meg McCready sitting on a packing case of tea, perhaps the last case in Varna, nursing a sore knuckle she had skinned in her haste to leave the house before she was fried alive. She had been able to rescue nothing. They were without clothes or a roof.

A practical approach seemed the only one possible. Mr Howard had two tolerably clean rooms in a villa on the outskirts of the town; he offered to give them up, to sleep with the French gentleman downstairs, a great cigar-smoker and entertainer of questionable ladies. Théo and Meg agreed at once. They also did their best to acquire some decent clothes and applied quite brazenly to those few real ladies still left in Varna for sympathetic help: some very nice underwear and a grey cambric dress for Théo was the result. For the rest they had to fall back, in the end, on the French gentleman's ladies, who were of quite another sort, as Mr Howard blushingly confessed; he had resorted to ear-plugs but was beginning to regret his sacrifice.

Major McCready rode over to see them one day and tried to persuade Meg to go back to Constantinople. She had never left him before, she said, she would not do so now. He looked harrowed and grey, not at all the man they knew, and his horror at the scenes of death and devastation in Varna made him very forceful in his arguments. But Meg was obdurate, puckering up her round cheerful face when he was reduced to shouting at her, but stating flatly she would stay with him come what may. She reminded Théo of Poll Batty, though rather more genteel and sentimental. She knew how to cry for effect certainly, and won her battle with the major the moment tears welled in her eyes; he had only seen her cry once before and he was reduced at once to shameless, pathetic concern.

Not so Alex, who was expecting tears and had fortified himself with rum and strong Turkish coffee to resist them. He arrived in the wake of the major, having galloped in a dust cloud all the way from camp going over and over what he had to say. He found Théo almost unrecognizable, worn to skin and bone, but alert and in good spirits, and with a more open, challenging expression than he remembered. She wore a blue skirt and a grey jacket over a white blouse, and she wore them as if they were her former exquisite gowns from the French dressmaker in St Helier. She had put her hair into a little silver net – given her by one of the Frenchman's ladies – and it was soft and fair and very pretty. Alex hesitated, liking what he saw, aware that amid all this stink and sweat she smelled of soap and lemons, though where she could have come by either in this blasted place was a mystery. Perhaps Lord Raglan and Headquarters were looking after her; it would be just like Millie Boswell to know Raglan, just as she had known Napier and the peripatetic Mr Howard.

He expected rebuke, he had neglected her shamefully. He had not seen her while he was at Devna and now, so much further away, he told himself he could not even think about it. He hoped she understood. His scrappy notes, the letters she had written him which had gone unanswered – those were a different matter. He might well blush for those.

'I had to come,' he said, rankled because Meg had left them alone with a meaningful look in his direction, 'I want you to go to Constantinople. Or Scutari would do. But I want you away from here. And I think you ought to know, if and when we're ordered to the Crimea, I won't take you with me. It would be absurd.'

Théo twisted her thumbs in her skirt and wished he would kiss her. It seemed such a little thing after so long apart, surely it was not unreasonable to hope for one kiss? But he did not look, contrary to Meg's expectations, as if he had that sort of thing on his mind at all, but only the difficulty of finding her a safe passage from Varna to Constantinople. He looked worried, and had cut himself shaving. His uniform looked much shabbier than when she had last seen it, bleached by the sun and impregnated with the ubiquitous dust.

'I wish you wouldn't worry about me. I can find my own way to Canstantinople if I have to go.'

'Of course you have to go.' He was determined to scotch any resistance, even the mildest. 'You can't stay here. Major McCready tells me Mrs McCready is to go with him if we follow the infantry; I can't understand him allowing it. Anyway, it means you'll be alone here, except for a maid and that peculiar little man downstairs. It won't do. I wish . . . I wish you'd go home to Rozel.'

She had not thought of Rozel for so long, the image that flashed before her instantly took her by surprise. She had not been homesick for a long, long time, being too busy trying to exist from day to day. She looked up at Alex, those few feet away that might have been a few miles, her green eyes very clear in her tanned face, the long Faurel nose somehow more prominent now her cheeks were hollowed so. If only he would show some sort of tenderness, some concern for her state of mind as well as her physical welfare. Of course she would be safer in Constantinople, but would she be happier? And if she was not, did he care? She took a step forward. Millie, she thought, was a great believer in making things happen . . .

'This is no place for a woman,' said Alex, irritated, suspecting she was about to argue with him, 'you aren't in a fit lodging and there isn't enough to eat, and the harbour's a midden. I wonder you're not dead of cholera. And we don't even know what we're doing yet, or what we're supposed to be doing in a week or a month. We're rotting up country on a ration that wouldn't feed half the number while rumours come and go like flies.'

Théo knew all about rumours. They had cluttered the streets of poor ravished Varna along with the offal and the ashes. She knew all about the suicides and the wives who had gone home, and the wives who might even now be giving birth in patched-up tents or under the gun carriages or out in the open. Well, that was not likely to happen to her, not in the circumstances.

'I'll do whatever you think best,' she said quietly. She could see he was surprised; he had obviously been expecting protestations.

'Perhaps this fellow Howard can take you back,' he said, 'I suppose he knows how to arrange a passage? What ship was it you came on? That young cub Monkton was asking me only yesterday and I couldn't remember.'

'The *Aphrodite*.'

'Gone now, I suppose?'

'Quite gone. She sailed the day after I arrived.'

'But not coming back, not carrying stores or anything?'

'Not that I know of. And I rather think Captain Griffith would charge well over the odds to take me on board again. I don't think he liked me a great deal. And I'm not sure he liked any sort of woman spoiling the look of his beautifully clean deck.'

She seemed inclined to levity, thought Alex. It was a side of her Caroline had warned him about but he had forgotten, this sudden descent to unbecoming levity when something important was being discussed.

'Well, whatever ship, you've got to leave Varna as soon as possible. Do you think I want you to stay here to die of dysentery or starvation?'

'Or boredom,' said Théo.

Before she left she was allowed to visit him at the house in Scuzhenst where Major McCready had taken a room for Mrs McCready. Théo wondered if Meg had been the moving force behind the invitation. They had a decent dinner, and Teddy Monkton was there, and two other officers. Alex tried to do most of the talking, in case Théo said something untoward and made a fool of him again, but he found he need not have worried, she seemed happy and at ease, fending off Teddy's too-obvious attentions with a new, attractive sparkle.

Inevitably the drink — there was a great deal to drink, it was the only thing not yet in short supply — and the pleasant atmosphere, the cheerful intimacy, the sense of comradeship in dire circumstances, brought about the result Théo had sometimes hoped for and sometimes dreaded. Alex forgot to remind her about a ship, about Mr Howard, about the necessity of engaging a decent, trustworthy woman, and carried her upstairs to the room they had been lent for the night. She felt gratified and apprehensive at once, a prickly combination. He was her husband, she must do her best to please him – another of Caroline's strictures – but the hurt of his neglect went very deep. She was his pleasure now but he did not care in the least if he were hers.

Meg had watched them depart with a satisfaction that made her remarkably rosy and emotional, so that cheering up young Monkton, who was consumed by shameful jealousy, was a very real pleasure. She felt that if she had saved nothing from the wreckage of Varna, she had perhaps saved Théo and Alex. She might have been less happy had she been able to divine Théo's thoughts as she climbed those stairs and then lay waiting in the narrow damp bed while Alex took off his clothes. He took them off quickly, partly due to the cold outside and the unexpected heat inside, but nevertheless the whole spectacle was ridiculous. Was it always like this, Théo wondered? If two people were in love and shared whatever passion two people in love might be capable of sharing, was it still like this? Was there anything more absurd than a man taking his clothes off in a hurry?

Lovemaking itself perhaps.

Afterwards she lay for a long time with the tears running into her ears while Alex slept against her shoulder. She did not know why she cried except for this dim feeling that she wanted more from marriage than this mechanical repetition of her wedding night, and that presumably desire did not have to be brutish nor the whole thing over so quickly. It was not that he hurt her nor that it was especially unpleasant, simply that it meant nothing. It was five minutes of an experience to be endured almost without thinking, the way she had endured the sights and sounds and smells of Varna this hot, memorable summer.

An hour passed. She could not sleep. From some shadowy, half-forgotten place Millie's voice announced: 'Life is nothing much if you don't put it to the hazard now and then.' Well, she had put hers to the hazard almost every day since leaving Portsmouth and to what purpose?

177

Alex shifted in his sleep and turned his face into the hollow of her neck. She put up a hand and touched his soft fair hair, with a deep, overwhelming pity. She was afraid for him.

She was afraid for all of them.

Mr Howard, who had intended to embark for the Crimea, found himself negotiating with some local fishermen on behalf of a parcel of women. He was not sure how he had come to be in this position, but wondered vaguely if things had begun to slide into chaos the moment he had opened Millie's letter . . .

The 'ship' he found to take them to Scutari was an elderly ketch that had gone aground on the shores of the Black Sea in Nelson's day and which the natives had patched up and used, with humorous alterations to the rigging, ever since. It rose and fell gently in the outer reaches of the bay, the stinking, putrid bay that was now crammed with transports and warships and craft of all sorts. Théo, in the bows of a small boat rowed inexpertly by Teddy Monkton, shaded her eyes against a squally glare to see it properly, and tried to look as cheerful as possible. She did not feel cheerful, she felt tired and weak. It was partly the poor diet, partly her late night finishing off her letters, and partly acute disappointment because Alex had not, as promised, found the time to say goodbye.

She knew that Teddy Monkton had probably ignored pressing duties to perform this last service for her, turning up hot and agitated just as she and the other ladies had almost given up hope. His indefatigable good nature and disarming innocence blazed from his reddened face, and Théo, who had thought she was schooled to withstand shocks and disappointments by now, had felt suddenly like throwing herself into his arms and weeping copiously down his immaculate jacket. She could reconcile herself to Alex's neglect but was somehow dissolved by Teddy's thoughtfulness, his touching, boyish concern. She had always reacted foolishly to any unlooked-for kindness, she thought.

Usually he looked at her with a brotherly delight, a great cheerful affection, but now he was preoccupied. Mrs Shales and Mrs Davenant were talking to him, which was distracting, and the shipping was thick and busy, necessitating careful and exacting navigation rather beyond his powers. He had been used to sculling on the Thames, not guiding an unwieldy old boat in and out of the ropes and anchor chains of the greater part of the British fleet, and the French, and a host of saucy native skiffs and caiques and the inevitable bumboats that cut across his bows without warning. He had stuck his tongue between his teeth and was pulling cautiously, his head screwed over his shoulder, while Théo called occasional warnings from her place as lookout.

And then a naval gig, apparently full of pokerfaced marines, shot at them from behind a wallowing transport. Théo cried out something totally incoherent, clutched the sides, and closed her eyes. Teddy bit his tongue, said something regrettable and out of character, and the two ladies were catapulted ungracefully into the bilge.

'Damn you! Can't you see?' demanded a carrying voice, and some kind of officer — it was difficult to judge from the horizontal — stood up in the stern of the gig. The marines did not turn their heads. The able seaman in the bows gave the rowing boat a hefty shove and commented that it was surprising it ever kept afloat, it felt like a sponge. Théo, righting herself, remarked conversationally that perhaps they ought not to go so fast or more accidents might happen before they reached the beach.

The officer might have been forgiven for taking her as one of a boatload of whores till she spoke. He craned to get a better look as the gig bumped along the side of her sad transport, and when he came level he removed his hat and gave her a creditable smile of apology.

'You're from the *Satyr*,' said the surprising young woman in the peak of the spongy rowing boat. 'Do you know a Mr Westover?'

The young lieutenant felt his colour rise. He did indeed know Mr Westover; he rather wished he did not. He said: 'Are you acquainted, Ma'am?'

'Perhaps you could give him a message.' She was leaning over as the boats pulled apart. 'Could you say that I hope he is well, that I'm sorry not to see him? My name is Mrs Trent.'

'Sponge!' cried Teddy Monkton, who had been at great pains to get any kind of boat at all. 'He could have sunk us, pelting along at that rate, not looking what he was at.'

They came alongside the ketch with inexpert commotion, the two ladies clutching each other and resigning themselves to waterlogged boots. Théo gazed up at the dark faces on deck, dark because they were unwashed and made even darker by apprehension; they had only been induced to carry ladies for a great deal of money. Behind them the anxious, welcoming face of Mr Howard bobbed and ducked, and his loud, contradictory commands went ignored.

'We'll meet again,' said Teddy Monkton as Théo, the last to leave the boat, made to get up, 'I'm sure of it.' It was a piece of bravado, he was not sure of anything but fear. She knew it. She gave him both her hands and leaned forward so that he could kiss her cheek. His lips were soft and shy.

'Of course we'll meet again,' she said.

She had one hand on the rope ladder to the deck and anxious, inquisitive faces were peering down to gauge her progress. She turned round again suddenly. 'As for you, the boat, all this . . .' and she looked about her at the horrible flotsam and jetsam nudging round them, 'what can I say but thank you?'

'Nothing,' said Teddy, flushed, grappling with his oars, 'you could say nothing. If I survive I'll come and see you at Scutari and if I don't . . . well.'

'Mrs Trent, Mrs Trent,' called a hearty growling voice, 'come up. Come up. They are eager to be away.'

She climbed obediently, not looking back, and Teddy cast off with a little more finesse than he had managed up till now, and pulled strongly for the shore, be damned to the other shipping, his eyes on her slight figure as she was helped with gallant clumsiness to the safety of the reeking deck.

They were creeping out over the smooth water when a dispute arose about provisions, Mr Howard having innocently supposed the ladies would have brought their own, his being meagre, and the Turkish sailors jealous of their slender store of rice and vegetables. For some minutes, during which heated remarks in several languages flew back and forth, the ketch flapped idly in the small wind, turning dispirited circles.

The outcome was a frantic search for another craft which might have spare supplies, not an easy task. Mr Howard had no Turkish and a weak stomach, even the bobbing about between transports made him ill, and the ladies had been unprepared for crises and looked terrified. At last a sack of rice and some flour, peas and onions were acquired, and Théo and Mr Howard sat on deck reckoning the price while the crew, suspicious to a man, brewed coffee and smoked.

'I do believe we're being hailed,' said Mr Howard suddenly, gazing to where a ship's boat cleaved the water away to starboard. 'Mrs Trent, my dear, do you see a man standing up and waving?'

She did. It occurred to her there was something familiar about the man and that his wave was both imperative and imperious. She said: 'I do hope it isn't their rice,' and underlined the total at the foot of her column of neat figures with a flourish.

The boat came nearer. Mr Howard felt impelled to stand up also and return a wave. He was reassured by the sight of British navy uniforms, one of which was clearly more authoritative than the rest. At least if there was some dispute, he thought, it would be in his mother tongue. Théo continued with her sums, working out whether their purchases would keep their stomachs filled until they reached Scutari. She only looked up when a gentle thud indicated the arrival of the naval gentleman, and when the head and arms of the officer had appeared over the ketch's side.

It was Joss.

She rose, clutching her accounts, the bags of provisions all round her in a ring. She had forgotten how tall he was, how deepset his eyes. All his worst features seemed exaggerated as if he had been ill or underfed; he seemed gaunt and his chin was dark as if he had not shaved properly. The Turks fell back on either side as if before a superior enemy and Mr Howard held out a trembling hand.

Joss looked at it and at its owner, at the agitated ladies in the bow, the general state of dirt and disrepair, and the rice trickling out of a tear in the bag at Théo's feet.

'My God,' he said, with a huge, affectionate smile, 'you seem to have fallen into bad company.'

16

He had received her polite message, he said, and the lieutenant had pointed out her ship among the others. He had not believed at first, said Joss, that Théophile de Faurel, who had been brought up on ships, would trust her life to such a rum old sieve as this. He could only spare a minute, he had a pipe fractured, his best officer down with a fever, and two sailing ships to get in tow within the next few hours. There were soldiers climbing all over the place like helpless, puzzled children, half of them not fit to travel, none of them cheerful, and they were packed into every available space and spilling out, even into his engine room. He would be glad to see them all off again, the poor devils.

Mr Howard took all this in from a distance, blinking. Théo introduced him along with the ladies, and then watched all three descend into the ketch's bowels to inspect the narrow wooden coffins assigned to them as sleeping places. Joss lodged himself on the low rail and stuck out his legs, scanning the anchorage and sometimes Théo's face with the eyes of a man used to judging tricky exits and entrances.

'How is your husband?'

She looked up quickly in case he intended to be sarcastic, but found him examining the deck with intense interest, scraping at the oozing caulking with the toe of his boot.

'He embarks tomorrow. It's a ridiculous business. I don't believe they even know where they're going to land. He thinks I'll be safer in Scutari.'

'It isn't any better than this place. Why not go on to Constantinople? Make yourself known to the ambassador.

182

Millie probably knows everyone worth knowing there. You look . . . as if you could do with some help.'

'I'll be all right.'

'Alone?'

'Well, I seem to have Mrs Shales and Mrs Davenant for company – and there should be a maid; Mr Howard elected to hire one but she didn't turn up. You ought not to scowl so at Mr Howard, he's a dear friend of Miss Cole.'

'He looks a bit like a dancing bear. I'm not sure being a friend of old Di is any recommendation at all; he might be as crazy as she is.'

She was conscious of moments ticking away, of his men waiting, of those two sailing ships waiting for the *Satyr* to take them in tow. She said abruptly: 'You have not congratulated me. You never even wrote.'

'Congratulations,' and then, as if he saw the shadow in her eyes, he reached for her shoulders and bent his head, kissing her firmly on each cheek. She was reminded, quite stupidly, of the way cousin Alexandre kissed her, with conscientious fervour and no real feeling.

'Thank you. You don't approve, do you?'

He straightened, looking across at the tall funnel of his own ship, almost hidden behind the masts and rigging of the ancient men-of-war. 'He was selfish to marry you and bring you out here.'

'I wouldn't marry him unless he did.'

'Then he's more weak-spirited than I thought. Why in God's name does he let you lay down conditions? You're on one of your crusades I see, thinking of all the poor wounded wretches whose lives you'll save. You won't you know, they won't let you. And you'll die of cholera.'

'I'm sure I shall have my deserts,' said Théo bitterly, reminded of Griffith and blushing suddenly, why she did not know.

'And what if Alex is killed . . .'

'I don't think about it.'

'Of course you do. Every woman here thinks about it. Haven't you seen those poor wretches on the quay begging to be taken in the transports? There isn't any room for them, there isn't any food. But God knows they don't deserve to be

183

left here like so much rubbish while their men die without them in the Crimea. You should never have come.'

'So I've been told several times. My mother, Louise, Millie, Alex . . . they were all against it. But it was what I wanted.'

'Well, I hope it's worth it.'

He brooded on the shipping again, seeing a thread of black smoke rise from *Satyr* to the sky. Then he rubbed one of his tarnished buttons; his uniform was spoiled by overuse and seawater and oil.

'I've never seen such a mess as this army, and we've got to take it to the Crimea without half its baggage and no transport and without any proper idea of how many Russians might be waiting for it. Heavens, Théo, you should have stayed on Jersey, a nice clean sort of place.'

The Turks had put away their coffee apparatus and were making the noises of imminent departure.

'Théo.' A hand was on her arm. 'Théo, I'm sorry. It's not my business. Of course you must be fond of him, you wouldn't have married without caring for him at all. Look, I must go.'

The Turks were scowling in their direction, surly – it was their ship after all – but cautious. Joss rammed on his hat.

'You ought to think seriously about Constantinople. Scutari's . . . deteriorating.' He had one leg over the rail now, an absurd pose, but none of the men below were smiling, nor were the Turks, who kept well back, their eyes fixed on his pugnacious jaw.

'Goodbye,' said Théo, who felt numb and tired, who felt she could not reach him, that they might have been strangers.

'I wish you luck,' said Joss.

And Mr Howard came fussing up the ladder to fetch the rice sacks, while the Turks, suddenly voluble, hauled up the sails.

Mr Howard was generous but fussy and short-sighted, and was not very entertaining company for three anxious women about to be delivered to the unknown. He was even more anxious himself, a stout English liberal surrounded by lithe, inscrutable persons of ancient lineage and dubious religious ideals. He kept his pistol primed. He also took comfort in the company of Mrs Trent, who was not the drab and uninspiring figure she looked in that sad, brown holland dress. He could not say what the nature of her appeal was, except that it had some element of the lost, deserted child about it. He felt protective towards her and yet he was still aware she needed protection far less than the other two ladies, one of whom was complaining unceasingly as they wafted in sickening lurches out into the Black Sea.

Théo showed him a picture of Alex, the precious picture she had slapped down so furiously in front of Captain Griffith. Even Mr Howard thought privately that the young man looked romantic and strangled at the same time, an illustration perhaps of how much suffering is necessary in order to appear truly dashing. He murmured something over it, trying to imagine this exquisite and dandified Lancer proposing to the quiet, unexceptional woman at his side; he failed, and as he did not wish to offend her, he handed the picture back with a positive shower of false compliments, every one of which she saw through as he uttered it.

'And the very tall, black-haired man in the naval uniform?' he asked. 'Who was he?'

'He . . . We share the same godmother.'

'Ah. A daunting person, to be sure. I would not like him as my enemy. The Russians had better look out, heh? Heh?'

He thought she might smile, but she did not. She looked tired and serious and remote. 'Oh,' as she turned away, 'he's not as fierce as he looks. He is . . .' but she could not think what he was, except a mass of warring contradictions. She shook her head.

She looked back towards Varna, a grey blur on the horizon, and whether she was thinking of her husband or her extraordinary god-brother Mr Howard could not guess. Perhaps she thought of both. Or perhaps, being a woman who took some notice of these things, she was thinking of the thirty thousand men who had set sail for the Crimea leaving their animals, tents, stoves, stores and medicine chests behind.

It is in the nature of things, Millie had said dryly, that in battle men are killed and wounded. And they had left all the bandages at Varna.

*   *   *

185

The first necessity, said Théo, was somewhere to sleep. It had not occurred to anyone else that this might present a problem. Scutari was dominated by the Turkish barracks recently given over as a second hospital and already filling rapidly with the cholera cases. The scruffy village was uninviting in all senses of the word. The ladies put up their umbrellas – a contemporary remedy against awkward situations and the gaze of impolite native populations – and wilted on the luggage. Mr Howard fumed ineffectually and felt queasy.

Mrs Trent, however, seemed to have stepped on shore a different woman from the one who had left Varna. It was impossible to say what might have brought about the change. Théo herself was mystified. She only knew that her hasty, clumsily tender parting from Alex, her disappointment on the quay, made so bitter-sweet by Teddy Monkton's obvious devotion, and the subsequent rough passage during which she had had to superintend the cooking and calm the ladies in their diabolical little cabin, had all put her in a mood that was an uncomfortable mixture of resignation and angry determination. Maybe it was as well; she seemed to have taken charge. It was she who settled with the Turks on the ketch, for Mr Howard was bemused, his face an unhealthy pale blur under his battered hat. It was she who struck off first for the village, holding up her skirts and avoiding the worst of the filth. She was wearing a grey wool gown that had belonged to one of the army wives who had died of puerperal fever at Varna: she did not think about it, she had little else that was not indescribably dirty and almost falling to pieces. She wore no bonnet and her hair, parted in the middle, was knotted severely on her nape.

The military commandant received her with astonishment and a chilling candour. 'There is nothing you can do here. There is nowhere you can stay.' And I can be as difficult as you like, said his eyes.

'I would not be permitted to help with the sick?'

'On no account. At neither hospital.'

'But my husband has asked me to remain in Scutari.'

'Your husband is entirely unaware of the conditions here. I shall do my best to accommodate you for this evening but tomorrow I must ask you to take ship to Constantinople. There are caiques to take you across.'

She eyed him across the room, smoothing her skirts. 'Thank you,' she said. 'What a nuisance we must be to you.'

The major looked sharply: he could not tell anything from her tone, that slightly foreign inflexion. He was irritated but admiring, he rather liked her. He offered her tea, a great concession, and even tried to make conversation while she drank it, sitting there in her plain grey dress with its white collar and cuffs like a quaker, a quaker or a nun.

He found her – and the two ladies with her whose husbands were in the artillery – a fairly clean room ten feet by ten which had been hastily vacated by a member of the supply department.

'Poor Mr Howard,' Théo wrote to Millie that night, by the light of a Turkish lantern and to the accompaniment of Mrs Davenant's deep, snoring,

Major Sillery could not help him – or would not. He said he must take his chance, there was nowhere to rent in the whole village. The poor man returned to the landing stage after we had left the major and found the wretches on the ketch had dumped all his baggage in the Bosphorus – he *would* leave it on board when it was plain they did not want him to. What was left was washing about in several feet of water being plundered by small boys and dogs. He was furious and heartbroken at the same time, and came lamenting back to us carrying the little he had been able to salvage. If it had not been such a disaster for him I would have laughed, he looked so comical, with a chewed-up carpet bag in one hand, his only surviving change of clothes slung round his neck, and some packages of eatables – waterlogged, of course – tied up in part of a fishing net. On his head he wore a terrible brutalized old shako he acquired visting the Lancers and on his feet some Turkish slippers. He was wet through to the waist. He has lost every penny of his money, which means he will not get a passage to wherever he wants to go – home? the Crimea? – until he has prevailed on friends in Constantinople. He had supper with us, much to the consternation of Mrs Davenant, who finds him 'rather too much' as she so delicately puts it. He was so very forlorn however that even Mrs Davenant relented enough to be quite pleasant to him and condescended to let him smoke.

We are not welcome here. It is always the same story. Soldiers' women are one thing but 'ladies' are quite another. There are men dying through lack of care in the General Hospital but 'ladies' are not allowed beyond the doors. There are a thousand administrative things to be done but 'ladies' would not understand how to do them. It seems to me some of the 'gentlemen' in charge of supplies should be ashamed to heap scorn on the poor women who could manage it all standing on their heads. One of the doctors, who was so good as to shake my hand and ask me how I did, had I just arrived from Varna – he, poor man, told me they have no tables at the hospital, no cooking apparatus, no fresh vegetables or decent meat. He said it very matter-of-factly as if indeed it had become a matter of supreme indifference, though across the water anything at all could be bought in Constantinople if only someone would authorize the purchase. Men arrive from Varna daily sick and dying, and nothing but rough treatment, rats, and beggarly rations await them here.

I have seen Joss. He visited me on the leaky old ketch, looking most ferocious and impossibly tall so that everyone shrank back, horrified. He does not approve of my marriage, he does not approve of my being here, and he does not approve of the war in general, all of which made him difficult company. I think he was shocked by my appearance, and though I believe he does not really care for ships – only their engines – he was obviously shocked by the ketch, which certainly looked as if it had never been cleaned nor properly mended for fifty years. It got us to Scutari though, at the expense of Mr Howard's health and the ladies' tempers: they were furious at being sick. Mrs Davenant is a very tough customer, both tall and righteous; we quake before her. Mrs Shales is very sweet and kind, not very old at all, and is terrified that her husband is already dead. She badly needs someone to cling to, that is her nature, and at the moment she is clinging unhappily to Mrs Davenant as I'm afraid I am no use, I am taken up with rations and finances and how to secure a caique.

Major Sillery looked in an hour ago – the others were already abed and asleep, despite the fleas – to tell me there has already been a battle, the cavalry either all dead or not involved at all, no one is sure. He thinks it would be prudent to ignore everything we hear until there is some official confirmation, and he is right, of course. There is no point sitting here growing frantic with worry.

I am down to my last shirt and have only one pair of stockings fit to wear. Mrs Davenant has lent me some gloves and a Bible, both together, so to speak, as if she feels I need brushing up morally as well as sartorially. But dear Bos, as Joss would say, please send me a box of new underwear and a riding habit, some shirts and some really nice soap. I have actually received – on my last day in Varna – a letter from Dr Frere, adorable old man, who exhorts me to wrap up against the coming winter, Crimean winters being unpredictable: a. how does he know? b. I am not in the Crimea but in Turkey. What are winters like here?

Her pen came to a stop. She cast her eyes over the sleepers on their straw mattresses. Of that curious mix of resignation and anger, resignation prevailed: there would be nothing for her in Scutari as there had been nothing for her anywhere else. All the excitement, the silly hopes, had died.

And tomorrow, she supposed, would bring ignominious retreat to Constantinople.

Tomorrow brought Mr Howard, near to tears, to lament again about his lost belongings and 'in the Celtic manner' Théo later told Millie, 'screeching and keening'; she had never heard a man make quite such a noise. The morning also brought a message that a caique was available and waited on their convenience, and a kind, brief note from Major Sillery wished them well.

Then Fanny Shales refused to go.

It mattered little that Mr Howard, abandoning his own grief in a greater cause, encouraged her to think of the cheerful life across the water, where the ambassador's wife held picnics on the shores of the Bosphorus and food and cakes of soap were nothing out of the ordinary. She raised damp imploring eyes and clung to Théo's hand, much as Mary Anne Brewster had done on the *George Fraser*. She was only twenty, she was frightened. She found Mrs Davenant overbearing and not all the promises of soft beds and superb dinners would induce her to leave Théo. She was pale and had had stomach pains: she dreaded the cholera. She did not feel up to a caique across a choppy stretch of water in the company of a woman she detested.

Théo repaired to Major Sillery, who could not offer her a room in his own house but found her three rooms in a squat, ugly villa on the far side of the village. It had been abandoned for some reason and could be had for practically nothing,

though its other rooms were occupied by an old man, some
hens, and a vicious little pony. Mrs Trent could not live there
more than a few days, said the major, perturbed, she must,
must go to Constantinople. Théo, who was at a complete loss
but was trying not to look as if she was, decided that she had
never run a disorderly house and was not going to begin now.
She engaged one of the poor army wives, whose husband had
died of cholera, as a maid, seeing that some gesture must be
made towards the conventions. Cooks there were none, so
Théo did what she could herself. Rice she could purchase,
and the occasional rabbit, and one day the toothless old man
across the courtyard gave her a stringy hen.

'We do not live in much style,' she wrote wryly to Millie
after three weeks,

This is not entirely due to lack of funds, though we feel obliged
to pay for Mr Howard, whose letters to Lord Napier have flown
across the Bosphorus and never been heard of again. When I
look out in the morning and see the city gleaming across the
water I feel as if we are all condemned to purgatory until we
can raise the passage money to cross; this is absurd as we could
cross tomorrow if we cared. Fanny has not been well however
though it is not the cholera. I am growing quite accomplished
at devising ever more recipes for the broiling, stewing, and otherwise disguising of camel: we like to think it is camel, we hope
fervently it isn't dog. Anyway, Fanny won't eat any of it, and Mr
Howard — who comes every day for a meal from his billet
with one of the staff officers — is losing his own appetite worrying about her. He has cast himself in the role of our protector
and will not accept the gift or even the loan of the fare to
Constantinople to chase up his funds at the embassy; he says he
is afraid to leave us. This is hardly good sense but what can
I do? I tell him he ought to go, could be back within twenty-
four hours, and he looks so hangdog and mournful I feel as
guilty as if I'd asked him to drown himself. He does try so
hard, poor man, though whenever he appears the price of our
'camel' rises to indescribable heights, for the Turks know he is
easy prey. He does not have much stomach for life here: the
filth, the poor fevered soldiers brought in every day now on the
transports, the food, anything. But he would never shirk what
he saw as his duty, fetches and carries with a superhuman
persistence, shields me from any nastiness about the streets —

190

and Heaven knows there is enough – and generally puts himself at our disposal.

The first wounded are arriving and in terrible condition. Dr Molloy, whom I met while calling on the commandant, came up to tell me about it this evening. He was exhausted and said that tomorrow they will be operating from dawn, he has never seen such suffering. He says he fears they can do little, there is not even an operating table in the whole hospital, and not enough beds, and all those cholera cases. Fanny worries me to question every pitiful half-dead soldier I see for news of Captain Shales but there has been no news of anyone – my letters from Alex have gone to Constantinople because someone told him Scutari was so terrible I was bound to have gone on, and although they have been promised by the staff officer who told me all this, they have never appeared. So we sit here uselessly twiddling our thumbs. We have been invited to dinner with Major Sillery but fear we must decline, we have nothing to wear and all our stay laces are broken.

I am feeling a little unwell myself today, a little faint and chill. I have not said anything to Mr Howard, he is inclined to hysteria like Clarice. He will insist I lie down so that he can bring me beef tea – made from 'camel' of course. If only we had some news, any news.

No news came the following day, only the sick and wounded from the battle of the Alma. To the consternation of Mr Howard and Fanny, Théo took to her bed, feeling sick, and refusing everything including beef tea.

'I do hope I may shortly write with better news,' Fanny wrote carefully as a postscript to the unposted letter to Millie, 'but Dr Molloy has been here in the last half hour and told us it is cholera. He says she is very strong and he will provide all the decent food he can, but it is pitiful to see her so.'

It was pitiful indeed. Mr Howard might have stood and howled like a dog but Fanny thrust him out, told him to find out if there was any post, to try for news of her husband and Captain Trent.

'It might cheer her up,' she said, lifting a tired pale face in which the hope was nearly extinguished, 'if I can make her understand. She doesn't fight any more. A letter might do wonders.'

Mr Howard personally felt that it would take more than a

letter to restore Mrs Trent. In a feverish and maudlin mood he made his way to the landing place, as if by gazing at the hospital transports he might accustom himself to brutality and death. And there, coming in like a gull on the stiffening breeze, was the *Aphrodite*, so clean and beautiful she might have belonged to another world.

The sound of her anchor cable was music. He jumped up and down ecstatically, shouting like a madman.

17

'Théo, Théo,' said Fanny Shales, 'here's Captain Griffith come to see you.'

They had told him not to venture too close but he walked straight up to the bed and looked down. Her eyes were open but she did not know him. If she had she would have struggled on to an elbow at once to come to verbal blows with him; he affected her that way. As it was she stared darkly and seemed already corpse-like, with all her roughly chopped hair, hacked off at the height of her fever, standing up in spikes all over her head. She made him think of a child, a sullen, rebellious child, all that had been agreeable about her face dissolved away to leave the painfully sharpened bones and hollowed cheeks. Reduced to its essentials her face was neither pleasant nor commanding, nor anything in between, but rather small and delicate and reproachful, like the faces of the scavenging orphans he had seen on the jetty.

Surely she needed fresh air and light? He glanced round. The windows were shuttered, the atmosphere oppressive. Fanny blushed, thinking it is a criticism of her nursing; she had known him at once as a man who could make her wilt with a look, a man outside her small experience — where she hoped he might remain. Mr Howard stood in the doorway, helpless and agitated. The commandant had been kindness itself, he told Griffith, and the old man across the courtyard had sent up hen after hen, he must have slaughtered his whole livelihood, but if Théo would not eat . . . And the weather had turned gloomy and cold, they dare not open the shutters for fear of a chill, and Dr Molloy said . . .

'Damn Dr Molloy,' said Griffith, spying the row of bottles on the shelf, 'none of that stuff will do her any good. She needs food and sunshine.'

Since it was beyond his powers to compel the sun to shine over Scutari, he did what he could by sending Albert.

The tough hens were seen no more. Sweet, succulent ones were brought in baskets from the coops on the *Aphrodite* for Albert to execute in the courtyard. Strange delicacies made their appearance: the best jam and marmalade and tea and coffee, boxes of sugared almonds for Fanny, plum cake for Mr Howard. They had forgotten, almost forgotten such things existed. And every day Griffith came and looked down at the patient so flat and faded under her blankets, exchanged some heated words in execrable French with Albert, and exhorted Mr Howard to scout the hinterland for fresh vegetables. Every day polite little notes came down from Major Sillery to know how Théo did, and every day they sent polite, non-committal replies, for she seemed to have passed into another world already, to have left them, though she still breathed and opened and closed her eyes and let Fanny wash and tend her with that frightening resignation, that unseeing stare.

Dr Molloy was not to be drawn. Any illness might have such an effect, he said, and she had been under great strain: the journey out, Varna, the lack of news from the Crimea. If she died now, he said, it would not, strictly speaking, be the cholera that killed her. Could they not do their best to get word of her husband, even to ascertain if he were still alive? Could they not find something to break into this dismal withdrawal, this shadowy country where she had retreated? They did their best, every day they did their best, but she was limp and shrunken and took no notice.

And then, one morning when Mr Howard had taken Fanny for some air — such as could be got now in that pestilential place — and Albert was in the room next door peering with an artist's exasperation into the depths of his cookpot and humming an old, old song about seagulls . . .

'*Qui est là?*' called a small, thready voice through the half open door.

He dropped his spoon, sprang into the bedroom. For a moment he could see nothing and then there were her eyes, shining with blessed intelligence, and her hands clutching strongly at the sheet.

'C'est moi, chèrie.' It seemed superfluous to say it, his smiling bulk, his white apron, could hardly be mistaken. He came nearer, the smile spreading. Another moment and he seemed all smile; she had never known anyone look at her with such joy.

She watched him dreamily as he opened the shutters a fraction and then went humming back to the stove to make her tea. The tune had taken her far away, to Le P'tit Clos des Pommes, to the maids beating the carpets in the bright sun and indoors Honorine, poring over the plans and the latest model from the shipyard, singing about seagulls . . . And Martagon, and Joss, and the respectful, rather astonished silence as she had finished and the last note had died away . . .

Later there was Fanny in a mauve braided dress – Captain Griffith had brought it, and others, without regard for size or suitability, but his guess had been remarkably accurate, or had Albert been snooping?

'We have had a caique-load of luxuries from Constantinople,' she said, doing her best to coax Théo's hair into curls, and failing. 'Heaven knows where he found the clothes. And wine. And fruit. Oh, and yesterday he brought a sackful of post that had gone astray and been rounded up with great difficulty – at least, there was always a great difficulty when poor Mr Howard went after it, but not so much when Captain Griffith tried. There are letters for you from England and Jersey. I'll sit you up after lunch and you can read them.'

She was too weak to be propped up, and by then too tired to read. Fanny read them for her, bending over, her soft brown hair lit by one of the *Aphrodite*'s lamps which hung from the ceiling. Millie wrote with the long galloping scrawl of someone perpetually in a hurry, her mind three lines ahead of her hand; it took Fanny a while to get used to the lack of punctuation, the furious deluge of apparently unconnected thoughts. Louise wrote great looping words, was frantic with worry, had enclosed a page from Marguerite, who was not well – 'overtired' the doctor said, there was no question of consumption, it was not in the family.

'She is bored and unhappy,' said Louise, 'as you were for

years. But she gave up the fight sooner than you did. But of course you are not bored or unhappy any longer, you are with Alex and maybe even on a battlefield. I can't imagine what it must be like.'

Fanny hesitated at this, looked up to find Théo's eyes fixed on the page she held in her hand; there was no letter from Alex in this sackful of post.

There were, however, letters from Miss Cole, Dr Frere, Pierre, Bon, and Joss. The note from Joss was a disgraceful thing of barely three lines written somewhere off Balaclava and with an oily pen. It hoped she was well and had found a decent lodging, she would be better off at Rozel. This made Théo laugh, something she had not done for so long she had forgotten how much effort it took, and she turned her face into the pillow overcome by the sudden, ridiculous weakness. When she opened her eyes again Fanny had gone and a man was standing there, a man who put a cool hand on her brow with the assurance of Dr Molloy but who was not Dr Molloy nor anyone like him.

'What do you mean by frightening Fanny to death? She thought you'd decided to die after all.'

'Where is she?'

'Albert is teaching her how to make *filets de poulet aux concombres*. They have plenty of *poulets* but no *concombres*. I expect they'll go on to the larks next, roast or stuffed or whatever.'

'It must be a crime to eat a lark. I've always thought so.'

'You aren't intending to die then?'

'Not if I can help it. I do feel,' and here she tried to get up on that elbow, she felt at such a disadvantage, 'I feel almost overwhelmed by your . . . your . . .'

'Selfless generosity? Chivalry? Tosh. You don't think I'd lend Albert to anyone unless it was in my interest, do you?'

It was impossible to be dignified while lying in bed too weak to lift a hand, thought Théo, though Caroline might have shown her how to do it. Caroline's illnesses, however, were all pretence. This was real, her arms felt so heavy, and her head. She could not think properly any more either, could not challenge his last statement at all. He would have to explain to her, patiently, as he would to a baby.

He explained nothing. He saw she was tired out. He picked up her thin arm and put it back under the sheet, and did up the top two buttons of her nightdress, and smoothed back her wild hair, and then he said good night and left her. He might have been her father, she thought, her last thought before she slept; but he was not her father and his familiarity was scandalous. Anyone would think it was scandalous, anyone . . .

Mr Howard had long ceased to think Captain Griffith's behaviour scandalous; deployed by an intelligent officer he had, so to speak, become for the first time a genuinely useful soldier. He was good with children and animals, it was only the adult world that left him baffled. Every two days he and Albert ran a soup kitchen for the orphans and such of the soldiers' women – mostly crammed into the hideous cellars of the great hospital – as cared to come. It was little enough to alleviate such misery, he would have liked to charge official-dom with a hatchet in order that these stinking, starving beings became a thing of the past, never more to disgrace the streets of an enlightened civilization. But he was no hero, action was beyond him. He could only distribute the soup, knocking away the marauding dogs with his umbrella, and keeping strict count of the bowls. He also learnt to row, an accomplishment he had never even considered before, and daily went out to the *Affie* for further supplies. Her crew treated him like a pet dog, rather untidy and rather foolish but with all the right intentions, but salved his sore ego – it was always sore after his bitter contemplation of the sick and starving on the shore – by congratulating him on the way he handled the boat, a Thames waterman was no comparison.

Fanny, who might once have been scandalized by a great many things, was now simply Fanny to the terrible Griffith and no longer ran to hide at his approach, though she could not stand up to him, was hideously afraid of his witticisms, dreaded his poking fun at her expense, and shrank from his touch. Unlike most men of her limited acquaintance, he thought nothing of taking her hand and leading her where he wanted her to go, or putting his arm about her shoulders to support her when she was collapsing from exhaustion – she had been at Théo's side all day and night for a week. There was nothing familiar in this, no underhand intentions, it came as naturally to him as breathing. But it made her uncomfortable and once it occurred to her she would like nothing better than to go to sleep in the circle of his arms, all his good sense and strength to support her for ever. She must lean on someone, she was more timid than Mr Howard. Théo was ill, Albert was not to be considered; the captain was her rock in this area of confusion. But Fanny, though young and afraid and ignorant, was not a fool, nor did he treat her like one. If only she had known he was vigilantly circumspect, that it was only because he thought of her as some sort of very young sister that he touched her at all. It was beyond him to change her now, to give her the necessary courage to face the world by herself, but he did his best. He saw she was secretly terrified of Albert so sent her to Albert for cookery lessons; once she was over the shock she was all delight. He asked Dr Molloy, with whom he was not on very good terms, to give her real praise for her nursing of Théo, a show of proper gratitude for a task excellently done – the doctor barely spoke to her when he visited, gave medical instruction but no encouragement. He must cease, said Griffith bluntly, to treat his patient as stone and her nurse as cardboard, the human spirit was not intended for such abuse.

Molloy, deeply incensed, managed a very pretty speech. He was rewarded by seeing the pink glow of joy spread over Fanny's face and her wide mouth tilt into the loveliest smile he had seen in years.

'You have sound notions, no doubt,' he said grudgingly as he and Griffith walked to the shore afterwards, 'but your manner leaves a great deal to be desired.'

'So they tell me,' said Griffith.

It was impossible to mistake Joss Westover, he drew the eye. Mr Howard felt decidedly conspicuous shooing him along the landing stage like a reluctant mahout. The wounded, the dying, the dead, brought from the hospital transports in the caiques, were all about them, but Joss seemed not to see them, and Mr Howard, who saw them only too well, averted his eyes as much as possible.

'How is she?' The dread question, to which Joss expected

a shake of the head. Indeed, on the voyage across the Bosphorus he had rehearsed this scene a hundred times and had composed his uncomposable face for the inevitable news. It was amazing then how all his careful strategies were disintegrated by Mr Howard's rapturous: 'Capital! Remarkable! She grows stronger every single day. Dr Molloy says nothing will hinder her recovery now. And Fanny is spared. And we have come by some cabbages.'

Since Joss did not know who Fanny was, and did not know how a humble cabbage might be prized in Scutari, which was overendowed with brothels, drink-shops and even tombs, but was lamentably short of vegetables, this latter news left him untouched. But Théo alive! And recovering! Since he had received Millie's letter he had not dared hope for so much.

'This place is worse than I imagined,' he said.

'Worse than it was. The sick and wounded from Balaclava are being landed now and there are no provisions made.'

'None?'

'Well, very few. The tales from the hospitals are unbelievable. I doubt any sane man would believe them unless he had had a whiff of the stench there and seen the graves. This place was a cemetery for Constantinople; I fear it may be the cemetery for the entire British army.'

'Some of the transports have gone on to Malta. And there are plenty of wounded in the field hospitals.'

'Thank God, thank God,' cried Mr Howard fervently, hopping along at Joss's elbow. 'They are better off taking their chance anywhere but in this hell here.'

Joss stepped over piles of refuse, the remains of a dead dog. Shock and disgust were etched in every crease of his face, and shock and disgust remained there right up to the time he stood at Théo's bedside and looked down at her sleeping face.

His first thought was that it was not Théo; his second that she might have been dead after all, she was so still. Then her eyes opened, the same uncanny green eyes he remembered, and the same spirit looked out of them at him, and she smiled.

'How grim you look. You are smoking with indignation.'

He sat down on the bed suddenly as if she had winded him, and said nothing for a few minutes, trying to come to terms with her altered looks. He had only obtained leave by the most monstrous deception, saying his sister was dying alone and unaided at Scutari, brazening it out with his captain who was already in the foul temper of a man who feels himself ill deployed in a senseless war, his ship at the mercy of fools and opportunists.

'I never thought to find you in a flea-ridden hovel,' he said. 'What is Alex thinking of?'

'If you think this is bad you should have seen it when we moved in,' she replied. She tried to sound cheerful but it was a false cheerfulness, she found it impossible to keep smiling. She had often thought of Joss sitting at her side like this, taking her hand perhaps, telling her . . . Telling her what? That the news of her illness had made him see how much she meant to him? That he wished he and not Alex had asked her to marry him? What nonsense! What silly, childish nonsense only fit for the pages of a romance.

He sat and looked at her, and his face told her everything. He had had a shock, thinking she was dead, and his natural reaction on finding her alive was profound relief and outrageous and unjustifiable anger. He had come out here for adventure, and by God she was having adventure, enough to nearly kill her and fetch him at vast trouble and expense across half a sea of disobliging ship-mongers and Turkish pirates. She had refused to stay at home reclining on her sofa, producing an heir for the house at Rozel, and now she had the gall to expect sympathy for being convalescent. The relief and the anger were too much. He walked to the window to look out.

He cared for her, she thought, but he would make no protestations of love, any kind of love, brotherly or passionate. He was an emotional man who let all his emotions show except that one, that single one; he had embraced Mrs Gurden so stiffly, Théo remembered, because he suspected her affection had been bought.

'Has Sophie written?' she asked gently, and saw by the jerk of his shoulders that she had indeed.

'Twice. And Millie has written telling me that Miss Barnard is terrified the girl will run away to Constantinople.'

'She very well might. She struck me as likely to grow bolder and more enterprising with age. But what,' as he turned to look at her, his eyebrows at acute angles, 'will you do with her? Her reputation will be in shreds. Even the flirtatious ladies at the ambassador's palace would look askance. You would have to marry her.'

He went a very deep red.

'She thinks I am going to ask her when I return to England.'

'Now why should she think that?'

'Because I let her get the idea into her head, it suited me. Why shouldn't I marry her? She has everything I need.'

'Martagon,' said Théo, 'all those ancestors in the Long Gallery. You have some kind of superstition about Martagon, don't you? You believe you can lay the ghosts if only you can call yourself master there.'

'What ghosts?'

'I don't know. Only you see them.'

He let out his breath slowly. He would not admit she was right. He would not admit he understood what she was talking about. But why should he deny himself a beautiful girl willing to fall into his arms, a girl with thousands a year and his ancestral home into the bargain? He did not love her, he did not think it mattered. He desired her – who would not? – as he was prepared, as presumably Théo had been prepared when she married Alex, to nurture whatever affection could be found. He would be the hero of a deliberate twist of fate, the rejected child claiming his inheritance. He thought of it perfectly seriously, it struck him as just and sensible. He was sure he could make Sophie as happy as the next man, and he would like to have children, children who knew from the very beginning where they belonged and who they were . . .

'*C'est impossible*,' said Albert round the door, 'I have not the ingredients for *poulet à la Marengo*.'

'Are we supposed to know what they are?' demanded Joss, looking with deep distrust at the round red face with its very French expression of resignation.

'Albert is a magician,' said Théo. 'If there is a mushroom in Scutari he will find it, and create a dish with it. The rest of the village lives off mud and mule, the soldiers at the hospitals they say live off nothing at all, and we . . . we think of *poulet à la Marengo*.'

'You should be ashamed.'

'You said that with a smile. But do you think I'm not, when

Mr Howard brings back stories of wounded men dying for want of bread and water? He and Albert have a soup kitchen for the women and children down near the beach but it seems so little, and no one cares . . . No one. Do you think there is anyone who will ever care enough to do something about it?'

'I can see you intend to when you're well enough. But the reports in the newspapers at home are stirring up some consciences, and Mr Howard tells me there are women nurses now at the hospital.'

Théo had heard all this before and was unconvinced. It was all very well collecting money in England for the troops in the Crimea but how was it to be spent, and who was to spend it? How would the Commissariat cope with public money — and private citizens — tinkering with the system?

It was beyond Joss. He did not see himself burned up with reforming ardour. He would brave a pit full of viperous regulations to save one of his own men but he did not see how he could do any good demanding better treatment for poor foot soldiers. He had always considered them a blackguardly lot, their own officers did not care about them, abused them in public.

He said as much to Dr Molloy, a small, harassed, pimply man of forty, from whom some thousands of these black-guards were hoping for proper treatment. They talked philosophically, in remarkable generalizations, and found themselves in broad agreement.

'I would have thought you might have more feeling,' accused Théo, who suspected he had but was suppressing it.

'Albert is off to the *Affie* for lentils,' said a voice, and Griffith walked in, wet with rain and smelling tarry, 'I think he said lentils. How are you?'

'Do you usually come into a lady's room without knocking?' asked Joss.

'Oh, he usually does,' said Théo, wondering if Mr Howard would stumble in and save them from the impending row. 'This is Captain Griffith who has . . .' Her disordered brain could not cope with the explanation, it seemed a little bizarre . . . 'Who has been kindness itself.'

Captain Griffith laughed, a harsh, cynical sound. He was

aware – who could not be? – that Joss's hackles were raised, but he made no effort to placate him.

'Oh, you are Westover, the great engineer,' he said, and only after a while, during which he banged out his hat in a shower of little drops and gazed about with infuriating mildness: 'I suppose you don't know anything about paddle-steamers, elderly, crank paddle-steamers? I'd give a crate of Burgundy for an honest opinion.'

The elderly, crank paddle-steamer had been the last hope of an impoverished shipowner, a lugubrious Scot called Campbell. Having been forced to sell his other three ships, his offices, his house – even the coal scuttles, said Fanny, overcome – to get himself out of debt, the *Tempest* had nearly finished him completely by running aground with a valuable cargo, uninsured and by now weeks overdue. As a last throw he had advertised berths for the Crimea – several companies were already doing so – so that for the extraordinary sum of seven pounds wives and husbands could be reunited or, for the more adventurous, the battlefields could be viewed.

The *Tempest*, that 'ill-natured tub' as her first mate called her, duly carried a dozen passengers to Constantinople, a dozen passengers with expectations pitched too far above reality for comfort – the owner's, the captain's, or their own – who complained of the weather, the food, the smuts, and the continuous shaking and pounding, of the steward's manners, of the angle of the deck, of the lack of after-dinner entertainment. Constantinople might have come up to scratch, if only from the sea, had they reached it, but the *Tempest* expired at the Dardanelles.

It was an expensive job, Campbell was a broken man financially and mentally, and the passengers, terrified of being marooned in a strange land, were vociferous in their demands to be repatriated. It had all been sorted out, of course, but *Tempest* still lay at anchor with only a boy in charge, a notice on her mast. Word got about, as word does, and Captain Griffith made his way down to see her, to poke at her pipes and her stinking bottom and her general disrepair. But he was a sailing man, could judge a futtock to a nicety but stared in blank ignorance at the paddle-steamer's rows of gauges.

'I can buy her cheap,' he told Joss over their meal on the *Affie* – they had gone on board to talk man to man, and taken Albert with them; the women could manage for one evening, said Griffith. 'I can fill her up for the passage home, get her ship-shape, and put her up for sale in England. I know someone who might be interested but he wouldn't touch her while she was out here, he'd want her safe at Gravesend. With the money I can buy a nice little clipper-barque, something sweet and fast for the Australian run. We'll have the heels of any steamer for a year or two yet and by that time . . .' His shrug was as expressive as Albert's. He would die a rich man with a fleet of forty, said that shrug, if the sea did not take him.

'I don't like paddles,' said Joss, who had a poor opinion of their capabilities and black memories of his earliest days in the navy hearing them thrashing in his dreams.

'But you'll give me an opinion? They say it'll be an expensive job to get her under way again, but she might just lack a few nuts and bolts – I don't know the first thing about steamers.'

Thus Joss spent the second afternoon of his leave scrambling about the *Tempest* while Griffith made notes, and he came back and reported to Théo that the ship was sound, would be good for another twenty years with some trifling attention, and that Griffith had made a derisory offer for her which he was fairly certain would be accepted.

Théo was amused by all this. Fanny was sure the two men had become firm friends, but Fanny had a trusting and ingenuous nature. Théo saw no sign of it, was aware that Joss, who made no claims to be a 'gentleman', had a tendency to look down on the captain for not being one, though he had sprung from a family – ship brokers and chandlers – quite as wealthy as the Westovers. Théo suspected it was the apparently natural hostility between royal and merchant navies, that though in general he wore his uniform with indifference, Joss could be relied on to adhere as strongly as any other officer to Royal Navy prejudices.

On the third day he was due to rejoin the *Satyr*. He said a protracted goodbye to Fanny, who had found him nothing but charming and could not understand why Mr Howard ran away at sight of him. He kissed her – Théo saw him through the open door – and Fanny looked rather distracted for a moment and went to hide behind Albert. Then he came to take his leave of Théo herself, but he only took her hand and dropped a self-conscious kiss on her knuckles, for she wore a strange look of withdrawal, of fierce resistance. He thought she had never been so far away from him in spirit since the night they had first met at Millie's ball, and he was at a loss to explain it, put it down to her illness: she was depressed, disorientated, sadly wasted and tired.

'I'll write to you,' he said, 'and if I hear anything of Alex . . . I'm being sent to join the Naval Brigade for a day or two as an observer, Heaven knows why. If news of the cavalry comes my way I'll send word as soon as I can. If I meet him I'll shake him till his teeth rattle. It seems to me . . .'

'Have you been talking about me to Captain Griffith?'

'No,' he said loudly and did not look at her. 'And that's another thing. Howard says the commandant is afraid there will be talk if you continue to put yourself so completely in the hands of an ill-mannered sea captain . . .'

'I haven't found him ill-mannered. Overbearing, irritating, argumentative, certainly. And who is there in Scutari who will "talk"? Only the poor soldiers. And what do they care?'

How passionately she spoke sometimes, he thought, backing away from the intensity of those eyes. He was glad he had got over that brief attraction – she would be the very devil as a wife. Thank God after all she was safely married to that lackadaisical fool Trent, who would never be able to control her, but who would have all the worry and the excitement. Thank God.

He let go of her hand. She did not stir him at all, lying there so thin and colourless, all eyes and lank short hair. Théo de Faurel might never have existed. This woman was not the Théo he had known in London, and they called her Theo, pronouncing the t and the h, whereas he had always called her Tayo.

'Goodbye,' she said, and did not even smile.

When he had gone she closed her eyes. She saw the wide flat expanse of sand in the dazzling sunlight, the boys running to catch her hands and beat down her blowing skirt, little Lou staggering along clapping, her curls all straightened by the breeze. And she saw La Croix clinging to the side of its hill, the garden door leading directly on to the lane that ran down to the harbour. And she saw herself in the little sailing boat she had borrowed so secretly, making swooping progress on the long even swell, all duties and obligations forgotten and the sour consciousness of Caroline's disappointment in her blown away on the glad wind.

All her life, except during those hours on the beach, or on the quay, or in the boat, she had looked forward to the future. Tomorrow she would learn how to look prettier, how to be more charming, tomorrow there would appear a man she might want to marry, tomorrow Caroline would praise her with real affection, or Alexandre would give her a share in the business, or the *Theophile* would be built, or . . . or . . . There had been no end to her hopes, secret, childish hopes.

It seemed to her now that only one survived: that Alex would come, unutterably glad to see her, that there might be a chance for this ill-starred marriage after all. She had made a score of excuses for his long absence, had even thought of him as dead – anything to explain it. Even tonight, exhausted and shaken, she still hoped . . . He *would* write, he *must* write . . . They would be reunited. Her likes and dislikes were strong ones, her loves overwhelmingly fierce, and she would not be put in a bottle of respectability and corked down. She wanted to travel, she wanted to sail, she wanted a ship; oh, she had always wanted a ship. Her ambitions were Bonespoir's. He had filled her head with his adventures when she was a little girl but like him her heart had already belonged to the sea and ships. Somehow she must reconcile this deep desire to escape to the sea with her duties as a married woman. It could be done; surely, surely it could be done?

After Joss had gone, and Albert, she got out of bed for the first time in weeks and sat in a chair, her head swimming. Fanny made her tea and came and sat with her, and they were still together, Fanny mending a tear in the mauve dress, when Mr Howard knocked timidly at the door and said he had been to the commandant to find out the truth of this Light Brigade business, this terrible muddle at Balaclava – and it was true, that fool Cardigan had lost the better part of the

206

cavalry, the 17th Lancers reduced to thirty or thirty-five men, he could not remember which. But it was all right, seeing Théo's stricken face, it was all right, Captain Trent had taken no part in it, he had been sick and feverish and was in the hospital at Balaclava. He was shrewd enough not to add 'or so they believe'; Griffith had impressed on him the necessity of keeping Théo cheerful, of giving her something to do as soon as she was up again – and here was the very thing: Alex alive and safe at Balaclava; when she was well she could go to him.

Why then did she stare at him like that, the shadows gathering in her eyes and her face paler than he had ever seen it?

'How long has he been ill?' she asked. 'Weeks?'

He shook his head, backing away, nonplussed. He could not give her any facts, hard, cheerful facts. When he dared to look he saw she had put her head on Fanny's shoulder and was crying quietly, but evidently not from relief or joy.

It was not the effect he had intended. He went away, chastened, and when he told Griffith what he had done later that night was nearly blasted across the Bosphorus by that volatile gentleman's temper. She would be off to Balaclava in the morning, said Griffith, and not strong enough to walk on her own two feet.

'Can you not insist she stay here? Oh, surely she takes notice of your advice?'

'Insist? Insist! I would never dare insist on anything where Mrs Trent is concerned. She would damn me to Hell with her eyes and go off in a huff, you know, one of those well-bred, starchy exits: a flick of her skirt is supposed to tell me what she thinks of me.'

'But she must not go to Balaclava yet,' cried Mr Howard, wiping his brow and gazing about the *Affie*'s saloon with the bewilderment of a trapped animal, 'she cannot! My dear sir, you *must* stop her – she will die!'

'Oh, I believe it would take more than Balaclava to kill little Mrs Théo. But I agree she should not go. However, I could not stop her short of knocking her out. You will have to stop her yourself, or get Molloy to put her in quarantine or something.'

'I had thought you cared about her welfare. You have been generosity itself,' declared Howard, desperate.

'Ah, but I told you it was in my own interests to be generous. The lady has connections with a very famous shipping line.'

'If I did not feel beholden to you, sir, I would call you a rogue,' said Howard.

'Please don't feel beholden to me in any way. Since your dilatory bankers remitted your money you have paid me back a great deal of what I spent. And call me what you like, I don't care.' And then, as an afterthought, lighting his pipe: 'As for her welfare — perhaps you should leave it to her husband, or Mr Westover.'

18

She was well again; she declared herself well again and went out. She was determined – how could anyone so mild be so determined, cried Mr Howard to Fanny, grieving over her in private – resolved to be doing something.

Scutari had deteriorated. It was Varna all over again. There were bloated carcases washing at the water's edge and a constant stream of sick and wounded, walking or on litters, going to the hospital. It was November. It was cold and wet. There was nowhere for them to go but the reeking corridors, packed in side by side, mile on mile. Théo heard that some nurses had arrived, a bold experiment resisted in almost every quarter, led by an indomitable Miss Nightingale, a lady with excellent connections. Dr Molloy told her with scorching disapproval that the woman had electric views on sanitation, would sweep them all away on a tide of scrubbing and cleaning. And she had made a start in the kitchens, these hellish caves of mismanagement, for if the medical men thwarted her in her nursing ambitions they could not thwart her in cookery.

'You are all fools,' said Théo bluntly, much as she had once rallied her charity ladies, 'you're fools to stand blindly by tradition and protocol. You ought to take help where you can find it and thank God. While you're resisting with all your might and clinging to worn-out prejudice thousands of men are dying for want of a blanket and a mug of tea.'

Dr Molloy looked sheepish, colouring a little. 'My dear Mrs Trent, you know the reputation of nurses – drunken, disorderly, immoral – and to think of letting them loose in a military hospital where every patient is a man!'

'I do believe,' snapped Théo, 'you're all worse than I imagined, not only fools but prurient, hypocritical fools too. Why not encourage the best, dismiss the worst, give them a fair chance? Are you hoping for drunkenness and immorality that you constantly talk of them? Do you dislike all women so?'

He was deep claret by now, avoiding her eye. He was not used to ladies who spoke their minds so frankly. She reminded him forcibly of Miss Nightingale, though he rather feared Miss Nightingale would prove the more terrible. At the moment this lady, this remarkable, chilling lady, was still being delicately diplomatic, like a tigress stalking her quarry through a gunpowder store.

'They could do a great deal of harm, you know.'

'Twenty-odd women among thousands of wounded men?' cried Théo, 'and if they saved ten lives would you not – should you not – go down on your knees and thank God?'

'My dear, that's a little strong. You have no concept of the situation at the hospital. Ladies have no place in scenes of such squalor. And the other women are not fit to be let loose on anyone, not even the healthy.'

He would not be moved. It was remarkable, thought Théo, how a man will cling so hard to an irrational prejudice he *knows* is irrational, as if by clinging to it he might give it sense. He took refuge at last in begging her to stay at Scutari until she had more definite news of Alex, at least until then, at least.

'Wait until your letters are answered,' he said, 'or go to Constantinople and wait there.'

'I shall certainly make Mrs Shales go to Constantinople,' she told him, 'Mr Howard will take her.'

'She won't go without you.'

'Well, she must. For I am going to Balaclava to find Alex.'

'I can see I shall have to enlist the help of Captain Griffith to make you see sense.'

'You'll have no joy in that quarter. Captain Griffith will not try to stop me. He is waiting to see me come by my deserts.'

'I beg your pardon, I do not understand.'

She smiled, offered no explanation. Her clothes hung on her, he thought, her hair straight and lifeless. He supposed he admired her a little, for clinging so tenaciously to life if nothing else, but he found her unattractive, difficult, excessively stubborn. And he did not like women who questioned his morality, who called him a fool to his face.

'I see you have made up your mind,' he said. 'I'll say no more.'

'Poor Dr Molloy,' with a direct look; how she always surprised him with these rare flashes of boldness! 'Confess you will be overjoyed to see the back of me.'

He went deep, deep crimson, was almost purple. And fled.

She had heard that more wounded were on the way after a terrible fog-bound struggle at Inkerman.

She had heard that Lord Cardigan lived on his yacht, only joining his troops by day.

She had heard that William Russell, the *Times* correspondent, was moving the bewildered populace in England with his vivid reports of the battlefields.

'You must move to Constantinople,' said Mr Howard, emerging from capes and cloaks and oilskins as from a chrysalis, 'a healthier and happier neighbourhood.'

'Sit in splendour and only think about the thousands dying, you mean.'

He had no answer. Indeed, he never knew how to cope with this dry, bitter Théo who lurked always beneath the kind, patient woman he liked so well.

'I do wish . . .' He was embarrassed, turned away a little so that in the gloom she could not see his expression, 'I wish your letters to Balaclava . . .'

'Perhaps he is dead.'

'I am sure you would have had word.'

'Yes.'

He glanced round and surprised pain in her eyes, but whether it was natural grief, or self-pity – to which he did not think she was prone – or understandable fear, he could not tell. All he knew was that his elegant little Mrs Trent was a fey shadow of her former self.

'Oh,' he said, groping in his pockets, 'I have a letter for you. It was sent down from the barracks hospital.'

It was from Miss Nightingale, who said that the situation, so delicate still, did not admit any more nurses to be 'acquired', however badly they were needed, but she thanked Mrs Trent for her kind wishes, for her encouragement, for her prayers; it began to look as if divine intervention might be necessary after all. She had begun to organize relief for the widows, the lost, verminous women and children in the cellars; she had nothing but praise for Mr Howard's soup kitchen, an inadequate but brave attempt to feed the five thousand without the requisite miracle. Perhaps in a month or so, perhaps at Christmas, if the situation had changed, she would be able to find something for Théo to do; and oh what use she could make of a sensible, steady daughter of a doctor, provided she could take orders . . .

'You really aren't strong yet,' said Mr Howard, aware that some disappointment had just diminished her spirit. 'Oh my dear, don't go to Balaclava. They say it's in terrible confusion. They say there's fever and starvation.'

It was not such a disappointment after all, Théo decided, tucking the letter into her pocket. She had not written with great expectations, only hoping that Miss Nightingale might consider her if more nurses were needed; she had to find her husband first, to assure herself he was well and properly cared for . . . that he was alive. Miss Nightingale's reply was sweetly apologetic and remarkably bracing at the same time, which was just what she needed. She had not been rejected without consideration, she had not been mocked or ignored.

'Théo!' and there was Fanny, breathless, smiling, her cloak blown open and her bonnet askew, 'Théo! There's a box arrived for you, a great box. Albert is bringing it up with the help of some Turks and the old man.'

It was the box from Millie, packed with the expertise of a woman who has often known what it is to want upon a battlefield. There was tea, and magazines, and books, candles, stay laces, flannel underwear, petticoats, a riding habit, shirts, cocoa, gloves, stockings, hairpins, eau de cologne. It was so unexpected and so welcome Théo sat down on the floor to unpack it at once, and found half a dozen letters tucked into

a felt hat on the top, letters from Miss Cole, Dr Crale, dear
man, from Sophie Barnard and Miss Barnard, from Mrs
Gurden – and from Caroline.

'She wrote to me at last,' Millie said in her own direct way,

'and so I send it on. If she will not write to you herself what is to
be done? She says she has heard from you 'infrequently'. Well, what
does she expect if she never takes the trouble to reply? As you will
see, she has taken up with a certain French gentleman, every other
line is Jean Louis this or Jean Louis that as if she were sixteen again
and quite passionately in love. It is certainly more than her usual
flirtation. I have the strangest feeling you are about to get a new
papa. Let us hope he carries her off to some remote château, or to
Paris, at any rate some place comfortably far from Jersey, and leaves
Louise in peace at last. The poor girl sounds distracted, for since
you left she has found herself – as you did, of course – in conflict
with Caroline more and more. Now you are not there to see to the
house, and the servants, and the provisions, it all falls to Louise,
and Louise apparently does not have your ideas of comfort and
economy. Your mother does not approve her methods – while not
lifting a finger to do anything herself – and Louise, growing bold
'in her old age' as she put it to me, will not accept her criticism
without retaliating.

Do I make my Caroline out to be a monster of selfishness? I
hope not. Though I would have no compunction in ducking her
in the Atlantic on the coldest day of the year for her sins, I really
don't believe she is at all malicious. She does not know the effect
she has. She is completely ignorant that her words might
make Louise unhappy. She would never think about deliberately
wounding anyone; she never thinks at all, except about herself.
She would be shocked if you were to accuse her to her face, and
it would be honest-to-goodness shock, nothing pretend about it.
Then she would call you an unnatural daughter, ungrateful, and
she would really mean it, you see, because she really does not
understand.

Enough of all this. How I wander on when I have half an
hour to spare and a new pot of ink. I have put in six packets
of hairpins, you will find, as I always thought nothing of note
could be achieved by a lady with her hair down her back, she is
never taken seriously.

Théo leaned back against the trunk, smiling, turning the
pages, while Fanny delved in the depths and came up with

crystallized fruit, chocolates, almonds. And there was a lace nightcap with a note pinned to it: 'For entertaining gentlemen while an invalid.'

'Millie has a puckish sense of humour,' said Théo.

Miss Barnard, on the other hand, had none at all. Her letter was stilted and formal: she hoped Théo was bearing the privations with fortitude. Théo handed it to Fanny to read and Fanny laughed.

'With resignation,' she said, 'hardly fortitude.'

Mrs Gurden hoped Théo was well and happy in the beautiful rounded and flowing hand she had been taught at dame school, and said that Joss had written – he was such a poor letter writer she had been overjoyed – and told them how Théo was determined to be at her husband's side at all costs. Théo, coming to this, felt the irony like a blow: she was not at her husband's side and she suspected Joss had mentioned it in a very different tone to the one his foster-mother implied. But then there was a piece about young Will having joined up – and after all, he had always talked of it, long before war was declared – and if Théo had any news . . .

'Mr Howard is going to Balaclava,' said a voice, 'and he's willing to take you with him. I persuaded him it was his duty to see·you safe to the hospital or wherever it is you're going.'

Théo put down her letters and looked up. Griffith was leaning in the doorway, the hairy face of Howard in the background. Fanny, who had been trying on the lace nightcap, gave a little shriek and sat back on her heels, blushing.

'Mr Howard was going to escort Fanny to Constantinople,' said Théo firmly. 'He promised me he would.'

'Only I don't want to go to Constantinople,' said Fanny, snatching off the cap so that one of her ringlets caught up in it. 'You will not get rid of me so easily. If you go to Balaclava so will I.'

'Well, it's all the same to me,' said Griffith, you will have to settle it with Howard. I simply came to tell you I am the new owner of the paddle-steamer *Tempest* and I'm bringing her up to Constantinople as soon as I can. The engineers are knocking and banging like monkeys, she should be fit to move in a day or so. If Balaclava fails to come up to expectation

I'll give you a passage back to England at reduced prices, sailing the week after next.'

Théo stood up. Why did she always feel at a disadvantage, that she must somehow or other struggle to look him in the eye or she would never be able to repudiate him properly?

'How generous of you! Reduced prices! From what Joss told me you ought to pay your passengers to take the risk,' and then, seeing that smile pulling the corners of his mouth, that kindling in his eyes, she added: 'Would you offer us a passage to Balaclava in the *Affie* at reduced prices?'

The smile was gone. He looked from her to Fanny, and back.

'The *Affie*'s loading cargo tomorrow. It took me all yesterday and all last night to get it: figs, raisins, dried fruits by the ton. Jimmy Dye is taking her back to Liverpool with the most disgraceful crew I've ever had set foot on a deck of mine, six of them straight from the prisons for sure, and all of them proper soldiers. Still, if anyone can get her home on time, the cargo intact, and no mutiny, it's Jim.'

'But you had three able seamen,' protested Mr Howard, 'who swore to me they would never leave you, that whatever ship you sailed so would they.'

'I am touched by their devotion. They are coming with me in the *Tempest*. They don't know the first thing about steamships but they're all good steady men and will keep the stokers in order. Stokers are the devil, so I've been told.'

He went out to confer with Albert, Albert who was so sorry he was to leave them, so *désolé* about the *poulet à la Marengo* he would never cook for them. He would not enjoy the galley of a steamship, he thought, but perhaps with seventy tons of coal in the hold he could look forward to a decent fire in the stove.

'I don't know what we are to do,' said Mr Howard, 'I hardly like to hazard you both on another ship like that . . . that monstrosity we arrived in. But perhaps if we take a caique across to the other shore we might find transport . . .'

'Courage,' said Fanny, 'of course we shall find transport.'

Since Théo had risen from her deathbed, since Albert had swept away her doubts about foreigners and complicated recipes, since the soup kitchen – at which she had timidly helped sometimes – and since she had learned to cope as best she could with several very different, obstreperous, demanding men, Fanny had grown infinitely more self assured. Her husband's letters, infrequent but very loving, always gave her fresh hope and strength. She did not believe Captain Griffith thought much of her – she knew nothing of his challenging Dr Molloy for her sake – but she did not mind, for he was not a man she could ever influence simply by being good and useful, which was all she would ever be. She suspected he liked women of strong character, women of resilience whose emotions could endure neglect and abuse.

'I'll take you to Balaclava if you can find me a ship to sail there,' said the gentleman himself, poking his head back in. It sounded like a challenge, though he spoke with mild cheerfulness as if he were overflowing with good intentions, they only had to ask.

Théo, who had gone back to her letters, and was engrossed by the outpourings of Sophie Barnard's feverish mind – Miss Barnard could never have cast her eye over this, it was outrageous! – looked up, hearing his words but making no sense of them; she was far, far away in the garden at Martagon, Nelson on her lap.

'Find a ship,' he repeated, not a muscle moving, 'then I'll take you.'

Her eyes cleared. She was back in her chair in the room in Scutari. 'Where would we find a ship?'

'Who knows? Anything will do so long as it's watertight and has decent canvas.'

'How much?'

His eyebrows rose gently. 'Charge you? Well . . . Since I shan't have a crew to pay and I'm not losing precious time – though I should keep an eye on those damn engineers – I don't think I need charge you, do you?'

Mr Howard wrung his hands. He could see Théo's sharp bones made sharper by indignation. He did hope, oh how he hoped, she was not going to rouse the devil in this man. It was so easily done, and she seemed to bring out the worst in him.

'It might interest you to know,' said Théo, 'that if I had a chart and a compass I could probably sail myself to Balaclava.'

'You probably could,' and he was turning away – so that she could not see him smile? 'But I have the charts and the compass and all the rest, and the wind is rising. Dignity's not worth much in a gale in a small boat, you know.'

She knew. Once she had nearly lost her life on the rocks, grappling with that belligerent lugsail, everything to do at once and only two hands to do it when four were needed. For a moment she looked up at him as a kindred spirit, someone else to whom the sea and ships were all-important, with whom she shared a special knowledge and respect.

His expression did not change. He was gone.

'It is extraordinary,' said Mr Howard limply, foreseeing a harrowing journey on the green billowing deep, nothing dry, and Mrs Trent and the captain at odds, 'how a man of good family can lack even the most superficial polish. Why, he never tries to be civil! But he has been before the mast since he was fourteen, he tells me. We must forgive him his rudeness, I suppose, and only thank God we haven't been exposed to such brutality.'

'Well . . .' said Fanny, startled.

'Quite,' said Théo, putting up Sophie's letter to hide her smile.

They found – Théo and Mr Howard together – the ancient ketch they had both hoped, perhaps, never to see again. Two of the crew had been struck by fever, the others dared not work the ship short-handed. Mr Howard, who had acquired some words of Turkish appropriate to the occasion, asked if she was for hire. She was, but it would be as cheap for the Englishman to buy her, said the owner, seeing he himself might never put to sea again.

They beat about the price like gulls about a carcase. Mr Howard, despite the cold, grew red and flustered, dabbing at his whiskers with a huge green handkerchief.

'Whatever you paid you paid too much,' said Griffith, inspecting her afterwards with the help of Chisholm Bonnet, one of the devoted able seamen, and a marlin spike. 'She's well nigh rotten. But she'll last a voyage or two yet provided she doesn't get rough weather.'

'Oh dear,' said Howard, who had not spent weeks on the

shores of the Black Sea without coming to know its moodiness.

There had been storms in the night, a royal gale. To sail north and west must be to sail into worse weather. 'We've been in worse than this, sir,' said Chisholm cheeringly, 'you could knock the bottom out of some we've known was you to jump about too energetic like. And masts, Lord the masts we've lost, torn out and sprung, and the spars broke, down in the Southern Ocean.'

Mr Howard had no ambitions regarding the Southern Ocean. He shrank away, listening to depressing murmurings below where the captain was discussing the whole miserable state of affairs with his second mate, a Mr Graham. This gentleman, a long-nosed, red-faced Scot, had once told off Howard for walking with dirty shoes upon the pristine decks of the *Affie* and leaving blank blank smudges: Mr Howard's ears had closed to the foul epithets. A Scot and a fiery Welshman, he thought now, with all the failings of the Celtic races: they would burn up with indignation in a moment, never forgot a slight, real or imaginary, and would draw your heart out of your breast with a poem or a song you later found out was a diatribe against the blood-sucking English; they were the best fighters in the world and they wept openly like children; they were stoical and resilient to a degree and they complained all the time.

'We will be there in two days,' said Théo gently, not guessing his prejudices but perceiving the pallor of nervous apprehension. 'Has Captain Griffith finished his inspection?'

'He says she's rotten. He says she will founder in rough weather.'

Since they had to shout above the wind, and the deck was tilting ominously this way and that, his words had an ironic ring to them. But Théo, who appeared able to walk without much inconvenience and did not have to grasp the rigging in undignified lunges to remain upright, only smiled sweetly.

'The sea holds no terror for you,' cried Howard, scrambling beside her as they made their way to the stern where they had tied on the rowing boat; would he ever get in it again, it leaped and wallowed so? 'Have you no fear at all of drowning?'

'My father drowned,' she said, 'and an uncle. And my great-grandfather. It wouldn't be true to say I'm not afraid.'

It was in the nature of some loves, she thought, to survive shock and fear, to be the fiercest the very moment they might kill you. She had known what it was to exult in a storm at sea.

'We cannot manage with only three men for crew,' wailed Mr Howard, 'I do not see how it can be done.'

But in the morning, a grey squally morning, the ketch stood out from Scutari into the Black Sea, the land fell behind, and all their worst premonitions were realized.

'Oh, how I wish you'd gone to Constantinople,' said Théo to Fanny, who was suffering in the stuffy cabin they had hastily washed and disinfected. 'You would do far better on deck, the fresh air would help.'

But Fanny shook her head and gave herself up to misery. Théo took off her petticoats and put on woollen drawers and a pair of Mr Graham's trousers under her skirt. He had handed them over at the request of his captain, who had sworn there was nothing more sensible in such conditions, but only Graham was anything near the right size. With an extra jacket, a scarf, and her heavy cloak, she felt up to the rigours of the deck.

'We seem to be all right,' was Mr Howard's faint comment as she emerged from the hatch, 'we are on course and the wind is . . . is holding. Or something. And she's carrying all the canvas she can without damaging herself,' he added, for he had been in tedious consultation with the mate upon the subject.

Théo glanced aloft. As an indication of the state of the timbers below the two rags of sails were hardly encouraging.

'Have you ever taken the wheel of a ship?' asked Griffith, appearing at her side and following her gaze, dropping his voice to say: 'I don't like to alarm poor Howard but we've water coming in at a spanking rate.'

'But you don't mind alarming a "lady".'

'Well, I would hardly have set out on this venture if I expected to drown. And so long as the pump can cope . . . It's an extraordinary thing, held together by prayers and spit says old Chisholm, who's keeping it going, a tribute to man's ingenuity and the low value he puts on his skin. But have you ever steered a ship?'

'Yes.'

'A Faurel clipper?'

'Once. Only once, and with my father's hands over mine. They wouldn't have thanked me for putting the ship on the rocks. But there was a schooner, and a strange old sloop out of Le Havre. My father took me on that too.'

'I thought your father was a doctor?'

'Oh,' with a fleeting, loving smile, 'a thwarted sailor. He was mad to do medicine when he was young, but of course he still had a half share in the company with his brother John George. His brother died young in an accident, *his* son Alexandre took his place, and so my father spent a great deal of time helping him get used to the business. I don't think they got on very well, and Alexandre had a great many new ideas; some Papa welcomed, some he resisted. Oh, Alexandre is very . . .' she gave a little laugh, remembering, 'very stuffy, very correct. He wanted innovation but not at the expense of taking risks. My father said there must be risk, that was what business was all about. There were . . . rows. Of course. Then Papa wanted us: Louise, Marguerite — my sisters — and I, to have a share in the business. It was the tradition only the sons inherited, and we had good portions anyway, but he minded about it, he wanted . . . I believe he wanted to keep part of himself in the company even after he was dead, do you understand? He loved the ships. For one very terrible week he even proposed I should go into partnership with Alexandre. I was only seventeen then. There was an outcry. Mama was horrified, Alexandre witless. The idea was put aside. I don't think Papa forgot it, it was just put aside until another time. Then he drowned.'

The man at her side was silent. He was watching the way the tired old canvas drew, the way the bow dug into the water. At last he said, more softly than she had ever heard him: 'I'm sorry. You missed him, of course. And you were not allowed in the business.'

'I was not allowed to set foot on a ship again. What have "ladies" to do with ships? Except to travel from place to place when absolutely necessary.'

He drew her to the wheel. He said nothing but Graham moved aside. Then her hands were on the spokes – such a poor, splintering wheel for this kind little ketch that had once spread ten times the canvas she was spreading now – and the spokes pushed against her palms as the great banks of water rolled under the keel, and the wind whipped her hood off, and the old feeling of peace and joy came back.

'Keep her . . . so,' and a cold hard hand covered one of her own.

Then he lodged himself somewhere behind her. She could smell his pipe.

'Watch her! Watch her. If she broaches to in this we'll be swimming to Balaclava. And I would stake my life on Mr Howard not being a swimmer.'

She smiled. The smile was not connected with his words but with a sense of freedom, personal and profound. She felt light-headed, feeling the little ship come steady under her hands, seeing Graham purse his lips under his forest of beard in reluctant approval. She was aware she had been granted a rare privilege, being allowed the wheel alone, that Griffith must have confidence in her ability; now when he corrected her course he made no move to guide her hands.

And then she remembered Rozel and her wedding night, and the sea on the rocks below the windows, and her certainty that she would sail again, but not in familiar waters and not with anyone she knew. Alex: she was sailing to find out if Alex was alive. She said: 'I must go below to Fanny,' and gave the wheel back to Graham, ducking away in a rush of spray for the companion.

They came to Balaclava on the last dying note of the storm that had nearly swept away the British army entrenched before Sebastopol, had sunk its stores and winter clothing in the outer harbour, and had wreaked havoc and destruction everywhere. Dismasted ships, general wreckage, spars, ropes, boxes – the ketch, listing badly and take in more water than the pump could cope with, pushed through them all into the inner harbour and came to rest.

There were vessels everywhere, crowded by the warehouses, tied up at the quays, anchored out in the fairway. There were barques and brigs, iron warships, steam tugs, the dread hospital transports.

'What an extraordinary place,' said Fanny, who was beginning to think she would never be dry or hungry again. 'What great cliffs!'

Théo handed her the captain's telescope. 'I do believe they were all right, when they said it was worse than Scutari.'

There had once been a fishing village – white houses? – but now there were huts and hovels, filthy and ruinous. The road that led up to the Heights, seven miles away, which looked down on Sebastopol and where the army was condemned to spend the winter, was a quagmire and would become impassable. And the harbour itself, full of the debris of the great storm and the worse debris of the battle of Balaclava, and all the amputated limbs and the bodies of the dead thrown out of the transports, and the Turks struck down by cholera, and the animals, and the entrails of animals killed for food, combined to form a ghastly scum.

'I feel ill,' said Fanny, and handed back the glass.

Mr Howard expressed the opinion they were better off on the ketch, a heavy judgement on what he could see of the shore for he had nearly died of fright and seasickness and had already vowed to purchase a berth in the *Tempest* and return to civilization and a good fire at the first opportunity. Griffith, however, brought their bags on deck.

'She's settling,' he said. 'You may stay if you like but I don't care to reckon on your chances if you get a mouthful of that soup. I know the master of the *Alice Ware*, that barque beyond the steamer there. If you're lucky he'll take you on board.'

They rowed to the shore, Mr Graham sunk into his beard, Chisholm Bonnet knocking the worst out of sight before Fanny could focus properly, Mr Howard with a handkerchief to his nose. Théo sat straight and still, her short hair invisible under a strikingly severe bonnet, the last of the clothes she had brought from England. It was cold, and her cheeks were pink from the wind. She did not care about their wild passage from Scutari – after that first morning when she had stood at the wheel she had felt tired and lost; she did not care about the state of Balaclava, about Mr Howard wanting to go home, or Fanny risking her life to stay at her side, or the vague possibility of clean dry bunks on the *Alice Ware*. She cared only that Alex was alive.

Griffith helped her out when they touched land. There were duckboards sagging into the mud. She gave him her left hand and the heavy ring slipped over her knuckle. He rammed it back without looking at her hand as if she was a child, hauling her the last yard to comparatively dry land.

But there was no dry ground in Balaclava any more. Balaclava was a swamp, and a swamp in which men and animals perished, of sickness, wounds, and starvation, and lay where they perished until someone could be beaten into clearing them up and putting them, most probably, into the harbour. There were all the old horrors of Scutari — the destitute women, the skeleton children, the scavengers — but they seemed even more hopeless here, more destitute, more cruel.

The General Hospital did not inspire confidence. Griffith took Théo there alone, having left the others to discover some means of communicating with the *Alice Ware*: 'Give Howard something to think of apart from himself,' said the captain heartlessly.

'I think you make too much fun of him.'

'He ought to be sitting by his own fire reading a book.'

They were being kept waiting. They were being treated in an offhand way. Neither Théo nor Griffith protested: it did not seem right to protest in a place so full of the sick and dying. After a long, long time they were ushered into a cramped office and a doctor looked in, asked a question, was gone again. Then someone else, in a blood-stained coat, and then a boy with a bucket, and a woman in a dirty apron. Then a man with a sheaf of papers in his hand, his face grey and his eyes scored round by weariness, came in and said, without introducing himself, without inquiring who they were: 'You're asking about a Captain Trent, 17th Lancers. I have him down here as dying on October 10th. I'm sorry. Is there anything else we can do for you?'

It was not supposed to be like this, thought Théo; she had been going to find him, had been going to take him back to Rozel. Alex, Alex . . . 'I don't love you. It would be unjust not to tell you.' Alex, Alex . . . He had been so young and sure of glory. From miles and miles away she heard Griffith's voice, controlled and hard, asking the cause of death . . . The cause of death . . . He couldn't be dead, she thought, he couldn't be dead. She had never really believed he would die.

'Cholera,' was the reply; she could hear pages fluttering. 'We've had so much fever, dysentery . . . I'm afraid he was put in a communal grave. Is this lady his wife? She's going to pass out . . .'

But she was not. She turned her face to Griffith's shoulder and felt his arms hold her fast above the void. She could hear the sound of his voice but could not make out the words nor if they were intended to reassure her or the hovering doctor. There was someone screaming somewhere, a high-pitched hopeless screaming, and the smell of blood and vomit. They had no time to offer consolation, she could understand that . . . Amid so much suffering who would not put on what armour he could find? The man's eyes were glazed with disinterest, he wished she was gone. He had nothing to show her but a name on a list.

This time she did faint, and Griffith caught her, swearing, and the doctor shrugged and went out.

19

There was a strong smell of Stockholm tar, rum and curry. The crew of the *Alice Ware* were doing their best to overcome the stench of the harbour with a greater one of their own, not so redolent of mortality. Indeed, they were all doing their best to counteract every dismal inconvenience and horror of Balaclava, from holystoning the deck every day to replacing, unnecessarily, all the running rigging, and, on the few dry days, painting ship, a brave and hopeless exercise. If they could have done so they might have lifted the old *Alice* bodily and carted her off to the top of the cliffs, to shore her up in a safe place where she would not be contaminated by that everlasting filth. As it was they did what they could to dissociate themselves from it, so that now their beloved ship rode like a white swan on a black and haunted lake, only her inaccessible bottom and chains fouled by corruption.

She had seen a great deal of the world had the *Alice Ware*, had once been a French privateer in the last days of the Bonaparte wars, rigged for speed and capering about at close quarters with nimble frigates and rich Indiamen. Then peace had altered her appearance, taken out her gundeck and given her proper holds, changed her vast spread of canvas for a more sober suit of sails. She traded in the China Sea, along the African coast, down to South America; she was nearly lost in the Roaring Forties, she ran aground in the Nile delta. Now she lay at anchor in the harbour at Balaclava, such a lovely harbour, practically landlocked, a lake reflecting the surrounding heights, and brought to this stinking, suppurating pond in a month. Only half a mile long and a quarter wide, it was inadequate to serve as a supply depot for the dying army. Of all the places the *Alice Ware* had been it was the one from which she would fly the quickest as soon as she had sailing orders.

Théo opened her eyes.

She was in a tiny cabin, fitted up with a bookshelf and a couple of hooks for a wardrobe. There was a window but the deadlight was firmly closed over it. There was Fanny's shawl on a trunk wedged up against the locker.

She could not remember how she had come here from the hospital. She knew Griffith had been harsh, quite unnaturally harsh, apparently as unfeeling as the doctor who had disappeared so abruptly, and he had half supported, half dragged her out into the air and told her to stand on her own feet, damn it, did she want to be carried? And nobody had taken any notice. There had been men everywhere, soldiers, French and British, and women, in rags most of them and none too proud to beg, but none of them had taken any heed, had stood aside as Griffith propelled her on and on, down and down, to the harbour. She recollected a boat, she had been sick ignominiously over its bottom boards. Griffith had said she might as well have tried to lean over the side, she could hardly make the harbour worse than it was. For the rest she had lost time and sequence and sense. How had she come aboard the *Alice Ware*? This must be the *Alice Ware*. She could not remember a ladder, or anyone there to greet her, Fanny or Mr Howard. There was just the bitter after-effect of Griffith's cold, unsympathetic practicality, his voice keeping her on her feet, his hands steering her forward, his exasperation and anger and disdain driving her, driving her.

There was no one in the saloon, a small, stuffy saloon, though the brass lamp was like the sun and a fastidious man, a more fastidious man than Mr Howard, might have eaten his dinner off the table without a plate. Théo crossed to the companion, but a blast of freezing air from the hatch drove her back for her cloak which she had forgotten. Then she climbed slowly, grappling with her skirts, and came out into an icy twilight, in which the lights of the ships and the lights of the town made a pretty sight, and all the refuse, human and animal, was hidden.

Captain McAlister saw her at once and left Mr Graham, with whom he was deep in a most interesting discussion about sharks and Fife and the conduct of the Highlanders at the Alma, to step briskly across his beautiful deck and berate her for being up and about. He stood on more ceremony than Griffith was inclined to do, took her hand when he introduced himself, expressed his grave sympathy with her loss, and in the next breath insisted she go below and rest and recover, she had had a fearful shock.

Below was Albert, installed as supernumerary steward for the trip back to Constantinople, a little more Gallic in his sympathy but commendably restrained, for he had long forgotten the nice distinctions between a cook and a lady. Mr Howard was asleep in one of the two port cabins, he told her, worn out by his excursions, overcome by the sights – and the heady smell too, no doubt. He had declared he did not wish to view the battlefields, that anyone who did was demented, deranged, inhuman. He had shut himself up and pulled the covers over his head.

Fanny – sweet, cheerful Mrs Shales – and Captain Griffith, Chisholm Bonnet as guard and messenger, had gone back ashore to see if any news could be had of Captain Shales – was it Captain? – in case he was on the Heights. If he was then Fanny could send up a message, could see him in the morning. Anyway, they would be back shortly, Captain Mc-Alister hoped, for it was dinner time and he was loath to eat without them.

A moment later and Mr Graham came below. He chatted amiably about nothing at all, brought Théo charts to show her the shape, the dangers, the desirability of this strange harbour between the sentinel rocks. She stood limply, taking nothing in, aware he was talking for the sake of it, that he was trying to occupy her mind. What had Fanny told him? Don't leave Théo alone, don't let her think about it?

She went to lie down again. She did not want to lie down but she could think of nothing else to do. The mirror she pulled out of her shabby carpet bag showed her a wasted face, more wasted from grief now than her long illness in Scutari. Caroline would not recognize her, was her first thought, and then: nor would Millie, who had dressed her in the sea-coloured silks and the charming décolletage, and nor would Joss.

But she did not want to think of Joss, nor of her shameful longing for . . . for whatever it was. Joss had sat at her bedside while Alex had been tumbled into that hellish pit. How could he have written her letters? He was dying, he had been dead. She put her hands over her eyes and rocked back and forth crying, not making any sound even while choking for breath, suffocating and blinded. She cried for a long time, while the *Alice Ware* prepared for the night, and Captain McAlister, rather soberly and accompanied only by Mr Graham, ate his dinner, and Mr Howard snored under his blanket. Then she took off her clothes and put on her cleanest nightgown and climbed into her berth. When they sent to ask her what she would eat she said nothing, she would like to be left alone, and when Mr Graham, presuming upon their long acquaintance and mindful of his captain's instructions, knocked softly to ask if she were all right, could he do anything for her, she did not reply.

By the time Fanny returned she was asleep, a hot, uneasy sleep full of strange dreams.

The cabin was scarcely bigger than a birdcage, said Fanny, but how clean it was! Her sympathy was real, her sorrow at Théo's loss acute, but she could not entirely suppress her own joy: her husband was alive, was coming to Balaclava as soon as he could. It was wonderful how Captain Griffith had shouldered aside the protesting minor officials, a whole clutch of staff officers in fancy hats and lace, august personages from the Commissariat, a whole drunken rabble, and a whole street – or so it had seemed – of vulgar, howling ladies of vicious habits. They had sent up a note to the artillery with a poor little boy – hardly more than a boy – on a skeletal mule, the last sound mule in the Crimea he had laughingly said, and hours later down had come a reply, almost at the last minute when they had given up hope. A fellow officer of dear Gregory's had come trotting in on a half-starved gun horse, his coat in tatters, sporting a huge beard twice as monstrous as Mr Graham's, and . . . and . . . and . . .

'I'm so glad,' said Théo; and she was though to her own ears her words sounded somehow false.

'And then there's something else,' said Fanny, mistakenly thinking that any diversion was better than none and that action was a better doctor than idleness: 'We discovered there are two officers in the hospital who were in the 17th with . . . with Alex. I don't know what one is called but the other is an Edward Monkton. Do you know him? He was wounded at the battle of Balaclava, in that wretched charge when . . . Théo, should you be up? You look so hot. You weren't well enough to come. I said as much to Captain Griffith last night and he was quite as brusque as usual, said you were quite old enough to decide your own destiny. It sounded very Welsh and poetic but I told him he was unfeeling, I was so cross, and he just laughed.'

'Once you would never have stood up to him.'

'Oh, I think I decided in Scutari his bark´was worse than his bite. He has always been most kind to me, even when he thought I was being feeble and ridiculous. I would not care to get on his wrong side though . . .'

Théo dressed, listening to Fanny's views on the captain's undoubted irascibility, continual and incomprehensible – it was all his years at sea, she concluded, no refinements, no decent company, no ladies of any sort: ladies must raise the tone of a gathering, did Théo not think so? – her more decided views on Mr Howard, such a dear and so helpless, like a baby; her opinion of Captain McAlister, who might also be improved by the company of ladies; and of Mr Graham, who had been disappointed in love and had suffered for it ever since to the point of misogyny, he could not bring himself to trust another female anywhere in the world.

All this was for effect as Théo well knew. Fanny hoped to deflect her mind from Alex. Instead she succeeded in giving her the idea that Teddy Monkton would benefit from a visit – supposing, that is, she was actually allowed inside the wards of the hospital – and that it was her duty to bring to Teddy a little of what she could no longer give Alex. A kind voice he knew, said Fanny, might do wonders.

A cloud of doubts and possibilities: could she bring herself to enter that place again? But there was an air of fatalism in

229

all this. She felt strongly that Teddy Monkton being alive and being so near was an omen.

'I strongly advise against it,' said honest Captain McAlister, thinking what a damn skinny sober wench she was to be sure, how on earth had Griff acquired her? 'The town is full of fever. You have been very ill, Mrs Trent, and you've had a shock.' He did not like to say any more, it was not for him to expatiate upon grief, its debilitating effect, its derangement of the senses. He was inclined to Griff's views that the best one could do was to leave her alone.

They left her so entirely alone that day that it might be supposed they thought her too weak and too deranged to be capable of anything. Fanny, in the best outfit Millie's box and their combined bags could provide, was away to a staff officer's house, a glorified hut on a hill behind the village, to meet her Gregory – Captain Griffith had arranged the venue as the most hygienic and private place that could be come by at short notice. With her had gone Chisholm Bonnet, who was a pig's whisker, Griffith said, from being her doting slave, an undignified role for a stout able seaman. With her too had gone Mr Howard, who felt it incumbent on him as the only true gentleman to lend all the assistance he could, though nothing but her appealing eyes could have driven him from the ship, he wanted no more of battlefields, bedevilled foreign towns, or assaults upon his tender conscience.

Mr Graham had also made for the shore, and as he had a hearty conscience that never gave trouble and all shores were alike to him, he went in a cheerful mood, humming through his whiskers.

'Well, there's no lack of brothels, he should be soon satisfied,' said Griffith, preparing to row over to inspect the half-submerged ketch and decide what to do with her. 'He has the lowest taste in women imaginable and then wonders why he is always at the mercy of quack apothecaries.'

Captain McAlister replied that it was remarkable how some men, apparently intelligent, failed to learn the crudest lessons of life – and Graham a Scot, and a certainty for a master's ticket before he was twenty-five.

'Do you think I should suggest Mrs Trent walks on deck?' he asked after a ruminative pause, during which he surveyed the debris washing against his lovely ship with an expression of utter hatred. 'With all this . . .'

'If I were you I'd leave her where she is and suggest nothing. And on no account let her leave the ship.'

'How could she? My gig has gone with Mrs Shales and the others, you are about to take the remaining boat, and all she'll have left is that damn cockle you brought over from the ketch. And by the way, why not take it back, it's fouling my paintwork.'

Griffith laughed up from the rowing boat, ready to cast off. It was a rather abrasive laugh, not at all humorous.

'I'd break it up for firewood, there's not a stick to be had ashore,' he said.

Teddy Monkton knew her but he could not bring himself to smile. He was emaciated, grey, exhausted, an old man. Théo knelt by the pallet, a stinking, lousy affair, and spoke very softly into the one ear he turned towards her so pathetically. For a moment she thought he would read all her pity and horror in her face, she had never struggled so hard for a simple expression of affection and pleasure. They had not wanted to let her in, they had been difficult and gloomy and infuriating, they said he was not responding to treatment, she might shock him into a decline.

She held his good hand.

'I wish I could go home,' he said; it was all he could think about.

'Your parents are on their way by steamer. You'll be home in a few weeks.'

He had lost an arm, had been cut about the face by an exploding shell, they feared for an eye. Théo put her arm across him, avoiding the bandages, and put her head down on his sound shoulder.

After a long time he said: 'I gave Captain Trent's personal effects to Mrs McCready. She . . . She is in Constantinople or . . . or gone home. The major died at the Alma, after . . . He was grazed by a bullet . . . The cavalry was not engaged at all, it was unlucky, an unlucky stroke. The wound festered. They sent him to the field hospital and then down here. And then the cholera grew worse . . . and he died.'

'Did Alex . . .'

'There wasn't much: a letter, a ring, some money. They gave them to me when I came down to see him, said he was dead.'

It only seemed yesterday, Théo thought, that this boy had been rowing her across the harbour at Varna, frowning with the effort, on an erratic course for the ketch. He was asleep now, an unhealthy, sweaty sleep. She stood up, mutinous, dry-eyed, empty of everything but the white-hot anger at the waste, the senselessness of it all.

She was glad of the bitter wind outside. She let her cloak fall open so that it struck through her and took her breath away. It seemed a clean and godly thing, that wind. She would not have minded had it killed her.

She met Griffith when she was nearly at the quay. He had been scouring the shoreline for the damned cockle and had found it at last, run up on the mud beyond the warehouses. He was in the smouldering rage of an autocratic man who has been disobeyed, but when he saw her it was sheer relief that ignited his whole tremendous temper.

She saw him, and she knew at once he was angry: there was a stillness about him that was formidable. She drew her cloak together again, feeling wretchedly cold now, and uncertain how to approach him. She was painfully aware she had left secretly, that they might all be worrying, that though Fanny had suggested she visit Teddy Monkton, Griffith had expressly forbidden it.

He was waiting in the lee of the buildings for her to come up, and she hesitated. Dear Heaven but it was cold, and more rain threatening. She clasped her cloak, at the neck, every bone in her body aching, and all her own anger draining away as she faced his. She felt limp and stupid, numb. She could make out his fair, greying hair under his peaked seaman's hat, the set, clean-shaven face; and she knew exactly how his eyes would be, no longer blue, but as always when he was in an uncertain mood a strange, excited grey.

'Hello, my sweet . . .' There was a drunken soldier at her elbow, only a little more healthy than the almost-corpses she had seen at the hospital. He was a military version of Mr

Graham, urgent in his desires and quite happy to gratify them anywhere providing it was out of the wind and had the modicum of privacy. His thin hand pulled at her cloak.

Griffith stepped forward and sent the man sprawling.

'Help him up,' cried Théo, the worst possible thing under the circumstances, 'you've hurt him.'

'He's drunk. Leave him alone.'

'He'll die of cold.'

'If I hadn't been here he'd have had you at the back of the warehouse and given you a penny for it and you're worried in case he dies of cold! God save us! Leave him where he is and come and get in the boat, you've done enough running about after soldiers for one day.'

She pulled against his grasp but he did not let go. The pain made tears come to her eyes. She was dragged after him down the quay to where his boat bobbed on the scum guarded by a beady-eyed boy in the red, cut-down trousers of a Zouave.

'Get in.'

She got in. She sat like a stone. He watched her as he rowed and his scrutiny was almost intolerable. She hated him. She had never hated anyone in her life before and the violence of it astonished her. She *hated* him. He had no right to forbid her to go to the hospital; if she had not seen Teddy she would never have forgiven herself, would have had it on her conscience for the rest of her life. And besides, she had needed to hear about Alex, and the major, and all the others . . .

'Didn't it occur to you to tell McAlister where you were going, to ask for someone to go with you? Wouldn't that have been courteous? Where were you dragged up, Mrs Trent, that you like to give your friends a good scare for lack of simple courtesy? McAlister was nearly out of his mind, Fanny's been in tears for an hour, and Mr Howard had you robbed and dead ten times over. Don't you care about their feelings? Don't you care about anyone except yourself?'

In the sullen grey of the late afternoon, the storm clouds gathering, she hoped he could not read her face. Ahead were the lights of the *Alice Ware*, newly hung out, and in two minutes they would reach her and this quarrel – if quarrel it was – would become public. He would think nothing of exposing every shameful strategy she had employed to leave the ship undetected, would think nothing of exhibiting her as an object of reproach and shame in front of everybody, would probably consider it her just desert – and he would probably be right, which made it all the more dreadful. She could not bear the thought of it. In fact, the thought of it stirred her to say hotly: 'I don't see you had any right to stop me going to the hospital.'

'It may amuse you to know I did it for your own sake, guessing what you'd find when you got there. I spent part of the morning arranging to sell the ketch for kindling, no sane man would attempt to restore her, and then I went up to the hospital to see if I could get news of this Teddy Monkton Fanny was talking about. He was asleep but I could see how it was. You can do no earthly good for him now.'

Her face flamed. She should have known his motives would be honourable, she had deliberately chosen to see them as irrational. If she did not like his manner it was still no reason for behaving with the petulant resentment of a spoiled child.

They came under the side of the ship. She felt sick suddenly: from the smell that rose from the water, from the exertion of rowing that leaking old boat across the quay, from seeing Teddy and being able to do nothing to help. It took her a long, long time to reach the deck, anyone would think she had never climbed up a ship's ladder before, and once she was there that same cutting wind made her shiver uncontrollably.

She could not stop shivering, even when Fanny had cocooned her in blankets and shut the cabin door on the hard looks from the occupants of the saloon: hard looks, undisguised anxiety, exasperation, grim speculation. And Fanny's solicitude made her doubly ashamed, for she *had* been crying, and no doubt too she had been burning with tender information about Captain Shales and no one in whom she could confide except Théo. Unlike the captain, however, she was not given to casting a friend's sins in her face, and simply did all she could to make Théo comfortable, begging and borrowing extra bedclothes, bringing a hot negus Théo could not drink, and folding up Théo's clothes.

'Captain Griffith warned me not to meddle and you see what's come of my not taking any notice,' she said unhappily at last, thinking how sad it was sound intentions had this

234

tendency to run amuck. 'I should have known *he* would have your welfare at heart, that he would do the best thing, the thing that ought to be done. He went to the hospital himself. Did he tell you? He must have been leaving as you arrived. I'm surprised they did not mention it to you. Anyway, I believe he has sent up to the Heights to the Naval Brigade to see if Mr Westover is still attached, to . . . tell him the news.'

Théo pulled the blankets tighter under her chin and turned her head so that all Fanny could see was the short brown hair and the hump of her shoulder.

'I wish he would leave me alone,' she said, with the irrational venom of a guilty conscience.

Fanny, being wiser than she generally appeared, took no notice of this show of ingratitude, but kissed Théo good night, and blew out the lamp.

The *Alice Ware* was under orders to sail the following day for Constantinople where she would take on a general cargo for the Thames. There was a great deal of fussing about to prepare the old lady for sea, most of it unnecessary, for they had been hoping for this release every day, every hour, almost since they had dropped anchor. The tensions of this last week, this most miserable week, were swept away, and the thought of washing off the last of the Balaclava scum with some breezy deep-sea sailing set every man smiling with irrepressible cheerfulness; even the two shabby replacements, neither of whom knew how to reef or steer, who had been sent on board at the last minute, two men having gone down with dysentery so bad as to become hospital cases in a matter of hours, even they were tolerably happy. And dinner in the saloon was a light-hearted affair, a deep unwavering content underlying the frivolous jokes, the spirited conversation.

Théo kept to her cabin and ate nothing.

Then very late, when they were all set to retire, and McAlister had gone off with his charts and his mate and his lugubrious carpenter, to plot his course, settle the details of the watch, and inspect for a last time the *Alice Ware*'s suspect knees, there was the heavy sound of someone on the companion ladder and Joss walked in, bringing with him the sharp damp smell of the freezing night.

'Of course she'll see you,' said Griffith, sending the steward Pollitt to warm some wine.

'I don't want to wake her. I'm much later than I expected,' and then, glancing round, 'I suppose she's all right?'

Fanny looked down at her hands; Mr Howard smiled with a terrible, false geniality; Griffith raised an eyebrow.

'She'll be all right in a day or two,' he said. 'She'll probably be better for seeing you. She might cry. I've always been told crying is good for the bereaved. Take a seat. Have some wine. Fanny will go in and see how she is.'

Joss, stooping under the deck beams, flung off his cloak and sat. There was a stove alight, a blessed warmth; it was burning the carefully chopped pieces of the damned cockle which had been condemned with reprehensible eagerness and executed in an hour: they were so short of fuel. He held out his hands to it. He had received Griffith's note this morning but had not been able to get away, had been shot at while leaving, had had immense difficulty coming by any transport, and was in a black depression. No words in the English language could convey how deeply he missed his engine room on the *Satyr*, thank God he could return to it on Monday, return to an orderly life, sanity, and the everyday, acceptable squalor of one of Her Majesty's warships.

In her cabin Théo could hear him answering questions, asking them, thanking Pollitt for the wine when it came. He had slipped back a little into the accent of his boyhood as he always did when he was upset, but Griffith was making an effort to draw him out by talking ships, not Joss's favourite subject though by degrees it brought him to a better frame of mind.

Then her door opened and he came in, shutting it behind him very quietly as if he were afraid she was asleep after all. She struggled to sit up, staring out at him from her blankets like a startled animal. Her hair did not seem to have grown at all since he had seen her last, and her face was, if possible, even more cadaverous, her eyes huge and, he felt, oddly shadowed, as if she were determined no one would come at a glimpse of her soul.

'I need not ask how you are,' he said, since there was no time to stand on any kind of ceremony. 'Mrs Shales tells me

236

you've attempted all manner of things beyond your strength. It's hard to expect a man to have sympathy if you go knocking yourself up on purpose.'

He wedged himself on Fanny's trunk and now he was directly under the lamp Fanny had relit she could see the new strain on his face, every line more deeply cut. There was the grey pallor of misery too, acute, unrelieved misery.

'Is it very bad up in the trenches?' she asked.

'The animals are dying, there's no forage; the men are dying, there aren't enough tents, blankets, rations. It's bad enough; you might say it was the outer reaches of Hell.' Only the outer reaches, said his eyes, January or February might see them in Hell itself.

'And *Satyr*?'

'She should be here in a few days. I hope they've missed me sufficiently never to want to part with me again.' And then, with the abruptness of a man who remembers his manners but is struck with awkwardness: 'I'm sorry about Alex. I'm sorry for the way he died. You must try to put it behind you, go back to Jersey.' He was reddening slightly, ashamed he should sound so trite, so very absurd.

But his words meant nothing. She was chill and numb where Alex was concerned. She did not feel like crying; she did not feel at all. It was as if her fainting at the hospital – she had never fainted in her life before – had been the extreme of her reaction, now there was nothing but calm, silent acceptance.

'I haven't heard from Millie for a good while,' Joss said, in a valiant attempt to ease the conversation to a more pleasant plane. 'Have you? It worries me a little. Was I cut off behind the enemy lines she'd contrive to get a message by pigeon, she directs the post by willpower, I swear.'

'No, I haven't heard since she sent me a box in Scutari.'

He fiddled with his cuff. For some obscure reason he felt ill at ease, he remembered feeling something of the kind in Scutari, as if everything he had liked in her had been destroyed and they could never again resume that close, affectionate relationship, almost brother and sister, that they had once shared.

'You are going to Constantinople?' he asked with a worried

frown, 'you aren't going to stay here? You're not well. And there isn't anything you can do.'

'It seems to me there's so much I could do,' and more softly, 'if I was allowed. But no . . . I have let all my ambitions go, I haven't the strength to fight for them. They were quite praiseworthy ambitions too. I expect I shall go home and take my place at La Croix, and by the time I leave off my black dress – if I ever do leave it off – everyone will have forgotten that I ever went away.'

The bitter mocking note was new. It was something else he found he did not like. A memory of the Théo he had taken to the Otmoor farm, a Théo at home on the settle with the children in her lap, strayed into his mind. He had lusted after her all night, he remembered, she appealed to him so in his fragile mood; and if she had been anything but what she was, and if she had been obviously willing, he would have sought the catharsis of making love to her, quite selfishly, and mindlessly, and furiously.

'Surely you don't have to go back to La Croix. What about the house at Rozel?'

'I couldn't live there.'

'You may feel differently when you reach home.'

'I don't think I have a home. I don't know . . .' – a blank, pale look – 'I used to think I would die if I left the island. I knew at the time it was silly, but there are some places . . . Some places get a sort of hold on us. It may be illogical but it is so. I do believe Fanny will always think of that dark and terrible little room in Scutari with affection because she nursed me out of the cholera there, and she would go back if she could just to look at it, for old time's sake. That is irrational, if you like. I used to feel like that about La Croix, I felt attached to it, almost physically attached the feeling was so strong; and even though I'd been unhappy there I didn't want to leave it, and with Millie in London . . . All I wanted to do was go back.' She paused, drew up her knees under the blankets so that she could rest her chin on them, and the light turned her hair to dusty gold.

'I don't feel like that any more,' she said.

'That's grief. It'll pass.'

The words meant nothing, she realized, he was mouthing

238

respectable platitudes because he could not think of anything else. It was as if the sight of her had suspended his intelligence, whatever wit he had possessed. He sat rather lumpishly, blinking in the lamplight, and she knew he wished he could get away. Once he had moved to take out his watch but had turned the gesture into an uncomfortable shrug as if his jacket were pulling across his shoulders. He, who had never minded offending her, knowing he would be forgiven, now feared to look at the time without giving offence. And she could not help him to be more open, more natural, not in this present mood of cold despair, resentment, confusion, deep, deep sadness.

'Will you stay on board when you reach Constantinople? Mr Howard has taken a berth on the *Tempest*, he tells me, but Fanny seems to think you don't care to travel any further with Griffith, she says you have fallen out. I can't stay I'd care to risk my skin on that smutty old barge whether I'd fallen out with the man or not, but you might be more comfortable keeping with friends.

'Captain Shales has asked Fanny to go home on her.'

'And will she?'

'I expect so.'

Joss fell silent. It occurred to him irrelevantly that he had never before had to make an attempt at civilized conversation with a woman in her nightgown. He was rigid with caution and conscience. He had no idea how to make her smile, nor even if he ought to try; he had no idea whether she was pleased to see him even, nor whether he cared one way or the other. He had come in answer to Griffith's peremptory note out of a sense of duty rather than affection. He had reflected on this during the long cold ride to Balaclava on one of the remaining pack mules; he had reflected and come to no conclusions. Perhaps affection and tenderness had been frozen out of him on the Heights, where apparently life was so cheap a whole army could be left to rot for lack of a few hours' forethought and the slightest attempt at decisive management; perhaps he had grown indifferent and brutalized, though a few weeks seemed a short time to bring him to such a pass. Perhaps the sight of Théo so shabby and low, almost as shabby and low as the poor women on the quay and in the soldiers' brothels, made him angry at her stubborn disregard of every piece of advice that had warned her not to come here: he did not feel any heating emotion but this dull leaden feeling might just be anger, sulky lumpen anger in the pit of his stomach.

'I must go,' he said after what seemed a century, contemplating the play of the lamplight on her straight hair without really being aware of it at all, without really seeing her. Perhaps if he focused properly she would see his distaste, he could find no better word for it, his distaste for her wretched position. He did not approve of women trying to be clever, or anyone come to that. Mr Howard would have driven him distracted within an hour, he was so nervously incompetent: Joss was impatient of incompetence. He would have recommended he return to his own sphere, his own close, circumscribed and cosy world, and left war to those with more reliable stomachs. If Théo had to come out East at least let her wait in some hotel or other, among women of her own kind and away from such desperate places as the General Hospital. Had Fanny said this boy Monkton, whoever he was, had his left side blown away?

'I must go,' he repeated. He had a strange idea Théo, whose eyes had never left his face, had read all his thoughts.

'Do you remember Millie's ball?' she asked as he stood up, gingerly in case he knocked his head. 'You didn't like me at all.' And you don't now, those eyes added.

'It seems a long time ago.' A long time ago she had been a small slender girl in aquamarine silk; she had had nice shoulders.

He ducked down with an embarrassed air, kissed her cold cheek, put a large hand over both her small ones.

'Get under the covers,' he said, 'you're like ice.'

And he went out, far more noisily than he had entered, partly because he was being careless and partly to relieve his feelings, whatever they were. He even banged his head on a deck beam as he was climbing the companion, and swearing at that, in a low incomprehensible murmur of lower-deck oaths which he never usually used, relieved him still further. It was absurd, he felt almost aggressive, inadequate to know his own mind or help Théo's distress. On deck he found

Griffith, bundled up against the cold and smoking a last pipe in company with McAlister. He thought they looked at him oddly, but in the dark he could not be sure.

'Persuade her to go home in the *Tempest*,' he said as he made his farewells, 'it would be the best thing she could do. There's nothing for her out here now that poor fool is dead.'

They shook his hand and saw him into the boat. He was used to getting in and out of small craft but this time he stepped off too soon and nearly ended in the dire broth of the harbour, only saved by the seaman nearest him grabbing his ankle and overbalancing him into the stern. It was as if he had been in too great a hurry to get off.

'I don't doubt,' said McAlister dryly, watching the boat pull away, 'he brought the poor lass succour and relief.'

Griffith knocked out his pipe. 'Oh, he has every attribute of a hero,' he said, 'except the capacity for affection.'

McAlister grunted. It was late. It would be as well to turn in while he could. The tug would be spitting and snarling alongside when dawn broke, expecting them all to do everything in double quick time, bumptious and impatient and fouling all the lovely white paint.

'A right cold son of a bitch, you mean,' he said.

The tug was there in the grey wreathing mist, sparks coming from her smoke stack, her master coming to lean over the bulwarks and curse indiscriminately at the *Alice Ware*, her seamen, her creaking windlass, her slow-witted mate. Fanny and Théo, who were keeping out of the way by the empty hen coops, watched the paddles thrashing frantically as she took the strain and the old barque began her slow passage to the sea.

'I wish I was not such a bad sailor,' said Fanny, gazing down the long reach of deck, creamy in the dawn, 'I wish I could say I was looking forward to going home.'

They were sharing a rug and were so heavily wrapped against the intense cold that they might have been bales of bedding someone had forgotten to take below. Fanny had been up early because she had a superstitious dread of leaving Balaclava, although she was perfectly resigned to it and would never think of disobeying Captain Shales' instructions. It seemed important she should watch the ruined town slipping away, that she should accord it some kind of personal farewell. Théo, hearing her go up on deck, had followed, and here they sat, side by side, mute for the most part, and each with very different thoughts and fancies.

They were in the outer harbour. Occasionally smuts from the tug blew back into their faces.

'I suppose we'll get even more of this in the *Tempest*,' said Fanny, brushing them from her nose. 'Is she as bad as Mr Westover makes out, do you think?'

'I don't know. I don't think I shall travel in her.'

'But Théo, you must . . . I won't go without you.'

'There will be fifty ladies and gentlemen on board if all the berths are filled. You'll have plenty of company.'

'But you must go. I'm sure Mr Griffith expects you to, and Mr Westover . . .'

'I would rather go in a sailing ship,' said Théo, which was the truth but in this case had a negligible bearing on the matter; she would rather not be subjected to Captain Griffith's dissection for longer than she could help.

They were leaving the outer harbour. The tug gave a melancholy hoot. There was the drum of feet, bare feet in general, as the order was given to prepare to make sail. And then they were out, out through that strange fissure in the cliffs, and lifting to the first of the swell. The sea was steely, far away in the distance the dim sails of two of the hospital transports bound for Scutari, and the *Alice Ware* heeled a little as the wind took her. The tug sank behind, hauling in the discarded tow; they could not even hear the splash of her paddles now, the blast of air and the rush of water drowned out everything. It was a good fresh breeze, nearly every sail was set. There was a general unspoken desire to reach Constantinople in record time: McAlister would do everything to achieve it but hazard his ship.

'Oh dear,' said Fanny, 'I knew we'd roll like this.'

'She wouldn't do it if she had a cargo,' said Théo, but in an odd, cracking voice. Behind them a voice was inquiring genially of some unknown if them ladies was coming below for breakfast, the coffee was hot, and cut along Jim and give 'em a reminder or they'll be froze solid to the bloody coops.

Jim cut along. He was a tall thin boy whose body seemed to have outgrown his head. His Adam's apple shot up and down nervously, and he begged to inform them breakfast was ready all on one high-pitched note.

'I don't think I feel like anything to eat' — Fanny rose unsteadily — 'but perhaps coffee,' and as the deck heaved she clutched at the boy who, taking fright, stepped back out of reach. She tottered aft, grabbing what she could until the mate, catching her on the roll, helped her to the companion.

Théo stayed where she was looking up at the yards and rigging, at the sails as their colour changed from grey to faded tan and the day broke properly at last over the uneasy sea. The smells of tar and sailcloth and salt water, of a good old ship working her way under a fair press of sail, were so familiar that for a moment it did not matter which ship she was nor where she was sailing. She walked to the side, hooking her arm round a backstay and hitching the rug plaid-fashion over her shoulder. What had she once promised herself? 'I will come back, I will not marry, I will sail again.' How foolish, how very, very silly. But then the girl on the beach had been a very different creature from this Théo afloat on the Black Sea. But after all . . . perhaps it was only at sea she was truly happy, though even that was a ghost of the old happiness now, a fractional lift of her heart. She looked down into the water, grey-green, cold, hissing back from the bow, and after a while the drift and spray wet her face so much there was no saying which was sea and which was tears.

The poor incensed Pollitt, who thought it shabby behaviour not to come to table when called, stuck his head out of the companion and asked a question of the man at the wheel. Griffith, who had been leaning on the taffrail, fixed him with a daunting eye and told him to mind his business below, the lady would come when she was ready; it was an exceedingly daunting eye: Pollitt gobbled a little, drew in his head, and retreated.

20

There are some people who can judge to a nicety when causing a sensation will be to their advantage. Millie had come ashore at Constantinople, had repaired at once to Lord Stratford de Redcliffe's magnificent residence, and it was said that even the myrtles and cypresses in the gardens were now bowing to the shock waves. He could not deny her absolutely, he could not profitably write her off as an eccentric, he could not — though how he longed to — refuse her an invitation to his receptions. She was not only a lady, she had the ear of grossly influential people, and so many and so immoderately chosen that her circle included friend and foe alike — friend and foe to himself, that is: no, it would not do to cross her. He was even forced to accept her travelling companions, an extraordinary tubular large-nosed squinting lady called Miss Cole, of whom he had heard from several learned gentlemen — it was as well she had a brain, she seemed to have little else of interest; a florid, tight-lipped gentleman, something like a new-fangled country squire — quite large estates but no interest in the land — called Barnard; and Barnard's daughter, a tall dark handsome girl with decided airs and a great deal of enjoyable spirit. They had all made a quick and dirty passage in an excursion steamer at quite evident expense: they had not only had the best cabins but the ship had made the fastest journey of the year, there was a distinct ring of bribery about it. They were in the East not to view the battlefields or turn Constantinople into the fashionable resort for 1855, but for varied, somewhat obscure reasons.

Millie Boswell had apparently come looking for her god-daughter, at least someone's daughter who was very dear to her, whose husband, a Captain Trent, might be supposed carrying out his duties before Sebastopol; but Mrs Trent had lately had the cholera and Captain Trent's whereabouts were unknown. Millie's anxiety had reached the fever pitch necessary for her to make a nuisance of herself in high places. The reports in *The Times* grew worse and worse. She could no longer sit in London twiddling her thumbs. So here she was calling on every officer available who might be expected to find an answer to her questions: how was Captain Trent and was Mrs Trent with him? Her strange colleague Miss Cole, on the other hand, was interested only in the flora and fauna of Asia, was apparently prepared to strike off into Turkey armed with a tent and butterfly net. She wished for permission to do this, written, unequivocal permission, and she haunted the embassy secretaries to this end. She picked up more words of Turkish in a week than some of them had acquired in years, and when they thwarted her as best they could, made herself known, without any letters of introduction, to the Turkish authorities, who took her credentials on trust, plied her with sticky sweetmeats and coffee, and listened sympathetically and with ardent curiosity to her remarkable plans.

Mr Barnard, who had been unwell at sea, poisoned by the smoke perhaps more than overcome by the more usual nausea, had come because his daughter had persuaded him. She was a persuasive young woman. Now she was a young woman and no longer a spoiled girl, her ability to get exactly what she wished from her doting parent had been strengthened considerably. She was an exact copy of her mother, for whom he had had a corresponding weakness, and besides, she was clever enough to know what appealed to him, to his sense of position, of self-importance, and of propriety. She was no longer the prejudiced, affected girl Théo had first met at Martagon. Joss had knocked her largest prejudices on the head and the lesser ones had tumbled down after them. Whatever her father thought was the purpose of their trip East, and she had given him a great many sound, oh quite remarkably sound reasons for it, her one desire was to marry Mr Westover.

Millie knew all this of course, for her anxieties about Théo had not blinded her to the undercurrents swirling about Martagon, whence came passionate, occasionally almost inde-cipherable letters begging her for news of her godson. Even Miss Barnard was brought to write along the same lines in the end, for she feared Sophie was worrying herself into consumption. When Millie announced her impending trip to Constantinople, Sophie had pleaded to come as companion, pointing out to her dear papa the educational value of such a journey, the fact that all manner of high society could be met in the East, that to be chaperoned by Miss Boswell would be an honour and a privilege, and that the doctors had said time and again she needed a change of air – *sea* air, did he not remember? If he saw through all this he chose not to make a fuss. He could not bear the thought of his only child fixing her attention on a man who was not only unworthy by birth but had a casual and cocksure manner as well. He could never like Joss Westover. On the other hand he had come by a better understanding of Joss's exact rank in the navy, of his likely salary, his income from his mother's small bequest, and his expectations. His expectations were splendid.

Mr Barnard was indeed a new-fangled country squire. He put his bad fortune down to the agricultural depression and did not see that a great deal was caused by his own neglect and his agent's voracity and incompetence. He did not know what a good field of wheat should look like, so was never astounded to be told the weather was to blame rather than the husbandry. Sophie's portion was assured, for it came mainly from her mother's family and could not be touched, but as to his leaving her anything more, or Martagon itself, that was now growing doubtful. Martagon was heavily mort-gaged and the rents still falling, the harvests still uncertain, and even the agent now quite moody, in the manner of those rats upon the famous sinking ship. Joss Westover's expectations – on his marriage Millie would allow him several thousand a year and after she died, oh, oh, a vast fortune, a heap of money, a nabobbery! – yes, Mr Westover's expec-tations could no longer be sneered at. He would have to be suffered at Martagon after all, dining off his own plate, damn him.

Millie did her best to discourage her entire entourage: she

wanted to travel alone. She had grave doubts about all three of them in any case, especially Sophie, who was proving – in her letters certainly but no doubt shortly in the flesh as well – to be a headstrong and argumentative. And Millie had no wish to see Sophie and Joss letting fly at a venture – for that was what she thought a marriage between them would be: untimely, ill considered, and sure to end in heartbreak.

In Constantinople she felt like a commanding officer whose troops, though professing absolutely loyalty, take every opportunity to act independently and without authority. There were several burning moments when she was ashamed to be associated with Miss Cole, who interspersed her imperfect Turkish with Latin tags much to the consternation of bewildered officials, and whose bonnets had apparently all been made by a South Sea islander who knew nothing of European fashions and could only work in raffia. There were even more moments when she wished some dashing young officer – and after all there were plenty of those – would carry Sophie Barnard away over his shoulder and cause such a scandal her future was assured. In fact, in the eight days she had been in Constantinople, she had had so few pleasant, quiet, reflective, enjoyable moments she was beginning to regret her decision to come – and still no news of Théo, who had certainly been at Scutari but had since vanished from the face of the earth. Only at breakfast, which she took in all weathers on the balcony facing the Bosphorus, did she have any time to herself.

She had been lucky enough to rent a small villa recently vacated by one of the embassy staff; it was indeed a very small villa, but it had lovely gardens and exceptional views. It was only hers for a fortnight, she had had to exert all her charm to get it, and December was no month for drinking early-morning tea in the open air. Still, the balcony was private – only Waterloo Jackson, whom she had vainly tried to leave behind, was allowed to set foot on it. And it was while she was sitting there on this the ninth morning of her stay, wrapped up against the wind and with her feet on a hot-water jar, her precious samovar hubble-bubbling with its usual menace in the room just behind her, and hot rolls and ham promised any minute, that she looked up and saw a stately little barque sliding in towards the Golden Horn, a white-painted ship, unusual in one that flew an English flag.

'Now there's a pretty sight,' she said to Jack, who bobbed up at her side suddenly with something smoking on a plate.

He looked, a disagreeable, disagreeing look. He had no time for ships, white-painted, black-painted, with engines or without.

'I'm not a-goin' on it,' he declared in an outraged croak, 'not on your life, I ain't. I'll sit here nice and dry and keep guard on that frippery kettle of yours.'

At which point the frippery kettle blew off steam in crescendo and by the time they had mopped up and mended, the little white barque was lost amongst the other shipping, rounding the point to pick up her moorings.

They were all bundled off the *Alice Ware* with as much haste as was consistent with good manners, for she was to take on her cargo immediately and fly, they would make her fly for sure, back to her familiar northern waters. Already McAlister had the glass trained on the nearest shore where there were some lighters putting off, decidedly lighters, though of a queer bastard Mediterranean sort of rig and manned by what he feared were men in turbans. He was sorry to say goodbye to Griffith, a true friend though a Welshman, and always to be relied on, though it was true he was an awkward man to have as a passenger, his keen eye missed nothing and his views on rigging were extreme – witness that over-sparred and over-canvassed little beauty *Aphrodite* – and did not accord with Captain McAlister's own. He was not sorry however to get rid of his other passengers, especially the women and the cook Albert who had not made himself popular on board at all, there being a lot of old-fashioned prejudice against the French along the lines of 'they wasn't on our side ever before, why should we trust 'em now?' and darker but unspoken prejudices about his sexual proclivities, which were uncertain.

As for the passengers themselves, they were rather glad to leave the ship, for they were in danger of being battened below to keep them out of the way, the sense of the *Alice Ware*'s urgency was so great. And the *Tempest*, at anchor in the far reaches of the harbour – indeed, they had passed her coming in – looked so respectable in a coat of new paint, black and red, her paddles picked out in yellow, and so large after they had expected something the size of the Balaclava steam tug, that they were quite eager to get aboard her; all except Théo, that is.

That she was mutinous and discontent, in a chaotic, wild mood, a living flame of indecision, contradiction, and pure anguish, Fanny knew, and Mr Howard knew in a dim, imperfect way, and Griffith certainly knew for he had been on the receiving end of her considerable flash of temper at breakfast when the question of transferring baggage to the *Tempest* had arisen. Though everyone else at the table had held a collective breath, Captain Griffith had been reasonable and consoling, as reasonable and consoling as a man could be who knows that reason and consolation are not required, that anything he might say would be taken amiss, and that violent longing, and a violent sense of loss, and equally violent dread, made Théo deaf to any argument whatsoever. He was very gentle when he suggested that, until the *Tempest* sailed, she would be wise to take a cabin instead of trying her luck ashore: Constantinople had filled up amazingly, there were tourists crammed into every space. He was equally gentle in making sure she did not see her bags transferred to the waiting boat so that, when it came to the point, she was more inclined to follow them than not, especially in view of Captain McAlister's rather brusque goodbye.

The *Tempest* reeked of new paint. She also reeked of coal, a great deal of which still littered the deck, rather spoiling the air of smart cleanliness she had had from the sea. Some very hasty redecorating had been going on below, where several oddly silent and lugubrious men in native dress – eunuchs, said the chief steward behind his hand to Albert by way of explanation – were polishing the glass and the ill-treated mahogany. There was no doubt she was a handsome ship, though butchered somewhat by prolonged neglect, her owner's parsimony, and the drunken nature of her last captain. Her new owner, equally parsimonious for he did not intend to keep her a day longer than was necessary, ordered that the major outlay was to be on food and laundry: Albert was to supervise the galleys and the tablecloths were to be spotless, the bedlinen good enough for the Queen.

'They won't notice the rust then, won't take it into their heads she might break in two and sink,' he said to Fanny, whom he found admiring the fancy mirrors in the first-class saloon.

'Oh,' cried Fanny, who had been so delighted with all this show of luxury she had almost forgotten such a thing could happen, 'oh, surely she won't do anything so terrible?'

'I suppose not,' he said doubtfully. 'At least, Mr Craddock assures me she won't, not yet at any rate.' Mr Craddock was her previous mate, kept on because he was sound, conscientious, old-fashioned and deeply knowledgeable about steam, and because he regarded the *Tempest* with unshakable adoration, refusing to leave her even when she had been practically abandoned at Gallipoli and he had not had a penny of his pay for six months. He was a great bluff shambling Whitby man, brought up in cobles and ketches, but he had been an early convert to steam and steam was his whole life. Griffith, who had the good captain's knack of getting the best from any type of man, gave him to understand he relied on his advice just so long as it was sound, he was sure it was always sound. Since the previous master had left the running of his ship entirely to Mr Craddock, avoiding every last one of his responsibilities, but had never reposed any trust in him whatsoever, Griffith's open, honest confidence quite won his heart.

Mr Howard, having stowed his luggage, took himself ashore to investigate the unlikely possibility of post. Fanny and Théo watched him go from the deck.

'He is so sweet,' said Fanny, 'so harmless and eager to please. I shall be sorry to say goodbye.'

But Théo was looking towards the bow where Griffith, Mr Graham and Craddock were in close technical conversation about ballast, drinking water, stokers' rations. There seemed to be odd diversions . . . cotton shifts . . . sodomy. Words, disjointed phrases blew back to Théo where she stood in the thin sunlight, gaunt and white in her hideous black dress. Then they looked sheepish, all three, and Mr Craddock consulted his list and Graham retreated into his Phoenician beard.

Griffith strolled towards her. 'The first of the passengers is to come on board tomorrow. Do you think she's fit to be seen?'

There were three gloomy and dull-eyed stokers sweeping up the coals. Fanny said: 'I think she's splendid.'

Théo said nothing.

'Have you decided what you are going to do?' he demanded, facing her squarely so that she could not avoid his eye.

'No.'

'Well, I have a proposition. Dear Mrs Shales, do excuse us. Mrs Trent and I have business to discuss,' and he offered Théo his arm, sweeping off his hat. She gave him a cold look, she could not bear to think how ungrateful she must appear and it made her seem even more proud and withdrawn. He did not retract his arm however so she took it, and he walked her to the companion, the noble staircase, and so below.

He had had the captain's cabin swept out, scrubbed, and made fit for a more fastidious mortal than its late occupant. Nevertheless a faint lingering scent of rum remained, like the last breath of a semi-exorcised ghost, and a pile of ancient tickets and ledgers and bills and manifests in one corner seemed to draw the eye as a reminder. Griffith swept his own ledgers off a chair and offered it to Théo, who sat gracefully but full of sudden unspeakable fright. What kind of business did she have to discuss with this man?

'As you know,' he began, his back to her and gazing out of the stern window across the busy waterway, 'I already have a buyer for this ship. Now what I really want is a good fast weatherly brigantine to trade to the West Indies and South America, as fast as the *Affie* but stiffer, roomier, and a great deal less temperamental. Now I know just the ship, she is laid up in the Thames for storm repair, but she's quite new and she cost a pretty pound to build and her owner's not yet so embarrassed by his expensive young wife that he cares to sell her at any price. He's interested but he's cautious, shall we say. Now when I've sold this ironclad and paid off the monstrous debt she's run up from here to the Dardanelles, and paid off other loans, and the victualling bills, I'll be left with half the probable price of the brigantine.' He paused, and watched a craft not unlike a vinco, with an eccentric combination of square sails and a lateen, slip in between the ships over by Pera. He did not really mean it as a significant pause, he was momentarily at a loss, for now it had come to it he was shy of asking her. He would not ordinarily have chosen such a time or place, but the likelihood she would not sail in the *Tempest* left him with little choice.

'I wonder if you would consider buying shares in the brigantine?'

There was a silence. Théo was staring very hard at his back, which told her nothing. Around his bent head she could see the pearly blue of the water, and his hair was gilded in the light, the short strong hair standing up where he had dragged his cap off hurriedly. Buy shares in a brigantine? What was he talking about?

'You're the daughter of a famous shipping house,' he said suddenly, turning round, 'you know what I'm offering. In return for the rest of the capital you earn a proportion of the profit on any cargo she carries — until I can pay you off, that is,' and he moved to sit on his official captain's chair, a colossal, neatly-carved monstrosity in no way suitable to his nature or his mood, 'if you wish to be paid off. If I make the investment profitable for you, you may even consider putting money into other ships, new ships even: I have a plan for a three-masted schooner, a grand lady, as fleet and kindly as you like, and cheap to man, far cheaper than the brigantine.'

She tried not to show surprise. She should not be surprised, surely, for this was what he had had in mind all along, this was why he had helped her at Scutari, and taken her to Balaclava, and had offered her a berth for England. She looked down at her hands lying so still in her black lap, the left one clenched as it so often was now, to keep the wedding ring from sliding over her knuckle. She contemplated her nails, very short and ugly since her illness, and the raw blister on one palm from rowing the damned cockle, and her thin and sinewy wrists.

'How do you know I can afford shares in the brigantine?' she heard her own voice saying.

'You were not poor, I gather from Mr Howard, before you married, and you now own property on Jersey. I can't conceive a daughter of the Faurels being short of a thousand pounds. That is the most I am asking for, a thousand. I would raise it myself but I have taken my credit to its limit, the limit of good business at least. But you . . . You understand ships, and the sea, and the trials of captains and cargoes. I believe now you might enjoy putting your money to such a use.'

He was leaning forward slightly as if he could compel her by the intensity of his gaze to look up at him, but she would not: in case he should see the deep, spreading joy that rose like the sun and struck even through her bones? A share, perhaps as much as a half share, in a brigantine: it was what she had dreamed, walking along the bay with her father, greeting the old fishermen, the boatbuilders, the dark, tarry Bretons; it was what she had dreamed watching the *Honorine* come slipping in on the merest breath of air, her reflection barely rippled in the water; it was what she had dreamed when Vautier had spilled the plans of the *Marguerite* across the office desk and had described her, French fashion, with his hands: so, so, and so.

'Of course,' Griffith said, 'your husband might not have approved.'

She raised her head at last. 'And of course you know that hardly matters now.'

He bit his lip. She had the impression that for once he was treading delicately, that he was unsure of how best to attack and even more of her likely response. He was an ambitious man, certain of his capacities and his virtues, though these might be counted on the fingers of one hand, and ordinarily he might have bullied her in the way he had found it profitable to bully other women. She knew his opinion of women was, in the main, far higher than Joss's, for instance, but perhaps each sex has inalienable instinctive prejudices which operate *in extremis*: we resort to the manners of crude, calculating nature, to apparent malleability, subjection, the promise of imminent surrender, to apparent arrogance, autocracy and omnipotent command. If he had wanted her body he might have tried this tack, but he wanted a thousand pounds and the hope of more, so he had hauled his wind and stood off, baffled, trying to judge her strengths and weaknesses on a level he had never considered before. He had it in him to be subtle, and he had a poet's judgement of feeling, but life had never yet required he sue a lady for her money.

'I meant no disrespect,' he said slowly, 'I know you cared

for him and he is recently dead. I know you grieve over that poor child you left at the hospital and hate yourself for being of no use to him, that this brings you to hate the world in general. But as to the money for the brigantine – I wonder if such an investment, such an interest might not be the best thing for you in the next few years.'

'While I dwindle to an old maid, you mean.'

'I didn't say so. You may marry again.'

'I doubt that, Captain Griffith.'

'But can we say the deal is assured?'

'I would rather have time to think it over. I am not yet sure of my position, of the . . . the property on Jersey. It may be the case I have no thousand pounds to give you.'

'I can't believe it.'

'Perhaps you should marry a rich young lady; think how prodigal your plans could be in such circumstances.'

He had thought he had her; now he had not. Théo saw the working of vague exasperation and the first spark of his quick temper under the bland exterior of his face. Then he stood up, reached into a cupboard behind him, and brought out a bottle and two glasses.

'I believe you should know this wine: see, it has Faurel Mannelier, wine shippers, on the bill that came with it. I thought you might care to take a glass with me before dinner – dinner will be at five, I'm afraid, Albert has put the fear of God into the galley boys and they hardly dare stir in case of thunderbolts.'

She watched the glorious red splash into the glasses, good old glasses garlanded with grapes and vine leaves that she remembered from the *Affie*. Out of the windows now the water had lost all its delicate colour and was the pearly white of an English sky after rain. Feet crossed the deck overhead, and a voice cried out something, and there was the faint, faint clang of a boat coming alongside.

'Were you so certain I would agree to do business with you that you bought the wine to celebrate?' she asked.

'No, no, it's Albert's choice. But I was tolerably certain you'd be interested. Are you interested?'

'I might be.'

'I need an answer by tomorrow.'

'Then I'll do my best to give you one.'

How Caroline would have applauded this studied temperance, this determination to give nothing away. 'For Heaven's sake, why must you be so obvious,' she had cried once, 'why must you smile on everyone, take everything on trust? And there's another thing . . . Jacques Passerel.'

'He is Goosie's nephew.'

'He is a fisherman. He is not the sort of boy you should know. Do I make myself clear? The next thing he will be taking liberties and you without the wit to stop him. You are not – do you understand? – *not* to go walking alone on the beach again.'

The cabin was shadowy, night falling. Griffith picked up his glass of wine – did his hand shake a little or was it her imagination? – and held it to the last of the light.

'What is the brigantine's name?' Théo asked.

'Name? *Wavecrest* I believe. I don't care for it myself. I like the Faurel tradition of naming their ships after women. But then it's not her name I'm after. And it could always be changed.'

'You'll change her luck.'

'Perhaps. It may be for the best, who knows? We could call her *Théophile.*'

'I don't think so,' with quiet deliberation so that he looked very hard at her through the gloom and made out nothing. 'There was another ship called *Théophile.*'

'What happened to her?'

'Oh, she . . . she was put in a drawer and forgotten.'

'Cousin Alexandre?'

'She was to be a steamship. He is deeply conservative and it was a long time ago: he saw it as a novelty and a bad investment.'

'A steamer! Oh no, not for you. A full-rigged ship, clipper built, a marvel in a fresh breeze and a mind of her own – that's what I would have chosen. But there you are, these niggardly puritans haven't the least idea of what's fitting, only what pays. It was dear Alexandre's father designed it, I suppose, in the days when steam was the thing to make men clutch their hearts and gape.'

'No, my father designed her, and she was entirely frivolous:

255

she was a sort of steam yacht, not for cargo at all. He said we would sail round the world in her.'

There was an awkward silence. Then he set down his glass with a click that sounded unnaturally loud and took out his watch and shook it furiously, peering down at it.

'It's late. I suppose you must go and dress.'

'If I had anything to dress in I would do so. Do you not join us?'

'I have a great deal still to do.'

'I'm sorry. I had hoped . . . You see, today,' and she rose, shaking out her sad, crushed black skirts, 'today is my thirtieth birthday.'

At any other time: in Jersey years ago, in Vautier's office, in any unlikely or likely drawing room – no, he was not a drawing-room man – at one of Dr Frere's impromptu musical parties, so hard on the ears and the feet, she might have taken his measure as far as she was able and said to herself 'I like this man', because whatever else he was he was not dishonest, nor, she suspected, disloyal to his friends. Now she could only be taken aback that she had surprised him into embarrassment, something she had never thought to achieve. It did not occur to her to even think of liking him. She felt he could see quite clearly the dubious mechanism of her inner being, the one we would all rather keep well hidden, and that although he could admire women in general and a few in particular, he found nothing admirable in Mrs Théo Trent at all. There again, she had hated him a little while since, with the hot, industrious hatred of helplessness and grief, and the shadow still remained if not the substance. So altogether when she looked at him she saw what she had seen that first night at Poll Batty's, a man whose company she would prefer to avoid, a man not of her class, her kind, and a man who did not care for either.

'Your birthday?' He managed to look grave and sweet, such an unexpected combination she found herself on his arm and at the door before she could think of anything else to say, anything at all to show him she would accept or reject his brigantine in her own time, 'Well, if it's your birthday we must rouse out Albert and tell him to start those galley boys. I doubt there's time now, but perhaps he could manage one of his infernal *poulets* this or that, given a good hot fire and the determination of genius. And we'll have the rest of the wine sent up. Dear God, what's that unholy howling?'

There was an apologetic scuffling in the dark passage and Mr Craddock appeared, resigned, drooping. 'Oh, beg pardon, sir. I came to say . . . I'll have the lamps lit directly.'

'What's that row, Craddock? It sounds like someone being waked.'

'Oh no, sir, not at all. I'm afraid Mr Graham has got athwart the eunuchs sir. He came over all Presbyterian and ranted at them for low vile dogs, sir, and they all took to wailing and beating their breasts. Oh, beg pardon, Ma'am, I didn't see you.'

'I'm sure,' said Théo gently, 'they aren't eunuchs at all. It is all a silly prejudice.'

'Well, you should know sailors are the most conservative souls alive. And they will have their little jokes.'

But it was Mr Howard they met at the entrance to the saloon, a Mr Howard transformed by ecstasy, electric with joy.

'Oh, Mrs Trent! Théophile!'

And behind him, rising to her feet with a shake, like a little bright bird settling its plumage, was Millie Boswell.

Perhaps Théo had never been so glad to see anyone.

'It was lucky you ran into Howard,' said Griffith on being introduced to this vividly-coloured apparition. 'We sail tomorrow. You would have missed Mrs Trent and been none the wiser.'

Millie considered him. She always found it interesting to meet a man only previously encountered in letters. Since Théo had never given her a physical description she could not quibble over that, but she saw none of the unpredictable violence of mood, the disenchanting irascibility she had been led to expect; she had known men of such temper before and they had had faces lined and creased in a very different manner, oh very different. She did not doubt he had a Celtic temper, quick to be moved, as quick to dissipate, but then Théo herself had that. Were they too alike then for a workable friendship?

'To tell the truth,' said Millie in a conspiratorial whisper, 'it would have been lucky not to have run into Mr Howard, for he was causing the most tremendous scene right on the steps of the ambassador's palace, so to speak. He had arrived in a sedan chair – the dear knows how many centuries old, a poor chipped thing with no cushions, and quite possibly stolen from the Sultan's garden shed, there are so many visitors in the city and no transport, well hardly any transport at all. I don't know what the row was about, but I think the bearers had overcharged him or were trying to, and he was quite enraged, let fly in Turkish, oh quite a native. Then the bearers called him a dog, a Christian dog, taking the bread out of the mouths of their children and a lot more to that effect, not threatening at all just a low monotone of accusation, though I'm quite glad he didn't understand at all, or didn't seem to. And then a Guards officer came up, bright red coat, fresh out from England by the look of him, and officious by nature as well as training, and there was a most entrancing set-to, with everyone talking at once, even the beggars from way down in the city seemed to have arrived to make something of it, and dozens of liveried flunkeys coming out to see what it was about, their eyes popping on stalks, and some earnest black-coated secretaries and clerks as scared as rabbits, and maids and all sorts craning out of upper windows where they had no business to be. Now if anyone within a mile could have missed all *that*, Captain Griffith, they would have needed to be deaf or quite dead, I assure you.'

He roared with laughter. It was as well Mr Howard himself was not there, having gone to pay off the caique that had brought himself and Millie out from the shore.

'He is the dearest man,' said Millie in conclusion, 'and strictly speaking he is Miss Cole's friend, not mine. But though his heart is sound, none sounder, his head is sadly wanting. It looks to me' – with a sudden sharp glance – 'as if Théo is ill.'

Griffith followed her eyes. 'I believe a great deal of it is shock. I've known men go silly from it on some voyages, even die of it. But I don't think she'll die on us now. I've been trying to divert her by offering her a share in a brigantine I intend to buy.'

'Ah, so that was your interest.'

'I beg your pardon?' He looked down at her with a baldly antagonistic eye but she met it squarely, still smiling.

'You could not imagine how grateful she is for your care and trouble. She swears none of them would have survived Scutari without you. But I'm afraid she has always been suspicious of your motives.'

'My motives were not entirely selfish, though I may have thought they were myself in the beginning. You cannot leave a parcel of lubbers like that with an easy conscience however hard you may try.'

'And the brigantine? What was her answer?'

'She says she will give it me before I sail.'

'I do believe nothing would give her greater pleasure, but perhaps your price was too high; there is no saying that dear silly boy of hers did not have debts. On the other hand' – looking him up and down – 'she may have grown older and wiser.'

He could not suppress a grin. They understood each other perfectly. He liked her thoroughly from the soles of her little kid boots – so unsuitable for slopping about the Golden Horn – to the curl of ostrich plume upon her bonnet, such a remarkable, foreign-looking, notice-me-or-be-damned bonnet.

'You are talking about me,' said Théo, coming over.

'Of course we were. We were saying how pleased we will be to shoot you over the side at St Helier so that we don't have to worry about you any more.'

Théo blushed, 'I have been a nuisance, I know that.'

'Never mind being a nuisance. Think what a dull world it would be if no one made any trouble. By the way, I do hope I'm invited to dinner, I cannot bear the thought of making ponderous commonplace conversation to Mr Barnard this evening. He does not eat until late, he thinks it is more fashionable, and it is getting to the point where tea comes in at midnight, poor Di snoring on the sofa.'

The ménage at the villa was explained. It was a ridiculous state of affairs, said Millie, for Mr Barnard never set foot outside except to take a turn about the gardens, he wished he was back in his study at Martagon – what brute arrogance

259

and narrowness of mind Englishmen could show at times – and Miss Cole chafing to be away by any means: scapho, felucca, sacoleva, raft even, just so long as she could get down to Izmir and strike off into the unknown.

'I shall be glad to go home,' said Millie with a sigh, 'I never thought I should ever say so. But years ago it was Jack and Polly and me, no constraints, no untoward responsibilities. But Captain Griffith knows how it is: you cannot leave a parcel of lubbers like that with an easy conscience,' and she twinkled in his direction, as arch and irresistible as she could be.

Her wish regarding dinner was granted. It was a birthday dinner after all, and worth waiting for, though they had to wait an unconscionable long time while the galley boys, who were not boys and were thin, amiable lascars, blown by who knew what ill winds from their native coast to the bowels of the *Tempest*, and Albert re-established an uneasy relationship. There were to be no more arguments over cockroaches and maggots, not in French, Portuguese, Hindi, Greek, Turkish or Mr Graham's rolling Scots; all the extraneous inhabitants of the galley had been ejected, Albert was in command.

Poulet indeed made an appearance, and small brown things like tiny roast potatoes, and various crisp green things in dressing, and cheese, and fruit, and a huge meringue shaped like a swan by way of a centrepiece; and there was the red wine, and white, and sound old brandy, and rum and water for Mr Graham, who never touched anything else and never would, though he travelled to Tartary and beyond. It was a meal of perfect, muted happiness, not high spirits for the woman in whose honour it was given was a very recent widow, sitting at the head of the long table in her black dress, but the charmed easy atmosphere of old friends reunited, of pleasant, animated, uncontroversial conversation, and a genuine desire to see many happy returns.

Afterwards, of course, it was too late for Millie to return ashore, and what point was there, when the *Tempest* had forty berths empty and all made up with crackling fresh linen? Théo felt light-headed as she kissed her good night, but she was not light-hearted. She lay for a long time in the dark in her berth thinking of the past and the future, the probable, possible future, and of the answer she would give Griffith in the morning as his first tremulous passengers came aboard.

A thousand pounds . . . A brigantine . . . 'I don't think so. There was another ship called *Théophile*.' 'It's not her name I'm after.' . . . Alex, did you care for me at all? Was it just the money, the connection with the Faurels? Mama never cared . . . She doesn't now. Even Millie looked embarrassed, desperate even when she told me there was no letter from La Croix, only one from Louise, dear, dependable Louise, wishing me well and telling me about the children and Clarice. I shouldn't care, of course. I shouldn't . . . 'You may marry again.' Oh, no, never, never . . . Never.

And then, on and on into the reaches of the night: a thousand pounds . . . a brigantine . . . If I say yes it is bound to be a disappointment, I shall probably never even see her, and he will lose all my money. I don't care about the money, but the ship . . . I want to be more than a passive partner, I want to sail in her. He would never allow it, never . . . It is different for women who are married to masters of deep-sea ships, they can travel where they like and no one thinks of it . . . but a lady, a lady with no . . . with no function, no reason to be there. He is no fool, and he dislikes women at sea, there are none on the *Aphrodite* nor ever have been, nor ever will be while he is master and Mr Graham mate. He would never let me set foot on her deck except a rare time in port, to admire her at the quay like a dead thing, not living and working out on the sea . . . So I will say no, and go back to Jersey and see what is to be done about Rozel, and maybe buy a little house in the south overlooking the sea, not too near La Croix, not too far from St Aubin. And then what?

A brigantine . . . A medium-sized, weatherly, profitable sort. A thousand pounds . . . Grand'mère sailed the *Martha* all the way from Madeira to South America once because fever killed the master and mate and bosun and half the crew. She said afterwards she had gone to take back some of the parrots. She had her two little boys with her and nursed them and steered the ship turn and turn about with the seamen. No one told her she was a lady, she must stay below . . . Perhaps Vautier will bring Alexandre round to let me buy a share in the new ship, she's framing up already, a brig Louise says . . . No. No, Vautier couldn't persuade him to anything, he and Alexandre are like two tom cats on the wharf, bristling and backing off. I shall never have another chance if I don't take this one . . .

I don't like him much, Griffith. I've never thought about it but I don't think I do . . . He sometimes treats me like an idiot child. But look at all he has done . . . All for a thousand pounds? If I don't want to be treated like a lady, like a woman whose ears must not be assaulted by anything indelicate, whose shoes must not be wetted crossing the street, who is incapable of anything but making herself presentable . . . If I don't want to be treated like that then he is the man not to do it. So why does his attitude make me so resentful?

But it was dawn, a slow stormy dawn creaming the horizon and lighting the golden domes of the city. It was only time for deep and convoluted introspection after a long night's sleep, and Théo had not slept at all. She could not now either, but dressed and went on deck, a dim deserted deck where the last smear of coal dust had been removed by vigorous swabbing and all the seats had been repainted for the passengers' delectation. She stood in the bow looking up the length of the bowsprit — not an ornamental addition but a working spar for the *Tempest* possessed two squat masts in addition to her engines. She felt disembodied: lack of sleep, the wine last night? She felt cold and uncertain.

'Beautiful, isn't it?' said a voice behind her, and Griffith was there, his hat pulled down hard on his face in shadow. 'But all ports come alike in the end: crimps, whores, drunkenness and thieving. I wouldn't mind sometimes if we never had to touch land.' There was a pause, and far over the water a chantyman struck up on a vessel about to get under way, there was the faint squeak of a fiddle, and the essence of familiar words floated over on the sharp breeze. 'Miss Boswell tells me you are staying with her and going home in the *Maryport* in five days' time. Fanny will be cruelly disappointed.'

'So will Millie if I sail without her. She came all this way to find me, Captain. What would you have me do?'

'Oh, I understand.'

He did, though he seemed determined to be graceless about

it. Surely he was not disappointed she was not to sail with him? She had thought he might be glad to see the last of her.

'I've been thinking over your offer,' and she turned to look out over the anchored ships again, and the colourless water, the land with its dark cypresses, its gardens, buildings, domes.

'And you are going to refuse it.'

From far away she heard her voice asking: 'How did you know?'

And he laughed, harshly, which was just like him, and flung at her over his shoulder as he strode away: 'Because you dare not accept. When it comes to the point you take refuge in the rules. Yes, you, you the virtuous Théophile, who wants something so badly yet when she has the chance to get it refuses for fear of what people might think ...' And he stopped, a good ten yards away now so that he was almost shouting, 'Isn't that why? In case they should say poor Théo has taken up with a common merchant captain?'

'It isn't true!'

'Yet you want a ship, why pass up such a chance? You love ships, you love the sea. You love them more than you ever loved that boy with the whiskers, or nursing the sick, or adventuring to battlefields. Well, turn me down. I don't care. But you will be a sour frustrated old maid one day when I am a prosperous shipowner, and more than that ... I shall be happy. You, Théo my heart, will never ever be happy, truly happy, in your life again.'

21

'Why?' asked Millie. 'Why? Why? Even I am not such an old fool I can't see it's exactly what you need. You had dreams of Faurel Mannelier once before Alexandre and Caroline put paid to them; this is not the same but it might turn out to be the next best thing, might turn out as good. Théo, what were you thinking of?'

'I don't know,' and perhaps she truly did not, standing on Millie's balcony looking across to Turkey between the cypresses; how far away the war seemed here, she thought, yet every day the hospital transports came, and the caiques took their dreadful burden across to Scutari.

'He isn't a man who offers twice,' said Millie shrewdly, a frown puckering her powdery brow. 'You have lost the chance for good.'

'He ought to marry a rich woman. I believe I told him so.'

'I am sure he appreciated your advice. Jack! Jack! Drat that scoundrel, where is he? You know, don't you, that Sophie has been invited to Lord Stratford's Christmas ball and is determined to go? The *Satyr* should be in by then and she is desperate Joss should see her in her Paris dress. Paris dress! It cost a great deal of money – between you and me, money that poor fool her father could ill afford – but it is nothing like so fine as your St Helier gowns, and all her underwear is straight out of a school box it is so plain and workaday. Jack!' This last incensed shriek brought Jack at the run, a malevolent gleam in his eye.

'I can't come no faster, I was rescuin' Miss C from those boys in the courtyard, all come up whistling and whining for scraps and money and old clothes. It don't do to encourage them, they're like vultures, never go away till they've picked the bones clean. And there she goes, every morning reg'lar as ever is, with her basket of things what they shouldn't have, making them all halloo and holler and praise Allah and all the rest. Then she wonders why her toes get trod on black and blue and her cap gets knocked in her eyes.'

'I don't want your opinion of Miss Cole's charity, I need you to see to this samovar,' said Millie, in tones more of distress than reproof, banging the offending article hard with a spoon. 'Théo, come in, you will freeze to death. Why, oh why is it so temperamental these days? It either will not boil or its boils too much and blows itself up.'

'It's gettin' old,' said Jack flatly, 'like the rest of us. And it's banged up and down on too many mules.'

Théo came in from the balcony and closed the door. Now that she was bathed and laundered and tidied into complete respectability, she only looked a little better than the extraordinary, over-thin, unprepossessing woman of the *Tempest*. A severe hairstyle did not help, nor did the black dress, so utterly unbecoming it might have been sackcloth.

The *Tempest* had sailed, Fanny in floods of tears, Mr Howard almost the same. Had any of them guessed what it had taken her to say her goodbyes? And goodbyes to Albert, whose delight at her recovery in Scutari warmed her memory still, and Mr Graham, who left off terrorizing his stokers long enough to kiss her hand, an unexpected, laughable, touching gesture: they had been painful too. And Griffith? He had not stirred to salute her, he had said a few words in a perfectly amiable voice, she could not remember what they had been, and asked Mr Graham to see her and Miss Boswell to the shore.

'My dear, breakfast. What am I to do about Sophie? And Di has obtained a very, very suspect pass to the interior, I am not entirely sure which interior, I can only conclude it is Turkey. I'm certain they've fobbed her off with it, she is driving them so distracted. And she has taken to wandering about the city alone, quoting the Koran, which I fear might be blasphemous or they will surely think it is, and Tacitus, and Saadi. You know, I do hate too much erudition in a

265

woman when it isn't accompanied by an iota of common sense. She knows Hebrew as well, it is really too bad. She plunges about the bazaars – I know all this because a Mr Fotherbridge usually brings her back, like leading home a stray sheep; he is one of the very minor officials at the embassy, so minor they overlooked his absences without a blink – yes, she is loose in the bazaars, asking awkward questions which of course no one understands, and quoting Latin and Persian which they take as an affront, *and* there is her odd eye, which is looked on very badly, a sort of mark of evil. I have told her and told her, someone will bundle her up and drop her in the Bosphorus soon, but she won't listen. Ah, but it bubbles! Jack, you old dog, it bubbles!'

They made a leisurely breakfast and, in general, a silent one. There was nothing more to say about Théo's refusal to contribute to the cost of the brigantine, nothing more to say about Alex, or Teddy Monkton, or anybody else. She and Millie had talked half the night, in the kindly light of one candle, and had talked themselves out.

Only: 'There's a woman here in Constantinople I must look up,' said Théo before Millie had left her and she had slept, 'Meg McCready. She has Alex's . . . Alex's things. I don't believe there's much but I would like to have them.'

'But of course,' Millie had said, 'if she's here we'll find her. She may have left them at the ambassador's, of course.'

She had not. There was no trace of her. In the end the self-effacing Mr Fotherbridge, who had taken Millie to his heart, found after copious inquiries that a Mrs Margaret McCready had been a passenger in a barque from Balaclava bound for the London river, and which had not called at Constantinople at all but had been expected to put in at Valletta. It was of no consequence, said Théo: a letter, a ring, some small amount of money, what did they really matter? At any rate they were safe with Meg, she would receive them in good time, there was no doubt of it. And Mr Fotherbridge, divining the studied disinterest of deep disappointment and regret, pulled his glasses to the end of his nose and gazed helplessly over them into Théo's pale face.

'My dear, if there is anything I can do . . .' But there was nothing else. He bowed over her hand when she left, curiously gallant, curiously old-fashioned in his black coat as if it were first cousin to a coat of another age and should have been set off with ruffles. He was very neat and short and talkative, a lawyer by training but brought by circuitous family troubles to occupy a humble station as a clerk. His face, a very lined, crumpled face like a sorrowful monkey, and his voice, deep and resonant as a cello, gave the impression of a good man brought low by circumstance. How strange, thought Théo, how men such as this find some sort of solace in respectful friendship with Millie, something they might never do with another man, or with another woman of a different kind. Or is it that she simply has an instinct for hunting out the kind hearts? And then: are kind hearts only to be found in the misfits, the misshapen, the unlikely? Are they given such capacity for love to make up for the defects Fate has tossed them? Or does battling with the defects make them more charitable towards others?

'You look puzzled,' said Millie, meeting her in the marble hall. 'Was Mr Fotherbridge difficult? He sometimes has bad moments, can grow quite passionate.'

'Oh no. He was kindness itself. It seems Meg took ship for Malta.'

'Yes, well, that is another thing . . .' began Millie, as they went outside and began to walk. 'There is no berth spare on the *Maryport*. I grew very distressed, gave myself airs in case it should just be the usual poppycock, but it seems there really is no room at all. So I have rearranged everything. We shall all leave together in the new year on the *Saint Helena*, Heaven knows what she is – "commodious and well-appointed" they assured me, looking as if lying were beneath them, a sure sign all is not as it should be. It was the best I could do.'

'So Sophie will have her Christmas ball after all.'

'Indeed she will, though she may have to dress in a tent. I am to give up the villa in a few days. However, it will give us time to see Joss again. The *Satyr* is due tomorrow. I believe she has been bombarding Sebastopol, I can't be sure. Nobody is sure. You would think the war was being conducted in China or Mongolia or the Sea of Japan, not just along the coast. Nobody knows anything, or wants to know anything. There are commissions set up already to look into conduct of one kind or another so everyone must scurry about looking busy and staying mum. My dear girl, sometimes I wish I could find an island somewhere where man has never set his beastly foot and live there quite alone.'

'Captain Griffith said he sometimes wished he never had to make landfall.'

'Well, I salute a kindred spirit. How I do dislike rain, especially, I am coming to think, Turkish rain. Put up the umbrella, we shall share it. What about that letter from Louise? You must tell me or I shall burst from vulgar curiosity.'

'I suppose it is really your letter.'

'Rubbish! She sent it enclosed for you, for me to pass on. And I believe it was something very special, she had written your name with a very desperate amount of ink and underlined it most emphatically. It was not bad news, you would have told me already. Was it good? Is Louise going to marry?'

Théo smiled. It was a strange, wistful smile. They picked their way over the stones and the mud for a while before she said quietly: 'No, not Louise. Mama.'

And: 'Thank God!' cried Millie, gripping the umbrella handle in a perfect frenzy of relief, 'I have prayed for it daily.'

Louise had written:

His name is Jean Louis Sayard de Baptiste, and he has a house in the Loire and another in Paris. He is much younger than Mama, I rather like him. When she is being her most pettish and annoying he simply ignores her, and once left her alone and took Pierre and the baby for a walk along the bay – can you imagine: Lou in a perambulator, Clarice bright scarlet, and this fine gentleman, *very* nice-looking and *impeccably* dressed, being dragged along by Pierre to see the fishing boats! But he is that sort of man, does not stand on ceremony at all, has a kind word for everyone, knows all about Goosie's rheumatism and goes out of his way to congratulate her on her sauces. At first I thought he was underhand, ingratiating, but now I don't think so. He has found the secret of Mama: he will not pander to her in the least. And I think she is in love with him and is terrified of losing him and so makes no complaint.

I am not very good at judging people's feeling myself, but I would say he was fond of Mama in his turn, not as fond as she is of him. He might not have taken it as far as marriage if she had not been a rich woman, or is that too cynical of me? Anyway, the wedding is to be after Christmas – what is there to wait for, Mama asks? Well, nothing, of course. I did venture once to ask if it were wise to tie the knot so tightly after only two months' acquaintance – he was introduced by Monsieur Brichard, the Paris agent – but all she said, quite mildly, was that age teaches one to know one's own heart and that she hoped I did not grudge her her happiness.

Now she no longer needs to live there, La Croix reverts to Alexandre. He has always wanted to live here, as you know, but he has found a new lease of charitable intention and says I may stay as long as I like. I am in two minds about it. I don't want to leave but perhaps I would be happier in a little house of my own. I have quite enough to rent what I like, and I will have Clarice and Laurente. How odd, but Laurente has refused to go with Mama and came to me in tears asking if I would keep her on as I have no maid of my own. Anyway, I seem besieged by wailing servants at the moment, for Goosie says she will never cook for Alexandre and all the others take her lead; even Luc, who has always been so passive, has grown quite belligerent about it and speaks of finding employment with someone more to his liking. Can you hear him saying it? No, no more could I until I actually did, if you see what I mean, and couldn't find anything to reply, I was struck so dumb and silly. I believe it is all a vague conspiracy and you at the heart of it, yes you. They all knew about Papa's plan to take you into the business, to buy you a share, and how it all came to nothing, and they all have quite Sicilian notions of vendetta, it seems to me, and that this refusal to countenance Alexandre at La Croix is all part of it. Mama's share of the business is another problem: Vautier has been here time and again begging her to be careful what she does. But Monsieur Sayard de Baptiste wants her to sell out, to sever all connection with the Faurels. It might be understandable dislike of having her always reminded of her first marriage, but it is irrational and he is not given to being that, I think. It is probably for the sake of the money, who knows how badly he might need it, and Mama will not be cheap to maintain. There I am being cynical again. I wish you were here, you would make me laugh at all of it.

Oh, Alexandre is frantic with worry about the company, of course. He cannot afford to buy her out and dreads a stranger doing so, and the alternative is to pay what he must by selling some part of the business. There is a great deal of competition, and there are fast steamers to contend with and rising wages and he has had no end of bother recently with an incompetent master: the *Marthe* was set on fire due to his carelessness and is almost too badly burned to be salvaged, all her cargo lost somewhere off Les Minquiers. He says if he has to part with any more ships he will not be able to fulfil his contracts, he must keep his contracts, that goodwill once lost is lost for ever etc. etc. I expect he is right, though it seems to me he trades much upon all the old contracts and does very little about the new ones he might have if he took a little more risk, and I don't mean foolish risk. The new brig looks like a whale with its bones picked clean; all work has stopped on her until Alexandre has Mama 'sorted out'. But she will sell, I know it, for Baptiste has told her to and his word is now her law. And she will deprive Alexandre of thousands and thousands of pounds and nothing to be done about it, Vautier says, nothing.

Sophie Barnard was most striking in deep pink, black braiding and black embroidered roses setting it off, and striking was what she wished to be: the *Satyr* had just been sighted. Well, it is what Joss wanted, Millie thought, and he would hardly be human if he was not pleased. But then there is Théo . . . What in the world are we to do with Théo?

'How quiet and . . . austere she is,' Millie had said in one of her rare moments alone with Di, 'like the girl I met off the Jersey mail boat when I didn't know what to expect. Do you think it's some form of guilt? Do you think she finds herself almost glad he is dead – no, that is wrong: glad she is free – and that she hates herself for it? She seems at odds with herself in some way or other, and it's not grief for Alex, that's for sure, though she does grieve for him, a deep, complex, obscure grieving. Oh well, I am a fanciful old maid. What do you think?'

'I think Joss will laugh her out of it.'

'Heaven forbid! They will probably fall to quarrelling. And I think from his letters – such dreadful scraps – that he is out of sympathy with her, he thought she was a fool to marry Trent and she's done nothing since to mend his opinion.'

'Well, and so she was a fool.'

'My dear Di, she was a puzzle of conflicting emotions. She

was trying to please Caroline and escape from her, trying to please herself for the first time ever, and trying to please Alex as well, because he was the first personable man positively encouraged to take an interest in her. Duty warred with inclination but this time duty did not seem so terrible – the man was not elderly, nor foreign, nor obviously a fortune hunter.'

Di considered, looking back over her own extraordinary past. The vision of a tall ungainly girl in blue, rescued from total obscurity in a dimly lit corner by an equally tall and ungainly boy with a jaw like a Hapsburg, rose to torment her. They had found dancing beyond them but were both at home with Newton and Pythagoras, though it was no mathematical law made his kisses so unforgettably sweet.

'Has she never been in love at all, d'you think?' she asked.

'The poor girl has never been allowed the luxury. The least hint of over-familiarity – that is what Caroline would have called it – and the young man is whisked away never to be invited again. It is next to impossible to be satisfactorily in love at so great a distance you are perpetually out of sight of your heart's desire; it might do for the engaged or married, for that presupposes some kind of courtship first, but it will not answer when the parties are separated after the very first dance together.'

The poor girl had come to this very conclusion herself while walking in the villa gardens in a shrieking wind that did a great deal for the complexion and nothing for modesty. She had always preferred being out of doors and after her long confinement in Scutari she sometimes felt, most vehemently, that she must go out at once just to breathe the pure air. The officer who had been waiting to occupy his villa had most opportunely been redirected up the Black Sea at the last minute, though his luggage had arrived, a colossal heap: 'He has brought his family plate,' cried Millie, viewing it as it mounted up piece by piece, 'and I'll wager the trunks are full of bedlinen, every quilt monogrammed.' The trunks were followed by more trunks, a saddle, a lady's saddle, and six hat boxes, what appeared to be a dismantled sleigh, two hampers of epicurean delicacies, and a servant in the dress of a brigand.

'He is from some tribe that lives near the Aral Sea,' said Di, who interviewed him at length in a succession of tongues, none of which he seemed to understand and some of which she understood less than perfectly herself: they eventually hit upon the excellent idea of conversing in jocular colonial English, much punctuated by sweeping, dramatic gestures.

'And what is he doing here when his master has been sent to Balaclava?' demanded Millie, who could take the inordinate mountain of luggage in her stride but who was not feeling like paying another person's servant.

Some strange mooing and mouthing – as to the deaf or the lunatic or dull foreigners – and some frantic gesticulation followed. It transpired the officer's orders had put him on board a Royal Navy frigate, that its captain had refused to even consider his baggage or servant, and that both had been left on the shore. And his name, said Di triumphantly, was Khazanmoo.

'So it may be for all we can tell,' said Millie, who had tried her mountain Turkish on him without success, 'but it makes no odds: he will have to be housed and fed elsewhere.'

He was not, of course. He took up residence in the kitchen, where he appeared to enjoy taking orders from Jack and made no trouble with the strange females who cooked and cleaned. On his second morning he had accompanied Miss Cole to the bazaars, walking at her side, though respectfully and with his hand on the dagger in his belt as if he made no bones about his office as bodyguard. Millie, who had watched them go with trepidation, watched them return laden with parcels and packages and even a carpet, exhausted but apparently content, with a sudden joyful relief. She took Khazanmoo on one side and quietly suggested that in return for a small sum of money he would look after the English memsahib who was very, very clever but like a child among the wily Turks. They were indeed wily Turks, declared Khazanmoo, stroking his beard, and he would guard the memsahib with his life, but he wanted no reward – and he drew himself up and backed off, the whites of his eyes showing horribly, to prove how affronted he was by any such suggestion.

Now, after four days, he was part of the household, Di never stirred outside without him, and he had accompanied

Millie to both embassy and shipping office and struck their respective staff 'all of a heap, though I expect it was the dagger that did it, he is not a large man after all,' as Millie put it.

It was Khazanmoo who came down the steps to the third cypress where there was a little iron and stone seat, and bent forward from the waist in something that was deferential but never quite a bow and said: 'There is a gentleman in the hall, Miss,' in exactly the modulated tones Miss Cole had taught him.

'Oh,' said Théo, who had been lost in some deep thoughts of the past, 'who is he?'

Khazanmoo shook his head. 'Officer. Coat just so,' and he stood like a Guardsman and puffed out his chest, sweeping one hand up and across to indicate buttons, insignia, maybe epaulettes. 'Ship,' and he pointed to the Bosphorus, 'big,' and he threw his arm upwards in an expansive arc.

'Miss Boswell?'

'Gone to tea.'

'Oh yes,' said Théo, remembering, 'she took Sophie to see Lord Napier. Very well, tell the officer I am coming.'

The officer however had not waited in the hall. They could hear him humming tunelessly in the long summer reception room to the left of the front door. Khazanmoo, who had strict ideas on the rules of hospitality, fingered his dagger. Théo put a hand on his arm.

'I know who it is,' she said. 'Go and tell Jack.'

At the sound of her voice Joss looked round. He had been standing by the long narrow windows looking out into the garden, his hands clasped behind his back, his expression one of hard-stretched patience, irritation, heat.

'I no sooner step ashore than I receive a message Bos is here, and then on the way up from the city I meet that insufferable Barnard going in the opposite direction. Good God, Théo, how many hangers-on has Bos got this time?'

'Oh, more than you would approve, I think, but she is coping very well. Mr Barnard brought Sophie out on the same ship and they have naturally clung together, and then there is dear old Di, and Jack and Polly and Khazanmoo, whom you met a minute ago, and . . . and me.'

'It was you she came for,' and to hell with the rest said his dark, ferocious look.

She stood a little way off, and she had reassumed that air of delicate elegance that had once been so characteristic of Théo de Faurel. The black did not suit her, the puritan hairstyle gave prominence to her decided bones, her sharp little chin, but here in essence was the Théo he had first met in Russell Square.

What is he looking at? she wondered, inwardly shrinking. He had been out of temper every time she had seen him out here in the East, not so much volatile and unreliable as sullen and withdrawn. It occurred to her now, watching him move from the light, thrusting his hands behind him again and glowering from under his black brows, that this was his way of coping with catastrophe, personal and national. He was not an animal of war, his blood was not roused by bugles and drums and the howling men set up to accompany them; even before Sebastopol with the artillery he had only been moved to pity and despair. He could not get back to his ship fast enough, and even her great guns did not cause him a moment's excitement: he did not even care to inquire at what they were shooting. As for his engines, they were another matter: there was nothing in the world could stir his passion perhaps like the working of a great machine. The navy did not matter to him, promotion was important only because it brought more pistons, pipes, more horsepower under his command, national pride meant little, it was not his nature to cheer his country right or wrong, it seemed to him both naive and wicked, and politicians meant nothing at all, they were Macchiavellis to a man. But even now, he could not entirely dissociate himself from the damage the guns above were inflicting, if any at all, that is, nor could he claim to be a pacifist in the uniform of a fighting man, nor could he forget his foster-brother Will was struggling for existence somewhere above Balaclava. He grew morose and most of his fellow officers tried to rally him in vain. Given half a chance and supposing it were possible, he would have taken off his uniform and gone back to Otmoor, taking the engine with him.

This was what Théo understood, seeing his shadowed face full of ill humour and exasperation. She told him Millie was out to tea with Sophie, that Miss Cole was resting, she had had an energetic morning buying tents, and that Jack . . .

'Jack, Mr Joss is staying for dinner. Is that all right?'

'The Barnards too tonight. You'll be a merry crew. Those women in the kitchen are doing strange things to half a sheep. What am I to do with the stuff in the hall?'

'Oh,' said Théo, pausing on the threshold and seeing the pile, 'Miss Cole's tents. I think you'd better ask Millie.'

'Tents?' cried Joss, inspecting them, 'what does she want tents for?'

'She is going into Turkey. Millie thinks we will never see her again.'

'Alone?' His eyebrows rose, he tugged at the strap that bound the two tents.

'Well, Khazanmoo has hinted he will not let her go without him. He doesn't seem greatly enamoured of his master Major Scott, who took him to India with him, a dirty heathen country says Khazanmoo and raining all the time; he also feels that since he was abandoned on the quay with no provision made for him Major Scott has forfeited any right to his loyalty.'

'But she can't go tramping off into Turkey with a bandit for company!'

'I'm very much afraid she can. And Millie says perhaps it will be the best thing for her, she has dreamed of an expedition so long and been disappointed so often. And after all she may not be robbed and murdered' – and here the first real smile Joss had seen for a long time – 'she may come home with a hundred more jars of pickled lizards.'

They were not exactly a merry crew at dinner after all. Mr Barnard had a cold, Miss Cole could talk nothing but maps, camels and Khazanmoo, and Joss refused to be genial. Millie did her best but her best tonight fell very far short of what was required, and so incensed was she at the gracelessness of her guests, she refused to leave the gentlemen alone at the end of the meal – which was just as well perhaps – and deliberately scandalized them by smoking a cheroot with her coffee.

Only Sophie rose to the occasion. She had dared to consult Théo about her dress, this remote, provokingly remote Théo of whom she was now half afraid, and had settled on the famous rose and black. She was wise enough, judging Joss's mood with some accuracy, to behave with simple unaffected propriety, spoke when she was spoken to, asked sensible questions, kept silent a great deal. It might be true to say that if he noticed her at all it was with approval, and once, though fortunately she did not see, with the eyes of a man who has been denied female company for a long time. Théo saw this hungry look and her heart turned over and sank without trace – or at least she had a strange feeling in her breast and then nothing, cold empty void. She longed to reach him through his misery, for she knew for certain it was acute, black misery; longed to make him laugh, to make him once again the cheerful, argumentative, clumsily innocent Joss of the past. But there was nothing she could say to dispel misery of such proportions, and if he wanted to make love she was not the woman he would choose.

And: I was wrong, thought Millie, squinting through the smoke of her cigar, she has been in love, or is still, or thinks she is. And he has no idea, the buffoon. Has he ever? Can he ever accept people may love him for what he is? And she blew a large cloud of smoke in his direction to make him look at her, which he did, with all the mild lazy affection of a man who, if he is sure of nothing else, is sure *she* will always be true. But then, thought Millie, he risks nothing for me, I am by way of being a dear old aunt: I pose no problems, cannot break his heart, do not challenge his manhood, asking nothing in fact but a few letters and a few visits. Dear God, don't let it be the only relationship he is capable of in this life! She puffed out more smoke, a positive blanket of the stuff, and Barnard looked at her through it with venomous, red-rimmed eyes. Another thought, as furious as the rest: there he sits, Heaven knows what's going on in his head, and if he marries that girl he will never satisfy more than a quarter of his heart, nothing of his intellect. And then: and look at Théo, all her natural affections screwed down for years, burning to love someone, and she has fixed on him and is in for nothing but unhappiness.

'Don't you think so, Millie?' finished Miss Cole, and at Millie's blank look: 'I was saying how generous Captain

Griffith was, could not have been more so. Without him Théo would surely have died in Scutari.'

'Yes,' said Millie non-committally, seeing Théo's instant look of angry withdrawal.

'Well, from what I hear he was thinking of himself as well as Théo,' said Joss, 'but I allow he is a sound seaman and has an eye for a bargain: that dreadful old-fashioned paddler will repay him handsomely if he gets her home without breaking her back.'

'Oh, he will,' said Théo quietly, 'he is nothing if not tenacious.'

'I think he sounds rather frightening,' struck in Sophie, who felt it was time she was noticed, 'ordering everybody about so. And not even a gentleman.'

'You will find,' said Millie crisply, 'that gentleman are born and not made, my dear. Not made, I mean, by social class or fortune or studying books of etiquette. I have known many a duke who was never a gentleman in his life.'

Through the haze her eyes met Barnard's again, and after a moment his fell. Joss suppressed a grin, his first grin of the evening, and his eyes lifted to find Théo gazing in complete consternation at the tablecloth, and as he watched she moved a hand to push away her napkin and her wedding ring – he had noticed how loose it was – slid down her finger and fell with a tiny metallic clink among the linen.

Nobody else noticed, he was sure, and yet he could have sworn that as she replaced it her hand shook and she blushed.

22

'It is a grisly farce,' said Joss, coming to the little ante-room where Millie waited by the leaping fire, 'all those poor wretches by Sebastopol won't be dancing tonight.'

'Indignation is a most wasteful emotion. There is nothing you can do about it, dear boy. If there was I would be the first to help you at the barricades, you know that. As it is you must take that dark look off your face and smile and sacrifice yourself for young Sophie's sake: it is to be the evening of her life.'

'She is quite hopelessly spoiled.'

'Oh, I don't think so. She has a penchant for her own way, certainly; so do we all. But she is abroad, she is in exciting company, and she is . . . a little in love. You must forgive her not thinking of your poor fellows in the snow before Sebastopol.'

He brushed specks of plaster dust off his uniform coat. The villa had a tendency to disintegrate when fires were lit, all the damp walls flaking gently whenever the air was stirred.

'We're late,' he said irritably.

'When have you ever cared about that?'

He did not care tonight; he did not care if they never reached the embassy. He left the room to see, ostensibly to see, if the boys had come with the lanterns, but he saw Khazanmoo already poised on the step peering out on the same errand so he turned aside into that long tiled summer drawing room that was almost a conservatory. There was a lamp lodged in the deep embrasure of the window and by its light he saw the slight figure in black.

'Théo?'

She turned. Indeed, she had heard his step on the tiles before he entered, and his step had told her everything: that he was quite absurdly and monumentally cross, like a child dressed up for a party he has longed to avoid, that he had decided not to be disagreeable to anyone, and that underlying all this, deep, deep where even he could not come at it, was an unalterable and abiding sense of shame at those of his countrymen who could make merry while their fellows died for lack of bread and a blanket. Such contrasts, such frivolous behaviour, such a deal of callous disregard are the way of a world, however. And Millie was right, nothing he could do would stop Lord Stratford putting on his best coat and waxing his whiskers and greeting his glittering guests; nothing he could do would in any way alter the confusion at Balaclava.

But he did not have to enjoy himself.

'I take it Sophie has not yet come down?' Théo asked gently.

'No. And Barnard keeps coming into the hall with his head wrapped in a muffler wondering why we have not left. Why is she such an infernal long time? She could put on her dress in a minute surely, she has Polly to help her.' And then, as if his mind still ran along these lines: 'I do hate you in black. Can't you leave it off?'

'Spit in convention's eye, you mean?'

'An unladylike way of putting it. Yes, I suppose that's what I mean. What does it matter? You're cooped up here until you sail, after all. Who is to see you?'

'The Barnards would be scandalized. I would forfeit all their sympathy.'

'I haven't noticed them being especially sympathetic. All *he* is worried about is money: Millie says Martagon will be under the hammer within twelve months. Can you credit it? All that good land being left fallow. He blames it on the repeal of the Corn Laws, on anything, in fact, except his own bad husbandry. Well what can he expect when he employs a man like Bartrum as manager? Unholy scoundrels the pack of them, stone-pickers and sow-gelders. There was a warren of them at Beckley when I was a lad and not one sober Monday to Saturday, too lazy to work for a living but quick enough to thieve for it.'

'I believe Mr Barnard is under the impression his Bartrum is the very model of a stout country bailiff, respected by the tenants and the cottagers alike.'

'Which only goes to show how bad a judge of character he is. And how he does not understand his own farm accounts, for they must tell a plain enough tale. He cannot blame everything on the Corn Laws, even he must smell a rat somewhere.'

He came and stood by her side, and looked down disparagingly at the black dress that drew all the colour from her face, and at that face with its strange eyes, tawny now in the glare of the lamp.

'I hope we are friends,' he said suddenly, remembering with a vague guilt his ill humour on the *Alice Ware.*'

'You and I? But of course we are. Why should you think otherwise?'

'I don't know. I suppose I had begun to think of you as a sort of sister, but then . . . You were so different in Varna, in Balaclava. It didn't seem to be you at all.'

'Oh, that was just the side of me you don't like. By and large I think you find me tolerable.'

She was teasing. The tawny eyes flashed green, the lamplight shone on her hair as she turned and lit the mysterious hollows of her face, so that for a moment she was transformed: he could see the girl of the aquamarine dress who had weighed nothing on his arm as he had swept her down the floor.

And that was another thing.

'I hope I do not have to dance,' he said.

She was smiling, her face ablaze with memory. 'Well, no girl who had ever danced with you could ever forget the experience, and that is something.'

His own face lightened, a trace of his old good humour was there and a more cheerful resignation. 'I wish you were coming,' he said, and surprised himself by meaning it from the bottom of his heart.

'It is going to be a splendid party. You will probably enjoy it. Perhaps it's the best thing after all, to try to forget the war for one night,' she said.

For answer he put both arms about her and rested his cheek on the top of her head, on the white lace cap that covered her gilded, springing hair. 'Wait up for me. I shall leave early. They have old Barnard to squire them about.'

It could have meant everything, or nothing. She was familiar now, and sensible, and she understood him: he would rather have spent the evening with her playing draughts and drinking cocoa, he was in need of just that kind of homeliness. On the other hand, his gratitude for just such sympathetic companionship had once nearly led him to make love to her, certainly to unchaste thoughts if not unchaste actions. He had not forgotten. She felt him take a deep uncertain breath, but when she looked up his face was creased with laughter.

'Sophie will never forgive you,' she told him.

'I'm not sure I give a toss for Sophie,' said Joss.

She waited, first in her room where she wrote to Louise and the children, wrote a page of careful congratulation to Caroline, wrote to Fanny in England – she would be nearly there by now – and dear Mr Howard. So many letters took a long time to write and a long time to read over: Millie's little travelling clock tinkled hour after hour. She waited, waited . . .

When she could not bear to sit still any longer she went down with her lamp to the summer drawing room again. She had no idea why she preferred this place to anywhere else, for there was not a stick of furniture except a marble-topped table under a sheet, and the rich tiles were dusty and cold. Though she was far from the clock now and could not hear the hours strike, nevertheless she was acutely aware of time passing. Near at hand was the frenzied beating of wings on the glass as insects were drawn to her lamp, and farther away a see-sawing high-pitched quarrelling in the back regions. At some point it seemed to grow so still and quiet she thought she could hear the waters of the Bosphorus, could certainly hear the measured thump-thump of her own heart. If he would only come, she thought, and they could share this last late hour and some wine and that sort of happy intimacy she had never known.

He did not come. She was roused from a state of torpor – it was cold in her retreat and she was very tired – by Di's voice booming beyond the half open door.

'. . . take a week to be introduced . . . so many distinguished people . . . General Pelissier . . . this Nightingale woman. Where are the others? No, never mind, pay off the chair, those good fellows. They ran almost, outstripped the boys with the lights. The others were left behind, Sophie so tired she could barely stand. I really do think Millie might have found some transport, another chair even.'

Théo doused her light. She stood in the dark like a conspirator while out in the hall that voice went on and on.

'So charming . . . but everyone wanted to dance with her. She refused four most gallant officers to stand up with Joss. They made an exceptional couple, both so dark and striking. Where is Khazanmoo, did you send him to bed? I am quite dead. Look, there they are, at the bottom of the path, I can see the lights. How sad poor Théo had to miss it all, but she could hardly go to a ball with that boy dead barely two months . . .'

And then footsteps, and voices, the link-boys determining a price, and a confusion of sound: the door shutting, Mr Barnard declaring, in quite a cheerful temper, that he thought he was in for congestion of the lungs, Joss's deep laugh, Millie's comment on Lady Stratford's dress – that vile green – and Miss Cole's braying good night, Jack asking if they were in need of anything, there was coffee upstairs.

Like a child Théo crept to the door and put her eye to the opening, seeing them climb the stairs to Millie's sitting room where the coffee pot would be waiting, piping hot, and tea too. Sophie was on Joss's arm, he was lost in her wide pink skirt with its flounces and clusters of embroidered pearls, and her bare shoulders brushed against his blue coat as he bent to hear what she was saying, her hand through his arm.

Like a child she put her hot forehead against the cold plaster and felt the tears run into her mouth. He had forgotten her. Well, of course he had, he was not in love with her, and he had no notion of her feelings for him. He never would have a notion unless she told him, unless she said, 'Joss, I love you' to his face and risked seeing him flushed, confused, embarrassed, risked his rejection, risked annihilation.

She went back for her lamp. Yes, that was better, she had dealt with the tears, tucked the stray hairs under her cap, was

Mrs Trent again, thirty years old, practical, perfectly behaved. If anyone saw her she would pretend she had been weeping for Alex. Dear God, what shameful hypocrisy! What a foul lie! The strong sense of her unworthiness, of sin, made her raise her chin and step out with determination, furious with herself and therefore the world. But as she passed Millie's sitting room door she heard the merry voices within, the clink of cups, the resonant laugh that could only be Joss, heard Sophie excited, Millie commanding, Barnard gruff and toler- ant, the wine in his head and his mood more and more expansive. And in that instant, poised in the light of the wall candles, feeling somehow as sore and bruised as if she had been in physical combat, she wanted to go home. She closed her eyes tightly. She wanted to go home.

But she had no home, she had to find one yet and make of it what she could. La Croix was not home, Alexandre would live in it now; Rozel was not home, she had never liked it and there were memories now, memories she would prefer left there, under the dust sheets; Russell Square was not home, though it would never be less than welcoming.

She walked on down the dark passage, and there, outside Miss Cole's door, sat Khazanmoo, cross-legged, his head on his chest. As she drew level he sprang up, silently. Could he read her face in the dark? He took the lamp from her hands and set it down gently on the side table, turning back to bend in his own peculiar fashion, a bow and yet not a bow, not a hint of subservience in it.

'Good night, Khazanmoo.'

She was not as brave as Miss Cole, she thought suddenly, as she closed her door. Or perhaps it was a matter of what one pursued. Happiness could not be found simply by looking, nor perhaps after all could adventure: Di pursued the *Reptilia* of Asia Minor and would probably discover both. There was probably no end to the ironies of life, the tragi-comedies of human existence; at least, so Théo might have thought at any other time, fortified maybe by one of Albert's *poulets à la Marengo*, a good meaty disagreement with Griffith, and a bottle of Bordeaux courtesy Faurel Mannelier.

As it was she unhooked her dress and stepped out of it, and sat on the bed in her petticoats, twisting her wedding ring.

Then she took it off and put it on the low table by the window, and stood there, looking out, until the rags of cloud in the east lifted on a new cold day.

The *Saint Helena* was there, was not 'commodious and well-appointed' and was to leave a day earlier than she was supposed to, she had to take on stores and water in Malta.

'Why Malta?' demanded Millie, who would have liked a huge, unquestionably well-appointed steamer, but no one cared to tell her, though it was plain as a pikestaff, Joss said, that she was keeping well out from land in case any of her hands jumped ship and he would make a guess her credit was not good, why else should she fly to Malta for provisions?

She was a brig, a very small, dirty, unsound brig with a list to port and the sorriest-quality rigging ever to leave a shipyard or a sail loft. Joss did not see them on board or he might never have allowed them to sail in her.

'I think Mr Barnard ought to wait for a steamer,' said Millie bleakly, looking about. 'He is a feeble sailor. If we have bad weather in the Mediterranean there's no knowing what will become of him.'

They had quitted the villa hurriedly, the shipping agent sending a boy, a skinny, insolent, expensive boy with a message, no time to lose, ship sailing in a matter of hours, where she lay, what colour she was, the master's name. The master's name was Banks and he was portly and impotent, his mate, a driving bully, running the ship exactly as he liked. He greeted his passengers with apparent pleasure, he was a lonely and misunderstood man who craved company, any company, especially that of handsome young women. He had his wish for a handsome young woman when Sophie descended gingerly into the saloon and the mate, standing to a sort of attention, glimpsed the lace frill of her pantaloons. He could not make up his mind about Théo, an unattractive widow, and not young any more. He was demolished by Millie, who said in the same breath as her frosty 'Good day' that his deck was a disgrace, it was greasy, she had nearly pitched on her nose, and what was the peculiar smell?

The smell reminded Théo of Scutari, of the cellars of the Barrack Hospital, of too many people in too confined a space and no privies, not even a decent drain. The reek on the deck of the *Saint Helena* rose from her bilge, for she was an old ship and over half a century and more a great deal of unmentionable waste had found its way to her bottom-most regions. A stormy passage in the Aegean had stirred it all up, like unsavoury soup in a great wooden pot, and shifted her ballast into the bargain. There was also a stinging, quite unmistakable addition to this stench from the heads, rarely hosed out or attended to in any way except when absolute necessity dictated it. Théo, who had seen at once what sort of ship she was, recognized both the under-smell and over-smell, but Scutari had made her tolerant, she gave no sign of being discomfited. The officers of the *Saint Helena* of course did not notice it.

'I hope he is going to wash his neck before dinner,' said Millie, staring dispassionately about the cabin she was to share with Théo.

'Captain Banks?'

'Well, with luck the mate will not come to table. Did you see his nails? Mr Barnard is sick already, thank the Lord, so will stay in his cabin — let us hope till England.'

As they got under way and Constantinople fell astern, as the old brig heeled over and her timber began to speak to the water and the force of the wind, it seemed possible he might never emerge from his cabin again. He was like Mr Howard, the slightest motion reduced him to jelly, to a grey-green, sweaty heap, groaning and suffering. Unlike little Mr Howard, he did not suffer as quietly as he could, but cried out for more blankets, or another hot brick, or a pail, or sal volatile, and when they had all been brought wished them all taken away again, quickly, they all made him feel worse. The steward, possibly the only cheerful, good-natured man on board, put up with all this without blinking, sailed in and out with an expression of pure benevolence, fetched and carried and arranged, and rearranged, and fetched something else, and finally, with the air of a man who is happy to have done his duty, informed the three ladies in the saloon that the gentleman had gone to sleep, bless him, and had they ever known anybody so cut up about a little bit of sea like this, why, he had known bigger waves on a village duckpond.

The Aegean dispelled any notion of duckponds, for a sharp squall whipped up the sea, and the brig, with her ballast displaced and her sail shortened too late, walloped over the water in great leaps.

'Do I look like a corpse?' asked Millie. Théo and she were the only two up, facing each other over a tattered draughts board.

'I don't think so.'

'I feel like one. If this goes on I shall have to retire in confusion like poor Sophie.'

'I don't think they were ready for such a wind,' Théo remarked, not putting more significance in the words than she felt was necessary. 'All that shouting was when they were trying to get sail off her.'

'It was a great deal of shouting, not so much commands as confusion.'

'Yes.' And a great deal of rope's-end too, and a helmsman who either lost his nerve or was given a wrong order, for he put his helm over when he should not have; more chaos.

The next day they had some fine sailing, for there was a wind from the north-east and they set what they could to take advantage of it. Even to Millie's lubberly eye the brig's suit of sails looked uncommonly patched, but in this bright cold, the sea hard, steely blue, they seemed to be cracking on. The terrible smell of the bilge was blown away, as was the equally terrible one from the sailors' latrines, the food was better than they had dared to hope, though of the boiled pudding variety, and Captain Banks had turned out less lecherous than he appeared and even more impotent than he appeared, deferring every decision to the mate. Millie, who suspected impotency of a general nature, began to feel sorry for him.

Théo, who had never sailed in such an ill-found brig, who had never known such a drunken crew, such a powerless master, watched the pitiful sails drawing as best they could and pondered on the probable state of the old girl's bottom, not scraped in twenty years, and the slovenly routine, hardly a routine at all, that told her she would be better off in a Greek fishing boat. She was glad Sophie kept to her cabin, not horribly ill but grey and exhausted, for the few sailors – pitifully few, not above a handful, and every last one unwilling

286

— cast speculative eyes aft; she was glad she was not pretty. The mate, finding her on deck most of the day, tried to ingratiate himself, any woman being better than none to an incontinent man baulked of the pleasures of Constantinople after an over-long passage from the Downs. He began with a heavy, patronizing air, elicited no obvious response, grew irritated, and tried another tack: would she care to learn how to navigate, would she let him show her how to take a sight, read a chart? It was a stumbling attempt to appeal to her mind since he had made no progress in his appeal to her flesh. It was inconceivable she should dislike and despise him, women of her class often found themselves unwillingly attracted to hard, handsome, bucko men, the like of which they had never met before. He persevered. Mrs Trent's eye became glassy. He persisted. Mrs Trent made a mildly caustic, intelligent comment on the brig's wake, which was nowhere near straight and true, and her oddly green eyes gleaméd slightly as she spoke. The mate made some excuse and went below, restrained enough to swear aloud only when he had reached the bottom of the companion.

'How was I ever persuaded to *buy* a passage in this hulk,' was Millie's heartfelt exclamation at dinner that evening, gazing in a state of shock at the greasy brown liquid just that moment served her as 'mulligatawny'. 'If Joss had seen her . . . Are you sure you ought to eat it? What are the floating lumps?'

'Be charitable,' said Théo calmly, 'and assume they are fowl. The captain himself delivered the *coup de grâce* to two of the dowdy hens from the coop this morning, I saw him. I believe he ate a whole one himself for lunch.'

'And he has gone to his cabin with stomach pains.'

For a moment they sat in a fog of spicy steam, onions, garlic and curry all about them. Millie said: 'I dare not risk it. I refuse to die from eating mulligatawny, it would be too absurd.'

And Théo, who had appeared once or twice to have reached a state of misery beyond the help of any mortal creature, suddenly looked up and laughed.

It had been this morning that had done it, she was thinking, this morning that had brought about the change. She had been standing watching the water slip past, the bright chilly water that reflected the bright untrustworthy sky, and Honorine's voice had spoken in her mind: 'It's the day you stop being interested you'll know things are really bad, the day the sun in your eyes and the wind on your cheek don't make you glad to be alive . . .' Well, she was glad she was alive. She was glad, glad. She had survived Constantinople, she had survived Joss's kiss of farewell, on one cheek and so enormously affectionate and innocent she could have wept; she had survived seeing the look that passed between him and Sophie, not so much of promise as of distinct willingness to pursue the matter further; she had survived Miss Cole's surprisingly motherly embrace, her stricture to 'Be good, but not at the expense of your own happiness. Look how delightfully wicked I am being and I have never felt happier'; she had survived Khazanmoo's formal salute, oddly enough the most moving of all her goodbyes, for his eyes had gazed directly into hers, like Griffith it was as if he could see her immortal soul, but unlike Griffith he seemed to like what he saw. He had wished her, as Di had schooled him, a good journey, but the stilted phrase held a significance and a genuine hope for more than her immediate voyage to England.

The mulligatawny removed, a sort of hash followed, adorned with dumplings, and a great dish of potatoes 'boiled to death' as Millie put it. After a while, after a long, long while of conscientious chewing and grave looks, she said carefully: 'I have convinced myself it is goat. Why are we jerking about like this?'

The plates were beginning to slide. The steward dashed in to put up the fiddles but was too late to save the potatoes, which had gathered tremendous momentum on the last roll. He was deft and efficient, he smiled as broadly as usual, and yet Théo saw a strange, beleaguered shining in his eye, as if he feared dreadful things to come.

They could not face the suet pudding, they sent it back with apologies. They knew perfectly well the cook and the steward would devour it between them and be the better for it. The choppy motion grew worse; another squall? asked Millie. She had never been very lucky in the Mediterranean, had come to view it as a benighted, unpredictable sea.

It was not a squall but a considerable blow. It had come on suddenly and kept coming, gusting with a playful ferocity that soon settled into a steady rage. Théo lay awake in her berth, aware Millie too was gazing anxiously into the noisy dark, though neither of them said anything. It was dawn, it should have been dawn but there was little to show for it yet, when some feeble whispering instinct drove Théo to dress, to rouse Millie, and to go next door to persuade Sophie into some clothes, any clothes, so long as she was warm.

'What is it?' demanded Millie, settling her bonnet: she would not be seen dead, she declared, without her bonnet.

'I don't know. The wind should change but ... I don't know.'

As if to prove her wrong the wind increased, a last violent blow to put the requisite finish to a stormy night. The brig, carrying too much sail as usual, for they had been creeping about this last half hour setting as much as she could bear — they were well off course and foresaw a sorry beating up and a deal of tacking to raise Malta even within three days — the brig dug in her bluff old bow and shuddered, and there was a glorious rending crack as her topsails blew out one after the other.

It was a miracle, Millie said afterwards, that anyone had had the presence of mind to launch the boats. It was a miracle too that there was time, thought Théo, but she did not say so. She rather admired the brig, for it was not her fault she foundered, and even then she did not lay right over but simply began to fill very slowly, the main hatch stove in by the falling topmast, as she lay at an angle. The helmsman was responsible, for he had let go of the wheel in panic when the sails had blown, had screamed when the mast had gone, and had bent double, covering his eyes. It was as well the *Saint Helena* was still stout enough, for all the neglect — or did she indeed have a cross-grained, bloody-minded nature? And it was as well the wind slackened the moment she heeled over.

For two long hours the Barnards, Millie and Théo swooped up and down short steep seas still within sight of the brig, which filled and filled but still floated, as if she would see them all damned first. Millie began to grow superstitious about her and their curious inability to get away from her, for every time they rose she was plainly visible, her remaining masts at an acute angle. But after a while, a long wet sickening while, she tried to ignore her and take more notice of the ship's boat, from whose rotten boards the steward was ladling a liquid not unlike the mulligatawny soup. His natural cheerfulness was subdued now in the face of the enormity of his task: his bailing was frantic to keep up with the quantities of water flung over the side and seeping up between the boards. At the oars sat the former helmsman and a morose lascar, pulling, not always together and not strongly, with a mechanical, dead motion, the result of shock and panic.

'Well, we seem to have lost both master and mate at least,' said Millie, stooping to see if there was anything she could use to help the steward in his thankless task. 'They both went into the other boat, no doubt.'

The helmsman looked at her, digested her words, and spat, without much energy, over the side.

'Where are we?' demanded Sophie, who was shivering and terrified but was bearing up, bearing up with a fine high colour and the beginning of devil-may-care desperation.

Théo asked the helmsman but the half-witted man did not know. He could not even remember what course he had been steering when the sails had blown out. Théo could not imagine what a master like Griffith would have to say to the man who had, effectively, caused his brig to sink, but then this boy — under the grime and the demeanour of a hard case, he was only a boy, seventeen or eighteen — would never have been allowed to disgrace the *Aphrodite*'s hold, let alone her deck. He had not had the ability — the cunning? the means? the courage? — to jump ship and so had stayed, along with those others too scared or too tired or too much under the mate's vindictive eye to try. It was not his fault he had lost his nerve, no one had ever taught him the names of the sails, though he had loosed and sheeted them home often enough, driven on by cheering oaths and the rope's-end. He found it difficult to keep to a course, dimly aware of both the science and instinct he lacked, and the *Saint Helena* had been sluggish and lopsided since her ballast had shifted. He gazed at Théo with a childish defiance as he rowed, a faint imitation of his dread

290

mate, but it was only show: his large hands were sweaty on the oar.

Mr Barnard had lapsed into wretchedness, his head sunk into the folds of his huge coat, a tarpaulin over his head. Under the coat, a blanket, and the boa-like folds of two comforters, he was still in his nightshirt, and the feet that rested side by side in the well were a delicate blue and white with cold. Théo thought she could predict a real congestion of the lungs if they could not raise some land or another ship within the next few hours. She had no idea where they were, for she had no way of knowing how far they had travelled during the night, pressing on under more sail than was safe. Certainly from the ship's boat, low in the water, no land was visible nor, in a sea full of busy vessels plying to and from the Crimea, was any ship; nor, when she stood up and looked about as they rose on a wave larger than the others, was the other boat containing the captain, the mate, and the remains of the crew.

In a while they were all hungry, a reaction after the adventures of the dawn, but there were only ship's biscuits and a sack of sultanas Millie had grabbed with some forethought as they had abandoned the brig. The tiny water cask was full of strange brackish stuff like small beer, and they shrank from it with one accord, and bunged it up again quickly, thinking virtuously that they would reserve it for when they were desperate.

The day was cold and grey. Though the storm had died out the wind blew strongly from the north and chilled them to the marrow. Théo began to think it would not be long before they were desperate, that desperation sets in remarkably quickly when one is wet, sick and cold. The helmsman was doubled up over his oar, his face a grey circle of exhaustion, and the lascar was gibbering under his breath, trying to stop the heavy old boat swinging round and being swamped.

Théo took over at the oar, the steward took over from the lascar, and Sophie and Millie crouched with a can and Mr Barnard's tall hat, bailing wordlessly and with serious, absorbed expressions.

And then, after another two hours, the lascar stood up and waved an arm towards the south and said: 'Ship coming', and they all looked up, but carefully, as if they were prepared for a shattering disappointment.

On the rise there was the tantalizing glimpse of a lateen; they sank again, rose, Millie produced a sail of her own in the shape of a whole petticoat; whipped off before the lascar's incredulous eyes, and streaming out a lovely, eye-catching white in the wind. They dipped and climbed, dipped and climbed, and still there was a lateen to windward and still it seemed as far away as ever. And then, just as Théo and the steward, pulling with real determination, had achieved a minute change of course that might, given a miracle of strength and furious activity, bring them to collide with the owner of the lateen, Millie gave a shriek of anxious delight and flapped the petticoat so wildly she lost her hold on it, so that it whipped away over the wave crests.

'It's changed course,' she cried.

'It' had not. It had simply lost way and was riding the angry sea, watching them, waiting for them to come up. She was a sperona out of Valletta who had been about her business in the Ionian Sea when she had been caught in last night's storm. She had sat upon the sea like a gull, as indifferent to the elements, as snug and warm. Now she was making her way home.

The Maltese were astounded at the bedraggled crew in the boat, were suspicious and then tender, carrying up Mr Barnard in one piece, so to speak, so that he was crammed into the deckhouse to dry out and warm like a great parcel, and distributing their meagre bedding to the rest. They produced some vile grease for Théo's hands, and resuscitated the helmsman, who was in a sort of stupor, and gave the pride of place on their small deck to Sophie, who was so beautiful.

And then they raised their sails and flew, with the ease of born sailors on their own sea, towards the distant speck that was the island of Malta.

23

The house was the same: small, shuttered, a not-at-home air about it. Théo snicked the latch on the iron gate and went down the short stone passage to the courtyard where a woman in a black veil was apparently singing to a speckled hen under her arm, and a child was running about on´a hobby horse. They both looked up at Théo's appearance, but with a dull, incurious inquiry: when she asked no questions they returned to their previous occupations as if she did not exist.

Théo rapped on the door but there was no reply. It gave a little under her hand so she pushed it and went in, and there was the remembered frowsty smell, something both fishy and earthy, a mingling of sardines, olive oil, a damp stone; and there too was a small brown bird in a cage, quite silent, and three cats who fled towards her, mewing piteously, and a very small, thin, bony boy of about ten. The lady, he said, was upstairs, he would fetch her.

There was a pause, during which the small bird jumped up and down and the air was charged with expectation; then footsteps, and the rustle of a skirt.

'Lord love us!' cried Poll Batty, swaying with emotion. 'Oh my! Little Miss Théo, my own darling,' and to Théo's consternation she found herself drowning in a huge, pillowy embrace. 'And there I was boxing the poor little lad's ears 'cos I thought you was some scrub after me strong box. Well! Well. Come along through to the parlour dearie, how often did we sit in that there room of an evening and me telling you it would all come right.'

In the parlour she turned for a better look, and her shrewd

small eyes missed nothing. 'Didn't come right after all, eh? I knew 'e was dead. A lady called and told me. Lovely woman she was, a proper heart and no airs. She left me a package for you. "You'll be seein' Mrs Trent 'afore I do," she says. "Ho", says I, "how can you be so sure? I don't reckon Malta's on her visiting list." "Well, I'm off home to Donegal," she says, "and that ain't on no visiting list either. But if she don't come 'ere by the new year send it on to the address on the wrapper and here's the money." She told me 'e was dead, see, but that she 'adn't seen you for months. And then one morning who drops anchor in Grand Harbour but my lovely Griff, comes up to buy me a drink, grim as a Tartar, just done the fastest passage from the Needles ever, every stitch of canvas on and God damn the consequences. I never seen him so touchy. Like a demon. I said it to his face. "You're like a bleedin' little Welsh demon," I says, "looking for poor kind ordinary folk for your breakfast." But he never said what was wrong. But he aint had much sleep, I can tell you that, he'd been drivin' that there *Affie* along like a devil ship. I saw our Mr Graham later in the Strada Reale and he said he was too tired for women, he'd not had a rest or a change of clothes for weeks. First from Constantinople to England, then back again with a cargo of timber. Never known anything like it, he said, and this with a captain who always sails with as much set as the ship'll take. Too tired for women! Things've come to a pretty pass if Mr Covenanter Graham has no time for women.

'So there he sits, my Griff, drinking off my best red as if it was water – and he's not a man to over-indulge, so *that's* odd – and I says, 'cos it come into my head and we're not talkin' of anything particular like: "I've got a package for Théo Trent, come from an Irish lady what knew her husband and had it when he died. Now if there's a man would know whereabouts the dear girl is it would be you." Well, I never seen him look so dark. "God damn Théo Trent," he says. Well, that was the wine talkin', I don't take no notice. "What's she done to you," I says, "to make you so sour? I give her into your keeping, trustin' you. What you done to the girl?" So he says nothing, and then he tells me – the bare bones like, oh I know when he's only givin' me the bones – about Varna, and Scutari, and goin' over on that stinkin' little collander to

294

Balaclava. Well, I know by now what you found when you got there, so I says: "You're givin' a high-flown heroic account of yourself but what was it all for? I never known you dangle after no lady before. You don't give no woman a second chance. But most partic'lar, you don't run after married ladies, that's one of your rules, and you don't break your rules, nohow and noway, not for anyone. So what's all this with Théo Trent?"'

Polly slapped her hand on her fat knee, and her eyes vanished in the creases of her huge face as she laughed. Then, seeing Théo's pale attentiveness, her grave containment, she said: 'He told me about gettin' you to help buy his brigantine, all legal and proper like, contracts and lawyers and all that, and you'd said no. Did I laugh? And if looks could kill, my dear, Poll Batty would be no more. He was furious, tore off in a rage too and only came back to apologize come morning and then he had a dreadful head, didn't dare move it, looked quite green. Never seen him like it. Never known him drink much. A temperate man in that though not always in everything else. Then I says: "Well, what am I to do about the package, the package what the Irish lady give me and I should send on?" And he thinks a while, sittin' out in the yard sippin' lemon juice and water like a lamb, and then he says: "Give it to me. I know where she is, I'll see if I can't get it to her. And if not I'll send it on. You keep the money you was given and buy some knick-knacks." So I gives him the package and off he goes.'

Théo stirred. 'How long ago was this?'

'How long! Why, bless you, yesterday. And if you want your parcel, my love, you have only to go down and get a boat out into the harbour and there you will see her, oh what a bird she is, the old *Affie*.'

At this point Poll clapped her hands together twice, much in the manner of an eastern potentate, and the small boy re-appeared, as silent and subtle as one of the cats.

'I found him on the waterfront,' said Poll as he vanished again for tea and cakes. 'What could I do? Little beggars most of 'em, sharp as knives, but 'e looked as if he had some good in 'im still so I took him on. But what a blessin' dear, what a blessin' you wasn't taken up by pirates when that old tub sank. There's still plenty of them about, Griff says; you can't change the 'abits of two thousand years, he says, not if you tries ever so.'

Théo, who had said very little about her shipwreck, wondered if the captain and the mate had been unlucky in this particular. They had not yet been delivered to Malta dead or alive. Not so Jack and Polly, who had only this morning been decanted on the quay with Millie's disproportionate heap of luggage from the ketch *Freda*, in which they had been forced to travel owing to lack of room in the *Saint Helena*. The *Freda*, Dutch-built, bluff and hearty, had ridden out the storm with a general contempt, ship, officers and crew happy to ignore it, for although these short wicked seas were not her home ground, nevertheless she could take all but the dirtiest weather, hurricane and typhoon, in her stride. Putting into Valletta for water, one of her casks being broken and now empty, her bosun had discovered that the *Saint Helena* was no more, but her passengers safe, if waterlogged, and one of them with pneumonia.

It was not pneumonia but Mr Barnard liked everyone to think it was, and kept Sophie ever attendant, running in and out with bottles and draughts of noxious-looking stuff prescribed by Dr Crashaw, another guest, a most welcome guest, at the hotel. It was now two days since they had been landed from the sperona and Barnard showed no signs of improvement, and when anyone mentioned going home he swore he never wished to set foot on a ship again, he would surely die. Millie, who had begun to call him, most uncharitably and with a most venomous curl to her lip, 'That Old Hypochondriac', had almost made up her mind to leave him in Malta. But she was worried about Sophie, Sophie who, flighty and headstrong or not, was proving to have remarkable patience, remarkable fortitude, even a remarkable capacity for being abused.

'What tyrants parents can be, to be sure,' sighed Millie, but there was nothing she could do, much as she longed to tip the cantankerous old rascal out of his hotel window and into the deeper parts of the Grand Harbour.

'So when will you leave?' asked Poll, squinting here and there at Théo's dress, its cut, its ornament, its probable worth.

'I don't know. We would go tomorrow if Millie had her way and Captain Charles of the *Hamilton Castle*, whom she knows from long ago, has offered us cabins; he is sailing at the end of the week. But Mr Barnard groans when he is asked, and Millie says she is overwhelmed by the responsibility . . . We are not a very happy party. You would laugh to see us, Poll, you really would.'

Poll rubbed her chin, that small chin lost in its folds of loose fat, that veritable dewlap. 'Dearie, I never laughs at folks in distress. But . . . Look, is that the best you've got to wear?'

'Oh this' – and a deprecating glance down at the threadbare wool – 'I'm afraid everything went down with the ship, everything of mine, that is. A lady at the hotel gave me this. I believe it was her maid's,' and Théo's eyes shone with deep, ironic amusement.

'Yes, well,' said Poll, straining to catch the return of the dilatory boy, 'I might have something in the cupboard more suited to a lady. After you left, your room was took by an officer's lady – ho, very ladylike she was – and he spent all he had on her, poor soul, and for precious little in return if I know that type of she-cat. She'd bin a lady's maid, knew how to turn herself out proper, knew how to speak, but not an ounce of gratitude, not one. But there you are. It's often the way. If a man lays hisself down too low under a woman's feet he's like to get trod on. She upped and went off one morning with a Guardsman. "What about your clothes?" says I. "Oh, sell them if you like," says she, little madam, "they won't be fit for where I'm going." And nor they wouldn't be, if she ends up where I reckon she will, they'd be a sight too good and that's a fact. I hope she's shiverin' in the mud at Sebastopol. That poor soft boy cried all over my best satin 'cos she'd left him. Anyway,' and here she broke off to clap again, imperiously, 'you can have what you want. She was much your size.'

The boy appeared, expressionless, with pale tea and fruit cake on a silver-plated dish.

'You don't take it amiss, my offering second-hand clothes? I never thought you was a girl to stand too much on her pride. They're better than those rags you bought when you was here before. I'll take you up after we've had a dish of this. Finest Chinese, Griff said, come by courtesy of some fancy London grocer. He said it was time I learned a bit of refinement. Was he pullin' my leg? I reckon I'm like them pirates, I've been at the bottle too long to give it up now.'

Afterwards they went upstairs and into the little room Théo remembered so well. There on the rail were half a dozen dresses, coats, skirts, blouses, all good quality, some extremely fine. It was not to be wondered that the young soldier, miserably overdrawn, had wept into Poll's broad bosom. Théo, who had no intention of standing on her pride, she doubted she had any left, chose a black merino skirt and a black velvet jacket, two snowy blouses intricately tucked and worked.

'If I see Griff I'll tell him you was here,' said Poll, as they descended and made their way to the street door, 'then he can bring up the package.'

Théo hesitated. There was a small frown between her brows. Poll said encouragingly: 'Perhaps the boy can bring it up when he brings the clothes,' with a broad, innocent smile that showed her few remaining teeth, as if she was completely unaware of some current, some strong drift of feeling, that was as irrational as it was violent. She did hope Griff had behaved himself, though if he had not she would be truly astonished: he would have broken every rule in his book. No, she could not believe it was that, and yet ... This deep, unspoken, but quite obvious desire *not* to meet Captain Griffith of the *Aphrodite* must have sprung from something: a quarrel about the proposed brigantine, by God he was no kind of angel roused; a quarrel to do with something else entirely, the dead husband perhaps?

'Come and take a dish of tea before you go' – with real feeling – 'I shall never drink the stuff up else and Griff will be hurt.'

'You're very fond of him.'

'Lord love you, and why shouldn't I be? I've known a fair basketful of sea captains in my time, some wanted this, some wanted that, but Griff, he never wanted anything, just to call, to buy a bottle of some decent claret – oh, I know me claret better than me tea – and to ask how things is goin', for old time's sake. If he owned forty ships and they made him a lord he'd still knock on my door, was he to know where to find me. Now and then, just now and then. He's got his bad side, worse than many maybe, but he don't forget old friends. I trusted him with you, didn't I? And you adrift in a wicked world with only your innocent face to see you through. I wouldn't've trusted no other man I know, not to do the right thing, come what may.'

'You make him sound,' said Théo, as they paused on the threshold of the street, 'like the very flower of chivalry.'

Poll threw back her head and laughed, and her whole body shook, fold on fold, her eyes disappeared, her black skirts shivered with delight. 'Flower is it?' she wheezed at last, hauling in breath on breath, her cheeks puce, even her ears scarlet. 'Flower! Well, I don't know about that. But I'd always try to have 'im on my side, that I would, else there'd be the devil to pay and no mistake.'

'Well,' said Millie wearily, 'Friday it is. Captain Charles implored me to sail as his passenger, even kissed my hand. Théo, I can't resist a man who kisses my hand without looking coy. And he is such a fine, sober, introverted man as a rule, anything so ludicrously out of character is so touching. He has promised to speak to the doctor, to talk man to man, as rationally as he can, to Barnard, and to stress that we may never get berths on another ship as fast, as well-found, and as ably manned. I told him to point out the fact that Sophie is being ogled by every officer in Valletta every time she goes out for air, that if she speaks to one, is seen to encourage any of them by the merest flicker of an eyelash scandal and hysteria will ensue. I'm not sure poor Charles is up to such brazen nonsense but I thought it worth a try: I have not found anything to move that odious man faster than the hint of scandal.'

'How is this?' said Théo, turning, smoothing her hands down the quality velvet of the jacket.

'The perfect fit. How generous of Mrs Batty, for she could have sold them for a great deal. You know you did not have to accept them though . . . We must shop tomorrow for all we need in the clothes line, I saved my money from the wreck if nothing else, and even if I had not, I know a great many people in Malta ... Turn round again. Yes, very nice. You would never have got such a perfect fit across the shoulder without its being made for you.'

Poll's boy had carried up the clothes, wrapped in tissue paper and oilcloth, that morning. With them had been a note from Poll, written in deliberate, flowing hand, to the effect that Captain Griff was away at the other end of the island about some business, she had sent down to Mr Graham for the package.

But the package did not come. The next day, Wednesday, Théo went shopping with Millie and Sophie, a thoughtful, subdued Sophie, for her father still cavilled at leaving his comfortable bed in the hotel and not all Captain Charles's blandishments were having the required effect. The shopping was only partially successful, giving them the feeling that they had battled valiantly but to little effect, that if they were indeed the victors they were far too tired to appreciate it. It seemed rather absurd to be buying nightdresses and nightcaps, hot-water jars and flannel petticoats; Millie could not find a petticoat as good as the one she had cast on the Mediterranean billows.

Jack compounded their general low humour by getting himself disgracefully drunk, and then getting into some violent quarrel with half a dozen of the shipyard chippies who knocked him about and left him dangling in a well, from which he was rescued by a buxom young woman with a stirringly sunny smile whose two large brothers pushed him home on a handcart. Millie told Théo privately that it was probably his revenge for having been left behind in Constantinople to follow on the *Freda*, he had considered it an insult; the fact that he might have lost his life had he sailed in the *Saint Helena* did not enter the argument.

Thursday came, the morning clear and sunny. For the first time the Grand Harbour was a sparkling blue, a cool blue, but blue none the less, and with an air of summery promise, of what it might look like under the relentless sun of July. Théo wrote to Louise, though she suspected she herself would arrive before the letter, and to Fanny. Ten o'clock struck on Millie's little clock – saved along with the money and keeping time valiantly though decidedly damp – and then eleven. Théo laid down her pen. Sophie looked in to say her father was awake and taking cocoa – Dr Crashaw had strongly advised cocoa as a restorative, and it also took away the after-taste of the medicines. She sat on a chair by the window, looking jaded and pale. Théo, leaving the little desk, crossed to her and touched her shoulder gently.

'There is really nothing wrong with him at all. Even Dr Crashaw says it was only a heavy cold. You know you ought not to let him worry you.'

'But I feel . . .' and she suddenly turned bright, wet eyes to Théo, reached for her hand, pushed her dark head into the folds of Théo's skirts like a child: 'I feel so guilty. I made him come, you see. I wanted to come. I made all kinds of silly excuses, and he took them quite seriously, and partly because of them and partly because he wished to have a rest from the lawyers – they have been making a meal of him, he says – he arranged to sail with Millie. It was all for . . . for Joss.'

She was really crying now, the tears running unchecked to wet the black wool of Théo's skirt. Théo smoothed back the waving hair and said: 'There's nothing to feel guilty about. And if . . . and if you and Joss . . . marry, well then, all your father's worries will be over, will they not? I doubt Joss will see you turned out of Martagon.'

The tears ceased. They ceased, Théo realized, because Sophie was concentrating on a more terrible vision, one too terrible for tears. 'He hasn't asked me,' she said in a small, firm voice, 'and if he does it will be because he wants Martagon. But I believe he will redeem Father's mortgages and get it that way, he hinted at it before he left. Do you know what I mean? It was . . . It was dropped into the conversation, just a word or two, so that Father knew there was that possibility, that Joss could afford to do it. Can he? I don't suppose you know. I know he has a small annuity and his pay, but this would be thousands. Would Millie lend it to him?'

'Maybe. Maybe not, not for such a purpose anyway,' replied Théo calmly, 'and I believe you're giving yourself a headache for nothing.'

'Oh, I do want to marry him,' cried Sophie, 'but to be married for Martagon! Or to be handed over as part of a

301

deal, sort of . . . sort of interest! Théo, I couldn't bear it. He's just like those Westovers in the Gallery, grasping, bullish sort of men, not feeling at all; he makes love to me as if one half of him wasn't there, was standing back and watching, and thinking: "Now, if I take this, and this, then I get Martagon." Oh Théo, I want to marry him, but sometimes I'm so frightened, there's a hard, cold Joss somewhere I've never met. And when I talk about Martagon, if I do, I hardly dare any more, he goes quiet, he . . . he withdraws.'

'Perhaps bastards are always touchy,' said Théo, remembering with a sympathetic smile.

'She has grown up, poor girl,' said Millie flatly when Théo recounted a little of this outburst just before dinner. 'How she has grown up. She will make someone a splendid wife. There's a great deal more to her than I ever thought.'

'But not Joss.'

'My dear, I am coming to the conclusion no woman will do for Joss. I don't know if he would be jealous and suspicious like a Spaniard, or horribly indifferent, but unless there is some woman can crack his defences, some woman can make him love her deeply, there is no hope for any liaison he may make.'

They went in to dinner, escorted by a French colonel whom Millie had cultivated for this purpose: she had known his father years before, a veteran of Waterloo, and, by some remote twist of genealogy, something very much like a fourth cousin twice removed. This gallant officer, tall, red-faced, distressingly un-Gallic, taxed their wit to its limits, for he spoke no English, and only Théo, after such an adventurous week, could speak French without having to cudgel her brains. After dinner he was persuaded to stay and play a game or two of piquet, a game fashionable in Millie's youth and very dear to her heart; a game which Sophie could not play, and which they promised to teach her. Théo excused herself, saying she wished to make inquiries about her package, for the *Hamilton Castle* was to sail at noon the following day, and she still had not received it.

She could have written a note, paid someone to take it down, but that would mean waiting for an answer. It was six o'clock. She might have to wait hours for an answer. She put

302

on her heavy new cloak, one of the few real prizes of their shopping expedition, put up its hood, and stepped out.

Poll Batty's house was not far from the hotel but was a great deal nearer the water, nearer the lower life of Valletta, the sort of life that always clustered about sea ports. At the turn in a steep street, where she could see over the harbour, Théo rested a moment, trying to see the *Aphrodite* through the blue evening, watching the lights being lit and a swarm of local craft plying through their reflections. And now, down again, to the left, balconies very close over her head, a furious din of raised voices somewhere within and to the right, a small prick-eared dog slinking away into the darkness of a doorway, and here was the gate and the stone passage and the empty courtyard lit only by a ship's lantern, a prize or a relic, hanging over Poll's back door.

She knocked. It was strange, she thought, how thoroughly behaviour could be conditioned: it would not have occurred to her to go inside without knocking. Yet she doubted anyone else afforded Poll that courtesy, that Poll was always 'upstairs' in order to overcome the inconvenience of importunate sea officers, good-natured and rowdy and sometimes not so good-natured and the worse for drink, crashing unannounced into her hall. But though Théo waited, no one came to her knock, even when she bruised her knuckles in a second attempt, and when she tried the door and it opened, there was no small boy running to intercept her, no cats either, and the singing bird had gone too.

In the parlour – anything less like an English parlour could not be imagined, thought Théo – there seemed to have been a hasty re-arrangement. The Turkey rug that had graced the tiled floor had gone, there were no cushions on the sofa and nothing on the table, no lamp, no ornament. Théo held up her own small lamp and swung it about. Poll had gone.

An unbelievable, abrasive disappointment left her weak, scarcely able for a moment to raise her light again, to pierce the pitchy dark beyond the doorway to the back regions. Then she moved forward, slowly, trembling a little, and made a ghost-like survey of the whole house, such a small house after all, such a still, musty, deserted small house. There were still pots in the kitchen, well, so there might be; there was still linen, and fresh, on both the beds upstairs; there was a closet full of Poll's clothes, enormous dresses, an acre of material in the skirts alone, and smelling rather strongly of that cheap, musky scent. But of Poll herself, or any valuables, or the intimate clutter of the everyday, there was no sign at all.

Théo began to go down. Three steps from the bottom she heard footsteps in the courtyard, male footsteps, not heavy but deliberate and unmistakable. One of Poll's sailors? He would walk straight in, thought Théo; there might be a misunderstanding. She blew out her lantern, retreated as many steps as she dared, and the door flew open, a voice yelled 'Poll!' and Captain Griffith passed across the hall and into the parlour. He came out again, treading with more care, his eyes adjusting to the dark, though it was too mortally dark for even the keenest human eye, what with the shutters barred and the door fast closed on the cobalt night sky. He had been expecting to find Poll in the parlour, instinct had carried him there, certain he was going to open the door on light and a warm welcome. Now he paused at the foot of the stone steps to the upper storey, and his eyes made out nothing, no single point of reference: he almost tripped against the bottom step, he was so adrift in his calculations. But his ears served him well enough: he could hear the cats wailing a long way off, and even the piercing shriek of a woman insulted, the coppery, muffled clang of her appropriate reply. Near at hand, nothing. But another sense told him he was not alone in the house, and that it was not Poll sleeping upstairs that stirred the hair on his scalp and tightened his fingers instinctively, it was someone above him, yes, but only a little way above him, on the stairs near the top. The faintest drift of warm, scented, clean – now that was unusual in this house – clean flesh came down to him.

Théo thought he could smell her fear. It did not occur to her that to be afraid of a man who had done so much for her, who had most probably saved her life, was more than ridiculous; she might have been a hunted doe, the tiger a leap away. For a whole minute of unbearable tension she stood stock still, at one with the blackness, her face turned automatically to the wall in case he should see its pale oval beneath the drooping hood.

'You might as well come down,' said Griffith suddenly, 'I can't see you but I know you're there.'

Still she did not move. The doe does not necessarily make a run for it simply because the tiger growls. But abruptly he flung himself up the steps, two at a time, and just as abruptly she instinctively threw herself back to get away, but her skirts hampered her, and the lantern, which swung out in her nerveless fingers and caught Griffith a blow on the side of the head. He swore then, and reached out, clutching handfuls of best-quality merino, and she slipped on the top step and fell, taking him down with her with a thin little cry of vexation and sheer terror.

He held her wrist while he struck a light. In the quick flare she saw that the lantern had cut his forehead, high up, there was a trickle of blood under his hair; she saw his eyes widening in disbelief; she saw disbelief give way to distress, acute, immeasurable distress, and then to anger, plain and simple, the anger of affronted masculine pride, of suspicion, of wounded dignity.

'Dear God, what are you doing creeping about in the dark, knocking me on the head? Get up. Let's see if the thing will light as well as give me a headache. Still after adventure, haven't you had enough?'

There was another spurt of flame, the lantern flickered and then glowed. Théo got to her feet.

'There's no one here,' she said absurdly. Reaction to fright had set in: she felt clammy and cold.

'No, well, I expect Poll's still on Gozo. I thought she'd be back by now, but you know how it is when you meet old friends . . . And what were you doing here, anyway? Graham said you'd been washed ashore in that blow we had last week, not much of a squall for a shipwreck, you must have been unlucky. He also said Poll was anxious you had this,' and he pulled a small package from under his coat, a very small package tied with string. A ring, some letters . . . Even so Théo had not been expecting anything so small.

She sat down on the top step to open it, spilling the contents into her lap. Griffith had gone into a bedroom, the bedroom she had slept in so uneasily all those months ago, and was busy unshuttering the window, letting in the cool fresh night.

305

Yes, there were three letters, all hers, and the heavy signet ring he had sometimes worn, and a banker's draught for a goodly sum, two hundred pounds, and a creased IOU from a Captain Bentham for fifty.

Was this all? A dim suspicion that it was not all, that other things: his watch, for he had possessed a fine one, had certainly had it with him; her picture in a tiny silver frame; all his cash, had gone missing in Balaclava. She was surprised the signet ring had been left untouched. She sat with her head bowed over it, turning it in her fingers, and then the pale gleam of the letters in her lap drew her eye, a reluctant, dry, anguished eye. It had been her last comfort, that he had not received her letters; and here they were, evidently read and then forgotten about, the creases in the pages were all hers, the paper was hardly crumpled from being turned over. He had read them, and put them in his pocket, and had not replied.

She raised a white and shattered face to Griffith's harsh inquiry. Yes, she was all right. It swam across her mind that he had suddenly feared they might be letters from another lady, not for her eye at all. And following this: it seemed to make him angry that she grieved over this pathetic package, this miserable little collection of nothing. She would destroy the letters, give back the IOU, deal with the draught, give the ring to Poll, yes, she would leave the ring for Poll, it was worth something. She did not want it. It lay heavy on her palm, winking in the lantern light. No, she did not want it. How strange. And she did not want the house at Rozel . . .

She was aware of a burning scrutiny. She looked up into a blaze of blue, intemperate blue, piercing to her very soul. She had never been looked at in such a way before, she could not interpret it, especially here, in this place, this absurd position, this very moment, she had no wit to interpret it. She understood simple lust, the Malta seafront had taught her about that, and the cellars of Scutari, and the alleys of Varna; she understood the arid, almost passionless coupling of her marriage; but she had never seen the strong desire of a man wretchedly in love.

But: 'I should go,' she said, attempting to rise, startled by the intensity of his expression. She had not wanted to meet him, she had hoped, some part of her had fervently hoped, never to meet him again. And this was why, this feeling of inexplicable panic, for she had no defences, he stripped her bare, bare of pretence and hypocrisy, pegged out all her mean and shameful fears and longings and dared her to dissect them and give them names. And she longed for his approval, for that meant safety, with him on her side she could overcome anything, just as at the hospital he had supported her, letting her hide her face in his shoulder; and she dreaded his being near her, speaking to her, for that meant disintegration: his last words to her on the deck of the *Tempest* had driven deep and true.

But why should she care? Why should she regret refusing his share in the brigantine? Her head did not regret it, only her heart. So why should her heart persist in having a say in the matter? He had not appealed to her heart, he had never appealed to her heart.

He caught her as she rose and pulled her into his arms. If she could have fled she would have done so then before he pinned her between him and the wall and began his practised assault. His mouth was gentle and persuasive, and she had never been truly wooed in her life since the sweet kisses of André Givard . . .

These were kisses with a deeper meaning. She lost all sense of time, of duty, morals, of self-control. How many women had he had in how many ports? How clever he was with buttons, it had taken her five minutes to do them all up . . . Dear God, she must fight, she must . . .

'Stop it,' he said, and 'Look at me,' but if she looked she did not see him, nor did she feel the cold north-westerly that blew in through the open window; not until afterwards, when it froze along the wide track of her tears.

24

A man who is deeply ashamed of himself might take refuge in righteous indignation, or the blustering anger that is the last of his pride, but Griffith took no refuge anywhere, had no room for any emotion but the one, was scoured to the heart by remorse as thoroughly as the *Aphrodite*'s decks were sanded and scrubbed each morning. He caught Théo up as she entered the stone passage, her cloak drawn about her in a defensive gesture, and his face was all bleak misery, his eyes as grey as the dawn that was even now breaking over the eastern sea.

'Don't speak to me,' Théo said, pressed back against the wall. 'It was you who warned me, wasn't it?' And then, in a rush, in case her courage deserted her before she could get it out: 'You thought you'd teach me my lesson. Well, you did it very thoroughly. I shall never wander about foreign sea ports in the dark alone again. You were always right: it's foolish behaviour for a lady. And there I was thinking I could trust you, that such a thing would never enter your head – it didn't enter mine. So I learned that too, never to trust anyone . . .' and she turned and made a quick movement for the gate, so that he had to stop her by putting a hand on her shoulder.

She shrank. Her fingers fumbled at the latch, made a mess of it, tried again.

'Théo, it was not meant to happen like that.'

'I didn't know it was supposed to happen at all.'

'No, but I had thought about it. I never thought to meet you again. Then Poll asked me what to do about the package

308

and I thought . . . I thought if I saw you one last time it would help clear my head.'

'You were angry because you were so sure I would put money in your brigantine.'

'Oh, damn the brigantine!'

'I told you,' and she turned, her back against the gate, 'I told you to marry a rich woman. Then you could assure any amount of investment, no need for contracts, and you could have saved yourself all that chivalry at Scutari . . .'

'It was you I was worrying about at Scutari, not some damn ship.' He had realized that at Scutari, it had come to him in painful waves; he had thought himself too old, too cunning, too experienced, to be caught by a woman. He had been resigned to a cheerful bachelorhood. If anyone had told him he would come to love a small, defiant body wasted by cholera, a pair of swiftly changing green eyes, slightly slanted, a long aristocratic nose, he would have laughed, would have conceded pity, a very proper human tenderness, but love? No, never love. But since he was too honest a man not to acknowledge the evident truth, he had to do his best to ignore it, a state of hypocrisy – in general he was not a hypocrite – and at inconvenient moments the truth broke out: he had been very much afraid at Balaclava that he would say something untimely, had been quite brutal with her, the only way he could cope. And he still did not know if she had truly cared for that dead soldier; it ought not to matter now the man was dead, but it did, and in any case women were apt in his experience to glorify even the most wretched, improvident skunk of a husband once he was in his grave . . . Seeing her looking at those letters, God knows what they meant to her, had set fire to all his frustrated emotion. He had not intended to make love to her, at least not to the natural end, only to bring himself to her attention, to make her properly aware of him.

And this was the result. She shrank from his touch. He had berated a fellow officer once for the sake of his dog, a little yellow bitch that had cringed away whenever the man had moved to stroke her, evidence of harsh treatment in the past: was he not ashamed, Griff had demanded, that here was a walking testimony to his cruelty?

309

And here was Théo, whom he loved, flat up against the gate in an effort to keep away from him, her face shadowed in the gloom of the passage but presumably filled with loathing. What woman would not loathe the man who had raped her? A lawyer might make a nice distinction between willing and unwilling in this case, she had not been paralysed with fear nor had she bit and scratched, but nor had she surrendered; not even the second time, when she was spent, exhausted by his implacability, by the uselessness of her own passive resistance. He was more than ashamed of that second time, he could not bear to think of it. He had tried to bring her to love him, and had failed.

And then, out of his shame and his misery – dear God, he had not felt so guilty, so thoroughly guilty of any sin since he was a boy in the days before he went to sea – the most inappropriate remark surfaced, and he gave voice to it before he could stop himself.

'I suppose you are going to marry that Westover.'

Incredulous shock on her face: he did not need light to see it. So she had wanted to, had she, and the gentleman unwilling. Well damn her, damn her . . . He didn't care. She could break her heart over any man she liked, it was certain she would never break it over him.

It was only after she had gone – he made no effort to stop her, to say anything else – that he found the contents of her package still on the stairs. He gathered up the papers – a bank draught, a large amount, it would have to be returned to her – an IOU, the letters. He turned them over in his hand. Then he sat down on the top step where she had sat and took one out: it was a perfectly ordinary letter, full of her daily life in Scutari: she must only just have arrived. It was affectionate, plainly dutiful and loving, but it was not a love letter. She might have been writing to her brother.

Captain Griffith never read other people's letters. He had been brought up to consider it a heinous act. Indeed, he put Théo's letter away with a hand that was not quite steady.

But then when one is in Hell already there is no real point in being virtuous.

*   *   *

It was Jack, as thoroughly sober as he had previously been thoroughly drunk, who brought the news to Millie that Théo had been discovered on the quay, had apparently been there all night, was unrepentant, did not see why anyone should be roused, was . . . in a mood. Millie raised her brows, not at the eccentricity of the way Théo had chosen to pass the time, but at this very mood, this vivid, furious, excoriating mood. She was bright and brittle and yet more alive, more intensely alive than Millie had ever seen her, and there was a kind of desperate happiness there too, more desperate than happy perhaps and very far under, but there none the less. There were also physical manifestations of a long, sleepless night: an inattention, a divorce from the present, bruises under her eyes.

There were real bruises elsewhere, but Millie did not see those. Théo made sure she did not, locking her door before she washed, washed with a thorough methodical application as if she could wash off memory too. But she was left with a sullen aching, and a complete weariness she would have to fight against all day, and a complete confusion of thought, a whirlpool of thought. It was better not to think at all.

She had always looked forward, or back: forward in the hope the future would deliver what the past had denied her, and back to the days of childhood when time's dimensions were otherwise. Now they were otherwise again. In Scutari, nearly dead, there had only been the present; last night there could have been nothing else, his hands and mouth pinioned her to it, driving all emotion but the emotion of *now* out of her mind. Did it take a mortal fever to do it, she wondered, and had she the symptoms of another, equally virulent one? He had said he loved her, several times, and she could not forget it, was not sure she could put it down entirely to the urgency of the moment, though Caroline had warned her men were sometimes quite irrational at such a time. He had not struck her as irrational. Through her haze of shock and disbelief and the effort of beating down the delight he conjured in her she found him many things but not, strictly speaking, irrational.

She could not face breakfast, made a paltry excuse. As she never made excuses Millie looked at her sharply, and then, in a half-hearted – she was not a prying woman – attempt to come at the reason for this extraordinary behaviour, she said: 'Has Sophie been talking to you about Joss? Poor girl. I have come to be quite fond of her, and he will never love her, Théo, never, I can feel it. I hope . . . I hope she did not make you unhappy.'

'How could she?' A straight, kind look, but the eyes, tawny now with this tempest raging away within, were too guarded for innocence.

'Well' – and Millie took a turn round her trunk, strapped up and waiting to be carried aboard the *Hamilton Castle* as soon as breakfast was over – 'I know you care for him.'

Again a flash of green-gold, a look, this time inscrutable, indecipherable. 'Yes,' said Théo.

'He wouldn't make you happy,' said Millie, and there was a desperate note to her voice, she was never desperate, not even in shipwreck or among Turkish bandits.

'No,' said Théo.

And: 'If you wants wittles you'd better jump to it 'cos they'll be clearing the board in one minute flat. And that there Old Hypochondriac is kicking up a right hullaballoo, says he won't go. Miss Sophie and the doctor are a-squarin' him up now but I bets you anythink you like he'll have the last word.'

'Jack . . .' Millie began warningly, but he had already vanished.

'Can we leave him behind?' asked Théo gently, putting her arm through Millie's and smiling into her face. 'Poor Sophie would be much more comfortable on the ship if she didn't have to run after him every minute.'

'Oh,' said Millie, and then: 'Oh!' with more asperity, and then a minute later, grasping Théo's hand before letting her go, 'Oh, how uncharitable we have become! But still, if he won't budge and the ship is to sail . . . I am not, I am not under any circumstances other than a declaration of war, going to miss that ship.'

Nor did she. She became overwhelmingly decisive, even vitriolic; this was the Millie who struck terror into the hearts of admirals and elderly generals who had not quailed before Napoleon. She told Mr Barnard, at least she flung the words in the direction of his pillow, the suffering heap beneath the bedclothes that might be supposed Mr Barnard, that she could not countenance leaving Sophie unattended in Malta when Miss Barnard had consigned her to her care – never mind the high-born ladies up the road, Lady this and Lady that, he had been ill, did not know Millie enjoyed their acquaintance and their confidence too. Sophie was to sail in the *Hamilton Castle* whether Mr Barnard cared to or not. This settled she departed in a rush of gorgeous peacock blue and choice emerald, to put on her bonnet and organize Jack and the porters.

Mr Barnard might still have wavered, but when Crashaw told him he too was sailing the following day, to replace one of the many doctors who had lost their lives at Scutari, his resistance finally gave way. He could not rely on the chambermaid, a thick-ankled, placid Maltese girl, or the hotel management to cherish him, and his purse was not as deep as Millie's; he could not afford bribery. He therefore allowed himself to be muffled up, swaddled almost, retiring under layer upon layer of flannel and wool until only his nose and eyes were left to distinguish him as a human being. Then they got him on a litter – 'Blow him,' said Millie crossly, 'why must he always make extra work?' – and carried him down to the harbour steps where the boat waited, a terrifying ordeal since his bearers pelted down the steep streets with the stretcher at acute angles. Millie said afterwards she never knew how he survived, but it only went to show he was not as weak as he made out: men rounding Cape Horn in a gale could not have clung more tightly to their ship than Mr Barnard clung to his tilting transport.

And there was the *Hamilton Castle* ready for sea, obviously a smart ship, for although it was the wrong time of year for painting, her white streak had been jealously renewed since she had been in the Grand Harbour and all the ports assiduously blacked. There seemed a great deal of her as they came gently alongside, more of her, anyway, than of that ill-fated brig, that *coracle* as Millie had called it.

Still: 'I hope this is the last ship I ever sail in,' said Sophie with feeling as they reached the deck, 'I am sure I shall always be dreadfully ill at sea.'

Captain Charles, greeting them with quiet good manners, pooh-poohed this rather too heartily; he was not a hearty man. He did not really approve of women as passengers, and as his ship was a general-cargo carrier he was not forced to suffer them aboard in other but exceptional circumstances. He could in fact carry eight passengers in some style, the *Hamilton Castle* being built along the lines of an old-fashioned Indiaman, but he never did, not even, it was said, when the owners went on their knees to him. For Millie Boswell, however, whom he had known as a boy – his late father had entertained a secret, long-lasting passion for her – the strict captain would swallow nine-tenths of his dearly held principles. Though it was difficult at this late date to see the girl his father had most salaciously dreamed of possessing, the essential Millie was unchanged; and if she declared herself too old for devil-may-care, her bonnets proclaimed otherwise. He kissed her, as he might an aunt, or an older sister, and he led her below with a cherishing smile.

The smile had faded by the time they cleared the harbour, for a flock of native boats had crossed his bows, the occupants singing and shouting out and apparently oblivious to the large vessel about to run them down, and besides that, the small scrawny widow who had come aboard with Millie was standing by the taffrail watching everything with a knowledgeable eye. He had never known a woman who could tell the difference between a shroud and a stay but he would have bet his year's pay this one could, and it made him uneasy. After a while, however, she turned to gaze astern to where the fishing boats were regrouping to tack in unison like pigeons, where there was the distant gleam of white canvas through the grey, uncertain light.

In a while Captain Charles, clear of the land and on course, his decks tidy, his first mate grinning with satisfaction, his sails drawing to perfection, moved rather awkwardly to stand beside Théo. He looked through his glass a moment.

'What you might call a flyer,' he said with a grunt. He could not approve her rig: he was a master who liked to get the best from any ship but he was not foolhardy.

'I rather think Captain Griffith bought her very cheap because she was considered too fine for a cargo carrier, and too dangerous,' said Théo steadily.

'You know him then? I have great respect for him as a

314

seaman. I hear she has made him some small profit, he has used her to best advantage, but my dear, she is like something from an age gone by, the days of my youth: look how long and narrow she is, look at the height of those masts, the length of that bowsprit. Thirty years ago she would have been a pirate or privateer. And I believe she was in the opium trade before Griffith found her, another trade that needs stealth and speed; a wicked trade. Griffith, he would have nothing to do with it, no. A hard man and drives a ship without mercy; well known for it, Mrs Trent. But a sound, likeable fellow. He started his own company years ago when he was not much more than a lad, had a partner, an experienced master, a treacherous sort too apt to look for easy money. Anyway, the partner died and left debts, Griffith hadn't known the half of them. It was enough to break any man's resolve, everything sold up, every penny gone. But a good master can always find a good ship, Griffith did, and made enough in a few years to buy shares in a tidy little brig, and then . . .' he raised his glass again, his mouth pulled down with comic resignation as he saw the *Aphrodite* set more sail. 'Well, it's not the vessel I would put my money in if I wished for a weatherly cargo carrier but there you are, she was cheap, laid up to rot, they say, and the man fell in love with her. Look at her now, a noble sight, isn't she? Even a plain man could not help being moved. He is a great seaman, Mrs Trent. He will make that thoroughbred pay her way against all the odds and in thirty years own a fleet of sober merchantmen that bring him handsome dividends, handsome enough, but he will always regret her, will always remember her with affection . . . Ships are like women, my dear, we love some and are kind to the rest. And the choice is not ours, it seems to me, the choice is made in Heaven.'

He fell silent, as if suddenly aware how long he had been talking. They both watched the *Aphrodite* coming up in a cloud of canvas.

'Well,' said Captain Charles, putting his glass in his pocket, 'we won't have *her* company for long.'

They were 'incommoded' – Jack's word – in the Bay, and met a brief, roaring north-easterly in the Channel which did them no good, but apart from this it was a good passage. Jack took charge of Mr Barnard two days out, for the ship's boy, all there was by way of a steward, took one look at him and fled, an understandable reaction. Jack's answer was to treat Barnard like a child, now and then rallying him with the cheerful oaths of a sergeant rallying his men in battle, ignoring his temper, and lacing his coffee and his cocoa with rum.

'If you ever turns me off,' he said to Millie, 'I knows what I can do, eh? Apply to look after old invalid gentlemen at some spa or other. He's a baby if you knows how to treat 'im.'

He was a baby still when they reached Russell Square, fretful when Jack was out of call. He insisted Jack accompany him to Martagon, he could not face the journey without help, and Sophie was no good at all, a most incompetent nurse. This, of course, was gross ingratitude, and also nonsense, but Sophie took it philosophically. She had grown rather too philosophical for her own good of late, said Millie gloomily, she had resigned herself to quiet spinsterhood in a cottage: she would not allow herself to be sold with Martagon.

Mr Barnard's worsening mood, reaching its lowest ebb the moment they tucked him in the carriage – Millie's carriage – and waved Hardy away with a certain trepidation, was entirely due to his reluctance to return and cope with his financial problems. But cope with them he must, said Millie bluntly, surveying the tide-marks of seawater on every dress as it was hung up, peering cheerlessly into the fishy bottom of her trunk, yes, cope with them he must, for Sophie's sake, for his tenants' sakes. Sophie had turned out amazingly well, had she not? A quick look at Théo, who was nursing the melancholy monkey.

Théo was still in the wild mood of the journey home, of that morning in Valletta. Her face, filled out only a little since Balaclava, was full of the old fierce hunger, and more and more, until Millie had come to the conclusion it must either be satisfied or it would kill her. So quiet and grey on the surface, so molten beneath: what was to become of her? She had decided to sell Rozel, and would not be moved, was as stubborn, as tenacious in this decision as in no other – but having done so, where would she go? Dr Frere had written, counselling caution, urging her think again before committing

316

an irrevocable step: such a splendid, lofty house, such an excellent position. She smiled over this letter, but was unmoved, unmoved, unmoved . . . She spent long hours with Alex's man of business, a cross-eyed, sharp, reptilian little man in rooms near Gray's Inn, and sometimes he came to Russell Square, to be primed with madeira and anchovies, stoked up, as it were, to greater feats of legal ingenuity. And in the end, the will proved, all property, annuities, pensions, interest, investments, debts, settled and settled for good, Théo still had her twelve thousand pounds, her five hundred a year left by Honorine, and whatever might accrue from the sale of Rozel.

Louise wrote:

If you come home before June, you will be able to stay with me at La Croix. I have taken the Lawrences' old house for a year, the one with green shutters just this side of St Helier, and I am supposed to be moving there in the summer. Alexandre has already been over La Croix with some workmen, talking new doors and wallpaper and the latest thing in kitchen ranges. Goosie was outraged, and shut herself in the dairy. Otherwise we have been very quiet, though Monsieur Vautier called the other day asking after you and shaking his head over the business. He says the *Marthe* has been written off, two more are laid up to be sold, and there is so little ready money Alexandre can barely pay the crews, he has had men jump ship in Bordeaux and Vigo for the sake of higher wages. There has been a great deal of short-sighted meanness over food too, and over repairs, rigging and sails. Vautier would have wept, I think, had he been a weeping man. He said if Grand-père Bon was alive he would have murdered Alexandre rather than have him put the ships and men at risk. I rather think old Captain Marchet was inclined to the same view for he has resigned. He gave his age as an excuse, but the whole of St Helier knows the true reason, and also knows the poor man will have a tenth of his proper pension and after thirty years' service to the Faurels. I am almost ashamed to walk near the harbour.

It is very peaceful without Mama. She has only written me two letters since leaving for Paris – she and Baptiste were married in Paris, a very plain affair, Dr Frere went; I am not sure he was invited, not formally at any rate, but he went, as if to assure himself they really were legally bound. I believe he wanted to satisfy his curiosity for the sake of the business, in the tenuous hope that if

Mama were not really married she might be persuaded to leave her money in Faurel Mannelier. Still, she is, and she will not, so there we are.

When you come perhaps we could go across to visit Marguerite, she has not been very well. It is a case of chronic unhappiness, says dear Dr Frere, who cares for all of us, I think, rather too much, but he says too that it is curable, that it must be curable, or he will give up being a medical man and take to farming potatoes. You and I, he says, must provide the remedy . . .

What had he said? 'You, Théo my heart, will never be happy, truly happy, in your life again.' It is curable, it must be curable . . .

'My dear Théo,' said Millie, who thought she was heart-broken for Joss, 'the spring is here, the trees are turning green. I believe it is time you went to Jersey.'

'Yes, I believe it is.'

And then, seeking to comfort, and still thinking of Joss: 'You don't have to pretend with me, my dear. I know how you feel. Oh, I do, I do. There is nothing in life so sharp as unrequited love.'

Théo did not blush. She turned a white, solemn face away from Millie's sympathetic eye.

'I know,' she said.

The island was a jewel, a vivid green surrounded by vivid blue and under a vivid sky. Théo watched it coming closer and closer, lost it momentarily behind the white mass of a barque's canvas, found it again even nearer, every building visible, and small black figures on the shore.

'Welcome home,' said Louise, wrapping her in lavender-scented softness, while the children clamoured at her skirt.

Clarice had a handkerchief to her eyes, and behind, his hat in his hand, stood Vautier, waiting to be noticed. Théo could see barely-disguised shock, affectionate pity in their faces, knew that she was too pale, neither pallor nor mourning suited her, and too thin, far too thin. Even Louise, now she had stepped back to see her properly, was looking concerned.

Luc was waiting with the carriage, grinning broadly, his face quite split in two with merriment. And he was animated all the way to La Croix, setting the horses to canter, something so strictly forbidden all these years no one had imagined the poor beasts remembered how to do it, and hallooing improperly at every dray and country cart they overtook. Louise, the wind in her face, held on to her bonnet with both hands, and laughed.

They came back to a trot, a vigorous, thundering trot all the same: St Aubin rang with the clatter of hooves. The children, who had been excited by the speed, tugged Théo's arm to look at this, or that, voluble, giggling, even the baby entranced, clapping her fat hands. Then they came to the steep lane, the garden wall, the sudden glimpse of the terrace, the new green of the wistaria, and the front door, flung open as the hooves struck sparks from the stones outside.

Goosie and Laurente were running out, talking at once, a good-natured keen witty colloquial exchange: they were as excited as the children. And now there was no standing on ceremony. Caroline was not upstairs.

Even so, even so . . . There was an air about the house as if already it belonged in spirit to Alexandre. Or was it simply, Théo wondered, that it no longer seemed to belong in any way to her? She paused on the half landing to look out of the window: what an intense green was the green of early May, as deep and clear and exhilarating as Millie's silks. Over the roofs she could see the masts and yards of several ships stark against the blue.

'I haven't touched anything,' Louise was saying, opening the drawing-room door as if Caroline might still be waiting. 'Mama took all her ornaments, her personal things.'

There was still a faint remembered fragrance, in spite of the blinds fully raised, the windows open to the strong breeze. Théo turned her straight back on the sofa and looked out at a more unfamiliar view: she had rarely been allowed to admire the scenery from this room. Now she could look down on the magnolia tree, on the children chasing Clarice round the shrubbery, and over the high wall into the town itself, other gardens, the lane to the quay.

'It seems a long time ago we walked on the beach at St Brelade and you were cross because Mama wanted you to marry Monsieur Varges,' said Louise, who had thought that

319

incomprehensible, passionate, rebellious Théo would be dead, killed in the Crimea perhaps along with Alex – had she loved Alex? Had she loved him at all? – and now found she was not, she was more alive than ever, gazing from the window at the distant masts of the ships.

'I had forgotten all about it,' said Théo.

'You wanted something to do: "I must have something to *do*!" you cried. I hope . . . Oh, Théo, I don't know what to say about Alex.'

'There is nothing to say.'

Louise, relieved, sank down on Caroline's famous sofa and plucked shyly at her skirt. If not grief, had guilt brought on this frightening new maturity? Had she really only married Alex to escape Caroline? Millie had said so. Millie had been very forthright on the matter, had been forthright to Caroline herself: Louise had heard them, not so much arguing as having a strong difference of opinion, and Millie with the upper hand, her tone accusing, even through two doors and across the landing. And there had been something about Marguerite. What had Marguerite to do with it?

'I don't remember,' said Théo suddenly, with a lightening of her voice which might indicate a lightening of her spirit, 'what Monsieur Varges looked like.'

'Oh, he was monstrously ugly, and old, sixty or sixty-five. And he was abominably hairy, like . . . like your Mr Howard.'

'Mr Howard was very sweet. He was like Millie's monkey, rather melancholy and out of his true element.'

A silence fell, in which they both listened for the ghost of Caroline. There did not seem to be anything, however, to cloud the lozenges of brilliant sunshine on the polished boards.

'She took the Aubusson,' remarked Théo with a wry look.

Louise smiled. It grew absurdly wide, as Luc's welcoming smile had done. Her face, her beautiful face, Théo thought with a great rush of affection, lit up with secret, guilty delight.

'Oh no, she did not. It was Papa's, a present from Old Bon, who had taken it from a French privateer that went on the rocks by Sark in the year of Trafalgar. So I decided it was a family heirloom, and I did not see that Alexandre was entitled to it, it is yours and mine and Marguerite's, and I got Luc and Goosie's grandson Jacques to roll it up and carry it into my bedroom where it will be quite safe until I move. Alexandre noticed it had gone, he even dared to mention it, but I pretended not to hear and said nothing and he must think Mama has it in Paris.'

'You have grown very wicked since I was away.'

'I know,' and one part of her was genuinely horrified at it, 'but I am not entitled to take anything, and nor are you, I suppose, and yet there is Papa's little writing desk – do you remember how he used to sit us on his knee and let us draw spiders on his best paper? And mice, and funny fat cats? – and it's very old and shabby, Alexandre will put it out or send it down in the cellar; and there is the brass parrot cage with the silver knobs on from India which Grand'mère left here just before she died; and there are the portraits of us as children – well, what will Alexandre want with those? He never liked any of us: he will hardly hang us on his wall. I don't mind about the house, I never did mind about the house, but I would like to take something for a keepsake.'

No, thought Théo, it did not matter about the house. The pain she had expected to feel was not there. Perhaps it had never been the house that was important, but what she felt it represented: love, safety, happiness. She had found all those things here, but long ago, and they had depended on people, not on the cold stone of La Croix; on her father, her sisters, on an eccentric French governess who had electrified her all one summer, whose lessons in mathematics had become lessons in navigation, so that old Bon, Vautier, the master of the *Marthe* had all become secretly involved, until Caroline had found out, had declared that she had never suspected latitude and longitude could be anything but innocent, had dismissed the governess, had confined Théo to her room. No: love, safety, happiness – she had never found any of them with Caroline.

Down on the lawn Clarice was twirling in a cloud of petticoats, attempting to hit a ball with a tennis racket, a ball bowled by Young Bon a little wide of the mark. There was a great deal of shrieking, more lace on view – she had always worn an outrageous quantity of excellent French lace, had once told Caroline, when reprimanded, that she had an elderly aunt in Valenciennes who sent her parcels of it, it would be unmannerly to give it away or keep it in a drawer, it would be ungrateful. The ball soared up and over the wall of sight. There was a silence, a great gazing about in mock innocence, a great doubling up with silent laughter. And then, as if at a signal, they ran giggling to the garden door and vanished in pursuit.

'You're like Old Bon,' said Louise, standing up and coming to look out, 'I can remember him always standing at the window staring towards the sea. He was born in this house but he never lived in it. Apparently, so Mama told me, he said you couldn't get a clear-enough view of the bay from here; I think she agreed with him but her motives for moving to where you could have one were not exactly the same. But I don't think he cared about houses, only about ships. After all, he chose Le P'tit Clos and it isn't anywhere near the sea, you can't even hear it unless there's a good north-westerly blowing. But how often was he there? A month here, a week there, a few days. And Grand'mère was in St Helier as often as not, in La Grande Maison with the parrots, overseeing the business. And *she* would have left everything for a cabin on a ship if Old Bon had asked her to, and she did, several times, and didn't even stop to lock up her jewellery.'

Théo raised her head, smiling. The sun was warm on her face.

'May I share your house with the green shutters until I decide what to do?' she asked Louise.

'But of course you must. I never expected you to do anything else,' and then, abruptly, irrationally inspired, 'But you have already decided what to do, haven't you?'

Théo nodded. It was a very definite nod, but no words accompanied it. Perhaps, thought Louise, thoroughly and unnaturally wise, there were as yet no words for what Théo had in mind, or perhaps it was superstition: voicing one's deepest desires could be so unlucky. She walked to the door, grimacing at the floor.

'It looks so odd without the carpet,' she said.

'Yes. Would Marguerite like to have it? And you could purloin the desk – who would tell Alexandre? And I could have the parrot cage.'

'Good Heavens! But why would you want it? It hasn't been cleaned in years. All the silver knobs are quite black.'

Théo came briskly across the boards. The sun had warmed more than her skin, or was this something to do with what happened in Malta, something to do with his wild protestations of love . . . She had not believed him. Of course she had not believed him.

'Why don't you have the portraits?' Louise was saying. 'You could hang them anywhere.'

'I would rather have the parrot cage,' said Théo, 'I will hang it in my cabin.'

There was a letter. It arrived thirty seconds before Alexandre, who came up the stairs blowing heavily, out of temper but trying not to look it, having just come from a regular out-and-out howling quarrel with Vautier, who had given his notice.

'What a nerve,' said Louise, seizing the teapot as if for protection, 'coming at breakfast. And he is such a formal stuffy prating clergyman of a man most of the time. If I called on him at breakfast he would be affronted.'

'Good morning,' said Alexandre. 'Welcome home, Théophile.'

She raised her cheek for his kiss, inclined sideways for the other one, said 'Thank you' primly, and slit open her letter.

One sheet of paper, two, three: the bank draught, the IOU, and a few words scrawled across a page:

I thought you should have these. I have taken the liberty of sending them though I know you hoped never to hear of me again. The brigantine is sold. She went for a great deal of money, too much. How wise you were not to trust me on that score. I cannot expect you to forgive me but never think I did not love you.

No signature, the full stop so divorced from the last word it seemed he had been tempted to add more and had resisted with the old impatience.

'My dear Théophile, I am so sorry you have been unwell,' said Alexandre, struck by her absolute stillness and the faint flush upon her cheeks.

'Oh, I am quite better now,' and she raised luminous eyes, quite beautiful eyes, sea-green and mysterious.

'Hmm. Still, the fine weather is with us and Goosie's

323

cooking will plump you up. I felt I had to call . . . Leonie is a little out of sorts and cannot come herself, so she begged me to see you as early as possible – hah, she did not mean *so* early but I had been at the office, Vautier is always there at seven, and was on my way to Bruchy's here in St Aubin. We offer our condolences, my dear, our deep sympathy.'

'Of course,' said Théo. She had folded her letter and put it next to her plate. The sun, coming through the tall windows, turned her hair to reddish gold, so that for a moment she was as fair as Louise. It was still only shoulder length and was gathered in a net under her black lace cap, but Alexandre stared at it for a full minute as if he had never seen it before. He had seen something very like it before, and like that sharp intelligence, that look of passionate inquiry; thinking about it, he was surprised he had not noticed the resemblance.

'Grand-père Bonespoir,' he began, as if, having seen the old man's ghost, he felt compelled to speak his name, 'er . . . the old gentleman would be sad to see what your mother has done to the company. Reduced! Reduced to almost nothing! Of course I am selling the house in St Helier now we are moving to La Croix, but all the same, it will be a paltry sum of money set against what is needed. We cannot fulfil our contracts, and there is trouble about wages, and I am on my way to Bruchy's to delay delivery of two new suits of sails, and defer payment too.'

The two sisters regarded him solemnly over the breakfast cups and the cooling toast. He detected an atmosphere of disdain: he could not hope for sympathy here.

'I will not see the end of Faurel Mannelier,' he said with uncharacteristic vehemence, 'I will not let that woman destroy us. I'm sorry, she is your mother, it is wrong of me to criticize her before you both, you might believe it ill natured, but she enjoyed my discomfiture, she will probably laugh at my ruin. She always hated the company, she wanted nothing to do with trade, nothing, and she is quite besotted by that beautiful, that outrageous young puppy. What am I to do? The *Honorine* and the *Marguerite* are too old to fetch any sort of decent price; indeed, I cannot even find a buyer. The others I can barely afford to keep at sea.'

He looked up at Théo. It was an appealing look. It was

met with polite vacuity. Perhaps, said her eyes, green flames in the gentle colour of her face, perhaps if you had not lavished the profits on yourself for so many years, had built new ships instead of buying new carriages, had been more enterprising over cargoes . . . It is only Vautier who has kept the business going.

As if she had spoken aloud he blushed a fiery red and stood up clumsily. 'And now this morning,' he declared, as bullishly as possible, accusing, affronted, 'Vautier says he wishes to leave.'

So the ship has really foundered, Théo thought, and the good captain is leaving her at last. She had once thought she would feel cold and sick if she ever lived to see this day, but she felt nothing, only . . . only, dear Heaven, the white heat of furious elation.

'I shall bid you both good day,' said Alexandre, but he turned at the door. 'I understand you are to sell the house at Rozel? You may be lucky over the price. I was talking to Fortescue yesterday and he knows of some English people looking for just such a place.'

'How kind of Mr Fortescue to concern himself in my affairs,' said Théo, though it was not said in sarcasm, he could not tell what her mood was. 'Ought he not to devote his whole energy to rallying the company after Mama's *coup de théâtre*? He is your lawyer, cousin, not mine.'

Her eyes met Alexandre's. She knew exactly why Fortescue had mentioned the house at Rozel. She knew, she knew. The delight engulfed her, she was on fire. But she must be careful, the face she offered for his exasperated scrutiny must be as bland as possible, as pale and sensitive and innocent as she could make it.

'I believe he only has your interests at heart because you are, after all, a Faurel,' Alexandre told her heavily. He had had very little practice at being ingratiating, except perhaps with his tailor, who was the best on the island but insufferably temperamental.

'I am sure he has,' and Théo smiled faintly, sweetly, as if she remembered Mr Fortescue with affection. 'And perhaps tomorrow, cousin, I may call on you. Will you be at home? And Leonie . . . I do hope she is soon recovered.'

'Good Heavens!' cried Louise as the door closed and they could hear those sober footsteps retreating down the stairs. 'How very odd! How very careful he was not to offend you, and you deliberately – oh, I'm sure you were – deliberately pricking him about silly old Fortescue. Théo, what is it all about?'

Théo picked up her letter. She held it very tightly in her hand as if it were from that she drew her strength and this flame of a mood, this peculiar wild happiness. Was it happiness? Louise frowned. How could she tell? This was her changeling sister, difficult, complex, changeling sister. She would never understand her. There was no point in trying.

'He wants my money,' said Théo frankly.

'What!' and Louise knocked her cup so that her lukewarm tea slopped into the saucer. 'What?'

'My money. Oh, dear Lou, you are completely in the dark!'

'Completely.'

'He wants me to invest my money in Faurel Mannelier, to . . . to bail him out. Don't you see? How opportune – just as Mama flees with half the capital I return a widow, quite a wealthy widow. He knows I have always been interested in the business – how sorry he must be now that he helped thwart Papa's plans for me – and he knows I am a woman, a . . . coercible woman. After all, only two thousand of my twelve is actually invested, and that in rather doubtful stock – a good lawyer would advise I withdrew it. A good lawyer would advise making that twelve thousand earn its living. What better, thinks dear Alexandre, if it earns him his too in Faurel Mannelier?'

Louise leaned back, took a breath, stared, frowned, went to speak, closed her mouth tightly, and then squeaked: 'I think he needs more than twelve thousand pounds,' which was all she could think of, and which seemed to make Théo smile more widely.

'Ah, but I don't,' she said.

25

The *Honorine* was thirty years old and had worked hard all her life.

'I don't know what you're thinking of,' said Vautier, tapping assiduously, now and again plunging a knife into the timber with a dispirited sigh, 'but I wouldn't recommend it.'

'If you don't know what I'm thinking of how can you advise against it?' demanded Théo, her skirts lifted above the wet and the lantern raised so he could see his way.

'She's *sound*,' admitted Vautier, looking down with comic distress at his wet trousers, 'and until recently she was cared for like a duchess. But all the same . . .'

'But all the same, in your opinion as a businessman, she is not a good investment.'

His small dark eyes swivelled. 'Was it as a businessman you asked me here, Madame? I had thought it was . . . I had believed it a whim.'

'A whim? In spite of what my cousin would like you to believe I am not subject to whims.' Dear Heaven, that sounded like Millie, she thought. 'I am not going to invest any money in the company or in these ships out of a sense of duty, or sentimentality, or because Alexandre says I must. I value your opinion, Vaudie; you say you are an old office dog but I know, and you know, and all the Faurel masters and mates know very well, there is no one can judge the state of a ship's timbers better than you, that long, long ago back in the time of my grandfather you were apprenticed a shipwright and that you first sailed with him as a carpenter. It is common knowledge in St Helier and Rozel and Gorey and all places between that you, personally, worked upon the Ark. Well?'

Her use of his long-forgotten pet name, something from the days when she had been carried to the quay on her father's shoulders and could not get her baby tongue round Vautier, moved him as the sight of her stepping off the packet boat had not moved him, and he had been glad enough then, in all truth. He came to take the lantern.

'Well, as your business adviser I would say she is old and slow and rather small, but she has years of life yet, she's newly copper-bottomed, and a less cautious captain than Linoir might get an extra two or three knots from her. At the moment her rigging is in a pitiful state, and her storm canvas is only fit for rags: Bruchy's loft was working her another suit but the order has been cancelled. Still, down here,' and he gazed about cheerfully at the foetid damp, 'there's nothing much to worry about.'

They emerged into a cleaner air, then to the sharp, gusting breeze on deck.

'You see what I mean,' said Vautier, staring upwards, his eyes shaded against the sun, and he was quite certain that she would see, he had enormous faith in her.

'Yes, it looks very sad. I wonder no poor seaman's lost his life.'

'She was always a lucky ship,' and the little black eyes gleamed suddenly. 'I told Mr Alexandre, lay up the *Celeste* not the old *Honorine*, the *Honorine*'s a lucky ship and we need luck now, we need the sort of fair wind she generally finds. And there are men will sail the *Honorine* who won't set foot on the *Celeste*, she's got the reputation, that one, of being accident-prone and unhappy. But he wouldn't listen. The *Celeste* was the newer, is supposed to be faster, and Linoir had been complaining about' – a quick nod at the poor rigging – 'about all this. Your cousin was glad to see the back of him.'

Théo gazed over at the *Marguerite* lying alongside, almost identical, two years older.

'Poor old Marchet,' said Vautier, following her eyes, 'it broke his heart. But he is nearly seventy, and though his record is outstanding he would have to compete for a ship against young ambitious men. Still, I'm sorry to see him retired. He had some years left to give us, Heaven knows he has been loyal. But as for the *Marguerite*, she's not been out of the water for five years, she works terribly in a big sea; she has been kept for coastal runs for some time past. No, no, don't consider her. She has never been right since she was floated off the beach – do you remember when Berryman put her aground?'

They went below again. A small ship but clean and roomy, a good sound watertight little ship, dry and weatherly and very, very old-fashioned. She was deep, flat-floored, had big single topsails, had a stern cabin with windows in the transom counter. She was the representative of a race of ships passing away, ships that had served their time well but were no good for the future. But the future was still a little way off, thought Théo, and now, now this week, there were cargoes to be moved from France and England and the West Indies and South America.

'You must advise me how much she is worth,' she said to Vautier, sitting down at the table in the big cabin to study the plans he had brought her from the office. 'I shall not ask you how much you think Alexandre will take for her, that would be too much like dividing your loyalties.'

He nodded. He understood her. Unlike Louise he had always understood her. Well, he was nearly an old man, he would not see fifty-five again, but it seemed to him he could not look forward to a peaceful old age, not if she needed him, this young tomboy upon whom he had once pinned all his hopes. He cleared his throat.

'I would advise you started very low,' he said, 'and did not rise at all.'

'It is that bad? And what about you? Has Alexandre accepted your resignation?'

'Yes.'

'Of course he would: he has no sense besides having no heart. Do you think you will retire to your little house by the harbour or do you intend to seek other employment?'

The reflection from the water below the big stern windows rippled over her quiet hands clasped on the detailed plans. Under her fingers were tonnage and capacity, every minute dimension, the original spidery exactitude of her rigging, and the date: 1825. But the *Honorine* and I, thought Théo, are only just beginning.

'I . . .' he cleared his throat again, 'I will have a very small pension, very small. Indeed, it is not strictly speaking a company pension, it was arranged by your father many years ago. So . . . I shall be open to offers, Madame.'

She was still looking down, tracing the words in their pool of watery light.

'If you work for me,' she said, 'I could not bear you to address me as "Madame", Vaudie.'

Her eyes were brilliant. If he had not been so overcome by relief he might have believed they were full of tears.

'No indeed, Miss Théo,' he said.

She went to Rozel and stood in the shouting breeze where she had stood with Alex, and looked down into the blue water, her true element. She did not go indoors. There were no sad memories after all, no ghosts to lay, but she did not want to leave this fresh blowy perfection, did not want to tempt fate. She would remember Alex with affection; what else could she do? She could not help being glad she was a widow but she was infinitely sorry he should have died to make her one. And guilt was no good, nor was helpless, enervating grief, the selfishness and stupidities of the past could not be undone, and she would never again think of what might have been: now was what mattered, and the future she could arrange as much to her own design as possible.

She climbed over the broken wall, snagging her skirt, and clambered carefully ten yards down the rocks. The smell of sun-warmed rock and weed, of restless salt water, rose and blew about her. She took off her loose wedding ring and held it, looking down at its perfect O for a moment, and then she threw it as far out as she could so that it was lost in the surge and pull of the outgoing tide.

'The weather has turned very warm this last week,' she wrote to Millie,

and Louise and I have been sitting in the shade under the magnolia tree wondering how Mama is enjoying her sparkling life in Paris.

330

Dr Frere is often here, making the most of it, he says, he will never be invited to La Croix again once Alexandre is installed. We have been dreadfully wicked and smuggled a great many odds and ends into the carriage for Luc to take to the house Louise has rented along the bay, including an Aubusson carpet worth a fortune which we are to give Marguerite, Papa's desk, various paintings, an oak coffer that belonged to Great-great-grandmother Faurel – in which, they say, she kept the family fortune – and a brass parrot cage Old Bon brought back from Calcutta the first year he was married; in fact, I do believe he did not even have a parrot to put in it at the time.

Yesterday, having dressed with great care – you cannot imagine how long it took me: Laurente and I were at it for hours – I took the carrige to St Helier and called on Alexandre for the second time. The first time he explained how advantageous it would be, for both of us, if I put my money into the company. As soon as we were alone he plunged in, rather too brash and hearty, all false smiles and encouragement. He thought I should be an easy conquest. I said I must think about it, I must consult my lawyer. He huffed and puffed a while but he could hardly advise me against it, it would look strange, but he bowed me out with a very bad grace, I could see him turning bright red with indignation. However . . . Yesterday I called at his house, and you would not believe how dignified I felt in a new black dress, very plain and full, and with my hair in proper ringlets for the first time since it was cut off. I do believe Leonie was frightened of me. She left us alone after a little, saying she would serve tea in a while, and she backed out of the door looking at me with a suspicious little frown. Alexandre, of course, thought I had come to put my life and property in his hands, and was unctuously charming – until I told him I had no intention of doing so but that I would buy the *Honorine* and also the new unfinished brig on the frame: that brig has been worrying him extremely, for he has not paid a penny piece for her yet and she is ready to plank up. Can you imagine his horror? Of course I was counting on it, and had waited ten days in torment before making my move knowing he would be the more furious the more desperate his financial state. And it is desperate. He has lived more prodigally than any of us guessed – he has always entertained on a grand scale, certainly, always had a house full of guests, using money which should never have been taken out of the company, and how dear Vautier staved off this evil day so long I can't imagine. Now I see why Mama's defection cost so dear. She might as well have taken one thousand pounds not thirty thousand and the result would have been the same. Alexandre has been trading on goodwill and make-do-and-mend for at least six of the last ten years.

So what of my offer, you ask: did Alexandre crumble at my feet? No, of course he did not, nor did I expect him to, but he worked himself up into a glorious, righteous rage and flung some very choice adjectives at my head: I am undutiful, selfish, uncontrolled, stubborn, and have no morals, not one. Poor Leonie rushed in after a while to see what the noise was about, and I stood up and said I ought to leave, I had not meant to upset Alexandre to such an extent. At that he became apoplectic. Leonie hurried me from the room. And so I came back to La Croix — my last day and night at La Croix, for today we are half moved and tomorrow will be completely so, cosily installed behind the green shutters.

Millie laughed as she read this, and then, hauling on the bell pull with the energy of one of Captain Charles's sailors hauling on a sheet in a brisk wind, she cried Jack: 'We must pack. We are going away.'

'Away where? We've not long been back. I don't fancy no more foreign parts for a while, I'm gettin' too old for all this caperin' about all round the compass.'

'Why must you always wrangle so? When I left you behind in Constantinople that was wrong too, you didn't want me out of your sight you said. Well, I am going to Jersey to see Théo. If you want to stay here you can and welcome.'

'Now, now,' and he actually looked ashamed suddenly, and hangdog, and apologetic, 'I didn't mean to get up your nose. Only you ain't so young as you were, neither.'

'I believe I can manage to stagger to Jersey one more time before I am confined to a chair for my declining years. Get up the trunks. Go!'

They grinned at each other. He went out noisily, just to show he still disapproved, but then poked his head back in: 'And I suppose you want the carrige ordered for this afternoon?'

'Don't be so ridiculous, we couldn't possibly leave before tomorrow at the earliest. And no, I shall not want the carriage. We will go by rail.'

'Well don't that . . . beat all,' exclaimed Jack.

Millie went to the drawing room, intent on some specific action, so intent that she left a row of open doors, a shawl and two handkerchiefs, a little gold slipper as she ran. Methodically, delicately, she detached the stuffed parrot from its perch and ran upstairs again, clutching it to her bosom in triumph.

'I do believe,' said Jack to Polly, as they watched this vision from behind the servants' door, 'she's gone as batty as dear old Di. It was that shipwreck that did it, all that injurious salt water gettin' inside her and plucked from the wave by them buggers of Maltese pirates. It's all very well when you're young and fresh, and so I've told her more'n once, but she's past all that' – a venomous look from under his eyebrows – 'and if she aint she should be.'

She had never been charming. How many times had Caroline told her she was not, could never be? But perhaps the charm Caroline spoke of was only the obvious kind to which Théo could not aspire, and there were others, more subtle or more unusual, at which she was accomplished.

Mr Fortescue, narcissistic Mr Fortescue, found himself defenceless before her. He found himself admiring her poise and her undoubted self-command. He did not remember her like this. He remembered her from long ago as a barefoot hoyden he had once had the misfortune to meet among the rocks at Petit Port while he had been engaged in some dalliance with a local girl, rather basic dalliance: he had prayed at the time Mademoiselle de Faurel had not understood what she had seen. Was it the memory, returned to haunt him, that made him so regrettably nervous? Or was it that Alexandre spoke of her with such undisguised contempt he had not been expecting this particular woman, this slow warm smile, this faultless dress and bearing, this shade of pale brown hair curling so prettily under the black bonnet.

'You know he must sell,' she was saying now; they had been closeted in the inner office an hour now, and he had drunk off three large glasses, very large glasses, of a fine old madeira, an exquisite wine, whereas hers was scarcely touched. It stood where she had left it, standing on the charts and drawings spread across the table, on the pages of sad accounts: Fortescue had been as frank as he dared, had hoped to confound her with figures perhaps. He had failed, she had understood them, understood the tale they told.

So: 'You know he must sell,' in that soft, reasonable voice.

'I cannot be less than honest,' and no, he found that after all he could not be less than honest though it pained him considerably, 'if he does not sell the company will be bankrupt. Even now it only needs one creditor to demand payment – and there are some almost come to it – and he will be undone.'

'So I understand. And if I buy the *Honorine* . . .'

'You are offering very little, if I may say so . . .'

'If I buy the *Honorine* and the new brig, and take shares, say, in the *Marie Jeanne*, which I believe is in Funchal loading a cargo for Swansea, how will that leave my cousin regarding the business?'

She knew exactly how it would leave him, down to a few pence. Mr Fortescue adjusted his spotted cravat and breathed in until the buttons on his elegant waistcoat creaked. He was weary, and the wine had taken the edge off his appetite for a long-drawn-out battle. This contained young woman sitting opposite with her small hands folded in her lap and her eyes staring steadily into his own was too formidable an adversary. Alexandre had been a fool if he had expected instant capitulation, or any capitulation at all. Even now Fortescue was not entirely sure how much the ships meant to her, and whether, if he tried anything high-handed or cast aspersions or treated her with anything but absolute respect, she would not stand up, bid him good day, and walk out without a qualm. He could not judge the depths of her shrewdness, he could only waggle a toe in the water and make perilous guesses.

'I would say that what you are offering would leave your cousin solvent,' and before her unabashed gaze he amended the statement to: 'solvent but struggling. However, he did mention an alternative . . .'

It was the refuge of the damned, the ultimate folly of a beaten man. The air in the office was already thick with Alexandre's reproaches and he did not know, could not know, safe by his own fireside while this unreasonable cold rain hissed down the chimney, that he was both damned and beaten.

'Oh, Mr Fortescue, and what was that?' She reached for her glass of madeira and he noticed that she wore no wedding ring.

'What would you say to a partnership?'

'Take my father's place, you mean?'

He had not been thinking of her father; he had not thought of Philip for years. He felt he had touched some chord, that here was a chance to work on her – all women were emotional creatures when driven hard, when *in extremis*. But when he looked again he saw that it was a smile softening her face, lighting her strange eyes with secret humour. She was certainly not *in extremis*.

'In a manner of speaking.'

'In Alexandre's manner of speaking? I would put in as much money as I possess for what would be, in effect, no more than a nominal partnership. I would have no active role in the business. I would not be allowed to question his policies, criticize his ships, talk to his captains, nor offer any advice. Oh, you need not look so aghast, Mr Fortescue, I am well aware of Alexandre's views on business, on women, and on Théophile de Faurel. He is a pale masculine version of my mother: how strange, when they were so at odds to think how similar was their outlook in life. Unlike my mother, however, he is not clever. You and I know he will never make money from the company because when he does he spends it at once and unwisely; even a profitable concern can stand such improvidence only so long. So I would either invest my money and be beggared, or invest my money as a powerless partner and be beggared. Do you think I could seriously consider such alternatives?'

She set down her glass, pointing to the plans of the new brig that lay under it, pointing at the sheet of figures she and he had pondered over a little while ago: the agreed cost, the cost of delays, the probable cost of her launch, the cost of fitting out, and so on and so forth.

'I am paying a good price for the brig, the full price. I have gone into it thoroughly but I have not quibbled over it. It is a great deal of money for a brig . . .'

'She is a hundred and twelve feet long, she is a large vessel, Mrs Trent.'

'A great deal of money even for a brig a hundred and twelve feet long and rather over-burdened with sail. Whose idea was it to have her built? This' – and a finger, a small blunt-nailed finger flicked the edge of the plan – 'is not a size, shape and rig to appeal to my cousin.'

'The company already owns four brigs as well you know . . .' he began.

'But not of this size and quality. This is a brig, Mr Fortescue, to beat all brigs,' and then, more gently, for she could not reveal her true feelings now, not after keeping her composure so long and with such intense effort: 'A little too much like a yacht, a racing yacht, for a trader perhaps.'

He knew nothing of brigs, barques, rigs, or racing yachts. He pursed his lips. 'Vautier approved the design. Mr Alexandre was in London at the time and he took it upon himself in his master's absence.'

'Yes, I see.' She had guessed it already.

'That man has always had too free a hand,' continued Fortescue, and then remembered too late how close Vautier had been to this young woman's father.

'I do believe it would have been better for my cousin had his hand been entirely free. Well,' and she rose, and her black silk skirts whispered their way towards the door, 'I must bid you good afternoon, since it seems we cannot do business.'

He put a hand on the knob but he did not turn it. 'Mrs Trent, reconsider,' he said thickly, for no parasite wishes to be instrumental in killing its host. 'How can we see Faurel Mannelier ruined?'

'You have been watching it for the last five years at least. Do you really expect me to be sentimental? I will not weep for my cousin, Mr Fortescue. Please open the door.'

She held her breath. An age, an aeon before he spoke. He looked remarkably haggard for a man who had just drunk three glasses of arguably the best madeira in the world.

'I shall recommend to Mr Alexandre that he accept your offer to buy the *Honorine* and the brig and shares in the *Marie Jeanne*. I will recommend it, strongly recommend it.'

He opened the door. There was no one in the outer office.

336

Could he escort her to the carriage? It was raining, miserable chilly rain, and she had no umbrella. But no, the carriage was only at the end of the quay, and it was kind of him but she would be quite all right, she did not mind for her bonnet, her dress, her curls.

She did not even feel the rain, it was just a coolness on her burning cheeks and the wind a cool breath for her starving lungs. Triumph and joy beat in her until they were starving again, until she was suffocated, speechless: she could not return the greetings of the men along the quay, she could only nod and smile. When she came in sight of the carriage she began to run, for the triumph could not be contained any longer.

Her progress was watched with interest by those who shouted 'Bonjour, M'selle' – she would always be M'selle to them and the spit of the old Faurels – for they had seen Vautier smiling yesterday for the first time since they could not remember when, and there was no knowing, there had never been any knowing, when the spit of the Faurels might come into her own.

The morning Millie struggled down the gangplank at St Helier with the warm southerly breeze in her face, Jack following with the picnic basket and Nelson, and then Polly with a mysteriously precious leather bag, was the day Théophile Marie Ursule Trent, née de Faurel, came into her own. Her papers of ownership for the *Honorine* and the brig, her contract for her share of the *Marie Jeanne* had been brought round by Mr Fortescue, a dejected Mr Fortescue, who had known his client's wrath. Personally he thought she had been generous, had shown as much dutiful sentiment as could be expected, bearing in mind past differences of opinion, past slights and omissions. She had offered a very low price for the *Honorine*, true, though no one else would have looked at her for any price, he suspected; on the other hand she had not asked for a halfpenny off the cost of the brig, a tidy sum by any standards, and she had settled for a very small percentage of the profits of the *Marie Jeanne*. Alexandre had nothing to complain about.

He was at La Croix now and complaining bitterly. Fortescue could not calm him, nor could Leonie. He said he never wished to set eyes on Théo again, ungrateful, wilful, scheming female.

'The poor man might die of congestion of the brain,' said Millie, sitting with Théo and Louise on the vine-covered terrace at La Maison Verte, the house of the green shutters. 'Have you no pity?'

'None,' said the sisters in unison.

'But what are you going to do with your ships?' asked Millie. 'These beloved ships. What a great battle you fought and won for them to be sure.'

'I am going to found a shipping line,' said Théo, 'but there is a great deal to do before they are ready. The *Honorine* has to be complete re-rigged. Vautier and I have been round her six times and so has the dear Monsieur Bruchy and there is really no other solution. Then the brig is being planked up, at a tremendous rate I know, but it will still take time, all the rest of the summer. And then I have been besieged by young men wanting to be mates, with certificates and without, and sweet old Marchet has been round hoping I will remember him — what kind of restrained, old-fashioned, diplomatic phrase is that? I shall give him the *Honorine* and make his last voyages happy ones.'

Louise and Millie exchanged significant looks, all smouldering light and eyebrows.

'You see how she is,' said Louise, 'she could be fifteen again and quite incorrigible.'

'And the brig?' demanded Millie. 'Who is to command the brig?'

They took her to see it, and she expressed great interest in the process of planking up, and in the cheery red-faced young men and old men crawling about with hammers and saws and buckets of nails. She also said she did not know there could be so much mud and wet sand in one small corner of Jersey, and would they not all be more comfortable in duck trousers and seamen's jerseys, and why should this brig appear to be twice as big as the one that had so shamefully sunk on them? They explained to her, pointed to the empty space that would be her holds, the emptier space that would be her saloon, her cabins, her deck house. Bemused Millie trailed at

338

their heels, absorbing strange snippets of information about masts and spars, gaffs, something booms, martingales. Nelson ran back and forth, back and forth, barking.

'Stop, stop,' she cried at last, when her eardrums and her brain and her watering eyes could take no more. 'All these details and yet I still don't know her name? Théo, you haven't told me her name.'

'It ought to have been *Théophile*,' said Louise, sitting down on a large piece of wood and shading her eyes from the sun's glare, 'but Théo said she was saving that for a big three-master, the most beautiful ship ever built.'

'I don't suppose,' said Millie sagely, 'she will ever build a more beautiful ship than this one, you know. Our first loves only grow dearer as the years pass.'

Théo smiled. Someone above was nodding and laughing: look at those three dears knee-deep in dirt and shavings, well, and how they do talk, pointing here and there. Well, the Faurels never had a brig as roomy, as thoroughbred as this one. No wonder M'selle was rosy, happy as a lark.

'It is a dreadful responsibility,' Théo was actually saying, gazing about, 'and the cost . . .'

'Marguerite is to buy a share,' said Louise, 'and so am I.'

'She is to be called *The Three Sisters*,' said Théo.

She had never written two such difficult letters, never. She sat and sat hour after hour, and the ink dried on the nib and her mind selected and rejected a dozen possible phrases, a score of possible words . . . When she had finished she was still not satisfied, but they would have to do, they would have to do or she would go mad.

And some weeks later in high summer she had a reply to her first letter, a reply from Her Majesty's Ship *Satyr* currently undergoing repairs at Gibraltar.

Dearest, dearest Théo,
What a kind letter to receive while sitting in a dark hole supervising the hopeless fools who purport to be mending my engine. I am so glad you are happy. Are you really happy? I am no hand at writing, cannot get my thoughts on paper in any sort of sequence, let alone feelings – but it sounded as if you were happy. And what about the

wise paragraph, the old maid advice? What can I say to that? Don't marry her, you say, for the wrong reasons.

Her father has written to me, a most abject, disgraceful sort of begging letter. But then I suppose I have asked for it, for I certainly gave him no reason to hope, when I saw him in Constantinople, that I might involve myself in his affairs on certain conditions. Is it not strange that now Martagon is mine for the asking I feel indifferent to its fate? I can't say when I began to feel like this but it was shortly after you and Bos left for home, and then hearing you were wrecked – we did not have any proper news of you in the Black Sea for over a week, and I was led to believe you had drowned. Then I learned that Will – you remember Will at Otmoor? – had been killed in the trenches on the Heights; he had avoided being starved or frozen to death to be killed by a sniper. It was a strange week altogether, unreal. When I heard you were in Malta and were safe nothing else mattered.

I have written to Mr Barnard telling him I will relieve him of nine-tenths of the land, provided I can have the Priory Farm to live in. I do not want Martagon. I do not want a brick of the place. Do you understand that, Théo? I have wanted to have it ever since I was a boy, but it isn't worth Will's little finger. Does that sound foolish? Sentimental? I don't know. But I mean to have a go at the estate and there is a new steam thresher not on the market yet but I believe it is a vast improvement on the old models. What odds do you lay I make a fortune as a farmer? They say it is not possible, but then I am determined on it. And Sophie? You said, you implied, she is too good for me, that I haven't even tried to guess her virtues, that she survived your shipwreck with aplomb, bailed the boat with her father's hat. You are right. Or are you? If I had not been such a touchy fool I might have asked you to marry me; I do not believe I ever gave you your due either, did I? But you will always write to me, won't you? Whatever happens, however you disapprove, you will always write? I believe I shall grow a grumpy old bachelor, living only for his engines and his wine cellar, and perhaps his godchildren. Will you present me with any godchildren?

And then, when she had begun to think she would never hear, Goosie knocked on her door late one evening and said a boy had come over from St Helier with a letter from the *Marie Jeanne* who was in and unloading, just in from Swansea where she had been delayed first for one thing, then another, and unloading as fast as she could in the summer twilight though everyone knew she had no more cargoes waiting.

Théo smoothed out the one sheet of paper. The sky was indigo over the calm sea and later there would be a moon. She ought to light a candle to read, or the lamp, but she simply turned the paper in her hand and looked down at the familiar tilting hand, strong and black enough to read even in the almost dark.

'I will not work as master on your ship. I will only consider a partnership in her. A brig does not sound much. I shall come and look at her when I have time.'

A brig does not sound much. He must know it was her life. Could he guess how little it might mean if he did not come, the brig, her life . . .?

She told nobody, she was secretive and evasive when she was questioned about a master for *The Three Sisters*; she carried on with the daily domestic round, she went to the orphanage with Louise, went to St Peter Port to visit Marguerite, organized huge picnics for the children, ate sardines on toast with Dr Frere. She wrote to Millie, sweltering in Holywell with all her domestic staff at loggerheads; she wrote to Fanny, in Bath and reunited with the captain; she wrote to Mr Howard in Hampstead and Miss Cole in the fruity crush of Izmir, trying to find a captain foolhardy enough to accommodate her and her collection for the voyage home; she wrote again to Joss; she even wrote to Caroline, a remarkably formal heartless sort of letter which she signed 'Your dutiful daughter' with a wry smile.

Then they sent up from the shipyard to say the brig was ready to launch.

And still he had not come.

26

The day was very hot. Théo went down the companion to the saloon and pulled off her straw hat, brushing back her stray damp curls. It was too hot for anything, the whole of Jersey languished behind drawn blinds. Even the quay was deserted, and the brig, moored alongside to finish her off, rocked gently on the glassy harbour swell.

She had walked down from the office, after a difficult and tacky interview with Alexandre, who was not pulling Faurel Mannelier together as he should, not now he had lost the help of the only man who might do it, who might sincerely want to do it. He had been only mildly vituperative, however, for it was too hot to argue with effect, and Théo was as irritatingly unmoved as ever, only offering, in complete and determined seriousness, to buy him out of the *Marie Jeanne*. Alexandre had called her a hussy, a word he regretted as soon as it was out of his mouth, for it was not only undignified but unjust, and he had sometimes felt she had not yet showed him her claws even, let alone her full mettle, that she could make him a terrifying adversary if she chose. And this was little Théo, the wayward, boyish afterthought!

She had left off her mourning at the end of June. She slipped quietly into grey, and then into the blues and greens that suited her best, and this morning she had worn a sprigged cotton, a French country dress almost, with a wide low neck, blue ribbons, and the pretty straw hat. She could not make herself look beautiful but she looked her best. It was one of the reasons Alexandre had tossed the word hussy at her, for it had annoyed him she could look so much better as a shipowner than she ever had as the youngest daughter of La Croix. It was an irrational annoyance, irrational in the extreme, but needle-sharp: he was on the verge of taking pleasure in the deep blush that spread up her neck and cheeks when something about her reminded him again of Old Bon. Perhaps that too was irrational. It frightened him though, for Old Bon had been as thorough and implacable in his time as Théo might prove to be in hers.

So here she was, fanning herself with the straw hat, sitting in the saloon of *The Three Sisters*, which would be ready for her sea trials in a week and had no master, the whole of St Helier was agog to know her master. And Vautier was harrying her, chasing her up and down, cackling his anxiety, sending her cryptic notes, demanding to know why no one was appointed. The master ought to be on board, might wish to make trifling changes in the rigging, might query her trim.

There were footsteps on the deck above where the pitch was melting between the seams it was so hot; the footsteps advanced and retreated and advanced again and then stopped. A smell of the tar and of tobacco, a male smell, wafted down the companion. Théo stopped fanning herself. When she put up a hand to push back her hair her forehead was beaded with perspiration. There was the creak of new wood giving to some weight or other, and the sound of a rope dropping on the deck. Then a shadow darkened the saloon and someone descended the steps slowly, carefully, his eyes adjusting to the dimness after the burning day.

'I always wondered,' he said, 'if one day you would pick up your life and do something with it. Polly told me right at the beginning there was more to you than met the eye.'

'You took a long time getting here,' she said, and it sounded remarkably unfriendly.

'I had a cargo for Marseilles and a friend to see in Port Mahon. I wrote you a note. I came as soon as I could.'

He looked round, opening lockers, peering at the deck beams, ignoring her. He was well dressed, very well dressed, and he held an elegant hat in his hand.

'You look prosperous,' she said.

'I won't have them thinking I'm a low-bred, uncertified

343

foremast jack. This is my best shore-going rig. I save it to impress bankers mostly.'

'And have you impressed any recently?'

'Not enough to get me a brigantine, no.'

He looked at her for the first time, looked at her properly. She fanned herself with the straw hat again, looking down.

'So you might consider a brig?'

'How large a share in her do your sisters have?'

'A quarter share. Three-quarters of her is all mine. And I have all the old *Honorine*, and shortly, I believe, all the *Marie Jeanne* which you must have seen in Swansea.'

'You have been a trifle ambitious. No, I did not see her in Swansea but my uncle said she was a smart brig with a competent master. Well, are you going to show me the rest of this one or have you changed your mind about offering me the job of master?'

She rose. He must not see her hand shake. She thought his eyes were grey, a bad sign. He was stringent, hard; how could she take him as her partner? Was that what she really wanted?

But she knew now what she really wanted.

She led him through the ship, mainly silent, offering information when it was asked for, otherwise letting the brig speak to him herself.

'Where is the *Affie*?' she asked at some point, when they had descended into the hold and re-emerged in the stifling heat, Théo rubbing her forehead and swinging the straw hat.

'Mr Graham has been promoted and has taken her to the West Indies.'

He was looking up, along, and then, without a word, swung himself aloft with the agile speed of a man who has been doing it all his life. When he returned to the deck and picked up his hat, which he had left on the deck-house roof, he said: 'She has some prodigious spars. What do you want to do with her? Win a race?'

'I assumed you would approve.'

'Well, it depends what she does at sea. She is built to carry cargo dry and safe, not tear along under everything she can carry.'

He went below again. For a moment she hesitated and then she followed him.

344

'When can I see the *Honorine* and meet this Vautier?'

'Tomorrow?'

She was at the foot of the companion, holding on. He was opening the cabin doors, one each side. The starboard one knocked against something, there was a metallic ringing, and he gave a smothered exclamation.

'What is it? Not a birdcage?' and then, forcing the door a little more: 'Good God, there's a parrot in it!'

'Oh no,' and she ran forward, smiling, 'no, it isn't a parrot. At least . . . It was a present from Millie. It's stuffed.'

She was a foot away from him. And suddenly all the hard formality, the hard rigid formality, melted away, and his sense of the ridiculous got the better of him and he began to laugh.

'You see,' said Théo, 'my grandmother had twenty parrots and that was one of her parrot cages, but Millie thought, after Grand'mère's experiences, that if one had to have a parrot at all it was better to have one which caused no trouble.'

He was still laughing. And in the middle of it he reached out and drew her against him, putting his mouth against her hair.

'Marry me.'

There were voices on deck. She could hear . . . She could hear the children, Bon and Pierre, and Clarice shouting '*Attention! Oh les vauriens!*' and the patter of running feet.

'Will you take on the brig?' Where could she find the strength to say it, she could feel his heart beating beneath that impressive waistcoat, and he was trying to raise her head.

'Oh damn the brig!' he said. 'Marry me!'

'Hello,' cried Bon, descending in a rush, his hair in damp spikes, 'Maman has decided to have tea on the beach. We came to tell you. She said you would be here.'

And: 'Yes,' said Théo.